Brickell Boss

Story of Love and Empowerment

Mac Harvey

Oceanfront Press—Miami Florida
ISBN: 9798218194307
Library of Congress Control Number: 2023909048
Title: *Brickell Boss*
Author: Mac Harvey
Digital distribution | 2023
Paperback | 2023

Dedication

This book is dedicated to my close Miami friends, it has been such an honor, blessing and privilege knowing that our paths crossed. As I've gotten to know you and watch what you do and how you do it, you've inspired me to be a better version of myself. You are truly the quintessential representation of what I call "Boss Entrepreneur Woman."

To all the hardworking, ambitious, goal-oriented women out there, who get up every day breaking those glass ceilings. Knowing that you are not alone, I know it's not easy in this patriarchal dominant society. Despite the circumstances you find a way to navigate the difficulty, to create the improbable, and manifest greatness. I marvel at your strength, gumption, and fortitude and remain fabulous while doing it. Your resilience and determination are an inspiration. You are blazing a trail for future generations of women and for that, I applaud you. Keep pushing forward, keep chasing your dreams, and keep inspiring others along the way. This book is dedicated to you, and I hope it serves as a reminder that anything is possible if we believe in ourselves and in each other.

Contents

Chapter 1

It was June 2nd 2020, Megan Babineaux a successful Wall Street Analyst from New Orleans, living in her Manhattan Soho condo with a gorgeous view that overlooks the city. As the city was in Covid lock down and nobody could leave their home.

Megan may have been able to work remotely from her Soho condo. However, she would likely have had to adjust to a new work routine, with virtual meetings and communication taking the place of in-person interactions. The economic uncertainty brought about by the pandemic may have also affected her work, as stock markets were highly volatile at the time.

Living in her luxurious Soho condo, Megan would have been fortunate to have a comfortable home to ride out the lockdown. However, the isolation and uncertainty of the pandemic would have still taken a toll on her mental and emotional well-being. She may have found solace in connecting with friends and family virtually, or through hobbies and activities that she could do from home.

After going stir-crazy sitting in her apartment, Megan decided it was time to connect with her closest friends and see how they were doing and managing work during this uncertain time. She sent out a group text to Bridget Berry, Elena Mazor, Sabrina Choi, Amber Alexander, Bethania Diaz, and Jacqueline James. The ladies had replied frantic, scared about their businesses losing money. Each of them sharing different ways of how they're coping while trying to find solutions to keep their business afloat. Bridget mentioned several of her real estate projects had halted, and investors were worried. Elena mentioned she couldn't see any of her patients and her staff was worried about their jobs. Sabrina luckily had been working long hours for her company at home as she prepared for several legal battles. Amber was not allowed to see any of her clients and nobody had placed any orders from her. Bethania was scared as she just started a new real estate job with so much uncertainty. Jacqueline had several clients that were panicked cause they didn't know if they could get their contracts finalized due to all sporting events shut down.

Megan had listened to each of their concerns. She remained calm, poised as she always was. She was an expert in crisis management but she knew this crisis had global impact everyone around the world. She started to generate an idea that would be able to help the ladies generate some cash flow during this time. She wondered if everyone would trust her, she told the ladies, "I have an idea that I believe give us a financial lifeline, but I will discuss with you on the phone."

She asked each of the ladies were they free tomorrow to video chat and discuss. They all agreed to video chat the next day and the ladies were eager at the idea of what Megan was going to present.

That night Megan drafted a proposal of the solution she was going to present and make it easier for each of them to understand. She was very excited and enthused about sharing this idea. She stayed up late that night making sure she was very due diligent in covering all of her bases of what she wanted to present.

<u>Megan Babineaux</u>

Megan Babineaux who hailed from the Garden District of New Orleans. She was the oldest of three siblings, and her father was a district court judge while her mother was a homemaker. Growing up, Megan was known for her intelligence and determination, excelling in her studies and extracurricular activities.

After completing high school, Megan went on to attend the prestigious University of Pennsylvania, where she earned a degree in finance. Upon graduation, she landed a job on Wall Street and quickly established herself as a top performer, earning accolades and promotions along the way.

Despite her success, Megan had never forgotten her roots, or the values instilled in her by her parents. She remained close with her family and returned to New Orleans often to visit and give back to the community. Megan's upbringing had undoubtedly played a significant role in her success, providing her with a strong foundation and work ethic that had propelled her to the top of her field.

Bridget Berry

Bridget Berry was born and raised in Nashville, Tennessee as the only child of her mother and father. Her father was also in the real estate industry and she grew up watching him work and learned the ins and outs of the business from a young age. Bridget was a smart and ambitious child, taking after her father's drive and determination.

Despite her father's involvement in the industry, Bridget chose to pursue a degree in Business Management from the University of Tennessee, Knoxville. After graduation, she moved to Orange County, California to start her career as a real estate developer. Over the years, Bridget worked hard to establish herself in the industry and had become very successful.

Bridget's personal life had had its ups and downs. She was previously married to a military man, but they recently got divorced. Although she was not very close to her father, she had continued to excel in her career and was always pushing herself to achieve more.

Living in Orange County, California. She built herself a successful real estate development company in the OC. She was an extrovert and a master networker, and Megan and Bridget had been friends for five years, having met at a conference in Las Vegas.

Elena Mazor

Dr. Elena Mazor, originally from Toronto Canada, moved to Beverly Hills after medical school where she practiced as an OBGYN. Elena was stoic and reserved, but witty, and Megan and Bridget met Elena when they went to a Laker game a few years back.

Elena grew up in Toronto, Canada as a middle child with two older brothers and two younger sisters. She was the quiet and shy type during her upbringing and didn't receive much attention. Her parents divorced when she was young, which contributed to her reserved personality.

The move allowed her to explore new opportunities and escape from the familiarity of her hometown. While in Beverly Hills, she developed a reputation as a skilled and knowledgeable medical professional, which earned her the respect and admiration of her colleagues and patients. Despite her success, Elena remained modest and unassuming, never seeking the spotlight or attention.

<u>Sabrina Choi</u>

Sabrina Choi was from Seoul, South Korea. Her family moved to New York when she was four years old. Sabrina's passion for the law led her to excel in her studies, and she graduated at the top of her Ivy League class. She was also the president of the Harvard Law Review, an impressive accomplishment in the legal world.

She was now a Corporate Lawyer for an investment firm that Megan formerly worked for. That was how her and Megan connected and became very close friends. Sabrina was very outgoing and charismatic, hardworking but always down for a good time.

Her father was a successful commodities trader, but Sabrina had her sights set on becoming a lawyer from an early age. She was an avid fan of the television show Law & Order and loved watching courtroom dramas.

Despite losing her mother recently to the pandemic, Sabrina had never forgotten the values and lessons she taught her, including the importance of being the best at what you do. As a corporate lawyer, Sabrina had applied these values to her work, and she had become known for her sharp intellect, keen attention to detail, and unwavering dedication to her clients.

<u>Amber Alexander</u>

Amber Alexander was from the Bay Area and lived in San Diego. She was once a professional cheerleader and a model. Now she was a successful Pharmaceutical Sales Rep, men couldn't help but marvel at her, every doctor in her network loved her, being drawn to her smile and sense of humor. One time she was accidentally mistaken for Margot Robbie. She and Elena became good friends since Elena was one of clients.

Amber was the youngest of her family and had two older brothers. She had always captured attention from the opposite sex, being known for her beauty and sense of humor.

Amber's father was a retired professional football player, and her mother was an accountant. Growing up, Amber was very close to her family, and her parents were very supportive of her career aspirations. She worked hard to pursue her passion for acting and modeling, and her talent and hard work have paid off with her success in the industry.

Bethania Diaz

Bethania Diaz was a Real Estate Agent from New Jersey who recently moved to Miami in search of a fresh start after coming out of a relationship back home. Megan was her client in Manhattan but hit it off as good friends, plus she was also the reason Megan owned a SOHO condo. Megan and Bethania remained close ever since, Megan recommended her to Sabrina so she could find a place in the city.

Bethania Lopez was born and raised in Hackensack, New Jersey as the oldest of three sisters. Her father was a Professor at Rutgers University, and her mother was a beautician. The family originally moved to the United States from Venezuela.

Bethania had always been passionate about health and fitness, and she'd been an avid vegan for years. She'd also very smart academically and attended Brown University, but she dropped out after only one year. This decision caused some friction with her father, who had high hopes for her academic success.

Recently, Bethania went through a difficult breakup when she discovered that her ex-fiancé had a change of heart and didn't want to get married. She was now newly single and looking to move on with her life. Despite the setback, Bethania remained optimistic and continued to focus on her career, health and fitness goals.

Jacqueline James

Lastly, Jacqueline James was from Chicago and currently lived in Atlanta as a Sports Agent. She grew up in the same neighborhood as Michelle Obama. She met Amber and Elena the same night in LA at sporting event that Amber ex-boyfriend was hosting. He was Jacqueline's client, so Jacqueline was there for her when Amber went through a tumultuous break-up.

Jacqueline was the youngest of two siblings, with an older brother. Jacqueline and her brother were known as the tall kids, often towering over their peers.

Jacqueline's father was a Journalist in the Chicago area, and her mother was a Nurse. They instilled a love of education and hard work in their children, and Jacqueline went on to attend Connecticut University on a basketball scholarship, where she earned her degree in Sports Management. She later became a successful sports agent, representing some of the biggest names in professional sports.

Jacqueline was known for her quick wit and sharp tongue, which had helped her navigate the male-dominated world of sports management. Despite her tough exterior, she was also fiercely loyal to her friends and family, often going to great lengths to protect those she cared about.

Bridget, Elena, Sabrina, Amber, Bethania, and Jacqueline were all excited to hear from Megan, and they quickly arranged a time to connect over video chat.

The next day, Bridget, the real estate developer from Orange County, was the first to join the call. Bridget greeted everyone with her usual enthusiasm and energy, sharing updates on her latest projects and networking events. Elena, the stoic and reserved, followed suit, cracking jokes and sharing her latest medical research findings. Sabrina, the corporate lawyer from New York, joined the call with her usual charm and charisma, making everyone laugh with her quick wit and infectious energy. Amber, the former cheerleader, and model from San Diego, dazzled the group with her stunning looks and magnetic personality. Bethania, the real estate agent who had recently moved to Miami for a fresh start, joined the call and shared stories about her new city and her latest listings. Jacqueline, the sports agent from Atlanta who grew up in the same neighborhood as Michelle Obama, chimed in with her usual candor and wit.

Megan and her girlfriends were catching up over a video call when the topic of being stir-crazy in lockdown came up. Bridget shared her frustration about the beach being closed, while Amber complained about not being able to get hair, nail, wax appointment. But the conversation took a hilarious turn when Elena added her two cents.

"Well, don't feel bad," she said, "I believe every woman around the country is suffering from that Amber including all of us. You get no sympathy from me!"

The group erupted in laughter at Elena's unexpected comment.

Jacqueline, tried to steer the conversation in a new direction by asking, "Ladies, what are we going to do?"

But Bethania had a different suggestion. "How about you come to Miami?" she said. "Everything in Florida is open."

Amber, always quick with a comeback, couldn't resist making a joke at Bethania's expense. "Does that include your legs too?" she quipped.

"Are you still on strike from all men?" Bethania wasn't having it. "I'm not going to dignify that with a response," she said. "Don't take your sexual frustration out on me!"

The group laughed at the lighthearted exchange, grateful for the chance to share a moment of levity during these challenging times.

"Ladies, I have a plan to make us some money while we are locked down. I was concerned for you guys after hearing you vent yesterday," Megan said. Megan shared her presentation through the video call and told the ladies she was going to help the learn how to Day Trade from home and make money. "The Stock Market is open ladies despite everything else being shut down. As you know this is part of what I do and I can definitely help you make some until things are back to some normalcy."

At first, the ladies were skeptical but each of them were interested in trying it with Megan guidance. Megan helped them set up accounts and told them how much money she recommends they should start.

Megan said to the ladies, "If I make you money tomorrow on your first day then I want us to take girls trip to Miami. I would love for us to live in the same city. We've talked about this for so long. What do you think?"

"Let's do it, Megan you've done so well at this over the years and I trust you," Bridget said.

"Uh hell yeah! At this point I don't have a choice," Amber said.

Sabrina, Bethania, Elena and Jacqueline said, "Let's do it."

The next day all the ladies gathered on video call with Megan just before the Stock Market opened. Megan had done some preliminary analysis of the markets prior to getting on the call. At the opening bell, Megan recommended to the ladies' what trades to execute and after about an hour into trading. The ladies were feeling the pressure of hoping that that their trades would make them so money. They were so shocked and elated that each of their trades had doubled in value. Megan told the ladies, "Make sure you close your positions and start packing your bags."

"I've never made that much money in one day," Bethania said.

"I was on eggshells watching my computer screen I have a great deal of respect for how you do this every day," Jacqueline told Megan.

"I switched from coffee to a cocktail watching my screen, I put all my money in one trade. I was so close to just drinking it straight from the bottle," Amber said.

So, Megan began to interject. She said, "Ladies, thank you for trusting me, let's go visit Miami I can't do this lockdown any longer."

"I don't know if I can take the Florida humidity," Amber said.

Jacqueline said, "Looks like you're not taking the California lockdown well either pick your poison."

"Amber when's the last time you've been on a date?" Sabrina asked.

Amber responded, "Fine, but as soon as I get there I'm making a wax, nail, spray tan, Botox and hair appointment. Bethania send me a few places where I can get my Botox."

Bridget asked the ladies, "Is this our girls' trip or are we thinking about actually moving? I don't know about you guys but I could use a change of scenery."

"What are the men like in Miami?" Elena asked Bethania.

Bethania responded, "I really haven't been checking out the men here I've been focused on business."

"Do you really think we're going to really believe that Mother Teresa response you just said," Amber said to Bethania. "As soon as we get to Miami, you're getting laid and I'm going to bring my feather duster to remove those cobwebs you've got built up."

Bethania said to Amber, "And I'm going to use my Dyson to remove the cobwebs you got built up."

All the ladies just started laughing on the call.

Megan and Bridget interjected, "Can we focus on the topic at hand?"

"Bethania you know I love you," Amber said.

Bethania said, "I love you too."

Bridget and Megan both, "Anyway, I'm going to convince the ladies heavily on the call let's do a group trip and check out the serious potential of living there."

"Let's just get a penthouse where we can all stay and let's just check it out," Megan said.

So all the ladies agreed to organize a group trip. So Elena asked a question, "What if we really like it and we want to move? I'll have to check with the licensing board to see what it's going to take for me to practice in Florida."

"Don't worry Elena, it'll be fine. and girls, no matter what, we're going to have each other's back," Bridget said.

"Ladies if we move to Miami only Bethania is bilingual, we're going to have to learn how to speak Spanish," Sabrina said.

"As soon as you meet a hot sexy Cuban guy that will give you all the motivation you need to teach yourself Spanish," Amber said to Sabrina.

"Good point but ladies that's do not get carried away we're just going to go and check it out see what it's like not as a tourist but as a potential resident," Megan said. In the back of Megan's mind, she felt so relieved knowing that all the girls were on board to take a trip.

Bridget suggested maybe they should try to stay away from the tourist areas and try to explore Miami as a local. They all agreed that was a good idea. Bethania suggested that she was going to make a list of places that she thought all the ladies would like to see and possible places where they would like to stay if they decided to move.

Elena was feeling uneasy about the move. She normally didn't respond well to change. She mentioned on the call, "Ladies, I'm still feeling a little uneasy about it."

Amber said, "Elena what's the problem? You're always mentioning how the dating is horrendous in LA. Use the disappointments in LA to motivate you to see Miami."

"You're right thank you girl," Elena responded to Amber.

Bridgette mentioned, "Ladies go have a good time and Bethania, we need you to show us the best places to have some fun as well."

"Yes, I want a strong Margarita the moment we land in MIA airport," Megan responded. Megan also mentioned, "Ladies we are newly single and some single too long, I won't mention any names, Elena."

The ladies chuckled then Elena responded, "I'm not like you guys I'm looking for my Prince Charming."

"In this dating culture Elena, just settle for a Prince Albert," Amber said to Elena.

"What's a Prince Albert?" Elena asked.

Jacqueline said to Amber, "Really? Leave her alone."

Amber said, "I'm just being honest. So Jacqueline, how's the dating life in Atlanta? Who's looking at your peaches these days?"

"I plead the fifth," Jacqueline responded.

"You see my point exactly. Ladies look, we are young, gorgeous, successful boss women in our prime it is time for a change. Let's give the Magic City a sample of what we are all about. Ladies, go pour yourself a drink and let's have a virtual toast," Amber said.

The ladies went and made themselves a drink and came back to the video call with a glass in their hand.

"Raise your glasses ladies, this pandemic will not define us, you only live once, cheers to Miami," Amber said.

All the ladies repeated, "To Miami."

Megan, Bridget, Elena, Sabrina, Amber, and Jacqueline were all preparing for their upcoming girls' trip to Miami during the 2020 pandemic. They were excited to get away from their lockdown routine and have some fun in the sun, but they knew that things would be different in the midst of the pandemic.

As they all started discussing through group chat their plans for the trip, Megan chimed in and said, "Ladies, we need to make sure we're taking the necessary precautions for this trip. We'll be wearing masks, practicing social distancing, and sanitizing everything."

"Girl, I already have my face mask packed, but I'm not talking about the medical kind. I'm talking about my Chanel mask that matches my purse," Bridget responded.

"And I'll be bringing extra hand sanitizer for all of us, just in case we can't find any at the stores," Elena added.

"I'm just glad we're getting out of the house. I can't wait to hit up the clubs and dance like nobody's watching," Sabrina said.

Amber chimed in, "Speaking of dancing, I've been practicing my TikTok moves for the trip. I'm going to be the next Charli D'Amelio."

Jacqueline laughed and said, "I'm just excited to finally wear my bikini and get some sun. I haven't been able to go to the beach in forever."

Bethania chuckled and said, "I'm at the beach working on this tan, I just closed on my second home since moving here. Ladies, bring your sexy attire."

As they continued to plan and pack for their trip, they all made sure to bring their masks, hand sanitizer, and other necessary items to stay safe during the pandemic. But they also made sure to have fun and enjoy their much-needed break from their lockdown routine.

The ladies decided they were going to stay in Miami for a few weeks and get a feel for the culture and all it had to offer. The ladies packed their bags and booked their flights. They decided they were going to leave a week later.

Counting down the days of their Miami trip, the ladies were looking forward to making some unforgettable memories and possibly starting a new chapter in their lives. Megan seemed to need this trip the most welcome as she missed working on the trading floor and interacting with her colleagues' things were very different in New York. She felt like New York just didn't seem like the New York she remembered when she first moved.

Bridget was very intrigued and enthused about what Miami had to offer. She felt like it could be a new territory for her to conquer in the real estate world. She had done some preliminary research and found that it seems that South Florida is a potential hot zone for plenty of opportunity. So, she was definitely eager to network and see who she could meet.

Elena still felt slightly a bit timid regarding the possibility of leaving the West Coast and coming to Florida. But she hoped that once she arrived with the girls, that Miami will win her over. There were times that she still volunteered at Mount Sinai to see if they needed any extra additional staff. She recently declined to volunteer as she wanted to take extra precautions before going to Miami.

Amber still felt extremely eager for a change of scenery and enthusiastic about seeing what the dating potential would be like. Fighting through her own personal issues, she was determined that maybe this was the change that she needed to get back on her feet. She had not told any of the girls that she'd been going through some financial trouble. Thanks to Megan helping her learn how to Day Trade, she felt a lot more financially secure paying off her debts while soaking up the Miami sun.

Bethania, since moving to Miami, had really been spending a lot of her energy and time at work plus she'd taken her workout regimen to a whole new level. She absolutely loved the vegan culture in Miami and had made a new girlfriend. Her name was Stephanie Toro. Bethania was very intrigued as to what she did for a living because she always had the nicest clothes, drove a nice car, and had an amazing condo in Edgewater overlooking the water. Bethania also noticed how

Stephanie was just immaculately gorgeous and always looked presentable.

It was Friday afternoon; Stephanie had invited Bethania to lunch on a yacht. It was Bethania's first time being on a boat so she was very intrigued at what that experience could be like. Bethania decided to come straight to the yacht after her morning appointment. As she walked up to the Marina looking for the boat, she already noticed Stephanie was in her Brazilian bikini.

Bethania said to Stephanie, "I thought we were having lunch."

"We are but it's Miami I'm having it in my bikini, did you bring yours?" Stephanie replied.

Bethania was feeling way overdressed, and Stephanie told her, "Welcome aboard I'm going to introduce you to my daddy."

"You're wearing that around your father?" Bethania said.

Stephanie turned around and looked Bethania directly in the eyes and said, "I said, 'my daddy' not my father."

Bethania realized in that moment, it all started to make sense how she was able to live her lifestyle.

As Bethania walked onto the boat, Stephanie introduced her daddy. His name was Amir Khan, a successful alternative energy and real estate investor from Dubai. He owned the yacht, and the home Stephanie lived in. Amir asked Bethania, "Where's your swimwear? It's going to get hot when we take the yacht out."

He told the staff, "Get her whatever she needs, she is our guest."

"I don't have any swimwear with me," she mentioned.

"Your bra and panties will do nobody will tell the difference. It's Miami, let me get you a drink what would you like?" Amir said.

Bethania realized if she was going to be in her bra and panties getting some sun on a yacht, she was going to really need a strong drink.

So as Amir handed Bethania her drink. He asked her a question, "What do you do in Miami?"

"I'm Real Estate Agent," she answered, taking a sip of her drink.

Amir asked for her card and then he said, "I'm going to make an appointment with you because I do want to buy more property in Miami."

Bethania never thought that she would be networking naked on a yacht. Certainly, wasn't on her bucket list.

Jacqueline felt extremely enthusiastic about meeting and networking in Miami. She also felt it was time for a change. She had always been a go-getter, determined to succeed in her career as a sports agent. She had built a reputation for herself in Atlanta but had struggled to find success in her love life. Despite her best efforts, she had yet to find a man who met her high standards and matched her drive.

So when Megan presented the opportunity to explore Miami, Jacqueline jumped at the chance. She was ready for a change and eager to see what the Miami dating scene had to offer. So excited, she even texted Megan on the side, "Megan girl you were reading my mind before I even said anything. Plus, it would be very nice for all of us to potentially be in the same city together."

The day had arrived all the ladies were heading to the airport ready to embrace what Miami had to offer and also excited to see each other.

Megan texted all the girls, "I'll meet you at the Penthouse safe travels ladies. I'm so looking forward to seeing all of you. Thank you so much for being open to the idea of exploring Miami."

Amber replied, "I might be the last one to meet y'all at the Penthouse I've already made a wax and a nail appointment as soon as I leave the airport. I will not be walking around looking like Chewbacca."

"Amber has a point let's all get pampered and freshened up for Miami," Bridget replied.

So, all the girls agreed. Amber was able to get all of them scheduled along with her appointment.

Amber also said, "I've got a hairstylist and a colorist coming to the Penthouse to do all our hair. It's on me. My gift to you. Safe travel my queens."

Chapter 2

As the flights begin to arrive in Miami airport surprisingly no delays. Megan had been eagerly anticipating her trip to Miami for weeks, and as she stepped off the plane into the jet bridge, she couldn't believe how smooth everything had gone. She had expected delays and long lines, but to her surprise, everything had gone off without a hitch.

The warm, humid air of Miami enveloped her as she stepped out of the airport terminal, and she breathed in deeply, savoring the sensation. She had always loved the heat, and the balmy Miami air was a welcome change from the chilly weather back home.

As she made her way through the airport, Megan's excitement grew. She was looking forward to spending time exploring the city, soaking up the sun on the beach, and trying all the delicious food she had heard so much about.

Her phone buzzed in her pocket, and she pulled it out to check the message. It was Bridget and Jacqueline letting everyone know they had made it safely and would be joining her soon. Megan smiled to herself, glad that she wouldn't have to wait long to start her Miami adventure.

Megan met Bridget and Jacqueline by baggage claim as soon as she approached them, the three of them embraced each other in a warm group hug. They were all thrilled to see each other after so long and the pandemic had kept them apart.

Megan was the first to break the embrace, and with a big smile on her face, she said, "It's so good seeing you guys! Jacqueline, your long, straight black hair and deep brown eyes look amazing girl. The pandemic has treated you well."

Bridget chimed in and agreed, "Yes, you look fantastic, Jacqueline! And Megan, your curly long black hair with hazel eyes and pretty smile looks amazing too!"

Jacqueline blushed and said, "Thank you, ladies! And you both look gorgeous too. Bridget, I love your curly-haired with bright green eyes, and Megan, I see you've been working that squat rack hard girl! You're such a spitting image of your mom."

Megan laughed at Jacqueline's comment, "Thanks! My mom would be happy to hear that. And yes, I've been trying to keep up with my workouts even during the pandemic."

Megan said to Jacqueline and Bridget let's get an Uber and get to the Penthouse and check-in I'm excited to see what the Penthouse and that view.

Megan, Jacqueline, and Bridget made their way out of the airport and decided to get an Uber to their condo. Megan couldn't wait to see what the penthouse looked like, and her friends were just as excited.

As the Uber pulled up to the condo, the three friends got out of the car and stared in amazement at the beautiful building in front of them. They couldn't believe their luck at being able to stay in such a luxurious place. When they arrived at this Brickell Penthouse, they were mesmerized at how gorgeous it was.

Once they entered the condo, they were even more impressed. The Brickell Penthouse was stunning, with modern decor and floor-to-ceiling windows that offered breathtaking views of Miami.

Megan was the first to speak up, "Wow, this is amazing! The view alone is worth the price of admission."

Bridget and Jacqueline agreed, and the three friends began exploring the spacious living room, bedrooms, and kitchen. They were all impressed by the attention to detail, from the high-end appliances to the luxurious bedding.

After a few minutes of taking, it all in,

Megan suggested, "Let's put our bags down and go out to the balcony. I want to take in the view and enjoy the warm Miami weather."

Bridget and Jacqueline nodded, and the three of them made their way to the balcony. As they stepped outside, they were greeted by a stunning panoramic view of the city skyline and the ocean.

They couldn't believe how lucky they were to be staying in such a beautiful place, and they spent the rest of the afternoon lounging on the balcony, sipping drinks, and catching up on their lives.

As Elena, Sabrina, and Amber made their way through the airport, they couldn't wait to see their friends and get the party started. They texted in the group chat to let them know that they had arrived safely, and Megan was thrilled to hear the news.

Bethania, who had just finished her last appointment for the day, also texted to say that she was on her way to meet up with the girls.

As Elena and Amber were walking through the airport, they ran into each other by chance. They hugged and complimented each other, catching up on their lives and how they managed to keep their figures during the pandemic.

Amber said, "Elena girl look fabulous, how do you keep that amazing figure?"

Elena said, "Thank you luckily, I've been working out at home and Bethania encouraged me to try vegan plant-base lifestyle. I was worried I would gain weight with the gyms shutting down."

Elena said, "You look so gorgeous, why are so many men starring at us?"

Amber said, "No honey, they're staring at you with that gorgeous long brown hair with hazel-green eyes I didn't notice you look this good under that white coat."

Amber's phone rang, and it was Sabrina calling to say that she was waiting for them at baggage claim. The three friends quickly made their way to the area, and as they reunited, they couldn't help but complement each other on how stunning they all looked.

Elena couldn't help but notice Sabrina's glow-up, "Oh my gosh, the glow-up is real, you look stunning!"

Amber chimed in, "I agree, what's going on? You guys look fabulous. I know it's been a while since we've seen each other, but my goodness."

Sabrina thanked them both, "Thank you, guys. Amber, you've always inspired me to be the best version of myself."

Amber blushed at the compliment, "Oh, stop it. But seriously, you guys look amazing. Elena, your legs look so good in that dress!"

They group hugged and caught up on each other's lives before heading to the Brickell Penthouse to continue their reunion and start their Miami vacation.

On their way in the Uber the driver tries to start hitting on them and Amber was getting annoyed while trying to talk to Sabrina and Elena.

The driver asked, "Would you ladies like to go tonight?"

Amber responds, "Sure I see you're into men." That uber driver remained quiet for the remainder of that ride. The ladies were anxious to see Megan, Jacqueline, Bridget, and Bethania as the driver unloaded their bags from the trunk.

As the driver unloaded their bags, Amber couldn't help but feel a bit embarrassed about her comment to the driver. Sabrina and Elena couldn't stop laughing about it and teasing Amber. They reassured her that it was just a harmless joke, and that the driver should have taken it lightly.

As they walked into the penthouse, they were greeted by Megan, Jacqueline, Bridget, and Bethania. The girls were all catching up and having a good time. Amber couldn't stop thinking about the awkward Uber ride and decided to tell the girls about it.

They all burst out laughing, and Bethania said, "Well, it looks like Amber has a new admirer." They all continued to laugh and tease Amber, but she couldn't help but feel a little embarrassed. Nonetheless, they all had a good laugh.

Amber said, "Ladies, let's go to the spa and get waxed and our nails done."

As they began to walk outside in Brickell, they all noticed that nobody was wearing their mask, it was like the pandemic never happened. No restrictions at all, complete utter freedom and they looked at each other and felt like they were in a different world.

Amber planned a fun afternoon of pampering themselves. They wanted to get their nails done, get a wax, and have their eyelashes done. They found a salon nearby and booked appointments for all six of them. As they walked into the salon, they were greeted by a friendly receptionist who led them to their respective appointments.

Amber went in first for her wax, and as she laid there, the technician was chatty and engaging, which made Amber feel comfortable.

Amber said, "Don't judge me it's been a while."

As the technician was in the middle of the wax, she suddenly sneezed, causing a wax strip to go flying across the room, sticking to the wall. Amber couldn't help but burst out laughing, which made the technician laugh as well. They both laughed so hard that they had to take a break before finishing the wax.

Bethania asked the ladies, "What is so funny while you're getting waxed?"

Sabrina said, "It must be really bad."

Bridget said, "Well I'm next I'm hope I'm not as bad as Amber."

Meanwhile, Jacqueline was getting her nails done and was trying to choose between two colors. She couldn't decide which one to pick, so she asked the ladies for their opinion.

Megan said, "try the stiletto French manicure" Jacqueline agreed, but as the technician started painting her nails.

Sabrina said, "I need to get a tan so badly."

Elena said, "I need one too."

Bridget mentioned that she researched spray tan place nearby.

Amber exited the wax room. "I'm down for the spray tan, ladies I'm back I feel refreshed like a new woman. Who's next?"

Jacqueline chimed in and said, "Ladies I don't feel I need to go by there, but I'll support you, I just want to lay on the beach and get a little darker."

Bridget responded, "Jacqueline you skin always looks fabulous."

Jacqueline said, "Thank you my dear, and so does yours."

Bridget, Elena, Sabrina, and Bethania were all getting their eyelashes done. The technician was very meticulous and precise, taking her time to ensure that each lash was perfect. As the technician finished, she turned to Bridget and said, "You have such beautiful lashes. I'm almost jealous!" Bridget smiled and thanked her, but as she stood up, she said, "Ladies, how do your lashes look? Are you all happy with the results?"

Elena immediately exclaimed, "I love mine! They look so full and long."

Sabrina nodded in agreement, "Yes, they're perfect. I feel like I could flutter them and fly away!"

Bethania chimed in, "I wasn't sure how they would turn out since my natural lashes are quite short, but I am pleasantly surprised. They look so natural!"

The technician smiled, pleased with the positive feedback, and replied, "I'm so glad to hear that! Remember to take good care of them, and they will last for weeks."

Amber asked the ladies, "Where do we want to go tonight? Did everyone bring their sexy Miami attire?"

Elena replied, "I feel like I need to go shopping."

Amber said, "Let me see what you have when we get back to the penthouse."

Megan said, "Oh yes I'm ready to let loose tonight ladies we need this."

Bethania mentioned she had a surprise. "I got a us a table at Kiki on the River."

The ladies were ecstatic and are looking forward to an amazing night out.

Amber mentioned to the ladies, "Before we head out tonight, let's all hit the gym first so we can feel good in our dresses tonight. I found us a nice gym with great reviews."

Megan said, "Wow we are really putting a lot in the schedule on the first day in Miami."

Amber said, "It will be fine trust me, we need to make up for lost time being locked down."

After their spa and spray tan session, the ladies felt rejuvenated and decided to hit the gym in Miami to continue their day. As they walked into the gym, they were taken aback by the sight of all the beautiful women working out.

Amber exclaimed, "Wow, look at all these beautiful women! I've never seen so many gorgeous women at the gym before."

Megan nodded in agreement, "That's exactly what I was thinking. What are we training on?"

Bethania explained, "Ladies, it's Miami. Some of the most beautiful women I've ever seen live in this town."

Amber admitted, "I'm inspired and intimidated at the same time."

Bridget, always up for a challenge, suggested they train legs and glutes. She added, "Ladies, I see men checking us out too. Let's show them how it's done."

Amber couldn't help but notice the abundance of women with amazing figures. "Jacqueline, so many women in here have a butt like yours," she said.

Jacqueline laughed and replied, "I guarantee you mine is all natural like the mangos down here."

Elena chimed in, "Amber, how does it feel to not be the only pretty girl in the room?"

Amber smiled and said, "It's humbling. This motivates me to step my game up. Ladies, let's show these women how to train and look fabulous while doing it."

The group got to work, putting in the effort to train hard while looking stylish and confident. They felt empowered by the supportive and energetic atmosphere around them, and they left the gym feeling even more confident and inspired.

After their intense workout, the ladies were feeling pumped up and energized. They vowed to keep up their fitness routine, so they headed back to the Penthouse to get ready for dinner. As they left the gym, Megan pointed out, "Ladies, it's clearly evident that we are going to have some serious competition in the dating scene if we relocate here."

Sabrina, always confident and positive, replied, "We'll just have to show these men that we offer something different other than looks. If they can't appreciate that, it's their loss." Elena and Jacqueline high-fived Sabrina in agreement.

Elena added, "What you see is what you get. I'm not trying to compete. I know my worth, plus I'm adding taxes."

Bethania, who had previously felt intimidated by the idea of dating in Miami, expressed her appreciation for the support of her friends. "Ladies, I love you guys. I so needed to hear that. I'll admit I was intimidated when I first moved here."

Amber, always one to encourage and motivate her friends, chimed in, "Elena, I agree. That's the spirit. Ladies let's remember that we are boss women. Let's never let any man or woman make us feel unworthy. If we move to Miami, we will run Miami. It will not run us. Let's go get sexy and head to dinner."

As the ladies prepared for a night out on the town in Miami, they faced a common dilemma - what to wear to look their sexiest.

Megan, Bridget, Elena, Sabrina, Amber, Bethania, and Jacqueline gathered in the living room of their penthouse, each with a pile of clothes on the floor and a look of uncertainty on their faces. "I have no idea what to wear."

Sabrina exclaimed, "I want to look hot, but not too flashy."

Bridget nodded in agreement. "Yeah, we don't want to look like we're trying too hard, but we also want to stand out."

Elena chimed in, "I want to wear something that shows off my legs but not too revealing."

Amber, always the fashionista, offered some advice. "Why don't we try on some different outfits and see what looks best? We can give each other honest opinions."

Bethania, who had previously felt self-conscious about her body, expressed her concerns. "I don't know if I have anything that looks good enough to wear."

Jacqueline, always supportive of her friends, reassured Bethania, "Girl, you have an amazing body. Let's find something that shows it off!"

Megan, being the leader of the pack said, "Elena with those sexy legs girl you can wear any of those dresses."

Bridget said, "Ladies let's go shopping tomorrow, Design District!!!"

All the ladies agreed to that tomorrow. The group spent the next hour trying on different outfits, sharing compliments, and offering constructive criticism. Some outfits were too revealing, while others were too conservative. After much deliberation, they finally settled on their outfits, feeling confident and sexy.

As they walked out of the penthouse and into the Miami night, the ladies turned heads and felt proud of how they looked. They knew that no matter what, they had each other's back, and they could conquer anything as long as they were together.

As the sun was set, they decided to head out for KiKi on the River for dinner and explore the Miami nightlife.

Megan, Bridget, Elena, Sabrina, Amber, Bethania, and Jacqueline had been planning a girls' night out in Miami for weeks, and they were all excited to finally make it happen. Bethania was considering a few different restaurants, but settled on Kiki on the River, a Mediterranean-inspired eatery with stunning views of the Miami River.

As they arrived at the restaurant, they were greeted by the hostess and led to a large table outside, overlooking the water. The group marveled at the beautiful scenery and the lively atmosphere of the restaurant.

Their server came over and welcomed them with a smile, handing out menus and explaining the specials for the evening. The group chatted and caught up on each other's lives as they perused the menu, each one eager to try something new.

Megan asked the ladies, "What are you guys' ordering?"

Elena said, "Ladies I don't mean to interrupt but why can he be on the menu?"

Jacqueline said, "Who?"

Elena said, "Turn around."

There he was a tall handsome gentleman bearded with a beautiful smile and well-dressed.

"He looks like Thor," Amber said.

"I'm sure you wouldn't mind playing with his hammer," Bethania said.

Elena said, "Take my advice ladies don't run with the pack, let's show Miami we're going to do it differently." So, Elena got up from her chair and made her way over to the gentlemen.

Megan asked her, "Get it, girl. I love this new Miami energy, what do you want to eat?"

"Seafood pasta," Elena said.

"All these beautiful women in here looking at him," Amber said.

Elena stopped, turned around and looked at Amber and said, "All these beautiful women expect him to come to them, are we going to run Miami or let it run us, plus this kitty is not going to lick itself?"

She proceeded to the gentleman at the bar. He was leaning over, ordering his drink. Elena said to him, "Excuse me, I couldn't resist. I wanted to come and find out who you are."

"Hello, I'm Colin and yours?" he said.

She said, "Elena."

Then Colin began slowly checking out Elena and Elena said, "Can I buy you drink?"

Colin was bedazzled at the question. He replied, "A gorgeous woman wants to buy me a drink. I can't remember the last time that's happened. You must not be from here."

Elena said, "Wow I made it that obvious? Are you here with anyone?"

Colin said, "I'm supposed to meet some friends for dinner, but they haven't arrived yet, what about you?"

Elena said, "I'm here with my girlfriends sitting over there. What drink are you having?"

Colin smiled and said, "I'm having a whiskey sour, but I wouldn't mind trying something new. What do you recommend?"

Elena, feeling a sudden rush of confidence, recommended one of her favorite drinks, a spicy margarita.

As they wait for their drinks, Colin and Elena chat and get to know each other better. They talk about their interests, careers, and hobbies, and soon discover they had a lot in common. Colin was a Software Engineer from New York, and Elena was an OBGYN from Los Angeles. They both shared a love for travel, trying new restaurants, and exploring new cities.

When their drinks arrived, Colin raised his glass and proposed a toast to new friends and exciting adventures. Elena clinked her glass against his and they took a sip, both enjoying the zesty flavor of the spicy margarita.

As they continued to talk, the rest of the group wondered how Elena was doing and wondered if she was coming back to eat.

"I've never tried to hit on a guy, but Elena has inspired me," Amber said.

Megan looked around and spotted her talking to Colin at the bar. She nudged Bridget and said, "Looks like Elena doesn't seem like she'll be alone in Miami."

Elena and Colin exchanged numbers and made plans to meet up again soon.

"I'm hungry so I'm go eat but text me later," Elena said.

"Don't you worry, I certainly will," Colin said.

She responded, "I'm hold you to it, ciao."

She proceeded back to the table and sat down with the girls, and they were elated and dying to get the scoop.

Elena said, "That's how you do it ladies and I'm starving."

"Spill the Tea," Bridget said.

Elena takes a deep breath and smiles, "Well, ladies, he's an amazing guy I love his Norwegian accent. His name is Colin and he's a Software Engineer from New York. We hit it off right away and had the most incredible conversation over drinks. He's handsome, charming, and we have so much in common."

The ladies lean in, eager to hear all the details.

Megan exclaimed, "Oh my god, that's so exciting! What's he like?"

Elena smirks and said, "Well, I was feeling bold, I just felt the urge to walk up to him at the bar and offered to buy him a drink. We started talking and the rest is history."

Amber added, "He is so cute, I saw you talking to him and had to nudge Bethania to take a look."

Bethania giggled, "Yeah, he was definitely a sight for sore eyes. I'm glad you made a move, Elena."

Jacqueline nodded, "Yeah, it's not every day you meet someone that interesting. So, what's the plan now?"

Elena took a sip of her water and said, "Well, we exchanged numbers, and he wants to take me out for dinner Sunday night. I'm thinking of saying yes, what do you guys think?"

Bridget chimed in, "Absolutely say yes! You only live once, and who knows what could happen. This could be the start of something great."

Megan ordered the grilled octopus, Bridget opted for the lamb chops, and Elena chose the seafood pasta. Sabrina went for the vegan eggplant, while Amber and Bethania decided to share a selection of small plates, including the tzatziki dip and stuffed grape leaves. Jacqueline, on the other hand, went for the vegan eggplant dish.

As they waited for their food to arrive, the group sipped on glasses of wine and laughed at stories from their past. They snapped pictures of the stunning views and the beautifully presented dishes as they arrived at the table. Amber and Jacqueline pulled out their phones and started sharing on social media the fun they're having.

As they ate, the conversation continued to flow, and the food was delicious. The lamb chops were perfectly cooked, the pasta was loaded with fresh seafood, and the vegan eggplant dish was a standout favorite among the group.

As the night continued at Kiki on the River, the DJ started playing some great music. The ladies were having a great time chatting, sipping on drinks, and enjoying the ambiance of the beautiful Miami waterfront.

Amber and Bethania were the first to hit the dance floor, swaying and moving to the rhythm of the music. The rest of the ladies soon followed suit, and before long they were all dancing and having a great time.

Sabrina and Jacqueline were dancing together, laughing and twirling each other around. Bridget and Megan were dancing next to them, with Bridget showing off her impressive dance moves, while Megan cheered her on.

As the night went on, the ladies continued to dance and enjoy themselves. Elena couldn't help but smile as she watched her friends having so much fun. She felt grateful to have such an amazing group of women in her life, who were always there to support and uplift her.

"Ladies I'm head to the restroom," Megan said.

Elena, Amber, Jacqueline, Bethania said, "I'll join you."

Meanwhile Bridget and Sabrina just got hit on by these two gentlemen.

They made their way to the ladies' room, chatting and laughing along the way.

When they got to the restroom, they noticed that it was crowded. Megan headed to the first available stall, and the other ladies waited their turn. As they stood there, they heard some commotion coming from one of the other stalls.

Suddenly, the door to the stall burst open, and out stumbled two women, clearly very inebriated. They started giggling and swaying, and before anyone could stop them, they fell into the sink, knocking over a stack of paper towels.

Elena, Amber, Jacqueline, and Bethania were caught off guard and started laughing at the absurdity of the situation. They tried to help the two women up, but they were too far gone.

Meanwhile, Bridget and Sabrina were out at the bar, enjoying their drinks and chatting with two gentlemen. They were completely unaware of what was happening in the ladies' room.

When Megan emerged from the stall, she found her friends doubled over with laughter. She asked them what was so funny, and they told her about the two drunk women who had stumbled out of the stall and knocked over the paper towels.

Megan couldn't help but laugh as well, and the group left the restroom, still chuckling at the absurdity of the situation. As they made their way back to the bar, they filled in Bridget and Sabrina on what had happened.

The ladies all had a good laugh, and Megan said, "Ladies I'm tired I'm ready to go to bed."

All the ladies agreed.

Megan also said, "Bethania please stay with us while we are here."

Bethania replied, "Ok but I need to pick up some things from my place."

Amber said, "I can't wait to show you guys what I have for us tomorrow."

As the ladies arrived back at the penthouse and were getting ready for bed, Amber and Megan were taking a shower. Jacqueline was still unpacking; Sabrina was in the kitchen getting a water. Elena was checking her messages and realized Colin had texted her. Bridge went to the concierge to get Bethania since she stopped by her place to get some stuff to stay with the ladies while they're in town. All of sudden as Bridget and Bethania got off the elevator, there was a guy that was passed out drunk in the hallway naked. It turned out there was a private party happening on the floor.

Bethania looked at Bridget and said, "Oh my, this is quite a situation we've stumbled upon."

Bridget nodded in agreement, "We need to get him back to his room and make sure he's safe. Do you think we can do it on our own?"

Bethania furrowed her brow. "He's naked I'm not going nowhere near that sausage, he looks pretty heavy. You try to wake him up and see if he can walk with our help."

They approached the man cautiously and tried to rouse him. After a few moments, he stirred and blinked at them blearily.

"Hey, can you hear us?" Bridget asked.

The man groaned and tried to sit up but swayed unsteadily and fell back onto the carpet.

Bethania and Bridget exchanged a worried look.

"Okay, we're going to have to get him back to his room," Bethania said firmly. "Bridget, can you grab his feet? I'll take his arms."

Together, they managed to hoist the man onto his feet, but he immediately slumped forward again.

"This isn't working," Bridget said, biting her lip. "We need to get help."

Bethania nodded in agreement, and they carefully lay the man back down on the floor. Bridget ran back to the penthouse to tell the others what's happened, while Bethania stayed with the man to make sure he was okay.

After a few minutes, Bridget returned with Elena and Jacqueline. "We called the concierge, they're sending security to deal with the party and help us get this guy back to his room," she said.

Elena nodded, "Good thinking. Let's stay with him until security arrives and make sure he doesn't try to wander off again."

Megan and Amber hear commotion going on as they put their robes on.

"What's going on?" Amber asked.

Elena said, "There's a naked guy in the hallway."

Amber and Megan look at each other and said, "What?!"

Elena nodded, "Yeah, Bridget and Bethania found him passed out in the hallway. We're waiting for security to come and take care of the situation."

Megan raised an eyebrow, "That's pretty wild. Did they say how he got there?"

Elena shook her head, "Not yet, but it seems like there was a private party happening on the floor. It's possible he wandered out of the wrong room in a drunken stupor."

Amber let out a sigh, "Well, I'm just glad we weren't out there when it happened. That could have been dangerous."

Jacqueline chimed in, "What an interesting way to end our night, It's a good reminder to be aware of our surroundings and always stay together when we're out."

Amber asked Bridget and Bethania, "So was he packing?"

"Barely, and it's not something we want to think about," Bridget replied with a grimace.

Bethania nodded in agreement, "We were not trying to look at his package but Amber I'm sure you want to add to your list of unsolicited penis pics."

Amber let out a small laugh, "Well, it definitely sounds like we're in for an interesting trip."

The group chuckled and shook their heads, realizing that unexpected situations could arise when you least expected them. But they also knew that as long as they stuck together and stayed alert, they could handle anything that came their way.

Bridget opened it to reveal two security guards, who quickly take charge of the situation and escort the man back to his room.

As they watch the guards disappear down the hallway, Sabrina spoke up, "I'm just glad everything turned out okay. Let's all get some rest now, we have a big day tomorrow."

They all nod in agreement and head to their respective rooms, glad that the situation was resolved, and everyone is safe.

Chapter 3

The next morning Jacqueline surprised the girls with ordering groceries and making everyone breakfast. Jacqueline knew that Bethania and Sabrina were on their vegan lifestyle, so she ordered different food for them.

"I've invited my new Miami friend Stephanie over this morning, I wanted you ladies to meet her," Bethania said.

Jacqueline smiles and said, "Good morning Beautiful Queens! Breakfast is ready, and coffee is brewing, Megan."

She gestures towards the table where a spread of different dishes was laid out.

"Bethania, I'm glad you invited Stephanie over. It's always great to make new friends and share a meal together," Megan said.

She walked over to the fridge and took out a carton of almond milk. "I made sure to get some vegan options for you and Sabrina, so feel free to dig in." Jacqueline poured the almond milk into a glass and set it down on the table. "I hope everyone enjoys the meal. Let's eat!"

The group began to eat and chat, getting to know Stephanie better. Elena said to Stephanie, "What do you do in Miami?"

Stephanie replied, "I'm Digital Influencer."

And everyone turned and looked at her mystified.

"Wow you must have a lot of followers," Amber said.

Stephanie said, "It's over a million, I get paid to promote different products to my followers."

"I don't know how I feel about having a million people know who I am," Megan said.

Sabrina said, "I've never of such a thing didn't know it had a coined term."

Stephanie said, "It's good money plus my daddy supports me too."

Jacqueline said, "Your father lives in Miami."

Bethania abruptly interjects and said, "Her Daddy not her father."

All the ladies said, "OOOOOOO."

Stephanie said, "He adores me, but I'm not sexually attracted to him but I'm in love with his credit card it's like we are soul mates."

In the moment, the ladies were perplexed and stunned so Elena said, "You have a man who's not your boyfriend or husband, but he gives your money?"

Stephanie replied, "Yes we have sex but I'm not into it plus he lets me stay at his penthouse in Edgewater, he travels a lot for business."

The ladies are taken aback by Stephanie's revelation. Jacqueline speaks up, "Stephanie, it's your life and your choice, but it's important to remember that relationships should be based on love and mutual respect. Money and material things should never be the foundation of a relationship."

Bethania nods in agreement, "I think it's important to prioritize your own self-worth and independence, instead of relying on someone else's resources. It's great to be able to enjoy the finer things in life, but not at the expense of your own dignity and respect."

Stephanie listens quietly, looking slightly uncomfortable. She said, "I appreciate your concern, but I'm happy with the arrangement I have with my 'daddy.' It works for me, and I feel taken care of. Plus, it's Miami it's part of the culture here."

Stephanie asked, "what do you guys do for a living?"

Megan said, "Wall Street Analyst from NYC,"

Elena said, "I'm an OBGYN in Beverly Hills"

Bridget said, "Real Estate Developer in Orange County California"
Sabrina said, "Corporate lawyer in NYC,"

Amber said, "Pharmaceutical Sales in LA."

Jacqueline said, "Sports Agent in Atlanta."

Stephanie is shocked to meet so many professional women and said, "Wow, you ladies are all so gorgeous accomplished, and successful in your respective fields. It's inspiring to see such strong and independent women. I really admire that. You don't see that in Miami it's very rare. Since I've lived in Miami, I've only met Influencers, Exotic Dancers, Personal Trainers and Real Estate Agents. How did you meet and become friends?"

Jacqueline smiled and responded, "Thank you, Stephanie. It's important for women to support and lift each other up, no matter what we choose to do for a living. We're all on our own journey, but we can all learn from each other and help each other succeed. To answer your question Megan and Bridget are close friends and the master networkers they brought us all together because they had tickets to see Made in America and watch Beyonce perform. We've been close ever since."

Jacqueline said, "Ladies remember that day what happened?"

Sabrina said as she stared chuckling, "Oh my gosh not again."

So, Jacqueline started telling the story to Stephanie.

"We were jumping up and down and singing along to one of Beyonce's biggest hits, 'Crazy in Love,' suddenly heard a loud ripping sound. We realized that Sabrina's tight pants had split open at the back, revealing her brightly colored underwear to the entire crowd. We started bursting out laughing as Sabrina frantically tried to cover up the embarrassing wardrobe malfunction.

"But the show must go on, and we continued to dance and have a great time despite the mishap. In fact, the incident brought us even closer together with a hilarious memory that they still talk about to this day.

"From then on, Sabrina made sure to double-check her outfits before any big events, and the group affectionately referred to her as the 'crazy in love' girl with the memorable wardrobe malfunction."

Megan said, "That's what happens when you start training that booty hard."

Amber added, "It's amazing how one event can bring so many different people together. I'm glad we all met that day and have continued to stay in touch."

Bethania chimed in, "And who knows what other adventures and experiences we'll have together in the future. I'm looking forward to getting to know each of you even better."

The ladies raised their glasses in a toast to friendship and support each other, and Megan said, "Anyone up for some beach time today? Who brought their sexy bikinis?"

Stephanie said, "I can text daddy and see if the captain can take us out on his yacht, the beach may be crowded today since it's the weekend.

Bridget and Megan said, "A yacht?"

Amber said, "I'm so down for the yacht."

Stephanie said, "We can sunbath topless, and the ladies looked at her with surprise and hesitation."

Sabrina spoke up and said, "Stephanie, while we appreciate the offer, it's important to respect each other's boundaries and comfort levels. I don't think all of us would be comfortable sunbathing topless, and that's perfectly okay. Let's enjoy the yacht and the beautiful views without feeling pressure to conform to anyone else's expectations."

Stephanie nodded and said, "You're right, Sabrina. I apologize for assuming everyone would want to do the same thing. We can still have a great time on the yacht without needing to take our tops off. Remember ladies it's Miami a judgment-free zone just do you and soak up the sun plus I don't believe in tan lines."

The ladies all agreed and got excited at the thought of spending the day on a yacht. They quickly got ready, packed their bags, and headed out to meet the captain.

As Stephanie, Megan, Bridget, Elena, Sabrina, Amber, Bethania, and Jacqueline arrived at the marina and walked to the yacht they realized they would be the only ones to have the yacht for the day with the captain and staff. They were ready to sunbathe and lay out and get some sun and enjoy the food and drinks on board.

The yacht was spacious with multiple decks and lounge areas, perfect for the ladies to relax and soak up the sun. They changed into their bikinis and headed to the deck to find comfortable lounge chairs.

Stephanie ordered some champagne and snacks to be served by the staff, and the ladies started chatting and enjoying the beautiful view of the Miami coast. Sabrina suggested they play some music, and Bridget connected her phone to the yacht's sound system, playing some upbeat tunes that made everyone start dancing and laughing.

Stephanie said, "I have a surprise for each of you and girls looked at each other as Stephanie goes down below. She comes back up and hands each girl a gift bag that has Brazilian bikini."

"This is my welcome to Miami gift to you, a friend of mine owns her own Bikini swimwear line and I model for her on her website," she said.

"Thank you, Stephanie," the ladies said.

"I'm go try mine on I love this material girl, you are speaking my language," Amber said.

Jacqueline and Elena agreed. They were excited too. Megan and Bridget said, "We're going to wear this next time."

Jacqueline was the first to come back up and the ladies we're like, "Jacqueline, you're so fine I love it."

Stephanie said, "Jacqueline I wish I had your butt; you look so good girl"

Jacqueline said, "Thank you ladies, I'm not use to my girls being this exposed but as hot as it is I feel so sexy!"

Amber and Elena made their back up in their new Brazilian bikinis.

"Stephanie, I love this, this takes sexy to another level," Amber said.

Elena said, "I feel like a Miami model in this."

And the rest of the ladies chimed in and said, "Wow, you both look amazing!" and "Those bikinis are so cute on you!"

The ladies complimented each other and took turns taking pictures and selfies to remember the day.

As they sailed along the coast, the ladies enjoyed some delicious food and drinks while basking in the sun. Stephanie, Megan, and Amber decided to take a dip in the ocean, and the rest of the ladies watched them playfully splashing each other and enjoying the refreshing water.

After a while, they returned to the yacht and continued lounging and chatting. Stephanie shared some stories from her travels as a digital influencer, and the other ladies talked about their work and personal lives. They laughed, joked, and bonded over their shared experiences, realizing how much they had in common despite coming from different backgrounds and professions.

As the day went on, the ladies watched the sunset from the 'yacht's deck and took some stunning photos and videos. Meanwhile, Megan asked the ladies, "What do you think so far about Miami? Do you think we can live here?"

Bridget replied, "I love the warm weather and the beach lifestyle, but I'm not sure if I can handle the traffic and crowds all the time."

Sabrina added, "Miami has some great job opportunities, especially in my field, but the cost of living can be high."

Elena said, "I think Miami is a fun and lively city, but I don't know if I could handle the humidity in the summer."

Amber chimed in, "I love the nightlife here, but I don't think I could handle the constant party scene."

Jacqueline said, "I could definitely see myself living here, but it depends on finding the right neighborhood and community."

Bethania, who had been quiet for most of the day, finally spoke up and said, "I love Miami, it's my home, but it can also be a challenging city to live in. You have to be ready to hustle and work hard to make it here."

Stephanie nodded in agreement and said, "Miami is definitely not for everyone, but for those of us who love it, there's no other place like it."

Amber asked Stephanie a question that shocked everyone. "Stephanie where do you get your work done? Your boobs look incredible, Miami makes me want to step my game up."

Stephanie said, "Thank you girl, text me your number I have my doctor on speed dial let me know what you need, and I'll make sure he takes care of you."

The ladies responded Bethania chimed in, "I've been considering a few enhancements myself, would you mind sharing your doctor's information with me too?"

Stephanie responded, "Of course not, I'll send his information to both of you."

Elena added, "I've been thinking about getting a breast lift, do you think your doctor does that as well?"

Stephanie replied, "Absolutely, he's one of the best in the city. I'll send you his contact information as well."

The rest of the ladies expressed their interest in the doctor as well, and Stephanie promised to share his information with all of them.

Megan said, "I love you, it's only been 24 hours since we stepped off the plane. Every city has its pros and cons. I know I'm the one who suggested that we try it. Bethania is going to show us tomorrow some nice places that we can stay at. Plus, I would love it if we can live in the same city and build our bond more."

The ladies said, "Absolutely, let's do it!"

They all agreed that it would be amazing to live in the same city and continue to build their friendship.

Stephanie chimed in and said, "I can help with finding some great places to stay and showing you around the city. Miami is a wonderful place to live, I've been here for a while now and I love it."

The ladies smiled and raised their glasses to toast their future plans.

As the ladies were leaving the marina, they ran into a group of gentlemen who were trying to hit on them. One of them invited them to come to E11ven tonight. "We have a table and drinks are on us."

The ladies smiled and politely declined the invitation, thanking the gentlemen for their offer. They explained that they had a long day and were planning on having a relaxing night in. The gentlemen wished them a good evening and the ladies continued on their way.

As they walked away, Sabrina said, "I don't know about you guys, but I'm not really into the club scene anymore."

The others agreed, and Megan suggested that they have a 'girls' night in with some wine and movies. The ladies were excited about the idea and started discussing what they should watch.

Stephanie said, "Ladies I have a better idea, I know exactly what you like. I can tell what vibe you would like."

The ladies all looked at Stephanie and said, "Really? What did you have in mind?"

Stephanie said, "I need you to dress up we're going to Living Room at the Faena Miami Beach."

Now the ladies were excited at the prospect of trying out a new place, especially after a day of lounging on the yacht. They quickly headed back to their Brickell Penthouse to get ready.

A few hours later, they all met Stephanie in the lobby, dressed to the nines. Stephanie led the way to her car, a sleek black Lamborghini, and they made their way to the Faena Hotel.

Jacqueline said, "Stephanie continues to impress me I didn't expect her to drive that."

Bethania said, "It's Miami honey don't be surprised what you see here."

The rest of the ladies said, "Sounds good to us!" as they made their way to the van.

As the ladies were riding in the van following Stephanie, Bridget asked, "What do you think about Stephanie?"

Megan responded first, "I think she's quite the enigma. She definitely has some powerful connections and seems to know her way around Miami. Plus, she knows how to show us a good time."

Amber chimed in, "I'm not sure what to make of her yet, but she does seem to have a good sense of style."

Elena added, "She's definitely got a mysterious air about her, but I like that she's taking us to some cool spots."

Sabrina said, "I'm always a bit cautious when it comes to new people, but I think Stephanie is interesting and I'm enjoying getting to know her."

Jacqueline added, "I have to say, I'm impressed with her knowledge of the city and the connections she has. She seems like someone we could definitely learn from."

Bethania nodded in agreement. "I think she has a lot to offer, and I'm excited to see what else she has in store for us."

Bridget smiled, "I agree, she's definitely keeping things interesting."

As they arrived at the Faena, they were blown away by the luxurious and elegant atmosphere. The Living Room was a beautiful lounge with chic decor and sophisticated vibes. The ladies found a cozy corner and Stephanie ordered some champagne for everyone. As they sipped on their drinks, they chatted and laughed, enjoying the beautiful ambiance of the place.

They were struck by the stunning beauty of the place. The living Room was an intimate, low-lit space with plush velvet chairs and couches, a grand piano, and a bar stocked with top-shelf liquor.

Stephanie led them to a corner booth, where they settled in and ordered drinks. The music was a mix of jazz, blues, and lounge music, and the atmosphere was electric.

Bridget told Megan, "I need you to turn around and look at this tall dark and handsome walking this way girl."

Bethania looked at Jacqueline. "Oh, my word."

The rest of the ladies chimed in.

Megan turned around to see a tall, well-dressed man approaching them. She whispered to Bridget, "He is quite handsome, isn't he?"

Bethania and Jacqueline giggled and exchanged glances, while the other ladies smiled and nodded in agreement.

Stephanie leaned over to Elena and said, "I think we have some potential for some fun tonight."

The ladies all laughed, and Elena responded, "You always know how to have a good time, Steph." As the man approached, the ladies took notice and waited to see what would happen next.

"You ladies look absolutely gorgeous," he said. Then he looked at Megan and said as he reached out to shake her hand, "I especially had my eye on you, what's your name?"

Megan said, "I'm Megan and yours?"

"Maxwell St. John," he said.

In the back of Megan's mind even his name is sexy. Megan said, "It's nice to meet you, Maxwell."

Megan even checked him out even closer and noticed his beautiful smile, that beard, and well-manicured hands, and noticed he smelled amazing. Her pheromone levels were elevated.

Stephanie whispered to Amber and Jacqueline, "I can tell he's not from here. Men that gorgeous and tall are rare in Miami."

Maxwell said, "I would like to invite you and your friends to my table, plus I want to get to know you more. My clients left early cause they have to catch an early flight. Would you like some Champagne?"

Megan said, "Sure, but first are you single? If so, we'll come join you."

Maxwell looked directly in Megan eyes and said, "Yes Single and ready to mingle I'll tell you more come with me."

As they made their way to Maxwell's table, all the ladies sat around his table and Megan sat next to Maxwell. Maxwell placed an order of Champagne for the table.

Then Megan asked Maxwell, "Tell me about yourself."

Maxwell said, "I live in Washington DC, but I have a home in Miami too. My company is Defense Contractor, I've been single for almost 2 years now, and I'm looking for someone who is intelligent, ambitious, and can keep up with me. I love to travel, go on adventures, and try new things. What about you, Megan? What do you do?"

Megan responded, "I'm Wall Street Analyst, and I love to travel as well. In fact, this trip to Miami was a girls' trip to get away from the pandemic lockdown and just have fun. My girls and I are deciding to relocate to Miami."

The rest of the ladies chimed in, introducing themselves and sharing a bit about their lives.

As the night wore on, Bridget, Amber, Bethania, and Stephanie had consumed a bit too much champagne and were feeling the effects. They started laughing and giggling uncontrollably, and their conversation became more and more nonsensical.

At one point, Stephanie tried to take a group selfie with her phone, but accidentally dropped it on the floor. Everyone laughed, and Bethania jokingly scolded her for being clumsy. Amber then decided to join in the fun and started doing a silly dance, which made everyone laugh even more.

Bridget then announced that she had to use the restroom, and Stephanie insisted on accompanying her, as she didn't want her to get lost. Sabrina, Elena, Bethania, and Amber decided to stay at the table and continue chatting with Maxwell.

As they walked to the restroom, Bridget and Stephanie were still giggling uncontrollably, and Stephanie accidentally bumped into a waiter carrying a tray of drinks, spilling them all over the floor. They apologized profusely, but the waiter was not pleased and gave them a stern look.

After using the restroom, Bridget and Stephanie made their way back to the table, where they found Bethania and Amber still chatting with Maxwell. They sat down and resumed their conversation, albeit a bit more subdued after their little misadventure.

As the night went on, the ladies danced, laughed, and chatted, enjoying each other's company and the luxurious surroundings. Eventually, Maxwell and Megan exchanged numbers and made plans to meet up again.

As they left to head back home to Brickell, they all agreed that Stephanie had picked the perfect spot for a night out.

The next morning Amber was feeling quite excited about the surprise that she had for the girls. Meanwhile, Elena and Colin had been texting, and kept her up late last night. She was also very excited about her date. Megan was happy to see that Maxwell had texted her, "Good Morning Gorgeous."

Two days into the trip and the ladies were ecstatic at the possibilities of what Miami had to offer them next.

Amber hired one of Miami's popular hairstylists to come and exclusively work on their hair at the penthouse. The girls were all excited about Amber's generous offer and couldn't wait to see the results. Amber mentioned, "Javier and his love Jorge are going to give a blowout and some color if we want it."

Elena said, "Thank you I need this before my date tonight."

"So do I," Megan said.

Amber said to Jacqueline, "Don't worry girl you know I thought of you too."

Jacqueline was impressed at first, she was hesitant but let's try it.

Amber mentioned, "They'll be here at noon so let's hit the gym this morning ladies after all that food on the boat and drinks last night I need to good workout this morning plus it's Miami we have to stay looking fabulous."

They ladies agreed, the ladies got ready and headed to the gym. As they were working out, they noticed some other people in the gym who looked familiar. Bridget approached them and realized they were a group of models who had just finished their photo shoot. Bridget struck up a conversation with them and before they knew it, they were all chatting and exchanging social media handles.

After their workout, they headed back to the penthouse to freshen up and get ready for Javier and Jorge to do their hair.

After settling in, Javier and Jorge arrived, and the girls got to work on their hair, trying out different styles and colors.

Then the ladies got a surprising door knock. Megan asked, "Who's expecting someone?"

It was a group of waiters who entered with trays of food. Amber announced that she had arranged for a private chef to prepare a special lunch for them. The ladies were pleasantly surprised and dug into the delicious spread of food.

Jacqueline said, "Amber, I love you girl, you really outdid yourself."

The ladies chimed in, "Yes, this is amazing!"

"Thank you so much, Amber!"

"I can't believe you planned all of this for us!"

"You are the best, Amber!"

Amber said, "No problem, ladies, I love our sisterhood, since Elena and Megan have dates tonight. Bridget, Jacqueline, Bethania, Sabrina let's go out tonight I can't believe I haven't met a guy yet."

Jacqueline said, "Sounds like a plan girl, let's get dolled up and hit the town tonight."

Bethania added, "I know a great spot in Wynwood where we can go dancing and have some cocktails."

Sabrina chimed in, "Yes, and we can take some fabulous photos in front of the colorful murals."

The ladies laughed and agreed that it was the perfect plan for a fun night out in Miami.

Bridget added, "Yeah, we should go somewhere with good music and dancing."

Amber responded, "What about LIV at the Fontainebleau Miami Beach. It's supposed to have a great atmosphere, great music, and a lot of cute guys. What do you guys think? I know it's a nightclub but let's try it and see if we like it."

The ladies agreed to keep an open mind.

Megan asked Javier and Jorge, "Tell us about yourselves, how long have you been together? What made you get in the hair business?"

Javier and Jorge smiled and started sharing their story with Megan and Elena. They explained that they had been together for 5 years and had started their own hair salon business together shortly after they met. Jorge had always been passionate about hair and had studied cosmetology in school, while Javier had experience in business management. They saw an opportunity to combine their skills and create a unique salon experience for their clients.

Jorge said, "We wanted to create a salon where people could feel comfortable and be themselves. We specialize in all types of hair, and we're always experimenting with new styles and techniques."

Javier added, "We also wanted to create a space where people could come and relax, have a drink, and enjoy the atmosphere. We believe that getting your hair done should be an enjoyable experience, not a chore."

After Javier and Jorge were finished, the ladies absolutely loved their new look. They said to Javier and Jorge, "We absolutely love our new look, you guys are amazing! Thank you so much for your time and your incredible talent."

Megan said to Amber, "Give us their numbers we will need you in the future."

After Javier and Jorge left, Sabrina mentioned she had a surprise for them. "Ladies, I have something fun planned for us this afternoon!"

Everyone leaned in with curiosity as Sabrina continued, "We're going to do a photo shoot on the beach with a professional photographer!"

The ladies cheered in excitement.

Sabrina said, "I have a friend of mine who knows a great photographer in Miami and was free to meet us plus we look fabulous I want to capture these moments with you guys."

The ladies were thrilled at the idea of doing a photo shoot and couldn't wait to get started.

Amber said, "Sabrina, this is such a great idea, thank you for putting this together. I can't wait to see how the photos turn out!"

Elena chimed in, "Yes, and we can share them on our social media to show everyone what a great time we're having in Miami!"

The ladies quickly got ready and headed to the beach. When they arrived, they were greeted by the photographer who had set up a beautiful backdrop with palm trees and the ocean in the background. The ladies took turns posing and having their photos taken, laughing and enjoying the moment.

After the shoot was over, the ladies were all buzzing with excitement and couldn't wait to see the final photos.

Sabrina said, "We should get together and have a viewing party when the photos are ready!"

The ladies all agreed and made plans to do just that.

The photographer captured stunning shots of the ladies lounging on the beach, playing in the waves, and striking fierce poses. The girls were feeling confident and beautiful, and the photos reflected their energy and spirit.

Later that evening, Elena and Colin had their date at a trendy rooftop restaurant with panoramic views of the city. They enjoyed delicious food and cocktails while chatting and laughing under the starry Miami sky. Megan and Maxwell also had a romantic evening, strolling hand in hand along the beach and watching the waves crash against the shore.

Amber, Bridget, Sabrina, Bethania, and Jacqueline decided to head to Wynwood then to the Fontainebleau.

While getting ready Sabrina said, "Ladies, I have a wardrobe crisis. The dress I was going to wear got ruined in my check-in."

Jacqueline said, "You know what that means."

Sabrina said, "What?"

Jacqueline said, "We have a reason to go shopping, what do you ladies think?"

Bridget, Bethania, and Amber cheered in agreement while Sabrina laughed and said, "I like the way you think, Jacqueline!"

They quickly finished getting ready and headed out to Brickell City Center to find the perfect dress for Sabrina. After trying on a few options, Sabrina found a stunning, form-fitting black dress that accentuated her frame and made her feel confident and glamorous.

Sabrina asked the ladies, "What do you think of this? I feel so sexy."

Bridget, Bethania, and Amber all agreed that Sabrina looked amazing in the dress, with Jacqueline chiming in, "Girl, you're going to turn heads tonight!"

While at the mall Jacqueline and Bethania noticed this very attractive group of gentlemen.

Amber said to the ladies, "They're checking us out and not bad looking at all."

Jacqueline said, "Ladies let's give them a sign we're interested."

Bethania suggested they all smile and wave at them, and the other ladies agreed. They turned towards the group of guys and flashed their best smiles, waving in a flirty manner. The guys caught on and started to smile back and wave, clearly interested. The gentlemen walked over and introduced themselves and they were speaking with a British accent.

The ladies were thrilled to meet the charming British guys, who introduced themselves as James, Harry, Charles and William. They exchanged pleasantries and started chatting, learning about each other's backgrounds and interests. The guys were in Miami for a vacation, and they were impressed with the ladies' sense of style and confidence. They all hit it off and decided to continue the night together, heading to a popular Fontainebleau in Miami Beach.

As they got into the Uber Black, James made sure to sit next to Amber and struck up a conversation with her. He asked about her interests and hobbies, and Amber found herself enjoying the easy banter between them.

Meanwhile, Jacqueline and Harry were seated next to each other, and Harry couldn't stop complimenting Jacqueline on her stunning beauty. He told her how he couldn't take his eyes off her all evening and how lucky he felt to have met her.

Sabrina and Charles found themselves engaging in a lively debate about art and music, with Charles expressing his love for jazz and Sabrina sharing her passion for contemporary art.

As for Bethania and William, he kept whispering playful and flirty one-liners in her ear, making her laugh and blush at the same time.

Harry told Bridget, "I have a friend of mine that's going to meet us, he's going to love you. You're so his type."

Bridget was intrigued and curious about this mystery friend of Harry's. She asked, "What's he like? Can you tell us more about him?"

Harry smiled and replied, "He's a great guy, really fun and outgoing. He's into fitness and loves to travel. I think you two will hit it off."

Bridget blushed a little and said, "Well, I'm excited to meet him then!"

Bridget group texted the ladies and said, "If we get separated, let's check in with each other regularly. Safety first, I love you." Then she asked how Elena and Megan were doing.

Megan and Elena responded, "We're doing great! Colin and Maxwell are such amazing guys. We're having such a good time with them."

"How's your night going?" Bridget responded, "Glad to hear you guys are having a great time! We just met some amazing guys, they're so much fun. We're heading to a Fontainebleau with them."

Megan said, "Please be safe ladies, and can't wait to hear details later! Love you."

When they arrived, James and Harry said, "We're going to a table to make it easier for us to stay together."

They replied, "Thank you guys," and followed the hostess to the table. Meanwhile Harry grabbed Jacqueline's hand and said, "Let's go dancing."

And Bethania and William followed them to the dance floor.

The girls shouted, "Work it Jacqueline!"

"Bethania show them how it's done girl!"

Jacqueline looked at Bethania and said, "Let's show these gentlemen how it's done!"

Bethanie and Jacqueline started dancing with Harry and William and the guys were impressed by the ladies' dance moves and the energy they brought to the dance floor. Bethania and Jacqueline were particularly in their element, showing off their best moves and keeping up with Harry and William. Meanwhile, at the table, James and Amber were engaged in deep conversation, getting to know each other better and enjoying each other's company. Bridget and the rest of the group were also having a great time, chatting and laughing together while sipping their drinks.

Harry's other friend arrived an hour later, and Harry introduced Cole to Bridget. Bridget said, in the back of her mind, *he looks like Liam Hemsworth.*

Cole sat next to Bridget and said, "Hi Bridget, nice to meet you. Harry has been raving about you all night. He said you're intelligent, funny, and beautiful, and I have to say he was right. How has your night been so far?"

Cole flashed Bridget a charming smile and his blue eyes sparkled in the club's lights. Bridget was absolutely smitten. Bridget blushed at Cole's compliment and smiled back, feeling a little flustered. "Thank you, Cole, that's really sweet of you to say. I'm having a great night so far, thanks for asking. How about you? Are you enjoying yourself?"

Bridget tried to keep her cool, but she could feel her heart racing a little faster as she talked to him. She couldn't help but think that Harry might have been right about Cole being her type.

Harry mentioned to Jacqueline, "Let's go out by the pool."

Jacqueline said, "You tired of dancing and putting your hands me already?"

Harry said, "Oh no I would love to put my hands all over you all night."

Jacqueline responded, "As lovely as that sounds and as much I love you putting your hands on places I don't normally allow when I first meet someone but I'm not that kind of girl."

Harry said, "I meant no disrespect my apologies how about we take a walk on the boardwalk?"

Jacqueline said, "In these heals, I can't darling."

Harry said, "How about I get us some drinks and set by the pool and enjoy the night?"

Jacqueline said, "I would like that."

Jacqueline told the ladies in the group chat, "Harry and I are going by the pool and have drinks."

Meanwhile Bethania and William couldn't seem to get enough of each other.

Bethania told him, "I love your sense of humor."

"I love making you smile," William said. Then he asked her, "Tu habla espanol?"

She replied, "Si."

Bethania said, "You're bilingual, me encanta El Senor William."

Bethania loved it

William grinned and replied, "Sí, I grew up speaking Spanish and English. It always come in handy, especially in Miami. I'm glad you appreciate it, Bethania. You know, I'm really enjoying spending time with you tonight. You have a beautiful smile and a great energy about you."

He took her hand and gave it a gentle squeeze. Bethania blushed and smiled back, feeling a flutter in her chest. "Gracias, William. I'm having a great time with you too. You're such a gentleman and you know just how to make me laugh."

They continued chatting and dancing, enjoying each other's company.

Charles and Sabrina liked each other even though she felt she was not a good dancer.

Charles asked her, "Would you like a shot? I absolutely love this dress on you."

Sabrina said, "Oh really? What do you like about it, Sir Charles?"

Charles said, "You have pretty stems, I feel like you wore that dress just for me."

Sabrina said, "If you keep being a good boy maybe someday, you'll get to see what's underneath."

In the back of Sabrina mind, she said, "I can't believe I said that but he's so cute though."

Sabrina was normally the conservative type, but she started having impure thoughts of what she would do to him. Then she started thinking maybe I had too much Maca Root in my smoothie today Sabrina said, "Let's go for walk. I want to get out of here."

Maxwell and Megan walked hand in hand, enjoying the peaceful sounds of the water and the beautiful Miami skyline in the distance. Megan turned to Maxwell and said, "This is just what I needed after a long week of work. Thank you for taking me out here, Maxwell."

Maxwell smiled and replied, "Of course, Megan. You deserve a break, and it's nice to have some alone time with you."

As they walked, they passed by some street performers playing music, and Meghan started to dance along. Maxwell couldn't resist and started to dance with her too. The two of them laughed and spun around, enjoying the moment.

After a while, they found a nice spot to sit and enjoy the view. They talked about their hopes and dreams and shared some of their favorite memories. Megan felt grateful for this moment and for having Maxwell by her side.

Rooftop bars were always a great option to enjoy the Miami skyline and Colin and Elena were excited to check out Rosa Sky Rooftop. As they stepped out of the elevator onto the rooftop, they were greeted by the warm evening breeze and the sound of a live band playing jazz music. They walked over to the bar and ordered their drinks, taking in the stunning views of the city.

As they sat at a table, Elena commented, "This place is amazing. I love how you can see the entire city from up here. It's so beautiful."

Colin smiled and said, "Yeah, the view is incredible. But honestly, I'm just happy to be here with you. You make everything so much better. It's even more of a magnificent view when you're a part of the picture."

Elena blushed at his words and took a sip of her drink. "You're too sweet, Colin. I'm really enjoying spending time with you tonight."

Colin couldn't help but be captivated by Elena's beauty, both inside and out. He felt a strong connection with her and knew that he wanted to spend more time with her.

After a while, they decided to take a walk around the rooftop and explore the different areas. As they reached the edge of the rooftop, Colin put his arm around Elena and pulled her in for a kiss, feeling the sparks fly between them.

They spent the rest of the night sipping their drinks, listening to the live music, and enjoying each other's company. As they left the rooftop, Elena couldn't help but think how lucky she was to have met Colin.

Bridget quickly typed a message to the group chat, "Hey ladies, do you think we should ask the guys what their real intentions are? I find it hard to believe that all these good-looking guys are single." The message was sent, and within seconds, the replies started pouring in.

Sabrina said, "I think that's a great idea, Bridget. It's always better to know where we stand."

Jacqueline chimed in, "Yes, let's do it! I want to make sure Harry is not just looking for a fling."

Bethania replied, "I agree, we need to know if they're serious or not."

Amber said, "I'm down, let's ask them!"

Bridget then turned to Cole and asked, "So, Cole, what are your intentions with me?"

Cole looked at Bridget, and with a serious expression, he said, "Bridget, I think you're an amazing woman, and I would like to get to know you better. I'm not looking for a fling or a one-night stand. I'm interested in something more serious."

Bridget smiled and said, "Thank you for being honest, Cole. I feel the same way."

The other ladies followed suit, asking the guys about their intentions. The guys all responded positively, stating that they were looking for something serious and meaningful. The ladies were relieved and happy to hear this. They spent the rest of the night enjoying each other's company, dancing, and having fun, knowing that they are all on the same page.

Megan mentioned, "Maxwell, as much as I would love to stay out with you much later tonight. The girls and I have a long day tomorrow we've got to go real estate hunting." Megan group texted the girls, "I'm about to call it a night with Maxwell and head back to the penthouse remember ladies we got a long day tomorrow Bethania is going to show us a lot of different real estate of where we would potentially like to live."

So Bethania, Jacqueline, Sabrina, Elena, Bridget, and Amber decided to call it a night after exchanging numbers with the guys and meet Megan back at the Penthouse.

On the ride home, Bethania asked the girls, "Do you think it's a little strange that all these good-looking guys are single looking for the same thing? I'm sorry ladies but I don't mean to sound like a pessimist it was a great night but it's a little too good to be true. Plus, they all live in the United Kingdom I don't know how I feel about dating someone long distance."

Jacqueline replied, "I know what you mean, Bethania. It does seem a little too good to be true. But hey, we just met them tonight, so it's hard to say for sure what their intentions are. Let's just take it one day at a time and see where things go. And who knows, maybe we'll find out that they're not all single or looking for the same thing after all."

Bridget added, "I agree with Jacqueline. We don't want to jump to conclusions just yet. And about the long-distance thing, it can be tough, but it's not impossible. We can always see where things go and take it from there."

Sabrina chimed in, "Yes, let's just enjoy the moment and have fun. We'll deal with any challenges that come our way when the time comes. For now, let's just focus on finding the perfect place to live tomorrow and making the most of our time here in Miami."

So as the ladies arrived back at the penthouse Megan had just arrived, taking her shoes off in the living room reflecting on the night as she decided to walk out on the balcony. The front door opened, and Jacqueline, Bethania Bridget Sabrina and Amber walked in. A few minutes later, here comes Elena in the door seeing that all the ladies were standing out on the balcony talking about their night. So Elena decided to join them.

Bridget said to all the ladies, "It was certainly one hell of a night."

Megan chimed in and said, "It was one heck of a weekend."

Jacqueline said, "How ironic we met a good-looking guy that was our type within 48 hours of being in Miami."

Bethania chimed in and said, "Since I moved here ladies there is a coin term in Miami it's called "only in Dade."

She mentioned that it meant things happened in this town that were so rare it only happened in Miami.

While the ladies were standing out on the balcony talking about their night and reminiscing, they could hear their neighbors below them having sex.

Amber said, "Well at least someone's getting some this weekend."

Megan said, "Amber, you're so naughty!"

They all laughed and continued to chat, but they made sure to keep their voices down so as not to disturb the neighbors. After a few more minutes, they all decided to call it a night and headed to bed, excited about the real estate hunting they had planned for the next day. They were determined to find the perfect place to live, and they couldn't wait to start their search with Bethania's help.

Chapter 4

The next day Bethania was working in the dining room preparing some different places she wanted to show the ladies. She already had an idea of the kind of places the ladies would prefer to stay at.

Bethania asked, "If I could find the perfect place for each one of you all today? Are you ready to make a deposit and lock the place down?"

The ladies responded, "Sure let's do it."

Bethania said, "I'm going to show you a few buildings here in Brickell then we'll go over to Edgewater and then we'll head over to Miami Beach. Because I know each of you wanted a place by the water. So, the first place they stop at is the Paramount building."

Bethania showed the ladies around the Paramount building, highlighting its stunning ocean views and luxurious amenities. The girls are impressed with the sleek design and modern decor, and they can already imagine themselves living there. Bethania explained that the building offers a range of apartments, from cozy one-bedrooms to spacious three-bedrooms, and that all units come fully furnished with high-end appliances and designer furniture. The ladies were excited about the prospect of living in such a beautiful building, and they eagerly asked about the pricing and availability. Bethania promised to follow up with the building's management and provide them with all the information they need to make an informed decision. Megan and Sabrina told Bethania that's my style.

The ladies' second stop was Brickell Key the Asia building. Bethania had heard great things about it, and she knew that it was a luxurious and exclusive building that would meet the ladies' high standards. As they walked through the lobby and saw the stunning views of the water, the ladies were all impressed. Bethania showed them a few units that were available, and they were all blown away by the amenities and features of the building. They made a mental note to consider Asia as a top contender for their new Miami home.

Bridget said, "I love this Bethania so far this is top of the list." Jacqueline chimed in, "I agree with Bridget."

Bethania showed the Aria and Paraiso Bay buildings to the group, Amber and Elena were particularly impressed. They loved the views of the water and the modern amenities that the buildings offered. Bethania made sure to take note of their preferences and requirements to help narrow down their options.

After Edgewater, Bethania recommended that they head to Miami Beach but took a scenic way across Venetian Island and the ladies loved it.

They drove across the Venetian Islands, the ladies marveled at the stunning views of the water and the beautiful homes. Bethania pointed out some of the most famous houses and landmarks, and the ladies were in awe. Finally, they arrived at their destination called Bentley Bay.

At Bentley Bay, the ladies were immediately impressed with the modern and luxurious building. Bethania showed them a few different units with stunning ocean views and high-end amenities, such as a rooftop pool, fitness center, and concierge services. Sabrina was thrilled with what they saw and decided to make an offer on a beautiful two-bedroom unit with a spacious balcony overlooking the ocean.

The ladies were surprised she was going to buy a condo and Sabrina said, "This will be an investment under my business plus ladies let's own some property here. Megan, you're on Wall Street you know the importance of investing." Bethania was ecstatic that Sabrina offered to buy the unit and immediately told the listing agent we'll take it.

Bethania still wanted to take the ladies over to One Hotel Residences and show them the vacant units.

Bethania drove the ladies over to One Hotel Residences, which was another popular beachfront property. She wanted to show them some of the vacant units that were available for sale. As they walked through the lobby and into the elevator, they were struck by the stylish decor and the modern design.

When they arrived at the units, Bethania showed them around and pointed out some of the unique features, such as the large windows that provided stunning ocean views, the luxurious amenities, and the state-of-the-art appliances. The ladies were impressed by what they saw and were eager to learn more about the properties.

After the tour, they sat down to discuss their options and see if any of the units were within their budget. Megan said to Bethania,

"I would like to put in an offer on the two-bedroom unit that faces the ocean." Bethania was shocked that she was getting two real estate offers in one day.

Bethania starts getting emotional she told the ladies,

"I was struggling trying to get acclimated in Miami it's hard doing business here at times."

Megan said, "Don't worry girl I love you we're going to take care of you and make you so much money." The ladies group hugged, and Megan turns around and looks at Sabrina and said, "Thank you, you inspired me today at first I was going to rent but you're right let's own in Miami."

Megan said to the ladies, "We're hard-working women we deserve this we've earned this."

Bridget said, "You're right Bethania I'll make an offer on the unit in Brickell Key I really like that."

Jacqueline told, "Bethania I'm going to make an offer at the Paramount Building."

Elena said, "I'll make an offer on the three-bedroom unit here in the One Hotel."

Amber said, "I want to make an offer at the Aria building."

Bethania starts crying as a Real Estate Agent nobody ever gets 6 offers in one day to buy properties. She thanked the ladies and said, "I can't believe this, you have no idea what this means to me. I'm so grateful for each one of you." The real estate agent congratulated Bethania and the ladies on their decisions and promised to work with them on closing the deals. The ladies exchange hugs and high-fives, feeling proud and excited about their new investments in Miami.

Amber said, "We have a lot to celebrate tonight ladies and Bethania I am so happy that you were able to get these deals." Bethania text Stephanie and told her the good news, and Stephanie said, "Let's all go out tonight and celebrate at Carbone." Bethania replied, "Isn't that the real exclusive restaurant that's so hard to get in?" Stephanie replies, "Yes I'll text Amir he has connections that can get us in." So, the ladies were excited to get a last-minute reservation at Carbone.

The ladies got ready for their night out, feeling excited about their real estate purchases and celebrating their friendship. They met Stephanie in the lobby of the building, looking stunning and ready to go. Amir would meet them there, and they all took a limo to Carbone, one of the most exclusive restaurants in Miami Beach.

When they arrived, the restaurant was buzzing with people, and they were immediately escorted to their table. The waiter brought them the menu and a bottle of champagne, and they all toasted to their success and friendship.

They ate their delicious Italian food, they laughed and reminisced about their night out the day before and their real estate purchases. Bethania was overwhelmed with gratitude for her friends' support, and she couldn't stop thanking them.

After dinner, they decided to head to a nearby rooftop bar to continue the celebration. They danced and drank, enjoying the warm Miami night and each other's company. It was a perfect ending to an unforgettable day.

Bethania the next day was so jubilant and ecstatic from what happened. She started thinking and says to herself,

"I'm going to work on my broker's license and have my own brokerage." She was so inspired by her friends it made her want to step up and take her career to the next level.

As the ladies gathered around for breakfast in the morning, now that they have become property owners in Miami.

Sabrina asked the ladies, "Do you think you could live in Miami as your primary residence?"

Megan said, "I believe I could be there are still times I would have to fly back and forth to New York."

Elena said, "I agree with Megan I would have to fly back and forth to LA, but I'll eventually open up my own practice here or I would just join a practice that's very well established."

Jacqueline said, "Miami would definitely be a primary residence nothing wrong with Atlanta but, Miami just fits this chapter in my life."

Amber said, "I would still have my territories around San Diego and expand here in South Florida so I would just fly back and forth a lot."

Bridget said, "I would have to fly back and forth too, but I do want to get involved in some real estate development projects in Miami.

Sabrina said, "it sounds like we're all going to be nomads for a little while as we're making our adjustment to the Magic City."

Bethania said, "I love you guys so much I know I can never thank you all enough for yesterday, but I just love how we selflessly care and elevate each other. We inspire and make each other better that's what real friendship is all about."

Jacqueline said, "I would drink to that that was so well said if I had a drink in my hand."

Bridget asked the ladies "What are some upcoming goals you ladies have next?"

Sabrina said, "I'm start investing in other businesses and launch my own line of skincare product."

Jacqueline said, "I will eventually start a nonprofit organization to help disadvantaged children."

Elena said, "Just to expand my practice to Miami."

Megan said, "I'm concur with Sabrina I'm start investing expanding my portfolio."

Amber said, "I'm start traveling more and visit new places." Bethania chimes in, "I'm continue growing her real estate business and help more people find their dream homes."

Bridget asked the ladies "Would you join me tonight in a networking event called Epic Talks Miami? You guys are so inspirational."

The ladies were excited about the opportunity to attend a networking event and show support for Bridget.

Sabrina asked, "What type of event is it? and what should they expect?"

Bridget explained, "Epic Talks Miami is a platform that showcases entrepreneurs, innovators, and leaders in various industries to share their experiences and insights to inspire the audience." The ladies were intrigued and eager to attend.

Megan suggested they should all wear something that represents their profession, like a blazer or a statement piece of jewelry. The other ladies agreed, and they began to plan their outfits for the event.

Bethania chimed in and asked, "If they should bring business cards to exchange with other attendees?" Jacqueline added, "We could also create digital business cards to share through our phones." The ladies were impressed by the idea and decided to create their digital business cards before the event.

As they continued to plan, Amber asked, "If they could grab dinner before the event?" Bridget suggested a nearby restaurant that serves healthy and delicious meals to fuel them for the night. The ladies agreed, and they set off to prepare for the networking event.

After dinner the ladies headed over to the networking event as they were walking around mingling introducing themselves to other business professionals and entrepreneurs in Miami. The ladies met some interesting individuals, Sabrina met a startup founder who was working on a new app that aimed to revolutionize the way people worked out. They talked about potential collaborations and ways to integrate the app into Sabrina's personal training business.

Megan struck up a conversation with a real estate developer who was interested in working with her to promote his latest luxury condo development.

Jacqueline met a successful restaurateur who was looking to expand her business and wanted to discuss potential partnerships and investment opportunities.

Elena talked to a fashion designer who was showcasing her latest collection at the event. They discussed potential collaborations and ways to promote the designer's brand on social media.

Amber met a social media influencer who had a large following in the beauty and fashion industry. They discussed ways to collaborate on future projects and potentially Amber's making an investment into the makeup line on the influencer's platforms.

Bridget networked with a group of young entrepreneurs who were working on a new tech startup. They talked about potential partnerships and ways to scale the business.

As the ladies were beginning to sit down in their seats and listen to some of the guest speakers.

Bethania receives a text from William asking, "How's your evening? When can I take you out to celebrate? It's been big week for you in business."

Bethania replied, "I'm at a networking event and thank you so much darling we can talk about it later."

William replied, "I know you are looking gorgeous over there. So what are you wearing? I'm jealous men are over there looking at you and I can't."

Bethania said, "I'll send you a selfie later to visually stimulate you, I have to go ciao."

Amber said, "I can't believe there are no hot guys here tonight."

Sabrina said, "Amber really?"

Amber replied, "What? I can't be intellectually and visually stimulated at the same time."

The ladies said laughing, "We know, Amber."

Megan adds, "But let's focus on the connections we're making tonight. Who knows, maybe we'll meet someone who can help us with our business goals."

Elena chimed in, "Or maybe we'll make some new friends who we can collaborate with in the future."

Bridget nods in agreement and said, "That's what networking is all about, building relationships and creating opportunities."

Jacqueline said, "You just met James what's wrong with him?"

Amber said, "James is great, but I can automatically tell he is boyfriend material. I'm just not sure if I'm ready to get emotionally involved. Plus, knowing that he doesn't live here in Miami and doing a long-distance relationship while we're still in a pandemic doesn't sit right with my love language. Also, ladies we're relocating to Miami I'm looking for Mr. Right Now, not Mr. Right. I was just locked down in my house in California. I'm not trying to be locked down again.

Elena said, "I understand on not being locked down and girl I support you."

The event was about to start and there were a few guest speakers, but the ladies didn't know who was one of those guest speakers. They announced the first guest speaker for tonight is "Bridget Berry" and the ladies were shocked, and Bridget didn't tell them she was going to speak about Real Estate Development. One her way to the podium she gets her heal caught on the floor and almost trips, but she recovers gracefully and starts her speech. Bridget talks about her journey in real estate development and how she was able to achieve success through hard work and perseverance. She shares some tips and tricks on how to invest wisely in real estate, and the ladies are impressed by her knowledge and confidence.

After the speech, the ladies meet up with Bridget and congratulate her on a job well done.

Sabrina said, "Bridget, great speech I had no idea you were such a pro in real estate development. You were amazing up there!"

Bethania adds, "Yes, I'm so proud of you. You inspired us all tonight."

Bridget said, "At first I was nervous about giving a speech, but you girls are my inspiration I can't believe I broke my heal."

So as the ladies were heading back to the penthouse, and they all got a text from their respective guy they met.

Jacqueline said, "Harry wants to get together and do something tomorrow."

Amber said, "James does too."

Megan said, "Let's host a game night and invite them over."

Elena said, "That's a great idea" so the ladies invited their guy over for game night.

Bethania said, "This is going to be interesting."

So, the next night Maxwell, Colin, Cole, James, Harry, Charles, and William all arrived at the penthouse for game night with the ladies. Bridget Megan, Bethania, and Deirdre cooked spread food and served drinks. While they were finishing up food, the guys were mingling and interacting and cracking jokes with the ladies.

Amber decided to break the ice, she suggested that they should play never have I ever. The group agreed to play the game and started taking turns making statements about things they had never done before. As the game progressed, the statements became more revealing and provocative, causing the group to become more and more comfortable with each other.

At one point, Bethania made a statement that surprised everyone, admitting that she had once gone skinny dipping in the ocean with a group of friends during a trip to Mexico. The guys couldn't believe it and were impressed by Bethania's adventurous side.

Jacqueline admits it she had a threesome with two ladies back in college, Harry said, "What I would give to be in that room and watch that."

The group laughed hysterically and then Amber started having some interesting impure thoughts in the back of her mind of how much she would have loved to have done that with Jacqueline.

Megan and Bridget had shared an interesting story at a conference and got hit on by the same guy at different times and both gave him their number. The guy invited Bridget out for lunch and Bridget told Megan you're going to come with me. They show up at lunch together and the guy almost had a heart attack.

Amber admitted she accidentally had anal sex.

She explains, "The lights were out and too much lube is a bad combination."

Everybody responded, "oh my god you poor thing."

Then it was Colin's turn, and he made a statement that left the ladies blushing. He revealed that he had once had a one-night stand with a stranger in a foreign country. The ladies were taken aback by Colin's boldness and couldn't believe he would admit something like that.

Meanwhile, Bethania and William played footsies under the table. Harry played with Jacqueline's leg. Colin sat next to Elena and pinched her on the butt. Cole caressed Bridget's leg under the table. The ladies tried to keep a straight face but secretly loved it. Bridget suggested they start with Cards Against Humanity. The game quickly became a hit, with everyone laughing and enjoying themselves. Bethania and Megan teamed up to take on the guys, with Deirdre and Sabrina offering their own witty responses.

After a few rounds of drinks with Cards Against Humanity, they moved on to other games like Monopoly and Jenga. It was a great night filled with laughter and friendly competition. As the night went on, the guys and the ladies got to know each other better, sharing stories about their lives and interests.

Amber and James decided to go to her room and have some more private time. Megan suggests, "Let's go to the rooftop."

Jacqueline said, "The guys don't have any swimwear."

Elena said, "Strip to your underwear it's Miami."

Sabrina said, "Not everyone is comfortable with that idea. Let's just relax and enjoy the view and company."

Bethania adds, "I have an idea, let's all take a dip in the hot tub. It's private up here, and everyone can just wear their underwear or swimwear if they prefer." The others agree, and they head up to the rooftop hot tub.

Bethania, Megan, Sabrina, Bridget, Jacqueline, Elena watching the guy's strip down as they were in their bikinis.

Bethania said, "Megan this was a brilliant idea let's see what they're working with." The ladies burst into laughter and cheers as they watched the guy's strip down to their underwear and jump into the pool.

Megan said, "I knew this would be a fun idea! Let's enjoy the night and have some fun!" The ladies joined the guys in the pool, and they continued to play games and joke around. Eventually, they all got out of the pool and wrapped themselves in towels, chatting and enjoying the warm Miami night.

They spend the next few hours enjoying the Miami skyline and each other's company while soaking in the warm water.

Amber and James notice it's very quiet in the living room they come out asking, "Where are you guys?"

James said, "We have the whole penthouse to ourselves."

Amber said, "It seems so they walk out on the balcony."

James decides to put his arms around Amber as he stands behind her enjoying the view. James starts kissing Amber on the back of her neck slowly towards her cheek. She turns around slowly as they begin to kiss James starts undressing her Amber starts to loosen his belt and unzips his pants. James said, "you want to do this right here?"

Amber said, "Are you afraid someone's going to watch us?" James takes off Amber's bra and slowly starts kissing her down her chest all the way past her belly button as he kneels on to the ground. Amber raises her leg up and puts it over his shoulder. As he continues to go down on her Amber can't believe how good James is with his tongue. As she runs her hands through his hair, she told James don't stop. No articles of clothing on Amber was fully nude on the balcony. Amber realizes she's about to have a very massive orgasm and can't control the high pitch of her voice.

James stands back up and hoists Amber legs around his waist and slowly begins to penetrate her. After Amber and James achieve orgasm, they realized it's getting late. Amber knows she's not ready for anything serious, but she didn't want James to leave either.

She asked James "Would you stay the night with me?"

James said, "I thought you never ask." he smiled.

Maxwell said, "Do you guys hear that?"

Megan said, "Shhhh, guys I hear it to."

Bethania said, "Wow somebody is getting their uterus worked tonight."

Jacqueline said, "Girl you crazy."

Elena said, "Let's go back to the Penthouse it's getting little windy up here."

So as the gang returns from the rooftop pool, they open up the door slowly. Bridget said, "Let's be quiet Amber and James might be sleeping."

To their surprise, Bridget, Elena Sabrina Megan Jacqueline Harry William Charles and Cole are completely flabbergasted at what they are witnessing happening on the balcony. Everyone freezes for a moment, unsure of what to do. But then William speaks up, "Uh, guys, I think we should probably give them some privacy."

Charles nods in agreement, "Yeah, let's just head back up and give them some space." The group quietly retreats to the rooftop, trying not to make any noise.

Once they arrive back up top, Bethania breaks the silence, "Well, that was unexpected. Now we know who was making all those noises?"

Megan giggles, "I guess they really couldn't wait until later tonight."

Jacqueline rolls her eyes, "I can't believe they were doing that out on the balcony where anyone could see them."

Bridget chimed in, "Well, they're both adults and it's their choice what they do on their own time."

Elena nods, "Yeah, let's just respect their privacy and pretend we didn't see anything." Yeah, let's not make a big deal out of it. It's their personal business."

Maxwell adds, "And let's try to be a bit more discreet in the future. We don't want to accidentally walk in on something like that again."

Sabrina smirks, "Or maybe we do."

Harry said, "This has been the most entertaining night of game night ever. James and Amber must have played truth or dare and dare went to the extreme." The group erupts in laughter and girls said, "Only in Dade."

Chapter 5

The next morning Bridget, Elena, Jacqueline, Megan, and Sabrina were anxiously waiting for Amber to wake up and share her night. While waiting with anticipation, Sabrina and Bethania decide to fire up her laptop to do some work.

As Sabrina and Bethania were working on their laptops, Jacqueline suggests they go for a morning swim in the rooftop pool. Bridget and Elena agreed, but Megan said 'she'll pass and decided to stay in the penthouse to see if Amber wakes up soon.

After some time, Amber finally emerges from her room with a huge smile on her face. The ladies eagerly asked her, "What happened last night?" and Amber coyly responds with "A lady never kisses and tells."

Sabrina playfully nudges her, "Come on, spill the tea!"

Amber finally relents and said, "Let's just say James knows his way around a woman's body."

The ladies all cheer and high-five Amber, happy that she had a great night. Bethania remarks, "Looks like Miami is treating us all pretty well"."

The girls all agree and head up to the rooftop pool for a morning swim and some relaxation.

Megan said, "Now that Amber has popped her Miami cherry, I wonder who will be next on the give it up express train."

The ladies respond, "Oh, Megan, you're terrible," says Jacqueline with a laugh. "Let's just focus on having a good time and enjoying each other's company. No pressure or expectations."

Bridget nods in agreement, "Exactly, we're all adults here and we can make our own choices. But let's also be safe and responsible."

Elena adds, "And let's not forget why we're here - to network and learn from each other."

Sabrina said, "Yeah, let's make the most of our time in Miami and create some unforgettable memories."

Then Bethania said, "I'm so ready to Reverse Cowgirl William it's been too long I haven't had any since my ex, plus I like how he stimulates me."

The other ladies look at Bethania with surprise, but Megan quickly recovers and said, "Well, now we know who's next on the express train!"

The others laughed and Bridget said, "Hey, no judgment here. You do you, girl."

Elena added, "Just remember to communicate your boundaries and be respectful of each other's feelings."

Jacqueline agrees, "And always use protection!"

Megan said, "Ladies you should check on your families let them know we're ok." The ladies all nodded in agreement and start grabbing their phones and called their families. Bridget called her mom and dad, and they were thrilled to see her and hear about her adventures in Miami. Elena called her mom and younger brother and told them all about the amazing views from the rooftop pool. Jacqueline called her dad and stepmom, and they were happy to hear that she was having a good time and making new friends. Megan phoned her parents, and they were all excited to hear from her and hear about the trip.

Sabrina called her dad and little sister, and they were thrilled to see her and hear about all the fun she was having. Bethania called her mom, and they chat about everything that's been going on and how much she's enjoying herself.

Bethania received a text from Stephanie, that said "I've invited you and your girlfriends to a masquerade party on Hibiscus Island tonight."

The group was excited at the invitation to the masquerade party. Bridget recommended they all go shopping for masks and costumes before the party. Elena suggested they split up into teams and make it a competition to see who can find the best masks and costumes.

Megan said, "That's a great idea! We'll have a prize for the winning team."

Jacqueline suggested they make it interesting and have the losing team do a dare at the party. Sabrina agreed, "Yes, let's make it fun and memorable."

The group would split up into two teams, with Bethania, Megan, and Jacqueline on one team, and Bridget, Elena, and Sabrina on the other. They head out to different shops and boutiques, looking for the perfect masks and costumes.

After a few hours of shopping and trying on different outfits, they would meet back up at the house to show off their finds. The winning team is determined by a vote, and it's a close call, but ultimately Bethania, Megan, and Jacqueline's team won with their unique and eye-catching masks.

As the night fell, they were heading out to the masquerade party on Hibiscus Island, ready to dance and have a good time. They arrived at the party and were amazed by the decorations, the music, and the people who were in their elaborate masks and costumes.

When they entered the mansion as guests of Stephanie and Amir. They were greeted by a sensual and erotic atmosphere. It was a dimly lit mansion filled with guests dressed in intricate masks and revealing attire, setting the tone for a night of uninhibited pleasure.

The ladies took in the surroundings, feeling a mix of excitement and nervousness in the bold and provocative atmosphere. They mingled with the other guests, sipping on exotic cocktails, and sampling the delicious hors d'oeuvres that were being passed around.

As the night went on, the music grew louder and the dancing became more sensual, with guests grinding and swaying to the beat. The ladies found themselves drawn into the erotic energy of the party, shedding their inhibitions, and joining in on the fun.

There were two guests at the party that walked up and touched Jacqueline and Amber inappropriately.

As soon as Amber and Jacqueline realize what happened, they immediately turn around and confront the men. "Excuse me, what do you think you're doing?" Amber said her voice laced with anger. Jacqueline stands beside her, glaring at the men.

The men just laughed and said, "Relax, it's just a party. We're all here to have fun, right?"

Bridget steps forward and said, "That's no excuse for touching someone without their consent. It's not okay."

The men just shrugged and moved away, clearly not understanding the gravity of their actions. The rest of the ladies gathered around Amber and Jacqueline, making sure they were okay.

Megan said, "Let's just stick together from now on and be aware of our surroundings. We don't want anything else like that to happen again."

The ladies nodded in agreement and continued to enjoy the party, but with a heightened sense of caution.

Megan turned to the group and said, "I don't know about you guys, but I'm not sure if I'm ready for all of this."

Bridget nodded in agreement, "Yeah, this is a bit much for me." Sabrina looked around, taking it all in, "I've never been to a party like this before. It's definitely a new experience."

Jacqueline said, "I think I'll just stick to watching for now." Bethania smiled mischievously, "I, on the other hand, would like to let loose and have some fun."

Elena looked at the group, "Well, whatever we decide to do, let's make sure we stay safe and look out for each other."

Before long, masks were being shed and clothes were coming off as the guests gave in to their deepest desires. "What is happening here? This is insane!" exclaims Bridget as she looks around at the wild scene. Elena seems to be enjoying herself, "Let's just let loose and have fun, girls! This is what Miami is all about." Amber nods in agreement, "Yeah, let's just go with the flow and see where the night takes us."

Jacqueline was a bit uncomfortable, "I don't know if I'm ready for this kind of party. Maybe I'll just sit this one out."

Bethania had put a hand on her shoulder, "It's okay, girl. You do what makes you feel comfortable."

Sabrina looks around, "Well, I'm definitely feeling a little wild tonight." Megan laughs, "That's what I like to hear! Let's make the most of this party! Miami it's judgement-free zone plus we're in mask nobody can see us." The ladies were swept up in the passion of the moment, exploring their own desires and indulging in the pleasures of the night.

Bridget said, "Ladies look, as they turn around there were women walking downstairs just only wearing a mask."

Amber said, "I know it's hot in Miami not that hot."

Elena laughs, "Hey, to each their own. Let's just focus on having a good time and not worry about what others are doing." Sabrina agrees, "Yeah, everyone is here to let loose and have fun. Let's just enjoy the party."

Jacqueline was a bit uncomfortable still, "I think I'm just going to head back to the penthouse. I don't want to be a buzzkill, but this party is a bit too much for me." Bethania nods, "I'll come with you, girl. No need to do anything you're not comfortable with."

Megan and Amber exchange a knowing look, "Ladies do what you need to do. We'll catch up with you later." The group decided to split up, with some continuing to party and others heading back to the penthouse.

Megan, Amber, Bridget, and Sabrina decided to walk around the mansion but then they walked upstairs. They accidentally entered into one of the rooms and found a crowd of people standing around watching a couple perform some sadomasochistic activity. What they saw made their jaw drop, As Megan, Amber, Bridget, and Sabrina walked into the room, their eyes widened. The couple was in the center of the room, with the woman tied up and blindfolded while the man wielded a whip. The onlookers around them were cheering and encouraging the couple, seemingly enjoying the spectacle.

The woman's body was covered in red marks from the whipping, and she seemed to be writhing in pleasure despite the pain. The man's face was twisted in a look of intense concentration and pleasure as he continued to whip her. It aroused the onlookers further, and they cheered louder. As they stood there, they could hear the whip cracking against the woman's skin and her moans of pleasure mingling with the cheers of the crowd. It was a shocking and intense scene, unlike anything they had ever seen before.

Megan, Amber, Bridget, and Sabrina felt very uncomfortable, but they couldn't take their eyes off the spectacle. The man continued to whip the woman, and she began to moan loudly, writhing as if unable to contain herself. Suddenly, the woman let out a loud moan and her body convulsed. She let out another cry and her body shook violently.

The man stopped for a moment, watching the woman. He was breathing hard and his body was covered in sweat, but he appeared to be very satisfied. The onlookers around them started to clap and cheer, and the man smiled and bowed. Then, he untied the woman and began to kiss her.

The woman's eyes were closed, and her limbs seemed to be lifeless. The man carried the woman over to a nearby sofa, and she lay there motionless, still tied up.

Bridget whispered, "Oh my god, what is happening here? This is insane." Sabrina covered her mouth in shock, unable to look away.

Amber took a step back, feeling uncomfortable and unsure of how to react. Megan stood frozen, unsure of what to do next.

After a few minutes, they finally managed to tear themselves away from the shocking scene and quickly made their way out of the room. As they walked down the hallway, they were all silent, still processing what they had just seen.

Finally, Bridget spoke up, "I can't believe that just happened." Sabrina nodded in agreement, "Yeah, that was a lot to take in." Amber said, "I think we should go back downstairs and try to forget about what we just saw."

As they walked out of the masquerade party, the ladies couldn't help but discuss the wild experiences they had just had. Megan said, "Bethania and Jacqueline you're still here?"

Jacqueline said, "It didn't feel right leaving you guys here so we were waiting outside and enjoyed a cocktail."

Bethania said, "That was crazy! I never thought I'd be part of something like that."

Sabrina added, "You missed what we saw upstairs it was definitely an eye-opening experience."

Elena nodded in agreement, "Yeah, it was definitely intense, but I'm glad we all had fun."

Amber said, "I can't believe we just did all that, but it was exhilarating!"

Megan laughed, "I have a feeling this trip to Miami will be one we never forget."

Bridget smiled, "We all needed this break from our regular lives."

On the way home Bethania said, "Tomorrow how about we go shopping for your new homes?"

Bridget said, "That's a great idea, Bethania. We could use some help making our new places feel like home."

Elena adds, "And it'll be fun to shop together and see what each of us likes."

Jacqueline chimed in, "I'm just excited to start decorating my own space and making it my own."

Sabrina agrees, "Me too, it's going to be so much fun."

Amber asked, "Do you guys have any specific styles in mind?" Bethania replied, "Well, we usually go for modern and minimalist furniture, but it all depends on your personal taste." Megan said, "I'm thinking of adding some boho vibes to my place."

As the ladies finished up their furniture shopping, Elena's phone buzzed with a text from Colin. Her heart skipped a beat as she read the message requesting her presence at his place. Elena wasn't sure if she was ready to take their relationship to such an intimate setting, but she also didn't want to give Colin the wrong impression by rejecting him outright.

Feeling conflicted and unsure of what to do, Elena turned to her friends for advice. She explained the situation to Megan, Amber, Bridget, Bethania, Jacqueline, and Sabrina, and asked for their thoughts.

Megan suggested that Elena take some time to reflect on what she wants and feels comfortable with before responding to Colin. Amber agreed, adding that it's important to communicate her boundaries clearly with Colin to avoid any confusion or misunderstandings.

Bridget recommended that Elena be honest with Colin about her feelings and concerns, while also being respectful and kind in her response. Bethania suggested that Elena think about what she wants out of their relationship and how meeting at Colin's place aligns with those goals.

Jacqueline encouraged Elena to trust her instincts and prioritize her own well-being in this situation, while Sabrina offered to be there for her if she needed support or someone to talk to.

After Elena listened to her friends' advice and considered her own feelings, Elena decided to respectfully decline Colin's invitation for the time being. She sent him a message thanking him for the offer but explaining that she wasn't ready for that yet.

After Elena respectfully declined Colin's invitation, Colin replied to her message saying that it's not what she thinks and that he appreciates her being upfront and transparent with him about her feelings.

He went on to explained that the wanted to surprise with a romantic dinner on the rooftop and that they would enjoy the sounds of the water together. Colin wanted to create a special and memorable experience for Elena.

Elena was surprised by Colin's response and the thought he had put into the surprise. She felt relieved and happy that she had communicated her feelings and boundaries clearly to Colin, and that he had respected them while still wanting to do something special for her.

She thanked Colin for understanding and respecting her decision and agreed to the dinner on the rooftop. Elena knew that she could trust Colin and that their relationship was growing in a healthy and respectful way.

As the night progressed, Elena and Colin enjoyed a lovely dinner on the rooftop and the sounds of the water created a soothing atmosphere. They talked and laughed, and their connection deepened as they got to know each other better.

Elena thanked Colin for a lovely dinner she told Colin "It's something about your vibe and aura you really just know how to relax me" Colin replied, "I'm flattered to hear, that wouldn't be a good sign if you weren't."

Elena smiled at Colin's response, feeling reassured by his words. She knew that she had made the right decision to give Colin a chance and was grateful for the time they had spent together.

"You know, I was hesitant at first about coming here tonight," Elena admitted, looking out over the water. "But I'm glad I did. You always know how to make me feel at ease."

Colin turned to look at Elena, his expression softening. "I'm glad you came too," he said. "I know we've only been seeing each other for a little bit, but I feel like we have a connection. Plus, I never met a woman who made the first move I admired your eagerness."

Elena nodded, feeling a warmth spread through her chest. "I feel it too," she said. "There's just something about you that feels different from anyone else I've dated."

Colin smiled, his eyes meeting hers. "I know what you mean," he said. "I feel like we can be ourselves around each other, you know? Like we don't have to put up any walls or pretend to be someone we're not."

Elena nodded, feeling a sense of relief washed over her. She had always struggled with feeling like she had to be perfect for the people she was dating, but with Colin, she felt like she could let her guard down and be herself.

"Thank you for tonight," Elena said, turning to face Colin. "It's been wonderful."

Colin reached out and took her hand, giving it a gentle squeeze. "Anytime," he said. "I just want to make you happy."

Colin asked Elena "Would you be interested in trying something you know even help you feel more relaxed around me."

Elena looked at Colin with curiosity. "What do you have in mind?" she asked.

Colin leaned in closer to Elena and whispered, "I've been studying meditation and mindfulness practices for a while now, and I think it could be something that could benefit both of us."

Elena was intrigued. She had always been interested in mindfulness but had never really tried it before. "I'm open to trying it," she said. "How do we start?"

Colin smiled, feeling excited about the prospect of sharing his passion with Elena. "Well, we could start by doing a simple breathing exercise," he said. "It only takes a few minutes, but it can help calm your mind and relax your body."

Elena nodded, feeling a bit skeptical but also willing to give it a try. "Okay, let's do it," she said.

Colin took Elena's hand and led her to a quiet corner of the rooftop, away from the noise and distractions of the city. He instructed her to close her eyes and focus on her breath, counting each inhale and exhale.

At first, Elena found it difficult to quiet her mind and concentrate on her breath. But with Colin's gentle guidance and encouragement, she eventually found herself sinking into a deep state of relaxation.

When they finished the exercise, Elena opened her eyes and looked at Colin with a sense of wonder. "That was amazing," she said. "I feel so calm and centered."

Colin smiled, feeling a sense of satisfaction at seeing Elena benefit from the exercise. "I'm glad you enjoyed it," he said. "Mindfulness and meditation can be powerful tools for managing stress and anxiety."

Elena nodded, feeling grateful to have someone like Colin in her life who not only cared for her but also helped her grow and evolve as a person.

Elena decided to text the girls and let them know "Don't wait up for me tonight." Then she offered a suggestion to Colin, Elena said, "I want to do some Therapeutic Sensate touch with you. I'm not going to have sex with you tonight, but I want you to experience the sensation of the power of touch by you allowing me to touch your body."

Colin was taken aback by Elena's suggestion, but he was also intrigued. He had heard of Therapeutic Sensate Touch before, but he had never experienced it himself. "That sounds interesting," he said. "I'm open to trying it."

Elena smiled, feeling a sense of excitement. "Great," she said. "It's a form of non-sexual touch that can help promote relaxation and emotional connection. We can do it fully clothed, and you can choose which areas of your body you're comfortable with me touching."

Colin nodded, feeling a sense of trust in Elena. "Okay, let's give it a try," he said.

Colin guided Elena to the living room, where he had set up a comfortable space with blankets and pillows. She began by showing him some breathing exercises to help him relax, and then she asked him to lie down on his stomach.

As he begins removing his clothes, she couldn't help but say in her mind I need you to focus as impure thoughts was crossing her mind. It's clearly obvious that Colin has never missed a day in the gym. She started with gentle strokes on his back, using her hands to apply pressure and release tension. As Elena worked her way down Colin's back, she couldn't help but feel a sense of connection with him. She had never experienced this level of intimacy with someone before, and it was both exhilarating and terrifying. She tried to focus on the task at hand, using different techniques to help release the tension in his muscles.

Colin let out a sigh of relaxation as Elena's touch became more sensual. He could feel her fingers dancing across his skin, sending shivers down his spine. He wondered if this was what it felt like to have an intimate connection with someone without the pressure of sex.

Elena began to work her way down to Colin's buttocks, applying gentle pressure and strokes. She could feel herself becoming aroused by the feel of his muscular body underneath her hands, but she tried to push those thoughts aside and focus on the task at hand.

As she moved down to his thighs, Colin let out a moan of pleasure. Elena could feel her own arousal building as she continued her massage. She moved her hands in small circles, applying more and more pressure until Colin was practically writhing in pleasure.

Suddenly, Elena stopped and looked up at Colin with a mischievous smirk. She reached her hand up to his face and gently caressed his cheek. "I think I've found all the tension in your body," she said softly.

"Now it's time to move on to something else if you're ready. "As she continued, she asked Colin for feedback on how the touch felt and adjusted accordingly. She also incorporated some light movements and stretches to help release any tightness in his muscles.

Elena takes a deep breath and reminds herself to stay focused on the task at hand. She starts with light touches on his arms and gradually moves to his chest and back, using different textures and pressures to create a variety of sensations. As she works her way down to his legs and feet, Colin seems to be completely relaxed and at ease.

Colin was surprised by how relaxing and enjoyable the experience was. He had never realized how much power there could be in non-sexual touch, and he felt a sense of deep connection with Elena as she worked on his body.

After the session was over, Colin thanked Elena for the experience. "That was amazing," he said. "I had no idea that touch could be so powerful. Thank you for sharing this with me."

Elena smiled, feeling a sense of satisfaction. "I'm glad you enjoyed it," she said. "I believe that touch can be a powerful tool for emotional connection and healing. And I'm happy to share it with you."

Closing Day

It was closing day for Megan and Sabrina on their beautiful units at Bentley Bay and the One hotel in Miami Beach. Bethania let them know they were lucky because they had motivated sellers that wanted to close fast.

Megan and Sabrina were thrilled to have closed on their new units at Bentley Bay and the One hotel in Miami Beach. They couldn't wait to move in and start enjoying their new home.

Bethania was a big help in the process, always keeping them informed and up to date on the progress of the sales. The motivated sellers certainly made things easier by being willing to close quickly, but Bethania's expertise and guidance had been invaluable.

As they toasted to their new homes with champagne, Megan and Sabrina couldn't help but feel grateful for the support of Bethania making it so easy. They knew they wouldn't have been able to make this purchase without her help.

Meanwhile Megan, Jacqueline, Amber and Elena their places in Brickell Key, Edgewater, One hotel, and at Paramount building was taking much longer to close than Megan and Sabrina.

Megan, Jacqueline, Amber, and Elena were feeling a bit frustrated as the closing process for their new homes was taking longer than expected. They had all found amazing properties in desirable neighborhoods like Brickell Key, Edgewater, Bentley Bay, and the Paramount building, but the paperwork and negotiations seemed to be dragging on.

They often vented to each other over group chats and phone calls, sharing their anxieties and concerns about the delays. Bethania, their trusted Real Estate Agent, was doing her best to keep them informed and alleviate their worries, but the waiting game was still tough.

Finally, after a week Bethania had been working so hard to get all these deals to close. The ladies were finally homeowners, they had their keys they were ready to move in. Megan's' first night in her new home she was sitting out on the balcony meditating and praying and just reflecting and being thankful for the moment. Sabrina's' first night was thinking about her mother and how much she wished she could have been here to see this. Bridget was so excited cooking in her new kitchen brings her fulfillment.

Amber was busy unpacking and organizing her things, excited to finally have a place to call her own. Jacqueline was soaking in her new bathtub, sipping on a glass of wine and feeling grateful for all the hard work that had led to this moment. Elena was snuggled up on her couch with a good book, feeling content and at peace in her new home. Plus feeling happy to be neighbors with Megan.

Bethania was motivated by the ladies; they had given her a sense of pride and purpose she made two goals for herself. First, that she was going to be a homeowner in Miami, and she wanted to start her brokerage. She no longer wanted to live with her roommate on West Ave.

As they all settled into their new spaces, they couldn't help but feel a sense of pride and accomplishment. They had worked hard to get to this point, and now they had a place to call their own. The late nights and early mornings, the negotiations and paperwork, it had all been worth it.

As they drifted off to sleep in their new homes, they were filled with excitement for the future and all the memories they would create in these spaces.

Chapter 6

Megan had text the ladies and ask them, "How does it feel to be an official resident of Miami?" Jacqueline replied first, "It feels amazing! I can't believe I finally have my own place in this beautiful city."

Amber chimed in, "I'm still in awe of the view from my balcony. It's surreal to wake up to such a gorgeous skyline every day."

Elena added, "I feel like I'm living in a dream. This city has so much energy and excitement, and I'm thrilled to be a part of it."

Sabrina replied, "I feel blessed to be able to call this place home. It's been a long journey to get here, but it's worth it."

Bridget texted back, "I'm so happy for all of us! We've worked hard to get here, and now we get to enjoy the fruits of our labor. Let's plan a housewarming party to celebrate!"

Megan said in the group text, "I have an idea that I wanted to share with each of you all but let's do it over brunch."

Jacqueline replied, "That sounds like a great idea! When and where should we meet?"

Amber adds, "I'm available this weekend. How about Sunday morning brunch at that 1 beach club at your place?"

Elena chimed in, "Sunday works for me too. And I've been dying to try that place! Even though it's located where I live."

Bridget said, "I'm in, but can we make it later in the day? I have a morning yoga class I don't want to miss."

Sabrina agrees, "I'm good with anytime on Sunday. Just let me know where to meet."

Megan responds, "Great! Sunday it is. Let's aim for 12 pm. I have a surprise for us all!"

It had now been three weeks since the ladies had stepped foot into Miami, Megan was ready to elevate the ladies to some new goals that she had been thinking about.

It was Sunday and the ladies decided to meet for brunch. As they all hugged and greeted each other. Megan proposed a way they can invest their money into the stock market where we can make some astronomical gains short-term. She mentions she's seeing a lot of movement with stay-at-home stocks.

Megan asked the ladies a question, "Can you imagine living a life where if you only worked because you wanted to and not because you have to? Think about it ladies I know we all want to be future wives and mothers but imagine having the ability to control your time."

The ladies listened intently to Megan's proposal, intrigued by the idea of making more money through the stock market like they did prior to coming to Miami. Amber said, "Let's do it I love the money I've been making money trading like you taught me."

Megan replied, "There's always risk involved with any investment, but I've done my research and I truly believe this is a good opportunity. Plus, we can diversify our portfolio to minimize risk."

Jacqueline chimed in, "I like the idea of having more control over my time. It would be amazing to have financial freedom and be able to work because when we want to, not because we have to."

The other ladies nodded in agreement, and Bethania added, "I think it's worth considering, but we should also do our own research and make sure we're comfortable with the risks involved."

Elena, who had been quiet until now, finally spoke up, "I like the idea of investing our money, but let's also make sure we don't forget to enjoy our lives in the present. We've worked hard to get where we are, and I don't want us to become so focused on making money that we forget to have fun and enjoy our time together."

Megan said, "Ladies I'm not trying to brag or anything, but you girls are like sisters to me and if I'm going places that's uplifting me I'm hoping that I can uplift you so we all can ride into the sunset together. In the past several months since the pandemic and the shutdown I've made more money than I have in the past five. There's a reason why I was able to pay for my condo without financing it. I became the bank instead of relying on one. I'm going to show you one of my investment accounts just so I can be transparent with you and show you how I can help you." Megan opened up her laptop logs into one of her investment accounts showed the girls from this investment right here I made over $3,000,000 that's what paid for my condo. I see men do this all the time on Wall Street I want to help you ladies do it just like how they're doing it. I always wanted a man in my life, but I never wanted to become dependent on one. So, I had to learn how to think like one.

The ladies were stunned by Megan's success and her willingness to share her knowledge and wealth with them. They were excited about the possibility of achieving financial independence and having the freedom to live life on their own terms.

Elena spoke up and said, "Megan, we trust you and we want to learn more about investing in the stock market. Can you teach us how to do it?"

Megan said, "I love you ladies and as long as you're willing to grow and elevate and become better let's do it together. I love that we motivate each other, and we make each other better in all retrospect's now let's get rich together."

Megan also makes a proposal to Bridget "Let's start a real estate portfolio here in South Florida. There's a lot of traffic slowly migrating to this part of the world."

Megan said, "Ladies I want us to own pieces of South Florida not just only our homes. There's only three ways you get rich the stock market, real estate, and running a business. We're doing all three. Sabrina, "You're a corporate lawyer in New York do you get reciprocity to practice law in the state of Florida? I want you to be our general counsel for this new business venture. Bethania get that broker's license we're going to work directly through you. Jacqueline, you have high profile clients in the sporting world that I'm sure would be very interested in working with us. Amber, you're good at sales I need you to help expand our marketing in our brand. Ladies let's raise our glasses and toast to new goals and new vision."

Bridget responds, "I love this idea, Megan! I am definitely in. And to answer your question,

Sabrina said, "Yes, I do have reciprocity to practice law in Florida. I would be honored to be the general counsel for our new business venture."

Bethania chimed in "I'll make sure to get my Florida broker's license updated as soon as possible."

Jacqueline said, "I know some high-profile athletes who would be interested in investing with us."

Amber said, "I'm excited to help with the marketing and branding efforts. Let's make this happen, ladies!" The group raises their glasses again and cheers to their new venture.

Megan said, "I love you ladies let's always watch our backs and always put our best interest forward I want us to make a lot of money but we're going to make it in a right way. I value our bond and integrity. I don't want to lose your friendship. I don't want to lose trust all I want is to build financial freedom. Let's always remain to be transparent and honest with one another and let's never allow our emotions to cloud our judgement. Cheers to that, ladies."

The ladies raise their glasses and cheer in agreement, expressing their appreciation for Megan's leadership and guidance. They all vow to work hard and support each other in their new venture, and to always prioritize their friendship and trust. They also discuss setting up regular meetings and check-ins to ensure they stay on track and make progress towards their financial goals. The brunch ends on a high note, with the ladies feeling excited and motivated about their new venture and the possibilities it holds for their future.

Before the ladies departed from brunch Megan said, "One last thing let's not tell anybody what we're doing we don't need to put this on social media we don't need to brag to our family and friends or who we're dating. Let's operate in silence and let the success make all the noise."

The ladies all nod in agreement and raise their glasses to toast to their new venture. They all feel empowered and excited to take control of their financial futures together. As they part ways and head back to their own homes, they can't help but feel grateful for each other and the bond that they share. They know that with each other's support, they can accomplish anything they set their minds to.

Bridget nodded in agreement, "I've been wanting to invest more of my money anyway." Sabrina chimed in, "I'm down too. It would be amazing to have more financial freedom." Jacqueline looked a bit hesitant, "I don't know much about the stock market, but I trust you, Megan. Let's give it a try." Bethania said, "Count me in! I'm all about making more money and having more control over my life."

Megan smiled, feeling excited that her friends were on board with her proposal. "Alright ladies, let's make some serious money and take control of our financial futures!" They all raised their glasses in agreement, excited for this new venture they were embarking on together.

Over brunch, they discussed different stocks and strategies, sharing tips and ideas with each other. They all felt motivated and empowered, knowing that they were taking charge of their financial lives and working towards a more secure future.

Later that evening Maxwell texted Megan to let her know he is back in town from DC. Megan feels some type of way she had not heard much from him, but she knows he's busy running his business. Maxwell asked her, "If she was free to do something tonight?"

Megan replied, "maybe but you've been on my naughty list." Maxwell said, "How did I get on your naughty list?"

Megan said, "I haven't heard much from you since you've been in DC, your DC girlfriend must be taking all your time. Did she confiscate your phone as well?"

Maxwell laughed and said, "No, she didn't confiscate my phone. I've just been busy with work and trying to balance everything. But you're right, I should have been better about keeping in touch. Can we make it up with dinner tonight?"

Megan said, "Thank you for admitting that there is someone else." I appreciate your honesty, Maxwell. However, I am not interested in being involved with someone who is already in a relationship. It's not fair to anyone involved. I think it's best if we end things here and move on."

Maxwell said, "I apologize if I've given you that impression, but there is no one else. I've just been busy with work and trying to focus on growing my business. I didn't mean to neglect you or make you feel like you're not a priority. Can we talk more about this in person? Maybe we can grab dinner tonight and catch up?"

Megan said, "Okay, let's do dinner tonight. you better make it up to me with some good food and wine." They made plans to meet up later that evening.

Maxwell decided to take Megan to Joia Beach, while the ladies were doing their own thing. Joia Beach is an upscale beach club located in South Florida with beautiful ocean views, luxurious amenities, and a lively atmosphere. When they arrived, Maxwell made sure to treat Megan like a queen, getting them a private cabana and ordering her favorite drink. Megan was impressed and grateful for the gesture.

As they settled in, Maxwell started to apologize for his lack of communication while he was in DC. He explained that he was dealing with some difficult business deals and didn't want to burden Megan with it. He also assured her that there was no one else in his life and that he was committed to their relationship.

Megan appreciated his honesty and apology, but also makes it clear that communication is important to her and that she needs to feel like a priority in his life. Maxwell agreed and promised to do better.

The rest of the day is spent enjoying the beautiful beach views, delicious food, and each other's company. The tension from earlier seems to have dissipated, and Megan is grateful for the opportunity to reconnect with Maxwell.

Amber decided to go downstairs to the lobby of her building to get her mail. She bumps into one of her neighbors that lives on her floor,

Amber walked up to her and introduces herself said, "Hello my name is Amber"

her neighbor replied, "Hi I'm Nicole, welcome to the Aria"

Amber said, "Thank you I love it here and the location."

Nicole replied, "I love Edgewater it's a nice convenient area." Nicole asks her "Where you from?"

Amber said, "I'm from San Diego, new to Miami but love the vibe here and you? "I'm from Buenos Aires I've been in Miami several years now."

Amber said, "Wow I feel like I'm meeting a Miami native, I'm not trying to hit on you but you're gorgeous. What do you do here?"

Nicole said, "Aww thank you and you as well, I'm a model." Amber said, "Oh wow I use to do some modeling, what agency are you with?"

Nicole said, "Fans Only." In the back of Ambers mind, she was surprised by Nicole's response and felt a bit uncomfortable. However, she maintains a polite and friendly demeanor and continued the conversation. She asked Nicole a few more questions about her modeling career and they chat for a few minutes before saying goodbye and going their separate ways.

Later on, Amber reflected on the interaction and realized that she made an assumption about Nicole's profession based on her appearance. She also realized that asking someone about their job can be a sensitive topic, and that she should be more mindful of this in future conversations. She decided to approach future interactions with a greater level of sensitivity and respect for other people's boundaries.

Amber decided to send out a group text to the ladies and let them know that she met her neighbor, and you wouldn't believe what she does for a living. Amber told them she's a Fans Only model, so Megan, Elena, Sabrina, Jacqueline, Bridget, and Bethania responded.

Megan responds first and said, "Wow, that's interesting. I've heard a lot about Fans Only, but I never knew anyone who worked for them."

Elena follows up with, "I've heard that Fans Only can be pretty lucrative. Do you know how much money she made?"

Sabrina chimed in and said, "I don't think it's really our business how much money she made. It's her job, and we should respect that."

Jacqueline adds, "Yeah, I agree. Just because she's a Fans Only model doesn't mean she's any less of a person. We should be supportive of her."

Bridget jumps in and said, "I think it's cool that Amber met someone with such an interesting job. It's always good to broaden our perspectives."

Bethania wraps up the conversation by saying, "I'm happy for you, Amber. It sounds like you had a nice conversation with your neighbor. Maybe we can all meet her sometime."

Amber said, "I'm not trying to throw shade or judge her situation, but I'm interested in having open dialogue about could you take your clothes for money?"

The group chat went silent for a moment, and then Megan speaks up, "Hey Amber, personal I couldn't, it's great that you're sharing your experience with us, but let's be respectful of Nicole's profession. Just because she's a Fans Only model doesn't mean she deserves any less respect or consideration than anyone else. We should support her and her choices, even if they're different from our own."

Elena adds, "I agree with Megan. We should avoid judging people based on their profession or lifestyle choices. Everyone has the right to make their own decisions and pursue their own interests."

Sabrina said, "And let's not forget that we're all adults here. Nicole is free to make her own choices, and we're free to make ours. It's important that we respect each other's autonomy and support each other's decisions."

Jacqueline agrees, "Yeah, let's not make assumptions about people based on their job. It's not fair or respectful."

Bridget adds, "I think it's important to remember that everyone has their own story and their own reasons for doing what they do. Let's be open-minded and understanding."

Bethania concludes the conversation by saying, "Thanks for sharing with us, Amber. Let's remember to be respectful and supportive of each other, no matter what we choose to do for a living."

Amber was quite surprised at their response, but it helped her to gain perspective on how to view the situation differently.

Bridget the next morning told the ladies know that all the necessary paperwork has been filed for our new business venture. Bridget also mentioned, "ladies we are officially incorporated to do business." Megan responded, "that is awesome now we can go to the bank and set up our business banking account I already have an accountant that we can work with."

Elena said, "That's great news, Bridget! I'm so excited to see our business take off. And having an accountant lined up is a smart move, Megan."

Sabrina adds, "Yeah, I think it's important that we have all our ducks in a row, especially when it comes to finances. It's better to be prepared than caught off guard."

Jacqueline said, "I agree. Having a solid financial foundation is key to running a successful business. And with our diverse backgrounds and skills, I think we're going to be unstoppable."

Bethania chimed in, "I couldn't agree more. I think we have a great team and I'm excited to see where this takes us. Let's keep the momentum going and make our dreams a reality!"

The ladies were excited that starting a real estate investment portfolio was a great idea, plus raising two million to start between all of them. Now they're excited to work with Bethania, who just got her broker's license.

Amber suggested that they start by identifying some potential investment properties in South Florida, and Megan offered to use her connections in the industry to help them find good deals. Bridget agreed to handle the financial side of things, and Jacqueline suggested that they develop a business plan to outline their goals and strategies.

Sabrina chimed in, "I reviewed all our documentation that Bridget has put together forming a legal entity for our LLC, to protect our personal assets and limit our liability."

Elena nods in agreement, "Yes, that's a good point. We need to make sure we're taking all the necessary steps to protect ourselves and our investment."

Bethania took charge and suggested they start with researching some potential properties and narrowing down their options based on their criteria. She also offers to set up some property viewings and connect with other professionals in the industry to help them make informed decisions.

They know it won't be easy, but with their skills, knowledge, and determination, they're confident they can make it a success.

As the ladies begin working in their home offices on their business along with still working their regular professions. They felt excited at the possibilities of what's to come, they haven't been too focused on dating. Bethania was excited to get a call from William since him, James, Harry, Charles, and Cole have been back in United Kingdom.

Bethania was taken aback by the news that William was flying back to Miami to see her. She was excited but also nervous, as it had been over a month since they had seen each other in person.

As William arrived Bethania loved his new look, he upgraded his still style and his new hair. She told him he looked like young Pierce Brosnan James Bond 007. In the back of her mind, she wouldn't mind being his bond girl. He mentioned he's now working for the British Prime Minister, and she told him she now has her own broker's license and starting her own Real Estate Firm. He responded, "We have much to celebrate."

He was also impressed to hear that Bethania had obtained her own broker's license and was starting her own real estate firm. He knew how hard she had worked to get to this point and was proud of her accomplishments.

William mentioned with a smile. "I'm so proud of everything you've accomplished, Bethania. Starting your own business is a monumental accomplishment."

Bethania smiled back at him, feeling grateful for his support. "Thank you, William. It hasn't been easy, but I'm excited for what the future holds."

As they continued to talk and catch up, they could not help but feel drawn to each other. They both knew that they had something special and wanted to see where things could go.

William said, "I know you have a busy schedule, and I don't want to interfere, but I want to plan an evening dinner boat ride to enjoy the sunset with you."

Bethania's eyes lit up at William's suggestion. "That sounds wonderful, William," she replied with a smile. "I would have loved to go on a dinner boat ride with you and enjoyed the sunset. "They made plans to go out on the boat the following evening and spend a romantic evening together. Bethania couldn't wait to spend more time with William and get to know him better. She was excited to see where their relationship could go and was grateful for the opportunity to spend time with him.

Bethania told the ladies what William had planned for their date and the ladies were all excited for her.

Bridget said, "I love it when a man puts some serious thought and knows how to plan."

Sabrina asked her, "What do you plan on wearing?"

Bethania replied, "Girl I seriously need to go shopping. He has upgraded his look with his hair and everything he looks like a sexy James Bond."

Amber said, "Bethania it's time to go to Design District girl I love it when I see a man takes great pride in his appearance."

The ladies all got ready to go shopping with Bethania at Design District Miami. As they walked through the upscale boutiques, they pointed out different items that they thought would look great on her.

Amber suggested a stunning red dress that would highlight Bethania's shape and make her stand out on the boat ride. Sabrina suggested a pair of elegant heels that would complement the dress perfectly. Jacqueline suggested a statement necklace that would add some sparkle to the outfit.

After trying on several outfits, Bethania finally settled on the red dress and paired it with the elegant heels and statement necklace. She felt confident and beautiful in her new outfit, and the ladies all agreed that William would be blown away when he saw her.

Amber said, "Bethania you look like a gorgeous hot Eva Mendez" Bethania laughed and said, "Thank you, Amber. That's very kind of you to say." She admired herself in the mirror, feeling confident and beautiful in her new outfit. The ladies continued to shop, finding accessories to complement Bethania's outfit and discussing their own fashion preferences.

As they left the store, Bethania felt grateful for her friends and their support. She couldn't wait for her date with William and was excited to see where their relationship would go.

So as Bethania finished up getting ready William texted her to let her know he sent a car for her to pick her up. As she waited down in the lobby to get picked up the car arrived the driver got out opens up the door and lets her in. As she arrived at the Miami Beach Marina there is William standing there looking dapper, she gets out of the car. William couldn't believe how gorgeous she looked.

He said to her, "It was definitely worth not waiting a second longer to come back to see you."

She says to him" I'm glad I inspired you to want to come back." Also, she told him, "I love the suit by the way."

He responded, "Thank you I may be a little too overdressed for the weather in Miami."

They boarded a beautiful yacht Bethania realized they have the whole boat to themselves.

Bethania asked "Where is the captain?"

William said, "You're looking at him."

She said, "Hold on this is your boat?"

He said, "No 'it's a friend of mine his dad has a boat in Miami. Plus, he owes me a favor."

William gave Bethania a tour of the yacht showing her the different rooms, the deck, and the amazing views of the Miami skyline. As the boat sets sail, they sit down to a delicious dinner prepared by a private chef. They talk and laugh, enjoyed each other's company as the sun sets over the ocean. William told Bethania about his work with the British Prime Minister, and she told him about her plans for her real estate firm. They both realize they have a lot in common, including their ambition and drive.

After they finished their meal, William surprised Bethania with a small gift, a necklace with a charm in the shape of a key, it symbolized the key to her success. She thanked him and tried it on, feeling grateful and touched by the gesture.

As they continue their boat ride, they dance under the stars, enjoying the cool breeze and the sounds of the waves. Bethania feels like she's in a dream and can't believe how lucky she is to be with someone like William.

Bethania said, "I hate it that we live so far away."

William said, "I know don't worry I'm working on a solution so I can be more closer to you."

Bethania asked William "Where do you see this going?"

William said, "I don't want anything less than for you to be mine."

Bethania said, "Drop the anchor"

William said, "We're pretty much in the middle of the ocean by Key Biscayne"

Bethania said, "Yes I know."

Bethania slowly starts taking her dress off and told William I don't want to go home tonight let's go down below as she walks in her bra and panties William follows pursuit.

In the master suite Bethania slowly started taking Williams clothes off she said to him "You smell really good." After she fully undresses William she told him to lay down. She asked William "do you trust me?" he said, "Yes" then she begins to tie his hands to the bedpost and his feet, she blindfolded his eyes with a heightened sense of stimulation riveting through his veins he doesn't know what she's about to do to him next but he loves it. Bethania leans over William and whispers in his ear, "I'm going to make you feel so good, William." She trailed her fingers down his chest, his stomach, and lower, until she reached his already hard member. She runs her thumb over the tip, eliciting a groan from William. Bethania takes William into her mouth and begins to suck, her tongue swirling around the head. William moans, pulling at his restraints, his excitement building. Bethania takes him deeper, her hand working in tandem with her mouth. William's breathing becomes ragged, his hips bucking up to meet her.

Suddenly, Bethania stops and climbs onto the bed, straddling William's hips. She removes her bra, revealing her pert breasts, and runs her hands over them. William strains against his restraints, desperate to touch her.

Bethania leaned down and into his ear and said, "You miss me?" He said, "Yes" and kisses him deeply, her tongue exploring his mouth. She sits up and reaches into the bedside drawer, retrieving a condom, which she tears open and rolls onto William's swollen member.

She positioned his tip at her entrance and sinks down onto him, taking him all the way to the hilt. Bethania kissed him passionately;

she started to run her fingers through his hair. He feels her soft lips on his skin and the warmth of her body against his they both cry out and Bethania is unable to move for a minute as she adjusts to him. Then she begins to ride, her hips rocking back and forth as she takes him. William thrusts his hips upwards into her, meeting her thrust for thrust, taking her.

Bethania leans forward, bracing herself with her hands on his chest. She can feel the pleasure building between her legs, needing to be released. She moans, her pleasure mounting. William bucks his hips up to meet her and suddenly, Bethania can't hold back anymore. She comes, her body shuddering. She rides it out, crying out and chanting William's name.

William can't hold on any longer. He pulls on his restraints and Bethania he moans softly and feeling a growing desire within him. After a few moments, Bethania sits up and looks down at him. She stares at him and smiles mischievously. "I want to take control tonight," she says. William nods eagerly, enjoying the feeling of surrendering himself to her. Bethania climbed off of him and slowly taking her time to explore every inch of his body with her hands and mouth. She moves down his body, kissing and teasing him until he's moaning with pleasure. Then she climbs back up and straddles him again, positioning herself so that he can enter her.

As they make love, the yacht rocks gently in the waves, adding to the sensation of being adrift in the middle of the ocean. Bethania moves with a sensual grace, taking William to the edge of pleasure and then pulling back, teasing him with her body until he can't take it anymore. Finally, they both climax together, collapsing in a heap of sweaty, satisfied bodies. As they lay there, panting and wrapped in each other's arms, Bethania looked up at William and smiled. She slowly begins to untie him and remove the cover from his eyes. "I think we're going to need a bigger boat," she said, laughing. William chuckled and pulled her closer, grateful for the chance to be with her again.

The ladies were wondering how Bethania's date went, they were starting to get a little concerned since she didn't text them any updates all night. Bridget decided to give Bethania a call the next morning just to check on her she finally answers.

She told Bridget, "I am just now getting home."

Bridget said, "oh wow girl you know it's after sunrise did you get stuck on the boat?"

Bethania chuckles and said, "No, we didn't get stuck on the boat. William just wanted to make sure we had a proper celebration, and it was amazing."

Bridget let out a sigh of relief and said, "Well, we were worried about you. But it sounds like you had a great time."

Bethania agreed and said, "I will fill the rest of the ladies in on the details later, but I just need to catch up on some sleep."

Sabrina and Bridget received a text from Cole and Charles that they were going to be flying back into Miami together and they really wanted to see Sabrina and Bridget. They've been keeping in contact and getting to know each other. Charles was a stockbroker and Cole was finishing his residency. He wants to be a pediatrician. With the lockdown restrictions still going on in the United Kingdom William Charles and Cole we're lucky to be able to leave but since William works for the Prime Minister, he was able to pull some strings.

Sabrina and Bridget were thrilled to hear that Charles and Cole were coming back to Miami and immediately made plans to meet up with them. They decided to have a casual lunch at a beachside restaurant and catch up on everything that had been going on in their lives.

As they sat down to eat, Charles and Cole shared their experiences of being in the UK during the pandemic and how they had managed to stay safe and healthy. Sabrina and Bridget, in turn, updated them on their new business ventures and how they were balancing work and their personal lives.

During the lunch, Charles and Sabrina found themselves having an intense conversation about their shared passion for travel, while Cole and Bridget bonded over their mutual love for children and the medical field. It was clear that they all had a lot in common and were enjoying each other's company.

As the lunch came to an end, Charles and Cole mentioned that they were planning on staying in Miami for a few weeks and wanted to make plans to hang out again soon. Sabrina and Bridget were thrilled at the idea and promised to make it happen.

It was clear that the four of them had formed a strong bond, and they were all excited to see where their friendship would take them.

Bethania had texted ladies and said, "She had a list of potential properties that they should take a look at that are great potential investment opportunities for their new business." Plus, they could grab lunch and she was eager to team about her last date with William.

The ladies were excited to hear from Bethania about her last date with William and were also intrigued by the potential investment opportunities she had found. They decided to meet up for lunch to discuss both topics. As they sat down at the restaurant, Bethania couldn't stop talking about her amazing date with William and how he had flown all the way from the UK just to see her.

Bridget and Sabrina were happy for her, and they couldn't believe that Charles and Cole did the same. Amber, on the other hand, was more focused on the investment opportunities that Bethania had found. She asked for more details about the properties and what made them a good investment.

Bethania pulled out her list and started going over the properties with the ladies. They were all located in up-and-coming neighborhoods with a lot of potential for growth. Some were commercial properties, while others were residential. Daniel had helped her research each one and had provided detailed analysis on the potential return on investment.

The ladies were impressed with the properties and decided to take a closer look at a few of them. They finished up their lunch and headed out to start their property search.

Megan and Jacqueline suggested we should make an offer on one of the properties based on the location. Bridget agreed and added that they should also take into consideration the property's potential for growth and development. Sabrina suggested they should do some research on the area's real estate market and current trends to make sure it's a good investment. Amber said they should also look into any zoning or building regulations that may affect their plans for the property. Elena chimed in, saying that she can help with the research and provide more information on the property's history and previous sales. They all agreed to move forward with the offer and plan to discuss further details with Bethania.

As the ladies finished up doing business for the day Amber shared with them that James had been very persistent and following up and keeping in contact with her. She mentioned, "He seems to really like her and wants to build something, but I am just not ready to get too serious with him."

She also mentioned, "I do really him but I'm so conflicted."

Bridget said, "Well, it's important to be honest with yourself and with him about where you're at and how you're feeling. If you're not ready for something serious, it's better to be upfront about that. But if you're conflicted, maybe you should take some time to think about what you really want."

Sabrina agreed, "Yeah, and it's okay to take things slow and process how you feel as you spend more time with him. Just be true to yourself and your feelings."

Megan chimed in, "And remember, you don't have to make any big decisions right now. You can take your time and see where things go." Jacqueline asked, "Are you conflicted due to how well he knows your body?"

Elena said, "That thought crossed my mind too."

Bridget jumped in and said, "Well, it's important to remember that physical attraction is just one aspect of a relationship. It's important to consider if you have a connection on an emotional and intellectual level as well. And if you do decide to pursue things with him, make sure it's on your terms and at your own pace." The other ladies nodded in agreement.

The next day Bethania received a call that mentioned the listing agent was interested and moving forward with the offer proposed. The ladies reacted ecstatically since they had just landed their first investment property.

Megan said, "I'm so glad that we've started this journey."

Bridget added, "Yes, and it's just the beginning. I'm excited to see where this takes us."

Sabrina said, "Me too. And we work so well together, I have no doubt we'll make this a success."

Jacqueline chimed in, "I agree. And with all our different backgrounds and expertise, we can bring so much to the table."

Amber said, "I'm just happy to be a part of it all."

Bethania said, "I couldn't have done this without all of you. I'm so grateful for this partnership."

Megan said, "ladies go pour yourself a glass so we can have a toast." They all raise their glasses to celebrate their success and toast to their future endeavors.

Chapter 7

Jacqueline texted the ladies and said, "Now that we are officially property owners in South Florida but we don't have any transportation we've been getting around using Ubers and cabs." Amber said, "You're right but Miami is such a small city it's like a small town you really don't need a car here."

Jacqueline said, "What do you guys think about getting scooters or how about an Electric Vehicle? Now that we're going around South Florida looking at potential investments, we should have at least some sort of mode of transportation."

Sabrina responded, "I think getting an Electric Vehicle is a great idea! It's environmentally friendly and also cost-effective in the long run. Plus, we can charge it up at home."

Bridget agreed, "Yeah, and there are a lot of incentives and rebates for electric vehicles, so we might even save money in the long run."

Megan added, "And we could even get one with enough space to transport any materials or supplies we need for the business."

Elena said, "Count me in, I think it's a great idea. Let's start researching some electric vehicles that fit our needs and budget."

Jacqueline said, "ladies it sounds like it's time for us to do some more shopping."

The ladies decided to do some market research on cars, they all decided let's just get a Model 3. The ladies loved their new cars, and it was very cost effective.

Amber said, "Now we don't have an excuse why we can't all work out together at the gym."

Bridget agreed, "Yeah, and we can even take weekend trips to explore more of South Florida."

Sabrina suggested, "We should plan a beach day trip soon. It's been a while since we've all hung out and relaxed together."

Jacqueline agreed, "That sounds like a great idea. Let's plan something for next weekend."

Elena chimed in, "And we should also start looking for our next investment property. We don't want to wait too long let's keep growing our portfolio."

Megan nodded, "Definitely. Let's keep an eye out for any good opportunities."

Megan suggested a good idea that she loved and was going to present it to the ladies.

She texted the ladies said, "Let's continue to research opportunities but I was reading that we can take a ferry from Fort Lauderdale to Bimini how about we all go to Bimini taken the size still do business there's nothing wrong with having your cake and eat it too."

The ladies are excited about Megan's idea and quickly respond with their agreement.

Sabrina excitedly said, "Yes, that sounds like so much fun! We can work hard and play hard."

Jacqueline said, "I've always wanted to visit Bimini. It's a great opportunity to explore a new place while still being productive."

Bethania chimed in, "And it's a chance for us to bond as a team and build our relationships outside of work."

Amber agreed, "I'm so down for this. Let's plan it!" The ladies begin to make plans and research activities they can do in Bimini while still staying focused on their business goals.

The day had finally arrived for the ladies' trip to Bimini. They had met early in the morning at the ferry terminal in Fort Lauderdale, excited and ready for their adventure. The ferry was big enough to accommodate dozens of passengers, but it wasn't too crowded, so they managed to find seats together.

As the ferry pulled away from the dock and made its way towards Bimini, the ladies took in the beautiful scenery around them. They could see the crystal-clear waters of the Atlantic Ocean, and the sun was shining brightly in the sky.

After a little over two hours, the ferry arrived at Bimini. The ladies disembarked and took a deep breath of the fresh island air. They were greeted by friendly locals who were eager to show them around and offer recommendations for places to visit.

They spent the day exploring the island, visiting local businesses, and meeting with potential investors. But they also had time to relax and enjoy the island's many attractions. They went snorkeling in the turquoise waters, ate fresh seafood, and sipped on tropical drinks while lounging on the beach.

As the ladies were relaxing on the nice warm sand beach Megan said "I have a surprise for you guys. I've made $500,000 investment to build more capital for our business. I did an aggressive call option on some stocks that have paid off quite handsomely well as I've been keeping up with how the markets have been during the pandemic. The good news is ladies that $500,000 investment has made us over $4 million it was risky, but it was worth it."

The ladies all jumped up with excitement and started hugging Megan, congratulating her on the success of the investment.

Bethania said, "That's amazing, Megan! You really know how to make those dollars work for us."

Sabrina added, "This is such great news, it's going to give us even more flexibility to pursue bigger opportunities."

Elena chimed in, "I knew we could trust you with our money, Megan."

Jacqueline said, "This is a game-changer for us, we can really take our business to the next level now."

As they continued to enjoy their day on the beach, the ladies started brainstorming ideas for how to reinvest their newfound capital. They discussed various industries and potential opportunities, weighing the pros and cons of each. Amber suggested real estate development in the Caribbean, while Jacqueline proposes expanding into the hospitality industry with a luxury resort. Bethania mentioned the potential for renewable energy investments, and Sabrina suggested exploring tech startups.

Bethania also shared with the ladies, "Thanks to you guys for motivating and inspiring me to be a better version of myself. I have accomplished my goals and now I am ready to be a homeowner like you all. I can't thank you all enough for believing in me even at times when I didn't believe in myself. My father and I haven't been on good speaking terms since he felt that me dropping out of college was going to be the biggest mistake of my life. But I realize the biggest mistake of my life was if I'd have stayed and never met y'all I will not be living this American dream of being the best version that I could ever be of myself."

The ladies all smiled and hugged Bethania, happy for her accomplishment and proud of her growth.

Jacqueline said, "You know, sometimes the people closest to us don't understand our dreams and goals. But that's why we have each other, to support and lift each other up."

Elena added, "And look at us now, we're all successful business owners and homeowners. We did it together."

Sabrina chimed in, "And we're just getting started. Who knows what else we'll accomplish as a team." The ladies' cheers to their success and toast to their future endeavors.

As the day started to wind down, the ladies gathered to watch the sunset. The sky turned pink and orange, and the water glimmered like gold. They talked about their experiences on the island and how they were excited to continue exploring new opportunities together.

On the way back to the ferry all the ladies received a text from James, Harry, Charles, William, Cole, and Maxwell. The ladies were so occupied enjoying Bimini taking photos and videos soaking in the moment they had turned off notifications on their phones and realized they had missed some messages.

Megan checked her phone and saw that she had few messages from Maxwell. He had been trying to get in touch with her throughout the day and was wondering why she wasn't responding. Amber, Jacqueline, Bridget, and Sabrina all checked their phones as well and saw that they had similar messages from their significant others.

Jacqueline said, "Oops, I guess we were having too much fun and forgot about our phones."

Amber replied, "Yeah, I turned off my notifications because I didn't want any distractions while we were here."

Bridget added, "I guess we should have told our guys that we were going to be out of reach for a while."

Sabrina said, "Let's just respond and let them know that we're okay and that we'll talk to them when we get back to the mainland."

Elena said, "Am I the only one who texted Colin and let him know I may be Mia for today."

Megan said, "I appreciate them checking in on us, but they are not our men yet if Maxwell was my man that's a different story."

As the ferry made its way back to Fort Lauderdale, the ladies were tired but satisfied with their trip. They had accomplished their business goals and had a great time doing it. As they looked out at the ocean, they knew that the future was bright and full of potential.

As Elena arrived home and got settled in she gives Colin a call she noticed that he was feeling sad on the phone.

She asked, "What's going through your mind Hun?"

He said, "He was really missing his family back in Oslo he hadn't seen them and so long even though we FaceTime it just not the same."

Elena thought of an idea and told him, "I want to see you, pack a bag and come over here and stay with me I don't want you to be alone tonight."

While Colin was packing a bag and getting ready to head over, Elena decided she's going to set the mood right and lit some candles dim the lights and play some soft music. She takes a shower and decides to change into some lingerie. As Elena finished getting ready, she heard a knock on the door. She rushed to answer it, eager to see Colin. When she opened the door, Colin was standing there with a small smile on his face. He noticed the dimly lit room and the flickering candles, and his eyes widened with surprise.

Elena asked Colin, "Would you like some wine?"

he said, "Absolutely."

Colin also said, "Elena you are truly quite an enigma I like it."

she replied, "I'm not your typical kind of lady and if I was a guy like you wouldn't find me interesting?"

Colins said, "Indeed, let's toast to that."

After they toasted Colin looked Elena in the eyes, leaned in and kissed her passionately. Elena's heart skipped a beat as she kissed him back, and they continued to embrace each other, lost in the moment.

Elena had set her wine glass down takes Colin by the hand escorts him to her bedroom. She slowly started to undress him.

As she took off his shirt, Elena traced her fingers over Colin's exposed chest, feeling his skin warm under her touch. She leaned in and kissed him deeply, their tongues dancing together in a fiery passion. Colin's hands roamed over her lingerie, feeling the curves of her body before he slowly peeled it off her, revealing her nakedness.

As they made their way to the bed, Elena couldn't help but feel a rush of excitement and anticipation run through her veins. She had never felt this way with anyone before, and the idea of exploring Colin's body and being explored by him electrified her.

As they lay on the bed, Colin took the lead, his hands exploring every inch of her body, sending shivers of pleasure through her. He kissed her neck, nibbling softly as his hands traced circles around her breasts. Elena moaned softly, her body arching up into his touch, her desire building with each passing moment.

Colin continued to explore her body with his hungry lips and fingers, leaving a trail of burning desire along her flesh. He kissed her neck, her collarbone, her chest. He took her nipple in his mouth before moving to the other, sucking it tenderly. Elena's eyes rolled back in her head. She never imagined that any of this would feel so good, so amazing. She was already on the edge of orgasm just from having his mouth and hands on her. She moaned louder, feeling the tension building up within her.

Slowly, Colin moved lower, his lips trailing kisses along her stomach until they found the thin patch of trimmed pubic hair where her legs met. Elena shivered as she felt his lips on her skin, an intense, agonizing pleasure that she had never experienced before. She gasped as she felt his tongue slide against her skin, his hands cupping her ass as he pressed his face into her.

Elena moaned and writhed under his touch. She couldn't with his lips, kissing her stomach and moving down to her inner thighs, savoring the softness of her skin, the way she quivered under his touch. Elena moved her hands over his shoulders, her fingers playing over his back, her nails gently digging into his skin as he traveled along every inch of her body. Soon, Colin found his mouth against her inner thigh, his tongue sliding against her skin, his kiss growing hot, his teeth gently nibbling at her.

Elena moaned softly as she felt Colin's mouth against her, his tongue sending a rush of pleasure through her. She ran her hands through his hair, slowly guiding him down, moving his head further into her, pushing him into her. Elena spread her legs for him, emotions of pleasure washing over her as Colin's tongue nestled deep inside of her, his mouth sending wave after wave of intense pleasure through her body. Elena's heart was pounding as she felt him against her, the pleasure building up. As Colin continued to explore her body, Elena felt herself reaching the brink of ecstasy. She cried out in pleasure as she reached her climax, her body shaking with intense sensation. As they lay there, lost in the afterglow, Colin looked at Elena with a smile. "You were truly amazing," he said. "I can't wait to explore more of you." Elena smiled, feeling happy and content. She knew that she had found someone special in Colin, someone who truly appreciated her for who she was.

The next morning, Elena and Colin wake up in each other's arms, smiling at each other.

Elena looked at Colin and said, "I'm so glad you came over last night."

Colin replied, "Me too. I feel so close to you." They spend the morning in bed, cuddling and talking about their hopes and dreams. Elena feels a sense of contentment wash over her, knowing that she has found someone who truly understands her.

Elena said, "After all that work you put on my body last night let me cook you some breakfast, I know you're hungry."

Colin said, "Wow you cook, Elena you are truly one of a kind." Elena said, "You better never forget that."

Later that morning Jacqueline received a call from Harry and said he'd arrived at Miami airport and wanted to surprise her to let her know he's back in town. Jacqueline is overjoyed to hear Harry's voice on the phone and can't believe that he's back in town. She quickly got dressed and rushed to the airport to meet him. As she makes her way through the crowds, she can feel her heart pounding with excitement.

When she finally spots Harry waiting for her at the arrivals gate, she runs towards him and jumps into his arms. They hug each other tightly and share a long, passionate kiss.

After they've calmed down a bit, Harry explained that he's been feeling homesick and really missed Jacqueline, so he decided to fly back to Miami for a few days. Jacqueline can't believe how romantic and thoughtful he is, and she feels grateful to have him in her life.

They spend the day catching up on each other's lives, sharing stories and laughs over a delicious meal at one of Jacqueline favorite restaurants. Harry surprised her with a beautiful bouquet of flowers and a thoughtful gift, showing her how much he cared about her.

Harry asked Jacqueline, "Do you like jet skis?"

She replied, "Yes I do What did you have in mind?"

Harry said, "Well, I rented a couple of jet skis and thought we could spend the day out on the water, exploring the coast and having some fun. What do you think?"

Jacqueline replied, with a smile, "That sounds like an amazing idea, Harry! I can't wait to get out there and feel the wind in my hair."

As they arrived at the Marina, Harry said, "I have a surprise for us tomorrow" I need you to pack an overnight bag and bring an outfit you would like to dress up in. I'm taking you to The Breakers tomorrow and get out of Miami.

Jacqueline eyes widen with excitement as she heard Harry's plans for the next day. She quickly agreed and started packing her bag when she arrived home also wondering what other surprises Harry had in stored for her at The Breakers.

The next day, they made their way to The Breakers, a luxury resort in Palm Beach. As they arrived, Harry led Jacqueline to a beautiful suite overlooking the ocean. The room is decorated with rose petals, candles, and a bottle of champagne on ice.

Jacqueline was surprised and delighted by the romantic setup. She turned to Harry and said, "Wow, this is amazing. What did I do to deserve all of this?"

Harry took her hand and said, "You deserve the world, Jacqueline. I just want to make you happy and show you how much I care for you."

They spend the rest of the day enjoying the amenities at the resort, including a relaxing couples massage, a private dinner on the beach, and dancing under the stars. It's a magical evening, and Jacqueline feels jubilant.

While Jacqueline and Harry were having fun, Megan sent out a group text to the ladies, inviting them over to the hotel rooftop for a day of relaxation by the pool. She set out some towels and pool float and orders some drinks and snacks for everyone to enjoy.

Shortly after, Elena arrived from their night together with Colin, and Elena shared the news of her fun evening she had. They all congratulated her and continued to enjoy their day by the pool, soaking up the sun and chatting about their experiences on the island.

Megan asked ladies, "How's work outside of the business?" Elena was working setting her a new OBGYN practice in Miami, Amber been expanding her Pharmaceutical Sales territory in Dade and Broward County.

Bethania said, "She has a meeting with her client Amir coming up since he wants to buy a condo on Fisher Island."

Bridgette said, "I'm focused on Real Estate Development Project in Coconut Grove."

Sabrina chimed in, "I've been working remotely for my firm in NYC but ready to start practicing law in Florida since the rest of the country is still under a lot of restrictions."

The ladies chatted about their plans for the weekend. Elena mentioned that she's going to spend time with Colin.

Amber said, "I'm planning to visit some family in Tampa."

Bethania said, "I will be attending a charity event at the Perez Art Museum."

and Bridget mentioned that she's going to a beach party in Key Biscayne. Sabrina said she made plans to explore some of the art galleries in Wynwood.

Megan listened intently and then added that she's been meaning to check out some new restaurants in Little Havana, and maybe catch a concert at the Fillmore. The girls started brainstorming more ideas for things to do around Miami, and they all agreed that they needed to make time for more fun and relaxation outside of work.

Amber asked Megan, "How's the dating situation with Maxwell? Spill the tea."

Megan said, "If I tell you, then you must tell us about what's going on with you and James since you were out on that balcony entertaining all the neighbors?"

Amber starts blushing, "How did you know about that? Did you guys see us?

All the ladies said, "Yes! So did all of Brickell" Amber is laughing hysterically.

Megan said, "Of course, we saw you. It's probably on YouTube by now. You were putting on quite a show. But let's get back to you, Amber. What's going on with you and James?"

Amber was embarrassed and said, "Well, we've been seeing each other I like him I'm just not ready for anything serious. He's a great guy and we really enjoy spending time together. We're just taking things slow and seeing where it goes."

Megan nodded and said, "Happy for you. As for Maxwell, things are going well. We've still talking as well and he's been supportive of the business. He's also kind and thoughtful. I'm really focused on building this business for us. I'm just not trying to allow for relationship to cause a distraction. What about you Sabrina have you and Charles getting hot and heated?"

Sabrina smiled and said, "Charles and I are doing well. We're taking it slow and enjoying each other's company. We haven't gotten too hot and heated yet, but we'll see where things go." She had a sip of her drink and looked out at the Miami skyline. "But like Megan,

I'm also focused on my career and making a name for myself in the legal and business world. It's important to have balance, but right now my focus is on work."

So, as they continued to talk Cole called Bridget and said he's at the Soho beach house and wanted her to come over.

She told him "I'm just at the One Hotel how about you come down here and join us Megan has all kinds of food."

Cole said he'll meet her at the One Hotel rooftop. She then turns to the ladies and said, "Cole is on his way over." As Cole joined them, they all catch up and chat about what they've been up to. Cole told them about his latest opportunity landing a job Mount Sinai in Miami and how excited he is about it. The ladies congratulated him and shared their own stories about their work.

Cole turned to Bridget and looks at her and said, "It seems like I'm going to be in Miami eventually full time, and I would really like to spend more time getting to know you."

Bridget smiled and responded, "I would like that too. I've really enjoyed spending time with you, Cole."

Then Cole turned to Bethania and said, "I need you to help me find a place here in Miami Beach."

Bethania smiled and said, "Of course, I'd be happy to help you find a place. What kind of neighborhood and amenities are you looking for?"

Cole replied, "I'm looking for something near the beach with a nice view, and maybe a pool and gym in the building."

Bethania nodded and said, "I know just the places to look. Let's get together tomorrow and start the search."

Jacqueline sent a group text and told the ladies it is very gorgeous up here Harry has truly outdone himself today. She sent a picture to the group text of the flowers that Harry got her. The ladies respond with excitement and admiration for the beautiful flowers.

Bethania responds, "Wow, Harry is really spoiling you! He must really like you."

Amber adds, "He has great taste in flowers! You're a lucky girl, Deirdre."

Elena chimed in, "Looks like you're having an amazing time. Can't wait to catch up with you and hear all about it."

Bridgette replied, "Those flowers are stunning! Glad you're having a great time, Jacqueline."

Sabrina sent a heart emoji and a message, "So happy for you, Jacqueline! Enjoy the beautiful day."

Cole is the only guy hanging out with the ladies, Amber asked him a question putting him on the spot, "What part of the UK did you grow up? Your friends James William Charles and Harry are so different than most guys in a good way in how you treat a woman. All these beautiful women here today and you haven't taken your eyes off Bridget. I love a man that doesn't have a wondering eye, A lot of men in Miami just want to sleep around with as many women as possible. What is it about me, Bridget, Jacqueline, Sabrina, and Bethania that makes you and your friends want fly across the Atlantic Ocean for us?"

Cole smiled and said, "Well, I grew up in London, but my parents are originally from Edinburgh in Scotland. As for your question, Amber, it's simple. When we met you ladies and started getting to know you each of you, we automatically knew you ladies were very different. Not only are you guys gorgeous, but you are women that are living with purpose. At this age and stage in our lives we're looking for women with substance that makes us want to be more then who we are. That's why James is crazy about you Amber and he's personally said Amber is the kind of girl that's so rare she's the kind of girl I'm looking for. I have a lot of respect for women, and I believe in treating them with kindness and consideration. I've always been raised to value honesty, loyalty, and integrity, and that's how I try to live my life. As for the ladies here today, you all have such unique qualities and personalities that make you stand out. We appreciate your intelligence, your sense of humor, and your ambition. And as for Bridget, well, she's just amazing in every way. What she is doing in such a male dominated profession is inspiring. I feel lucky to have met her and I'm looking forward to getting to know her better."

Cole also said this, "You guys are single not because you don't have any options, you're single by choice. I look at you ladies as high value women and when you're high value you're not just going to be with just anyone. As a man I feel that way about myself there's a reason why Rolls Royce's are not parked in every driveway."

In the back of Amber's mind, she was very surprised that James saw her that way it's making her feel like she's going to rethink pursuing and being with him.

Elena Megan Sabrina and Bethania smiled looked at Cole and said, "very well said thank you Cole cheers to that."

Amber said, "ladies I need to use the ladies room care to join me."

The other ladies nod and follow Amber to the restroom. As they freshen up and touch up their makeup.

Sabrina turns to Amber and said, "So what's going on with you and James? You seem surprised by what Cole said."

Amber sighs and said, "I don't know. I mean, I've been interested in James for a while now, but I didn't think he saw me the same way. Hearing that he does is making me rethink things. I don't want to get too invested if it's not going to go anywhere, you know?"

Bethania chimed in, "Well, you won't know if you don't take a chance. Maybe you should talk to James and see where he stands."

Amber nods thoughtfully and said, "You're right. I think I will."

Megan said, "This has me wondering how Maxwell thinks of me, does he see me like the way Cole, Harry, William, James, and Charles looks at you guys?"

Bethania chimed in, "Well, why don't you ask him? Communication is key in any relationship, especially when it comes to understanding each other's intentions and feelings."

Sabrina agreed, "Exactly, Megan. It's important to be open and honest with each other about your thoughts and feelings. If you're curious about how Maxwell sees you, the best thing to do is just ask him. That way, you can have a clearer idea of where you both stand."

Elena nods in agreement, "And remember, it's important to approach the conversation with an open mind and a willingness to listen to each other. Don't be afraid to express your own thoughts and feelings as well."

Megan nodded, "You guys are right. I think I'm going to have a conversation with him and see where things stand between us."

Megan decided that she was going to invite Maxwell over and talk to him and Amber decided she wanted to see James. They both decided they were going to cook a small meal at their house and have a more private intimate conversation.

Later that evening, as Maxwell arrived at Megan's he was feeling a little perplexed at the last-minute invite and didn't know what to expect. When he walks into Megan's amazing condo that she has finally finished her interior design makeover he is mesmerized at what he sees when he walks in.

Maxwell was awestruck by Megan's beautiful condo. He looks around at the sleek and modern furniture, the carefully curated artwork, and the tasteful decor. He could tell that Megan had put a lot of thought and effort into making her home a reflection of herself.

As they settled in for the evening, Maxwell couldn't help but feel a little nervous. He's always been attracted to Megan, but he's not sure if she felt the same way. He started to wonder if he's been too subtle in his flirtations, or if she just sees him as a friend.

Megan noticed that Maxwell seemed a bit nervous, and she tried to put him at ease. She complimented him on his outfit and told him that she's happy he could make it. They start talking about their favorite restaurants in the area and share stories about their travels.

Megan asked Maxwell a direct question "When you see me what do you think? What type of woman do you see yourself with?

Maxwell took a moment to collect his thoughts before answering Megan's question. "Well Megan, I see a beautiful, intelligent, and ambitious woman who knows what she wants in life. You have great taste and style, and you are always up for trying new things. As for what type of woman I see myself with, I'm looking for someone who is kind, honest, and loyal. Someone who is passionate about their career and has a strong sense of self. And I think you embody all those qualities. I've enjoyed spending time with you and I'm looking forward to getting to know you better."

Maxwell asked her "When you see me what do you think? What type of man do you see yourself with?"

Megan smiled and took a sip of her drink before answering. "Well, Maxwell, when I see you, I see a successful and ambitious man who knows what he wants in life. And as for the type of man I see myself with, I want someone who is driven, kind, and has a good sense of humor. I want someone who can challenge me and help me grow, but also someone who can support me and be my partner in all aspects of life. He can't be possessive and controlling, he's got to learn to be very secure in his foundation. I operate at a very high frequency so I need to make sure he can tune into my channel and understand and respect it."

As the evening went on, Maxwell started to feel more comfortable. He's enjoying spending time with Megan, and he can't help but feel drawn to her. He decided to take a chance and told her how he felt.

"Megan, I know we've been friends for a short time, but I have to be honest with you. I've always been attracted to you, and I can't stop thinking about you. I know we have a great connection, but I just wanted you to know how I feel."

Megan looked surprised but also pleased. She smiled and said, "Maxwell, I'm glad you told me. I've been feeling the same way, but I didn't want to ruin our friendship. I think we could have something special together."

Maxwell felt a rush of relief and excitement. He can't believe that Megan felt the same way he does. They clink glasses and share a toast to their newfound romance.

On the other side of Biscayne Bay, Amber and James are having a candlelit dinner at her place and James loved her place and what she cooked.

James complimented Amber on the lovely dinner and said, "This is amazing, Amber. You have such great taste in everything, from your home decor to your cooking. And not to mention, you look absolutely stunning tonight."

Amber blushed at the compliment and said, "Thank you, James. You always know how to make a girl feel special."

James responds, "Well, you are special, Amber. You have a rare combination of beauty, intelligence, and kindness that I find very attractive."

Amber smiled and said, "I feel the same way about you, James. You have such a strong work ethic and passion for what you do, and it's truly inspiring. And the way you treat women with respect and care is so rare to find these days."

Amber asked James, "What are you looking for in your next relationship? Where do you see us going?"

James takes a sip of his wine and looks at Amber with a serious yet gentle expression. "Well, Amber, what I'm looking for in my next relationship is someone who shares my values and aspirations, someone who I can build a strong foundation with. I want a partner who is honest, loyal, and supportive, and who I can trust with my heart. As for where I see us going, I'm not sure yet, but I do know that I enjoy spending time with you and getting to know you better. I think we have a lot of potential, and I'm willing to see where things go between us."

He takes another sip of his wine before continuing. "But I also want to be clear that I'm not looking for anything casual. I'm looking for something real and long-term. I don't want to waste my time or anyone else's time. So, if you're not looking for the same thing, I want you to be honest with me. I value open and direct communication, and I think that's important for any successful relationship."

Amber responded and said, "Thank you James, I apologize for being closed off I didn't think I was ready for something serious. I realize I need to find someone who saw me seriously. I've always felt like men only saw me as a pretty face and body, but you see me differently. In my past I've been with men who were in love with the idea of me and not with me. I realize they really didn't know me at all."

James smiled at Amber and took her hand, "Amber, you're much more than just a pretty face and body. From the moment I met you, I could tell that you were someone special. You're intelligent, driven, and passionate about what you do. And you have a big heart, which is something that I value greatly. I see a lot of potential in our relationship, and I'm excited to see where things go between us. I want to build something meaningful with you, and I'm willing to put in the work to make that happen."

James nodded in agreement and said, "I think it's important to treat others the way you want to be treated. Amber, I want to be the best version of myself. I want to make you happy and support you in everything you do."

Amber looked at him and said, "I believe you, James. I want to be there for you too. We can be each other's rock and grow together."

James said, "Since you cooked this amazing meal I'm going to clean up and do the dishes."

Amber smiled and said, "Thank you, James. That's really sweet of you." She watched as James started to clear the table and do the dishes, feeling grateful for his thoughtfulness.

She complimented James and told him, "You look like a sexy Brad Pitt in meet Joe black right now."

While James was in the kitchen standing over the sink washing the dishes, Amber stood up quietly started undressing herself. As she looked at James with such passion intensity and desire, she said to him "James would you like some dessert?"

James looks at her with surprise and sees her standing there. He pauses for a moment as his eyes stared at her body, taking in the sight of her, before responding, "Of course, Amber. I would love some dessert."

Amber smiled seductively and walked towards James, her naked body glistening in the dim light of the kitchen. She stood behind him and wrapped her arms around his waist, pressing her chest against his back and feeling the warmth of his body against hers.
James turned around and faced Amber, his eyes full of desire. Without saying a word, he lifted her up and placed her on the kitchen counter, running his hands over her curves and kissing her deeply.
Amber moaned softly and ran her fingers through James's hair as he kissed her neck and trailed his lips down her body. She arched her back and let out a gasp as he took her nipple into his mouth, swirling his tongue around it and causing a shiver to run down her spine.
James looked up at Amber and said, "You taste so sweet, Amber. I could spend hours exploring every inch of your body."

He grabbed Amber's hand and led her to the bedroom. He leans in to kiss her again and whispers in her ear, "You look stunning tonight, Amber. You take my breath away." They continued to kiss and explore each other's bodies, lost in their passion and desire for each other.

Amber turned on some soft music and dims the lights, creating a romantic atmosphere. She then starts to kiss James passionately, letting him know how much she desires him. James reciprocates her passion, his hands exploring her body as they make their way to the bed.

The next morning Sabrina texted the ladies and asked them, "How they're doing how was their night? She lets them also know she is now licensed to practice law in Florida and can be the legal liaison for the business.

Elena responded, "Congrats Sabrina! That's amazing news! We'll have to celebrate soon."

Megan chimed in, "Yes, congratulations! And to answer your question, my night was wonderful. Maxwell came over and we had a great time."

Bethania mentioned, "Glad to hear you had a good night, Megan. As for me, I had a relaxing night by myself. Sometimes that's just what I need."

Amber smiled as she reads the messages but decides not to share anything about her night with James. Instead, she texted, "Congrats Sabrina! That's great news! Let's plan a dinner to celebrate soon."

Bridget said, "I'm so proud of you ladies I love all of you all and Congrats Sabrina! I love how we are crushing our goals remaining focused and finding love in the process."

Jacqueline agreed, "I couldn't agree more, Bridget! It's amazing to see how far we've come and how we're all pursuing our dreams while still supporting each other. And Sabrina, congratulations on your new license! I know you'll do great as the legal liaison for the business."

Elena chimed in, "Yes, it's been an incredible journey, and I'm grateful to have each one of you in my life. Let's continue to support and uplift each other as we pursue our dreams."

Megan added, "I'm just so happy to have such amazing friends who inspire and motivate me every day. And congratulations again, Sabrina! Your hard work has paid off."

Chapter 8

Bethania made an announcement to the ladies about an event coming up in Miami called Miami Swim Week. I would like to go to several events and watch the ladies walk the runway modeling different swimsuits. This would also be a great way for us to network plus I have found us another investment property that I believe we should take a look at.

Elena chimed in, "I love that idea, Bethania! Miami Swim Week is always so much fun and a fantastic opportunity for us to network and find new investment opportunities. Count me in!"

Megan agreed, "I'm in too! I can't wait to see this next investment property!"

Amber added, "I think it's a great idea to attend Miami Swim Week, and I'm excited to see the latest swimwear trends. Bethania, I trust your judgement when it comes to investment properties, so let's definitely take a look."

Bridget said, "I'll definitely get us some VIP tickets there's one event I want us to go to at the Faena forum."

Sabrina was very excited about Miami Swim Week but she's also enthusiastic that Charles was going to take her out to celebrate her latest accomplishment. He wanted to take her to see the Opera in downtown Miami. Later that evening Charles arrived at Sabrina's place to pick her up. As Charles gets out of his Porsche and walks into the lobby of her building Sabrina is absolutely mesmerized about how good looking, he is in his suit, she says to him, "Sir aren't you Idris Alba, but you told me your name is Charles."

Charles chuckles and responded, "Thank you gorgeous I'm not Idris Alba, although I do get that a lot. I'm loving this dress, are you ready to celebrate your latest accomplishment?" Sabrina blushed and thanked him before they headed out to the opera.

During the show, Charles leaned over to Sabrina and whispers in her ear, "You look absolutely stunning tonight." Sabrina feels her heart flutter as she looked back at him with a smile. After the show, Charles took her to a fancy restaurant for dinner and they spent the evening talking, laughing, and enjoying each other's company. Sabrina feels grateful to have someone like Charles in her life who not only supports her in her career but also knows how to treat her like a queen.

As they arrived home at her place Sabrina told Charles have valet park your car. I want you to stay with me tonight.

Charles looked at Sabrina and smiled. "I would love nothing more than to stay with you tonight," he said. As they entered Sabrina's condo, Charles told Sabrina that her condo was stunning and that he loved how she had decorated it. He takes a moment to take in the panoramic view of Miami from the floor-to-ceiling windows and compliments her on her taste. Sabrina beams with pride and invites him to sit down and relax on her plush couch. She pours him a glass of wine and they toast to her success as a licensed attorney in Florida.

Sabrina told Charles I'm going to get out of this dress and slip into something more comfortable, I'll be back.

Charles nodded his head and watched Sabrina walk towards her bedroom, admiring her beauty. He takes a seat on the couch in the living room and looks around, taking in the stunning view of Miami. As he waits for Sabrina, he can't help but think about how lucky he was to have met her.

Sabrina slowly walked back out wearing a short satin robe still in her black YSL pumps. She told him "I admire your consistency, your energy, your desire to want to be with me and for always being a gentleman. My home is my protected space and knowing that you're here you're in very sacred territory. Thank you for always making me feel like a queen. I know at times I get caught up with work because I'm very passionate and I love what I do. I wanted to take my time and let my guard down with you."

She told him to stand up she looked at Charles in his eyes and said, "Remember when I told you if you're lucky enough you'll get to see what I have on underneath." As she slowly unties the robe Charles can't believe how magnificently gorgeous Sabrina is it's more than what he ever imagined. He slowly removed the robe off of her and just admired every crevice of her body. He is deeply enthralled and mesmerized at how toned her body is. He said to her, "I can't believe just how natural and gorgeous your body is how beautiful you are. Sabrina told him "This is for your eyes only."

Sabrina told him I want you to take your time and enjoy this moment tonight you've earned it. As he runs his hand down her body over her breath slowly just taking in the moment. As he slowly begins to kiss her on her neck.

Sabrina lets out a soft moan, her body trembling with anticipation. Charles picked her up and carried her to the bedroom, laying her down on the bed. He takes a moment to just look at her, admiring her beauty and the way the moonlight dances across her skin. He leans down to kiss her again, his lips exploring every inch of her body.

Sabrina lets out a gasp as Charles moved his way down to her breasts, taking one of them into his mouth. She arches her back, her fingers running through his hair as he continues to pleasure her. Charles then moves his way down to her thighs, spreading her legs apart as he kisses his way up to her center.

Sabrina moans loudly, her body trembling with desire as Charles expertly uses his tongue to bring her to the brink of ecstasy. She grips the sheets tightly, her body writhing with pleasure as she reaches her peak.

Charles then climbed on top of her, his hard body pressing against her soft skin. He kisses her deeply as he enters her, his hands gripping her hips as he thrusts deeply inside of her. He can feel her tense as she comes around him, her nails digging into his back as her pleasure mounts.

He keeps moving deeper and deeper inside, her moans echoing around his ears as he takes her over the edge, her body quaking with the intensity of their shared passion. Charles then moves up to kiss her again, his body throbbing with desire for her, for this moment.

Sabrina trembles as she feels him move inside, her hands running up and down his hard body. She kisses him hungrily, her tongue probing his mouth as he moves with relentless passion.

The night is filled with passion and desire as Sabrina and Charles indulge in each other's company. The soft glow of the city lights seeping in through the windows adds to the romantic ambiance of the room. The sound of their bodies moving together fills the air, as they lose themselves in the moment.

Afterwards, they laid together in bed, the sheets twisted around them. Charles pulled Sabrina close to him, holding her tightly as they bask in the afterglow of their lovemaking. He whispers in her ear, telling her how much he cared about her and how lucky he feels to have her in his life.

Sabrina smiles, feeling a sense of contentment she hasn't experienced in a long time. She knows that she's found someone special in Charles and looks forward to continuing to build their relationship together.

Megan sent a message to the ladies in the middle of the night, she would like to meet with them for a late brunch to discuss business and then do some shopping for Miami swim week events.

The next morning, the ladies met for brunch at a trendy spot in Miami Beach called Planta. They catch up on each other's love lives, Sabrina sharing about her romantic evening with Charles and Bethania updating the group on the investment property she found.

Megan said, "ladies the first line of business I want to discuss with you all is the cash flow and how well we are performing. I know the real estate side of things is slowly building but the investment side is paying us handsomely well." She reaches in her purse hands each lady a white envelope.

Megan continued, "So as of this month I would like the business to start paying each of you all one-hundred grand a month. I have spoken with our accountant, and I know you all are going to say well that side of the business you've pretty much done all the work." The ladies were very shocked with a jubilant look on their face.

Megan continues "we started this venture together we profit together. Remember when I told you all you can work because you want to not because you have to that's the goal. When we started this venture all I wanted was a sense of belief in each other and you believed in me."

Each of the ladies were getting emotional with tears of joy and happiness in that moment they have crossed a major milestone in life of now they were truly living an American dream and what it felt like to now have control over your time.

Bethania said, "to the ladies what I have learned is when you are in the company of right people who truly love and support you and want to help you grow you can achieve and accomplish such amazing things, I truly love you guys not because of what we accomplished but who we are.

Jacqueline agreed, "I couldn't agree more, Bethania. It's not just about the money, it's about the relationships we've built, the trust we have with each other, and the shared vision we have for our future. This is just the beginning, and I can't wait to see what else we can accomplish together."

Bridget nodded in agreement and said, "We are unstoppable when we work together. I am so grateful for each one of you and the support we have for each other. Let's continue to crush our goals and live our best lives."

Sabrina wiped away her tears and said, "I couldn't have said it better myself. This is a moment we will never forget, and I am so blessed to have you all in my life. Let's raise a toast to our success and to each other."

Megan smiled at the ladies and said, "I'm so proud of all of us, we've worked hard to get here and it's only going to get better from here on out. We have each other's backs, and we are unstoppable when we work together." The ladies share a group hug, feeling grateful for each other's support and their success in their business. They feel like they can conquer the world with their friendship and hard work.

The ladies looked at each other in disbelief and gratitude, thanking Megan for her generosity and leadership.

Jacqueline said, "Megan, you are truly amazing. Thank you so much for everything you've done for us."

Bethania mentioned, "This is a game changer for all of us. I'm so grateful to be a part of this team."

Sabrina chimed in, "I couldn't agree more. This is an incredible opportunity for us to continue growing and thriving together."

Amber simply smiled and said, "Thank you, Megan. You're a rockstar."

After a few moments of excitement and gratitude, Megan said, "Alright, now that we've got that settled, let's talk about Miami Swim Week. I've got some events lined up that I think we'll all enjoy. And I've also found a few properties that I think are worth checking out. So, let's finish brunch and hit the shops, ladies."

After they finished their meal, Megan takes the group to some of her favorite boutiques to shop for Miami Swim Week events. They found some stunning pieces, and Megan uses her keen negotiating skills to get them some great deals. They leave the shops feeling excited for the upcoming events and confident in their newfound fashion finds.

Bethania had to cut the shopping trip short since she had to meet with Cole and help him find his new place. They went to see several beautiful beachfront properties, including a few in the historic Art Deco district.

Bethania and Cole spent the day touring different properties, trying to find the perfect place for him. They walked through a few spacious and luxurious beachfront apartments with stunning views of the ocean. They also visited a few cozy bungalows in the historic Art Deco district.

Finally, after hours of searching, they found the perfect place for Cole. It was a modern and stylish apartment, just a few blocks from the beach. The apartment was spacious and had an open layout, with large windows that let in plenty of natural light. It also had a beautiful balcony where Cole could relax and enjoy the Miami sunshine.

Bethania and Cole were both thrilled with the new place, and Cole couldn't thank Bethania enough for her help. He knew he could not have found this apartment without her. They hugged and parted ways, promising to celebrate with drinks later in the week.

As the sun was beginning to set over the Miami skyline the ladies all arrived home thinking about this monumental occasion and turning point in their lives. Some were thinking about what they would do with their first big paycheck from the business others were just relishing in the moment of finally feel like they have crossed a major marker in their finance journey and basking in that feeling of financial security.

So, it was the first night of Miami swim week and the ladies decided to go to an opening event in Miami Beach. Their first time experiencing a swimsuit event in South Florida all the ladies were so amazed at the high traffic of people that are in town for this event.

The ladies walked into a large and luxurious venue filled with vibrant colors and lights. The walls were adorned with artwork and there were multiple bars serving up delicious cocktails. The sound of upbeat music filled the air as models strutted down the runway, showcasing the latest designs in swimwear.

Sabrina couldn't help but notice the diversity of the models and the different styles of swimsuits on display. Megan was busy networking with different designers and investors, while Bethania and Amber were busy discussing potential investment opportunities in the area.

Elena happened to see Maxwell at the same event and says to herself, "Wow Miami is a small town." She was wondering who that woman was that Maxwell was talking to then she looks at Megan and tried to get her attention. Then she walks over to Megan and said, "Excuse us for moment, did you know Maxwell is here?"

Megan was perplexed and shocked and said, "He didn't mention anything to me that he was coming but I didn't ask him either." Elena and Megan decided to walk over and see Maxwell.

As they approached Maxwell, he noticed them and greeted them with a warm smile. "Hey ladies, what a surprise to see you here. Are you enjoying the event?" he asked.

Elena responded, "Yes, it's quite amazing. And to whom is this lovely lady you're talking?" pointing to the woman next to him.

Maxwell introduced her as his business partner. She said, "Hi I'm Abigail Lawson" as she shakes Megan and Elena hand.

Megan said, "I'm Megan Babineaux" and "Dr. Elena Mazor." Elena said, "I like your accent Abigail where you are you from?" Abigail said, "I'm from McKinney Texas."

Megan said, "You're very pretty Abigail, I love your red hair. How long have you and Maxwell been business partners?"

Abigail smiled and said, "Thank you so much, Megan. Maxwell and I have been working together for a few years now."

Elena chimed in, "That's amazing. Another part of our business is also in the real estate industry, but we focus more on residential properties and vacation rentals."

Maxwell interjected, "It's a small world, isn't it? Who would have thought we'd all run into each other here at Miami Swim Week?"

Megan nods in agreement, "Definitely a small world. It's great to meet you, Abigail. Maybe we can all grab a drink later. I would love to find out more about how you and Maxwell met.

Abigail smiled and said, "That sounds great. I would love to get to know you all better."

Elena turned to Megan and said, "Do you think there's something going on between Maxwell and his business partner?"

Megan said, "Did you see her? He never mentioned to me he had a business partner that look like Jean Grey from X-men. Plus, they're both attractive I wouldn't be surprised."

As Miami Swim Week event started the ladies took their VIP seats as they began watching some of the models walk out on the catwalk. Amber and Jacqueline pull out their phones and start recording but in the back of Megan's mind she was a little bothered by what she saw with Maxwell.

Megan couldn't help but feel a little uneasy about Maxwell's mysterious business partner, Abigail. She wondered why he never mentioned her before and why he seemed so secretive about their partnership. Despite her concerns, she decided to focus on the event and enjoyed the show with her friends. She was impressed with the creativity and boldness of the swimsuit designs and couldn't help but feel inspired to incorporate some of the styles into their own fashion line.

After the fashion show, Megan checked her phone and noticed that Maxwell had texted her and he's invited her, and all love her girlfriends to come over to have a drink at the Seville hotel in Miami Beach. He said he wants Megan and the ladies to get to know Abigail.

As the ladies were getting ready to leave and head outside, they asked Megan, we noticed you were feeling uneasy earlier, and I think Maxwell saw that too.

Amber asked her, "How are you feeling?" Megan shows the message to the other ladies.

Megan took a deep breath and said, "Honestly, I'm not sure. I just feel like there's something off about Maxwell and Abigail's relationship. It could just be my imagination, but I can't shake this feeling."

Jacqueline chimed in and said, "I know what you mean. Abigail seemed a little too close to Maxwell for just a business partner." The other ladies nodded in agreement.

Elena added, "We don't want you to feel uncomfortable, Megan. If you want to skip the drinks with them, we completely understand."

Megan thought for a moment before responding, "No, it's okay. Let's go and see what they have to say, and they all agree to go, excited for the opportunity to network and socialize with new people in the industry. They quickly freshened up and head over to the Seville hotel."

When they arrived, they are greeted by Maxwell and Abigail, who are already seated at a table in the hotel bar. The ladies all introduce themselves and take a seat, ordering drinks and appetizers. The conversation flows easily, and they all chat about the fashion show and the Miami scene.

As the night went on, Megan started to feel more comfortable with Abigail, and they started talking more about business. Abigail shares some insights on the fashion industry and talks about some of the challenges she has faced as a female entrepreneur. Megan is impressed by her knowledge and drive and starts to see her in a new light.

Overall, the night was a success, and the ladies leave feeling grateful for the opportunity to meet new people and expand their network. Megan felt especially grateful for the chance to connect with Abigail and hopes to continue building a relationship with her in the future.

As the night wore on and the fashion show came to an end, the ladies decided to head back home and get some rest before the next day's events.

The next day Bethania this sent the ladies an address of a real estate piece of property that she thought had a real good upside potential. She knew the owner, he's looking to sell so she sent the ladies the address and said, "let's meet here and check it out."

As the ladies arrived, they noticed it's a whole apartment building of multiple units, the owner is there to meet them an older gentleman looking to retire and move to Key West as he introduced himself.

Bethania greeted the owner warmly and introduced herself and the other ladies. She then asks if they can take a tour of the property to see the units. The owner agrees and begins to show them around the building, pointing out the different features and amenities of each unit.

As they walk around, the ladies discuss the potential of the property and its investment value. Amber and Jacqueline asked questions about the rental rates and occupancy, while Elena and Megan inquired about any necessary renovations or updates.

After the tour, they all gathered in the lobby to discuss the potential of the property. Bethania asked the owner about his asking price and any negotiations he may be willing to make. The owner reveals that he is motivated to sell and is open to offers.

Megan decided to meet with the ladies outside.

Megan said, "I love the location it does need some work this is over 10 different apartments."

Jacqueline said, "I know a good contractor they did great work for one of my clients is homes here in Florida."

Bethania said, "I know a good property management firm that can help if that's something we want to explore."

Elena said, "It's close to a school district which means this will be good for tenants with children."

Megan asked Bethania "What's the asking price?"

she said, "It's 1.5m."

Bridget said, "Let's look at the cash flow statement, we need to see that all the tenants have been current with their rent."

Bethania said, "There's a lot of real estate development that's going to happen in the next five years in this area."

Megan said, "let's offer him 1.25 tell him we'll do a cash deal. If he says yes Sabrina how soon can you get the contracts and bill of sale drafted up?"

Sabrina responded, "I can have the contracts and bill of sale drafted up within the next 24 hours. We can also make sure to include any necessary contingencies to protect our investment."

Megan nodded in agreement and said, "Great, let's move forward with the offer of 1.25 and include a contingency for a thorough inspection of the property." The ladies all agreed, and Bethania said she will contact the owner and make the offer. They all leave feeling excited about the potential investment and the possibility of expanding their business.

Bethania and the ladies walk back over to the owner, and they make him a cash offer for 1.25 mil even though he wants 1.5.

The owner seems hesitant at first, but Bethania and the ladies explain the benefits of a cash offer and the potential for a quick and easy sale. After some negotiation, the owner agrees to sell the property for 1.35 million, a compromise between the original asking price and the ladies' offer. The ladies agreed to the new price and the owner agreed to provide all necessary paperwork for the sale. They shook hands and agree to close the deal withing week.

As Megan and the ladies walked to their car she said, "congratulations ladies another one in the bag. once this thing closes let's get that contractor you know Jacqueline and set up a meeting." Megan also said, "Ladies I'm hungry let's go get something to eat." Bridget interjected and said, "Yes ladies I have a business proposal that I want to share with you all."

As the ladies arrived in Wynwood for lunch, Megan said, "Bridget I'm curious about your business proposal."

Bridget proposed, "That we start a mortgage division of the business. The real estate market is hot right now in South Florida. Let's become a bank, ladies here is the proposal breakdown that I have."

Bridget continued "I'm working on obtaining necessary licenses and certifications to operate as a mortgage lender in the state of Florida. I've done all the research that's required this could easily be a way to create another financial pipeline for the business."

Bethania said, "Wow Bridget, this is a great idea. We could offer our clients a one-stop shop for all their real estate needs. Having a mortgage division would give us a competitive edge in the market. How much capital do we need to get this started?"

Bridget responded and said, "That we would need to have at least $500,000 in capital to meet the minimum requirements for a mortgage lender in Florida. We can use our existing business cash flow to get started, but we might need to investigate outside funding options as well." The ladies agree that this is a smart move and that they should start working on the necessary steps to make it happen.

Megan looked at the ladies and said, "You know what y'all can take time if you want to think about it but Bridget has presented a brilliant idea. Let's do it ladies I want this business to be more than a successful business we are building a legacy."

Megan told Bridget "Don't worry about the money I'll make sure we have it. Sabrina, you're our Chief Compliance Officer. You can help Bridget with make sure we are aligned in getting that division stood successfully.

Amber said, "Ladies I absolutely just love us but I never asked you all what drives you to be so successful?"

Megan said, "For me, it's about financial freedom and independence. I want to have the ability to live life on my own terms and not be tied down to a traditional 9 to 5 job. Wall Street and Real estate has given me that opportunity."

Elena chimed in, "For me, it's about making a positive impact in people's lives. I want to create beautiful spaces and provide housing options that people can truly call home."

Jacqueline nodded in agreement and added, "For me, it's also about the financial benefits, but it's also about leaving a legacy. I want to build something that can last for generations and provide a better future for my family."

Sabrina said, "For me, it's about the challenge. I love taking on new projects and pushing myself to be better. Real estate is such a dynamic industry that is always changing, and I find that exciting."

Bethania said, "I come from a humble background, and I have seen the power of real estate in changing lives. I want to help others achieve their dreams and goals through real estate investing."

Bridget concluded, "For me, it's about building something that can make a difference in the world. Real estate has the power to transform communities and improve people's lives, and I want to be a part of that change."

Chapter 9

The next day Bethania received a call from Stephanie and asked if she's available to talk.

Bethania said, "Sure you sound like something is wrong?"

Stephanie said, "I thought about a lot what your friends said I'm just not happy anymore with Amir, I wanted to talk to you cause if I tell my friends they're going to judge me and think I'm crazy."

Bethania told, "You're grown woman and I'm not here to judge you for your choices."

Stephanie told her, "I'll admit I was jealous of you at first, you moved to Miami and created the American dream for yourself, you're very inspiring I never believed in myself that I could do that."

Bethania told Stephanie "Thank you and I'm glad I can inspire you, but I was like you when I met Megan, Bridget, Jacqueline, Amber and Elena. I watched these powerful ladies do amazing things they inspired me to level up and be better version of myself."

Bethania also told her, "If you want to be a better version of yourself you have to surround yourself with the right people that are going where you're trying to go, I learned early on in life how important hanging out with people that have no goals, drive or vision can be and it led me down a road of sabotage."

Stephanie said, "I know that statement is true cause I've watched how you've elevated, at this stage of my life I wouldn't even know where to start."

Bethania asked her, "Where do you see yourself in the future? What type of woman are you trying to be?

Stephanie took a moment to think and then responds, "I want to be a successful businesswoman like all of you. I want to have financial stability and independence, but more than that, I want to make a difference in the world. I want to create something that helps people, that makes their lives better in some way. I just don't know where to start or how to get there."

So, Bethania thought of a suggestion, and asked Stephanie, "How about you come in and work with me in my office and you be my assistant? I need one anyway because business is really picking up."

Bethania continued, "I'll take you under my wing and be your mentor. I need you to be consistent. I need you to be reliable and I need you to be ready to put in work. Stephanie how do you feel about that?"

Stephanie was excited and grateful for the opportunity and said, "Bethania, I feel honored that you would even offer me such an opportunity. I am interested in working with you and being your assistant. I promise to be consistent and reliable and to put in the work required. I am ready to learn from you and to grow both personally and professionally."

So later that day the ladies received notification from Charles, William James Harry and Cole. They are taking a private plane ride to Saint Barts for a few days and would like the ladies to come with them. Megan asked if she could bring Maxwell and Elena asked if she could bring Colin.

The guys agreed that Megan could bring Maxwell and Elena could bring Colin along on the trip to Saint Barts. They made arrangements for the private plane and accommodations, and the ladies packed their bags for a fun getaway. As they board the plane, they can't help but feel excited about the adventure that lies ahead.

As they arrived in Saint Barts, the ladies were amazed by the crystal-clear waters and picturesque views surrounding them. They are taken to a luxurious resort with stunning ocean views and the scent of fresh flowers in the air. The group was welcomed by friendly staff who showed them to their lavish villas with private pools, outdoor showers, and breathtaking ocean views.

The ladies can't believe how stunning the place was and can't wait to explore all the amenities the resort has to offer. They were greeted with welcome drinks, snacks and began to unwind and relax after the flight. They decide to spend the day lounging by the pool, soaking up the sun, and enjoying each other's company.

Maxwell told Megan, "Let's get changed and go out on the beach and get in the water."

Megan smiled and nodded in agreement. She quickly changed into her swimsuit and meets Maxwell on the beach. As they walked towards the water, Megan observed the beautiful scenery around them. The crystal-clear water, the white sandy beach, and the warm sun on her skin make her feel at ease.

As they entered the water, Maxwell took Megan's hand, and they started to swim out towards a nearby coral reef. They put on their snorkeling gear and dive down to explore the underwater world. Megan was amazed at the vibrant colors of the fish and the coral reef.

After a while, they swam back to shore and relaxed on the beach, sipping tropical drinks, and enjoying the warm sun.

Megan turned to Maxwell and said, "This is just what I needed, a break. I'm happy you decided to come."

Maxwell smiled and replied, "I'm happy to be here with you. It's important to take some time to relax and enjoy life."

Then Maxwell and Megan noticed Charles and Sabrina with Colin and Elena were coming to join them. Maxwell greeted Charles and Sabrina while Megan welcomed Elena and Colin. As Amber and James, William and Bethania, and Jacqueline and Harry arrived, the group greeted each other with hugs and excitement. They all decided to hang out on the beach and enjoy the beautiful weather. They all settled down on the beach chairs, enjoying the sun and the sound of the waves. Charles suggested they should plan a group activity for later in the day.

Bethania suggested they rent a yacht and go for a sunset cruise around the island. James and William agreed, saying it would be a great opportunity to see the island from a different perspective. Colin and Elena were thrilled with the idea and started discussing the different types of yachts they could rent.

Meanwhile, Megan and Maxwell decided to take a stroll down the beach. They talk about how grateful they were for their friends and how much they enjoy spending time with them.

Maxwell told Megan how much he cared for her and how lucky he felt to have her in his life.

Megan blushed and said she feels the same way about him.

As the sun started to set, the group gathered to board the yacht. They all marvel at the stunning views of the island as they cruise around, sipping on cocktails and enjoying each other's company. The sunset is breathtaking, and they all take pictures to remember the moment.

The yacht docks back at the marina, and the group decided to continue the night with dinner at a local restaurant. They all dressed up and made their way to the restaurant, chatting and laughing along the way. They sat down to have a delicious meal, enjoyed each other's company and made new memories together.

After dinner, they head to a nearby bar to dance and enjoy the nightlife in Saint Barts. The music is lively, and the energy is high as they dance the night away. Some returned to their villas in the early morning hours, exhausted but exhilarated by the unforgettable experience.

Sabrina suggested to Charles before going back to the villa "Let's take our clothes off and get in the ocean."

He said, "you lead the way and I'll follow." As they leave their clothes by the shore, Sabrina runs into the ocean first and Charles slowly walks behind her. Charles takes Sabrina and lays her slowly on the sand as they're passionately kissed while the ocean waves crashed against their bodies. They both felt alive and free in the moment, letting go of all their worries and just being present with each other. Charles continues to kiss her passionately while Sabrina runs her hands down his back. Then she wraps her legs around his body. They both know they have a strong connection and can't wait to see where it leads them. As they lay there, they both felt grateful for this moment and for each other.

As they caught their breath, Charles and Sabrina gazed into each other's eyes and smiled.

Sabrina spoke first, "That was amazing, Charles. I feel so connected to you right now."

Charles nods in agreement, "Me too, Sabrina. Being with you feels so natural and easy."

Colin and Elena headed to the pool to cool off and enjoy the warm evening air. They lounge on pool chairs, sipping on cocktails and chatting about their day.

William and Bethania decided they were going to take a nice hot shower together. They turn on the hot water and step into the shower together, the steamy water enveloping them both. William leaned in and kissed Bethania deeply, his hands roaming over her body. Bethania moans softly as she runs her fingers through his hair.

As the water cascades down their bodies, they lose themselves in the moment, forgetting about everything else around them. They take turns washing each other, savoring the intimacy and connection between them.

Megan smiles and nods as she follows Maxwell into the villa. Once inside, Maxwell lays out a towel on the bed and gestures for Megan to lie down. He starts to gently rub her shoulders, working out any tension and knots that he finds. Megan closed her eyes and relaxed under his skilled touch, feeling grateful for this intimate moment with him.

After a while, Maxwell leans down to kiss Megan's neck, causing her to let out a soft moan. He continues to work his way down her back, eventually reaching her lower back and hips. Megan feels a rush of pleasure as Maxwell's hands move over her body, and she can't help but let out another moan.

Maxwell leaned in closer to Megan, whispered in her ear, "You're so beautiful, Megan. I love you." Megan smiles, feeling her heart swell with love for this man. She turned around to face him, and they shared a passionate kiss. As Maxwell kissed Megan, his hands roamed over her body, exploring every curve and dip. Megan moaned into his mouth, her desire for him growing stronger with every passing moment. Their kiss deepens as Maxwell slides his hands under Megan's shirt, feeling the softness of her skin. She arches into him, her body hungry for his touch.

Breaking their kiss, Maxwell stood up to undress. Megan watched, her heart racing as she takes in his muscular form. When he was completely naked, he climbed back onto the bed and pulled Megan into his arms. They kissed again; their bodies pressed together as they explored each other's mouths.

Maxwell's hands slide down Megan's body, stopping at her hips. He pulls her closer, grinding his hard length against her. Megan gasped, feeling a jolt of pleasure shoot through her. She wraps her legs around his waist, urging him on.

Maxwell moved his hands to Megan's breasts, kneaded them gently as he slowly pushed into her. Megan's breath hitches as he stretches her, his thickness filling her up.

Maxwell started to move, thrusting slowly at first, then faster and faster until they were moving together in perfect rhythm. Megan closed her eyes and moaned, spurred on by her desire for Maxwell. She can feel herself reaching the edge, the building pleasure inside of her threatening to overwhelm her.

Maxwell's thrusts become more urgent, harder, and faster. He runs his hands over Megan's body, desperate for every inch of her.

Suddenly Megan cried out, her whole body tightening as she came. Maxwell moved faster, desperate to find his own release, and then moaned loudly as he found it.

Maxwell collapsed onto the bed, breathing out deeply and pulling Megan close to him. He kissed the top of her head and stroked her hair, unable to find the words to express how he felt.

As Cole and Bridget draw a warm bath, they sip on glasses of champagne and talk about their day. Bridget shares her excitement about the potential mortgage division for their business and Cole told her how proud he is of her for pursuing her goals.

As they settled into the tub, Cole started to massage Bridget's shoulders and neck, easing the tension from her muscles. Bridget lets out a contented sigh and leans back into Cole's arms. Bridget loves the touch of Cole hands all over her body.

Cole continued to massage Bridget's shoulders and neck, working his way down her back. Bridget felt her body relax under his skilled hands and she let out a soft sigh of pleasure. Cole kissed her neck, his lips trailing down to her shoulder as he continued to massage her.

Bridget turned to face Cole and they shared a deep, passionate kiss. Cole pulled her closer, running his hands through her hair as their bodies pressed together in the warm water. As they explored each other's mouths, their hands roamed freely, tracing each other's curves and contours. Bridget could feel the heat building inside her, her body responding to Cole's touch.

Cole broke the kiss and looked deeply into Bridget's eyes. "I love you," he whispered, his voice filled with emotion. Bridget smiled back at him, feeling overwhelmed with love. "I love you too," she replied. Cole's hands continued to roam over Bridget's body, moving lower and lower. He cupped her breasts and kneaded them gently, eliciting a soft moan from Bridget. As he leaned in to kiss her neck again, his fingers slipped between her legs, finding her already wet and ready for him.

Bridget gasped as Cole moved his fingers in slow circles, teasing her with just the right amount of pressure. She arched her back, pressing herself closer to him, wanting more. Cole sensed her desire and slowly slipped one long finger inside of her, watching the reactions on Bridget's face to gauge his progress.

Bridget moaned again with pleasure; her mouth now slightly open as she pressed her hips forward to meet his rhythm.

Cole slipped another finger inside and continued probing, drawing out Bridget's pleasure. Bridget moved her hips in time with his fingers, caressing his chest as he worked. She kissed him as he fingered her, wanting to be as close to him as possible. She could feel herself building toward orgasm, her hips beginning to move faster and faster.

Suddenly, she felt Cole's fingers move faster, rubbing her in just the right way. Bridget moaned into his mouth as she felt the orgasm building inside of her, her body suddenly feeling completely free of tension.

Cole watched Bridget's face as she came, her mouth open in pleasure, her eyes closed. He could tell that she enjoyed the way that he touched her, and he felt a deep sense of pride at knowing how he made her feel.

Bridget felt a rush of desire as Cole's hands roamed over her body, sending shivers down her spine. She slowly begins to straddle him. As Bridget straddles Cole, she runs her fingers through his hair, deepening the kiss. Cole groans softly as he feels Bridget's body against his, the warmth of the water intensifying the sensations. They continue to kiss and touch each other, lost in the moment.

Eventually, they break the kiss and look into each other's eyes, smiling. "I love you," Cole says, his voice filled with sincerity.

Bridget smiles back at him. "I love you too," she said, and they kissed again, sealing their love for each other in that moment. They spent the rest of the night wrapped in each other's arms, the sound of the waves lulling them to sleep.

As Jacqueline is taking a shower Harry is on the balcony enjoying the view then Jacqueline quietly walks outside, and Harry notices Jacqueline has no clothes on. As she bends over on the balcony, she told Harry "Do what you want." Harry said, "With Pleasure." As the water streamed down Jacqueline's body Harry leaned forward and began to lick her from neck down her back to the bottom of her lips.

As Jacqueline was bent on the balcony Harry slowly kneeled behind her as he thirsts to want to eat her from behind. Harry started to eat her from behind as he gently licks her. She moans to let Harry know she liked what he was doing. Their bodies were shaking as their sexual pleasures escalated their sensation.

Harry felt a sudden surge of desire course through his veins as he gazed at Jacqueline's naked body. He had always found her so sexually stimulating but seeing her completely exposed before him was a whole new level of temptation. His hands touched her silk-smooth skin.

Jacqueline tilted her head back, her eyes closed as Harry's hands explored her body. She let out a soft moan, the pleasure she was feeling almost too much to bear. Harry's fingers trailed down her spine, his lips tracing back towards the path to her neck.

Jacqueline turned around and faced Harry with a hunger in her eyes that matched his own. She pressed her body against his, feeling his hardness pressing against her stomach. Harry's hands found their way to her hips, pulling her closer as their lips met in a fiery kiss.

They broke apart, gasping for air as Harry lifted Jacqueline off her feet, carrying her into the bedroom.

Amber and James decided they're going to try something different, Amber wanted to be James's dominatrix for tonight. As Amber takes control, James complies with her every demand. Amber commanded him to kneel before her and he obeyed, feeling a rush of excitement at the power dynamic between them. Amber then proceeds to use various tools and techniques to explore James' limits and push him to the edge of pleasure and pain. James trusts Amber completely which allowed himself to surrender to her control, feeling completely submissive to her every whim. After their intense session, they collapse into each other's arms, feeling a deep connection and intimacy from the experience.

The next morning each of them was snuggled cuddled in their beds as the sun rose slowly over the ocean. Each of them realized the connection they had with each other has elevated. Bridget and Cole's relationship had taken a significant turn towards romantic love, while Megan and Maxwell have deepened their existing emotional and physical intimacy.

Jacqueline and Harry also felt a stronger connection after their balcony encounter, and Sabrina and Charles felt even closer after their passionate night on the beach. Amber and James had a fun and exciting night exploring a new dynamic in their relationship. William and Bethania felt closer than ever after their intimate shower together.

As they slowly woke up, each one of them smiled knowing they had shared something special and unforgettable with each other. They all agreed that this trip to Saint Barts had brought them closer together as friends and as lovers.

As each of them were getting ready to get the day started, the ladies had texted each other about meeting for breakfast. So as each couple was arriving at the table to be served, they all greeted each other. As they sat down to enjoy breakfast together, they couldn't help but smile and exchange knowing glances. There was an unspoken understanding between them all that something special had happened the previous night.

Amber asked everyone, "So how was the rest of your night what did you guys end up doing?"

Megan and Maxwell looked at each other with a smile before Megan spoke up. "Well, we went for a stroll on the beach and then ended up back in the villa where Maxwell gave me a massage," she said with a grin.

Bridget and Cole exchanged a look before Bridget spoke up. "We took a nice long bath together," she said, her cheeks turning slightly pink.

Charles and Sabrina looked at each other, and Sabrina spoke up. "We went for a swim in the ocean," she said, giving Charles a playful smile.

Elena smiled and said, "Colin gave me a massage and we enjoyed a nice bath together in our villa." Harry grins mischievously and said, "Jacqueline and I enjoyed the view from the balcony and had some fun outside under the stars."

Amber looked at everyone, impressed with their adventurous and romantic night. "Sounds like everyone had a great time," she said with a chuckle. "We tried something new," she added, glancing at James with a mischievous grin.

Harry stood up at the table and told everyone, "The reason why we planned this trip. Charles William Cole James and I had talked about wanting to do something special for you ladies. From the moment we met you all we were completely blown away with the type of women you are. We absolutely love your character, the synergy, the chemistry that you guys have for each other.

You ladies are truly super women to us." Harry turns and looks at Jacqueline, grabs her by the hand.

Harry told her "From the first moment I saw you in that mall in Brickell I was like who is this beautiful gorgeous young Halle Berry woman walking through here. I want to ask you to be my woman."

Charles looks at Sabrina, William looks at Bethania, Cole stares at Bridget and James turns to Amber. Each of them desired to be exclusive with their woman.

The ladies were all surprised and taken aback by the sudden confession from the men. There were tears in their eyes as they realize how much the men truly care for them.

Sabrina looked at Charles and said, "I feel the same way. I want to be exclusive with you too."

Bethania nods her head in agreement, "Me too, William. I've never felt this way before."

Bridget smiled at Cole and said, "I would love to be your woman, Cole."

Amber looked at James and said, "I'm so happy to hear this, James. I feel the same way too."

Colin even looked at Elena and said, "I want that with you too"

Elena smiled warmly at Colin and said, "I would love that, Colin. I feel the same way about you."

She took his hand and gave it a gentle squeeze.

The atmosphere at the table was electric as each of the men expresses their desire to be exclusive with their respective partners. The women were overcome with emotion and gratitude, feeling incredibly lucky to have found such wonderful men.

Amber looked at James and said, "I've been waiting for you to ask me that for so long." James chuckles and leans over to give her a kiss.

Bethania turned to William and said, "You know I'm already yours, right?" William nods and said, "I just had to make it official."

Bridget smiles at Cole and said, "I'm so happy right now."

Cole took her hand and said, "Me too, Bridget. Me too."

Sabrina looks at Charles and said, "I can't believe this is happening."

Charles took her hand and said, "Believe it, Sabrina. I want to be with you."

Jacqueline looked at Harry with tears in her eyes and said, "Yes, Harry. I want to be your woman." Harry leaned in to kiss her, and the rest of the group cheered and applauded.

Megan and Maxwell were so flabbergasted and surprised at what had transpired and had them feeling overwhelmed. They look at each other, both with tears in their eyes, and Maxwell takes Megan's hand.

Maxwell said, "I know this is unexpected, but I can't imagine being with anyone else. You are the most incredible woman I have ever met, and I want to be with you and only you."

Megan nodded, feeling the same overwhelmed love for Maxwell. "I feel the same way," she said, squeezing his hand tightly.

So afterwards the ladies decided to take a break and walk together and just kind of reminisce and take in the moment and see how each other was feeling.

Megan said to them, "I love you to death and I love that we're happy not only that we are happy with the men that were with but we're happy with each other. We are living in a very fortunate serene utopian kind of existence. I couldn't have imagined when we all decided to move to Miami that we would be standing where we are right now. We're operating at a much higher frequency and by us elevating ourselves we found good men that could tap into our frequency. They just wanted to love us and support us, not control us, they're not insecure by who we are but secure in who they are."

Bethania chimed in, "I completely agree, Megan. I feel so grateful for this moment and for all of you. We have a special bond that is so rare, and I cherish it so much. And I feel so lucky to have found William who understands and supports me in every way. We can be ourselves around each other and that is so important in a relationship."

Bridget adds, "And I feel the same way about Cole. He's my rock and I know I can count on him for anything. I feel so lucky to have found someone who loves and accepts me for who I am."

Sabrina nods in agreement, "Charles is the same way with me. He's my partner in everything and I know I can always rely on him. And I love that we all found these amazing men together. It just feels like everything happened for a reason."

Amber smiled, "Yes, it really does. And James is just the perfect fit for me. He challenges me in all the right ways and supports me in my goals and aspirations. I couldn't have asked for a better partner."

Elena chimed, "And I feel the same way about Colin. He's just so kind and caring and I feel like he really sees me for who I am. I'm excited to see where our relationship goes."

Megan said, "Not only do we have the right support system within each other, but we have it with our partners and that motivates me to take the business the goals that we have and take it to the next level."

Bethania nods in agreement, "I feel the same way, Megan. Having this kind of love and support in our lives is a blessing. It makes me want to be a better person, not just for William, but for myself and for all of us. We've come a long way and I can't wait to see what the future holds for us."

Elena adds, "I think it's important to have a strong support system in all aspects of our lives. It not only helps us grow and achieve our goals, but it also helps us navigate through the challenges that come our way. I'm so grateful to have all of you in my life, and Colin too of course, and I know we will continue to uplift and inspire each other."

Bridget chimed in, "I think it's amazing that we not only found great partners, but we also found great friends in each other. We have each other's backs, and we are there for each other through thick and thin. I'm grateful for all of you and for the love that we share."

Bethania shared with the ladies "I've decided to hire Stephanie as my assistant I'm going to mentor her. We can expand her role and I think she'll be a good assistant as we build out the business more." The ladies nod in agreement and congratulate Bethania on taking the initiative to mentor and support someone else. They all agree that it's important to lift each other up and help each other succeed.

Chapter 10

As the ladies arrived back in Miami feeling jubilant, rejuvenated energized motivated and inspired. The feeling of having strong handsome men by their side supporting them they felt a sense of confidence and security. They knew that they had found something special in each other and in their partners.

As they settled back into their routines, they continued to work hard towards their business goals, but with a newfound motivation and drive. They supported each other every step of the way, both in their personal and professional lives. They knew that they had each other's backs, no matter what.

Megan decided to host a business lunch so they could talk about the status of the business. As the ladies arrived this time, they have a new member joining them at the table. Bethania and decided to bring Stephanie.

As the ladies sit down to start the business lunch, the ladies welcome Stephanie to the team. Stephanie looks nervous but excited to be joining them.

Stephanie said, "Thank you ladies, you've inspired me to better myself I'm going to start working on my Real Estate license."

The ladies all smiled and congratulated Stephanie on her decision. Megan asked for updates on the business and the ladies started discussing their current projects and plans for expansion. Bethania mentioned that she has been working on a new marketing strategy and shows the ladies some of her ideas.

Elena shared that she has been working on improving their social media presence and has been seeing positive results. Amber mentioned that she has been networking with other businesses in the area and has made some valuable connections.

The ladies continued to discuss the status of their business and what they need to do to take it to the next level. They talk about the importance of branding, marketing, and networking. Bridget suggested that they start attending more networking events to get their name out there and meet potential clients.

Amber suggested that they should also consider expanding their services and perhaps offer some new packages or promotions to attract more customers. Elena chimed in and suggested that they should focus on building strong relationships with their existing clients and offer them incentives to refer their friends and family.

Stephanie said, "After listening to you guys discuss business, I've taken a lot of notes. I know you said you guys are launching a new division. I know several people in the suburbs that are looking to refinance their homes. Also, Bethania, a couple of Amir's friends are looking to buy on Fisher Island, but I told them this morning you just got back in town, and I set up a meeting this afternoon since you're free. So, what I can do is I want to host an event to introduce you guys and invite a lot of people that could really benefit from what do you guys are offering."

The ladies are impressed with Stephanie's initiative and ideas.

Megan nodded and said, "Stephanie, that sounds like a great plan. We really appreciate your help and support. It's amazing how you're already using your network to connect us with potential clients."

Bethania smiled and said, "Stephanie, you're such a go-getter. I love it. Let's have that event."

Stephanie felt a sense of fulfillment and satisfaction from being able to contribute to the success of the business and help the team in any way possible. She knew that by using her skills and connections, she could make a real difference and play a valuable role in the growth of the company. The feeling of being part of something bigger than herself and working towards a common goal with the other women gave her a sense of purpose and belonging that she had never experienced before.

Megan mentioned to Sabrina "I have to fly to New York to handle some things regarding my home this week apparently you want to fly with me I know you mention about needing to get home to check on your family."

Sabrina said, "Absolutely let's do that I want ask Charles to join me I want him to meet my family."

While at the meeting Jacqueline received a notification from Harry that his parents are going to be flying to Miami and he wants them to meet her. Jacqueline was nervous she'd never been in such a serious relationship where the guy introduced her to his family. Plus, this is Jacqueline first interracial relationship so it's a lot to process for her.

Jacqueline responded to Harry saying, "That's great news! I'm excited to meet them. Just feeling a bit nervous since it's my first time meeting your parents and it's a new experience for me. But I really like you and I want to make a good impression."

Also, while the ladies were eating Sabrina decides to text Charles and ask him to come to New York with her to meet her family. This will be the first time Sabrina has been in a serious relationship that has elevated to a point where she was ready to introduce someone to her family. In the back of her mind, she still felt sad with the loss of her mom not going to be there to meet Charles.

Charles responded quickly, saying that he would be honored to meet her family and that he's happy to support her in any way he can. He also mentioned that he knows how difficult it must be to not have her mom there, but that he'll be there for her, and they can honor her memory together. Sabrina felt a sense of comfort and gratitude knowing that she has such a supportive and understanding partner.

Just before the ladies adjourned lunch Stephanie had one more thing she wanted to present. She says she knows a great photographer that can do some good business professional shots she wanted to work on building the social media marketing campaign.

Stephanie said, "As you know by me being a Digital Influencer I have over two million followers now that I can really help broaden you guys' brand plus, I don't see why you guys as gorgeous as you look should be on a Miami billboard."

Megan said to Stephanie "I think you are very brilliant you've only been on the team just a short period of time and your value proposition is already invaluable. You're already thinking of things that we didn't even think about. I love how solution-oriented you are. I am very honored that you decided you wanted to come work with us. The first thing I want you to do I want you to put together some numbers of what it's going to cost us to launch that sort of campaign."

Bethania, Sabrina, Bridge, and Amber also chimed in with their agreement and appreciated Stephanie's contribution to the team. They all agreed that her ideas and enthusiasm were valuable assets to the business, and they look forward to seeing what she can bring to the table in the future. Megan suggested that they set up a meeting to go over the numbers and discuss the marketing campaign in more detail, so they can decide if it's a feasible option for the business at this time. The ladies all agreed, and Stephanie is thrilled to be given the opportunity to take charge of such an important project.

Stephanie was anxious and excited, and she was ready to get back to her Home Office to start planning for the event and the new marketing campaign for the business. Stephanie started working on the budgeting of how much it will cost to host the event and launch the new marketing campaign. It was like she had something that she needed to prove to herself, and this was an opportunity where she felt like she was going to grow and evolve by being around such inspiring individuals. She'd never felt like she'd had anyone she could ever look up to but now these ladies were like older sisters that she always wished she could have had.

Stephanie pulled out her laptop and began to research different photographers and social media marketing firms to get an idea of the costs associated with launching a successful campaign. She also started to create a budget for the event, factoring in the cost of the venue, catering, and decorations.

As she worked on the budget, Stephanie realized that she may need some help to accurately estimate the costs of the marketing campaign. She decided to reach out to some of her contacts in the industry to get their input and advice.

Stephanie spent the rest of the day working on the budget and reaching out to her contacts. She was excited about the opportunity to contribute to the success of the business and was looking forward to presenting her ideas to the team.

Meanwhile, Bridget just received some devastating news regarding her father having some health issues and needed to go home to Tennessee to figure out what's going on. The first person she turned to was Cole, as she was getting emotional on the phone talking to him.

Cole told her "I would like to go with you to support you and be there with you."

Bridget was touched by Cole's offer and felt grateful to have him in her life. She thanked him and told him that she would let him know when she had more information about the situation with her father. Bridget was feeling overwhelmed and unsure of what the future held for her family, but she knew that having Cole by her side would make a big difference. She started planning for her trip back home to

Tennessee, hoping that she could be there for her family and help her father in any way possible.

James surprised Amber by saying he had planned a spontaneous date for them later that night. He wanted to take her to Ball and Chain and do some salsa dancing. Amber was thrilled by the surprise date and loved a spontaneous date with James to Ball and Chain. She loved dancing and hasn't had the chance to go salsa dancing in a while. She spent the rest of the afternoon getting ready, picking out the perfect outfit and doing her hair and makeup.

While Elena was home working in her Home Office Colin messaged her to say he was close by.

He asked her "Would it be ok if I stopped by?"

Elena said, "I would love to see you. So as the concierge let him up, he brought her a surprise bouquet of red roses, he knows how much Elena loves flowers.

Elena was emphatically surprised she said, "These are beautiful what's the occasion?"

Colin told her "When you're beautiful and special there's no occasion needed, I just wanted to surprise you."

Colin told her "I wanted to run something by you because I've been thinking about this for a while. I know you've been looking to expand your OBGYN practice in South Florida plus you're working the business. What do you think about starting your own online OBGYN telehealth business right from your Home Office?"

Colin also said, "You know since I'm a Software Engineer, I can just build it for you if you're interested as my gift to you."

Elena was surprised and intrigued by Colin's idea. She had been looking for ways to expand her practice and reach more patients, and telehealth could be a great solution. She asked Colin more about his thoughts on the matter and how he envisioned the business working.

Colin explained, "With the rise of telemedicine, there is a growing demand for online OBGYN consultations, especially in a busy and diverse city like Miami." He suggested that Elena could offer virtual appointments for routine check-ups, prenatal care, and even postpartum consultations. He also pointed out that with the flexibility of telehealth, Elena could easily balance her work with her other business ventures.

Elena was impressed with Colin's idea and his willingness to help her build the telehealth business.

She thanked him and said, "That it's a great idea" and she would like to explore it further. Elena also appreciated his gesture of offering to build the platform for her, and she told him that it's very kind of him.

Elena suggested that they start by doing some research on the feasibility of the idea and the potential market for online OBGYN telehealth services. Colin agreed, and they spent the rest of the afternoon brainstorming and planning. She was excited about the prospect of expanding her practice this way and grateful to have Colin's support and expertise. She knew that starting a new business venture could be challenging, but with Colin by her side, she felt more confident and motivated to make it a success.

Bethania was working late at home finalizing the latest deal for the apartment building that the business had just acquired. William knows when she's occupied with work, she sometimes forgets to eat so he had some vegan food delivered to her place.

William sends her a message that said, "I know you're working late and having a busy day, but I went on and had some food sent your way.

Bethania responded to William's message, "Thank you so much, babe! You really didn't have to do that, but I appreciate it. I've been so caught up in work that I almost forgot to eat today." Bethania felt touched by William's thoughtfulness and it put a smile on her face. She decided to take a break from work to enjoy the food William had sent her way.

Maxwell called Megan and told her he's ready to sell his home in the DC area and be full-time in South Florida. He told her that I want to be closer to you I'll just have to fly back and forth to DC but it's worth it. He also mentioned that he's been looking at some houses in North Miami but would like to work with Bethania to find his next home. Maxwell has also requested Megan's input on his next home. He felt as if this is a home that both are going to spend a lot of time in.

Megan thanked Maxwell for letting her know and told him that she'll let Bethania know about his interest in finding a new home in North Miami. She also told him that she's excited about the prospect of him being in South Florida full-time and that they can spend more time together. They discussed potential neighborhoods and the type of home he was looking for, and Megan assured him that Bethania was an expert in the North Miami area and would be able to find him the perfect home. Maxwell thanked Megan and said he can't wait to start this new chapter of his life.

Jacqueline had been at home thinking a lot about meeting Harry's parents but she's even going into deeper thought about him meeting her family. She's nervous because a lot of thoughts have run across her mind, she worried that maybe she's overthinking. She grouped text Sabrina and Bethania and shared her concerns as they are also in an Interracial relationship. Jacqueline wondered how they are processing it. Especially Sabrina now that she's taking Charles to meet her family.

Sabrina replied to the group text, which said that she understands how Jacqueline feels, and that she also had a lot of worries and concerns when Charles was going to meet her family.

Sabrina said, "that it's important to remember that her family loves her and wants her to be happy, and that they will support her in her relationship with Charles." Sabrina also suggested that Jacqueline talk to Harry about her concerns and see if they can come up with a plan together for how to approach meeting each other's families.

Bethania chimed in, saying that she agreed with Sabrina and that communication is key. She also suggested that Jacqueline try to focus on the positive aspects of the situation and remember that love knows no boundaries.

Jacqueline said, "Thank you ladies I was just overthinking things way too much but you're absolutely right love has no boundaries all that matters is my happiness and how he makes me happy."

Amber sent a message to all the ladies asking them, "Are you guys interested in joining James and I for some salsa dancing tonight." I know it's spontaneous, but we deserve to take a break and have a little fun. The ladies all respond enthusiastically, with

Bridget said "I've always wanted to try salsa dancing! I need to get my mind off of things."

Bethania chimed in, "I know a few moves myself, I can teach you guys."

Megan mentioned, "I'm in, let's do this!"

Sabrina and Elena also express their excitement.

Jacqueline said, "I'm not the best dancer, but I'll give it a shot." They all agree to meet up later that evening at Ball and Chain for a night of dancing and fun.

Later that night, James picked her up and they headed to Ball and Chain. The atmosphere was lively, and they could not hear the music from outside. As they entered the club, Amber felt the energy of the crowd and couldn't wait to start dancing. The crowd was diverse and energetic, and the overall vibe was infectious. The ladies couldn't help but feel swept up in the excitement and energy of the place. The colorful decor and the live music made them feel like they were transported to another world. They couldn't wait to hit the dance floor and let loose.

They find a spot near the dance floor and start dancing to the music. James is a great dancer and Amber feels herself getting lost in the rhythm of the music. They dance the night away, laughing and enjoying each other's company. Amber feels grateful to have such a thoughtful and romantic partner.

As they take a break from dancing, James surprised Amber by ordering a round of mojitos for them. The cool minty drink is the perfect refreshment after all the dancing they've been doing. They sit down and chat, enjoying the lively atmosphere around them. Amber couldn't help but feel happy and carefree, forgetting all her worries and just living in the moment.

As the night went on, they continued dancing and having a great time. The ladies had joined them, and they all danced together as a group, cheering each other on and having fun.

At one point, James pulled Amber close to him and whispered in her ear, "I'm so happy we could do this together. You make me feel alive."

Amber smiled and kissed him, feeling grateful for this moment of pure joy and happiness. As the night winded down, they made their way back home, tired but happy. They both fall asleep with a smile on their faces, looking forward to more spontaneous adventures in the future.

As Bridget, Megan, and Sabrina head to the airport for Tennessee and New York. Bridget decided she wanted Cole to come with her for support and Sabrina was excited to have Charles meet her family. Maxwell told Megan he'll be in DC on business but once he's finished, he'll join her in NYC.

Megan told Bethania, Jacqueline, and Amber; we'll miss you guys but hold down the fort.

Bethania said, "Safe Travel ladies and Stephanie has emailed us the budget proposal for the marketing strategy."

Jacqueline said, "Tell Stephanie I love the format, tell her excellent job."

Amber adds, "Don't worry, we'll make sure everything runs smoothly while you're away!"

Bethania nods and said, "Yes, enjoy your trips, and let us know if you need anything from us."

Jacqueline adds, "And take lots of pictures to share with us when you get back!"

They all gave each other a hug and wished each other a safe trip. As the three ladies head off on their adventures, Bethania, Jacqueline, and Amber dived into the budget proposal and start working on the marketing strategy.

As Megan arrived back in NYC for the first time since becoming a new homeowner in Miami Beach. She walks back into her place for the first time in a long time and realizes that she was more thankful to have made the decision for a transition. She felt humbled by the pandemic, if that hadn't happened it wouldn't have allowed her to be where she is today.

Megan took a deep breath and looked around her New York condo. She remembered all the late nights she spent working here, the stress and pressure of her job weighing heavily on her shoulders. But now, as she looked out at the city skyline, she felt a sense of calm and peace that she hadn't felt in a long time.

She thinks back to the beginning of the pandemic when everything seemed uncertain and scary. It was during that time that she had a realization, she didn't want to go back to her old life, she wanted something different. She wanted to take a chance on herself and make a change.

She took a leap of faith and moved to Miami Beach. It wasn't easy, but she was determined to make it work. Started a business with her girlfriends, and even found love. Looking back, she realizes that if it weren't for the pandemic, she may have never taken that chance.

As she sit on her couch, she felt grateful for where she was now and excited for what the future holds. She knows that there will be challenges ahead, but she's ready to face them head-on, knowing that she has the support of her friends and loved ones.

When Bridget arrived home back in Nashville, she was happy to see her mom and family but was very concerned for her father's health. Also, she's happy to introduce Cole to her family and being the support, she needs right now. Everything Bridget learned about Real Estate Development and how to be successful she got from her father.

Bridget's father was her role model and mentor in the real estate development industry. She was grateful for all the knowledge and wisdom he had imparted to her over the years. She couldn't imagine a life without him, and his declining health was a source of worry for her. She spent as much time with him as possible, and she and Cole were a constant source of support for her mother and family during this difficult time.

As she sat with her father, Bridget couldn't help but reflect on all the lessons he had taught her about business and life. She was determined to carry on his legacy and make him proud. She knew that he would want her to keep pushing forward, even in the face of adversity. And so, she resolved to use her skills and knowledge to continue developing real estate projects that would make a positive impact on communities.

With Cole by her side, Bridget felt empowered to face whatever challenges lay ahead. She knew that he would be there for her, and she could count on him to help her through the tough times. As she looked at her family, Bridget felt grateful for their support and love. She knew that they would help her carry on her father's legacy and make a difference in the world.

Elena, Bethania, Jacqueline, and Amber dived into the budget proposal and started working on the marketing strategy.

Elena said, "Let's have a meeting at my place and invite Stephanie. I would like her to present the budget proposal for the new marketing strategy. Also, ladies, I have an announcement I've decided to do my OBYGYN Telehealth business from home so I can continue to work both businesses from my office."

Bethania responds, "That sounds like a great idea, Elena. It would be good to have Stephanie present the proposal in person so we can ask any questions we may have. And congratulations on being able to work from home for your OBYGYN business! That's a big accomplishment and I'm happy for you."

Jacqueline chimed in, "Yes, congrats Elena! Working from home will give you more flexibility and control over your schedule. And having the meeting at your place will be great too, I'll bring some snacks and drinks for us to enjoy while we work."

Amber added, "Elena I'm so happy for you that's great news. When Bridget, Megan and Sabrina return let's host you a Business Shower, it's like a baby shower but for your new business. I'm excited to hear more about the marketing strategy and to work on it together. Let's make sure we schedule the meeting soon so we can stay on track with our goals."

So, Charles and Sabrina arrived in Sag Harbor NY to visit her family. Her father decided to move away from the city after losing her mother. Sabrina still has a heavy heart even when she sees her family and knows her mother is not there. When they arrived, she introduces Charles to her family, this is the first time she's ever introduced a significant other to her family.

Sabrina's family warmly welcomed Charles and made him feel at home. Her father was happy to see her and proud of the woman she has become. He showed Charles around the house and shared stories about Sabrina growing up. Sabrina's siblings also greeted Charles and were excited to get to know him.

Despite the happy reunion, Sabrina couldn't shake off the feeling of sadness knowing that her mother wasn't there to share this moment with her. She felt her absence deeply, and it made.

As Sabrina and Charles walked in the house, they are greeted by the rest of Sabrina's family. Her siblings, aunts, uncles, and cousins are all there, eager to meet Charles. Sabrina's father hugged her tightly and welcomed her home. Sabrina can't help but feel emotional, thinking about how her mother should have been there to meet Charles.

Charles introduced himself to Sabrina's family, and they all chatted for a while. Sabrina's aunt invited them to sit down for dinner, and they all gathered around the table. Sabrina's father leads a prayer, and they begin to eat.

During dinner, Sabrina's family asked Charles about himself, his interests, and his family. Charles shares his story, and Sabrina's family seems to be interested in what he has to say. Sabrina feels grateful that her family was welcoming to Charles.

After dinner, they all gathered in the living room to watch a movie. Sabrina cuddled up to Charles, and he put his arm around her.

Sabrina's father comes over to them and shares with Sabrina how much he loved her and that he's happy she's found someone special.

Sabrina can't help but feel overwhelmed with emotions, missing her mother, but also feeling grateful to have Charles by her side. She's happy to have introduced him to her family and feels like she's taken a big step in their relationship.

Colin was ecstatic to share some good news with Elena, he just got official word that Norway is rescinding its restrictions and allowing international travel so he can see his family. So, he stopped what he was doing with work immediately gave her a call and she answers and told her the good news but he also asked her he wanted her to come with him to Norway so he can introduce her to his family.

Elena was thrilled to hear Colin's good news and was happy for him to be able to see his family after such a long time.

When Colin asked her to come with him to Norway, she was taken aback for a moment but quickly regains her composure and said, "Colin, that sounds wonderful! I would love to meet your family and experience Norway with you."

She then thinks for a moment and adds, "Let me check my schedule and see if I can take some time off work, but I am definitely interested in going with you."

Colin was excited to hear Elena's response and agreed to give her some time to check her schedule. They both hung up the phone with smiles on their faces, excited for the possibility of traveling together.

So later that evening Stephanie, Bethania, Elena, Jacqueline, and Amber gathered at Elena's house to meet and have dinner and discuss the new budget proposal for the marketing strategy. Before they begin Megan and Bridget and Sabrina video conference in to listen in before Stephanie makes her first presentation, she was nervous and never have done this before. Before she begins, she has a drink to calm her nerves.

The other ladies can sense Stephanie's nervousness and try to offer words of encouragement.

Bethania said, "Stephanie, we know you've put a lot of hard work into this proposal, and we're excited to hear what you've come up with."

Elena adds, "Yes, we trust you, Stephanie. Just take a deep breath and give it your best shot."

Stephanie took another deep breath and began her presentation. She went through the proposal, explained each section and how it fits into the overall marketing strategy. As she speaks, the other ladies nod and take notes, impressed with the level of detail, and thought put into the proposal.

Once Stephanie finished, there was a moment of silence before Elena breaks it by saying, "Stephanie, that was fantastic! Your presentation was clear and concise, and the proposal itself is well thought out. I believe we have a solid plan to move forward with."

Stephanie was absolutely elated at the positive feedback that she's getting from all the ladies. It's a very emotional moment for her right now. It's the first time she felt like she was around people that believed in her and they're giving her the right type of support system. She felt very confident in herself, this had always been something that's been hard for her, and she struggled with self-confidence.

The other ladies agreed, and they spent the rest of the evening discussing the proposal and making plans to implement it. It's a productive meeting, and everyone leaves feeling excited about the new marketing strategy.

Elena decided to make an announcement to all the ladies that Colin has asked her to go to Norway with her to meet his family. She said she's going to take her laptop with her and continue to work but just wanted to run it by everyone just to make sure it was ok as she knows they have so much gone on with the business.

The ladies congratulated Elena on the exciting news and expressed their happiness for her. They also assured her that it's okay for her to continued working while she's away and that they will support her in any way they could. They reminded her that it's important to take breaks and enjoy life, especially during special moments like this. They offer to help cover any tasks or responsibilities she may need assistance with while she's away.

Elena was overjoyed and eager to start packing and meeting Colin family and seeing what Norway was all about.

She texted Colin that night and let him know "I'm coming with you to Norway when are we leaving?"

Colin was thrilled to hear that Elena was coming with him to Norway and he immediately replied, to her text, "That's fantastic news! I can't wait to introduce you to my family and show you around. We can leave next week if that works for you?"

Elena said, "Yes I can't wait, I'm start packing now."

As for Colin and Elena to head to Norway, she was so ecstatic and can't believe the moment has arrived that she was going to be meeting his family. She was overjoyed and excited for the long plane ride all the way to Oslo. Colin mentioned to her. "I got first class tickets making it a little bit more romantic as we enjoy the plane ride."

Elena blushed and smiled, feeling grateful for such a thoughtful gesture from Colin. She leaned over to him and said, "Thank you, Colin. This is going to be such an amazing trip. I can't wait to meet your family and explore Norway with you."

As they settle into their seats on the plane, Elena can't help but feel a mix of nervousness and excitement. She's never traveled to Norway before, and meeting Colin's family was a big step in their relationship. But she trusts that everything will go well and is looking forward to making memories with him.

Once they arrived in Oslo airport as they retrieved their bags and got in the taxi to head towards Oslo. Elena looked out of her window and enjoyed the scenic ride, Colin said, "We're going to stay downtown near the Royal Palace." As they arrived at the hotel, Elena stood outside and marveled at the Royal Palace and how beautiful it was.

Colin couldn't help but smile as he watched Elena take in the beauty of Oslo. He took her hand and led her into the hotel lobby to check-in. As they walked to their room, Colin points out some of the popular tourist spots they could visit while they are in Oslo. Elena was so grateful to have Colin as her tour guide and couldn't wait to explore the city with him.

Colin told Elena, "We are going to have a dinner with my family they are so eager to meet you." While they were getting ready for dinner Elena was feeling little nervous deciding what to wear. Colin noticed Elena's nervousness and reassured her that she looked beautiful no matter what decided to wear. He even joked that his family would be more interested in getting to know her than what she would be wearing.

Elena laughed and relaxed a bit, feeling grateful for Colin's support. She picked out a nice dress and they headed up to the rooftop for dinner with Colin's family. The views of the city were stunning, and Elena was excited to meet the people who mean so much to Colin.

As the hostess escorted them to the table Collins family had already arrived a little early so excited to see Colin since it's been so long. They couldn't believe how gorgeous Elena was. Elena couldn't help but feel a little nervous as she sat down at the table with Colin's family, but they all greeted her warmly with smiles and hugs.

They immediately made her feel welcomed and part of the family. They began to chat and share stories, and Elena felt grateful for the opportunity to get to know them better. Colin's mom made some traditional Norwegian dishes for them to try, and Elena was pleasantly surprised at how delicious they were. As the evening went on, Elena felt more and more comfortable around Colin's family, and she knew that this was the beginning of a beautiful relationship.

The next day Colin wanted to Elena some place special that brought back a childhood memory. Colin took her to Vigeland Park, upon their arrival she was immediately in awe of the sculptures that surrounded her. The park was full of beautifully crafted bronze and granite sculptures created by artist Gustav Vigeland. She saw statues of men, women, children, and even babies in various poses and positions.

The most impressive sculpture she saw was the Monolith, a 46-foot-tall column made of 121 human figures stacked on top of each other. It was a breathtaking sight to behold, and Elena couldn't believe the amount of work that must have gone into creating it. As she continued to stare at it, Colin was behind bent over on one knee as she turned around, she's shocked that Colin holding a beautiful princess cut engagement ring.

Colin looked up at Elena with tears in his eyes and said, "Elena, I know we haven't been together for very long, but from the moment I met you at Kiki, I knew you were the one for me. You made me a better man and I can't imagine my life without you. Will you do me the honor of becoming my wife?"

Elena was completely surprised but overjoyed at the proposal, and without hesitation, she said, "Yes!"

Colin slipped the ring onto her finger, and they hugged each other tightly, tears streaming down their faces. It was a moment they would both cherish forever.

Colin told her that as a child, he used to come to this park with his family all the time and that it held a special place in his heart, that's why he wanted to do it here. Elena was touched by the sentimental value of the proposal location and hugged Colin once more. They walked around the park, taking in the beauty of the sculptures and basking in their love for each other. Colin told Elena about his family's tradition of visiting the park, and they made plans to come back again one day with their own family.

As they left the park and walked hand in hand, Elena felt overwhelmed with happiness and gratitude for Colin and the life they were building together. She couldn't wait to start planning their future as husband and wife.

Chapter 11

The first night of being an engaged woman Elena could not sleep completely jubilant and elated still feels very surreal trying to crystallize the moment. Even though she and Colin took several pictures in the park she posted some on her social media and sent some to her family. Knowing there is a six-hour time difference where she's at she wanted to wait to tell the ladies later.

Colin was lying down when he turned over and realizes Elena was not sleeping at all. She's just been staring at her engagement ring.

Colin noticed that Elena is awake, and he asks her, "What are you thinking about my love?"

She turned to him with a big smile on her face and said, "I can't stop staring at my ring! It's so beautiful, and I can't believe we're engaged!"

Colin smiled back at her and said, "I'm so glad you love it. I wanted to make sure it was perfect for you."

The ladies were still sleeping back home she took a picture of the ring and sent it to the group chat. As soon as the other ladies woke up and checked their phones, they were all excited to see the message from Elena with a picture of her beautiful engagement ring. They quickly replied with congratulations and asked for all the details of the proposal.

Stephanie said, "OMG Elena, this is so amazing! I can't wait to see the ring in person when you get back!"

Bethania said, "I am so happy for you! Colin is such a great guy, and you two are perfect for each other."

Jacqueline said, "Congratulations Elena! You deserve all the happiness in the world."

Amber said, "Wow, that ring is stunning! I'm so happy for you, Elena!"

Elena replied to the group chat, "Thank you so much, everyone! Colin proposed at Vigeland Park yesterday, and it was so beautiful and special. I can't wait to tell you all about it in person when I get back!"

Stephanie later that morning was processing some very difficult news. Amir and her decided to part ways and he told her he wanted her to move out of his home. He felt like she's spending too much time working on these new ventures and she doesn't want to spend any time with him.

Stephanie told Amir "I'm here I just no longer feel comfortable being with you, I'm at this stage where I want to focus on myself."

Amir tried to convince Stephanie to change her mind, telling her how much he loved her and how he was willing to work on their relationship. But Stephanie knows deep down that it's time for her to move on, to focus on her own personal growth and success. She thanked Amir for the time they had together, but ultimately told him that it's best if they go their separate ways.

After the conversation with Amir, Stephanie feels a mix of emotions, sadness, regret, but also a sense of relief and freedom. She decided to take some time for herself, to process everything and figure out her next move. She thought about reaching out to her friends for support, but also knew that she needed to rely on herself and find the strength within to move forward.

So now while dealing with the marketing campaign and planning for the company's first event for the mortgage side of the business, she now has to find a new home. She doesn't want to tell Bethania or the girls she felt very determined that she's going to do this on her own and only rely on herself and not rely on anyone as she goes through this difficult transition.

Stephanie took a deep breath and decided to focus on her work for the time being. She knows she needs to find a new home soon, but she doesn't want to rush into anything. She wanted to make sure she found a place that feels right for her and fits her budget.

As she continued to work on the marketing campaign and plan for the company's first event, Stephanie tried to keep her mind occupied and not let the breakup distract her. She knows she can't let her personal life interfere with her professional responsibilities.

She hired movers to come get her stuff out of Amir place and she was going to temporarily put it in storage. In the meantime, she had a friend who was a general manager at a hotel so she was going to stay a few nights there. Work from the hotel and stay focused because she had a lot to prove to herself and to Bethania and the business that she can do this.

Stephanie checks in at the hotel and starts to unpack her belongings. As she's doing so, she thinks about the next steps she needs to take to start fresh. She pulled out her laptop and started searching for potential apartments in the area. She wanted to find a place that's affordable but also safe and comfortable.

After a few hours of research, she found a couple of apartments that she likes and decided to schedule some appointments to go check them out in person. She's determined to find a new home and make this transition as smooth as possible.

Stephanie was starting to feel confident as she found out about the new website for the business which is going to be launched at the end of the week. She has been working on the social media campaign that would bring followers and slowly building the new business social media page and then Stephanie has a very special surprise that she wanted to share with the ladies when Bridget and Sabrina and Megan are back in town this week.

As she finished up her work for the day, Stephanie took a moment to relax and clear her mind. She takes a long hot shower and orders room service for dinner. While she waits for her food, she decided to call her mom and tell her the news about her breakup with Amir.

Her mom was supportive and offered words of encouragement, reminding her that she's strong and capable of overcoming this challenge. Stephanie felt a sense of relief after talking to her mom and started to feel more optimistic about her future.

After dinner, she spent some time going through her belongings and decided to donate some of her clothes to a local charity. She wanted to simplify her life and focus on what's important to her.

The next day Bethania was scheduled to meet with Amir to look at a new place he wanted to buy on Fisher Island. She had a list of places she wanted to show him. When they met, they greeted each other.

Bethania said, "Well I'm surprised you didn't want to invite Stephanie to come look with you."

Amir responded with a sigh, "Stephanie and I are no longer together. She moved out of my place yesterday."

Bethania's eyes widened in surprise, "I had no idea, Amir. Are you okay?"

Amir nodded and said, "I'm fine. It just didn't work out between us. I'm here to focus on business today. Let's get started on our tour of the properties."

Bethania nods and they proceeded to look at the properties together, discussing the pros and cons of each one. However, Bethania can't help but think about Stephanie and how she's doing. She made a mental note to check-in with her later and see how she was holding up.

After Bethania finished her meeting with Amir, she sent Stephanie a text to meet for lunch. Stephanie received the text from Bethania and replied that she would love to meet for lunch. She quickly freshened up and headed to the agreed-upon restaurant to meet Bethania.

As she sat down, Bethania looked at Stephanie and asked how she had been doing. Stephanie took a deep breath and told her about her recent breakup with Amir and her plans to find a new apartment.

Bethania listened attentively and offered her support, telling Stephanie that she can count on her for anything she needs. She also told her about some potential leads she has for apartments and offered to help her with the process.

Stephanie was grateful for Bethania's kindness and support, feeling a sense of relief knowing she had someone to lean on during this difficult time.

It's Friday, the start of the weekend, Megan, Sabrina, and Bridget have all arrived back in Miami. Jacqueline, Amber, and Bethania were excited to hear they were back in town and decided let's meet at the Standard Hotel Miami Beach for lunch and cocktails to catch up. Megan had requested that we invite Stephanie.

Bethania sent a message to Stephanie inviting her to meet up with the group at the Standard Hotel Miami Beach. Stephanie was hesitant at first, but she decided to go and meet with her friends. She puts on a cute outfit and heads over to the hotel.

When Stephanie arrived, she saw the ladies were sitting at a table, chatting, and laughing. She felt a bit nervous, not sure how to approach them after what happened with Amir. But as soon as she sits down, they are happy to see her, and they start catching up on everything that has happened since they last saw each other.

Stephanie gives Megan Bridget Jacqueline Bethania Amber and Sabrina an update on letting them know the new website has been launched they could see it from their phones, she also told them the social media presence is growing and she has another surprise for them, but they all have to take an Uber ride downtown together to see it.

The girls were all curious about Stephanie's surprise and excitedly agreed to take the Uber ride downtown. As they made their way to their destination, Stephanie told them that she's been working on securing a partnership with a popular local restaurant for their upcoming mortgage event.

The girls were impressed and congratulated Stephanie on her hard work. When they arrived at their destination, Stephanie led them to a building and told them to wait outside for a moment. A few minutes later, Stephanie emerges with a set of keys and led the group into a beautiful and spacious loft space.

Stephanie explained that she's been working on securing this space for the company's first official event, and it's going to be a night to remember. The girls were all blown away by the space and couldn't wait to start planning the event.

Stephanie also told them I need you to go to the rooftop, I'm going to show you something. Once the ladies get to the rooftop Stephanie told them to look to the left, the business is on a gigantic billboard downtown. You can see Megan, Amber, Bridget, Sabrina, Jacqueline, and Elena on the billboard with the name of the business website.

The ladies are amazed and impressed by the billboard. They all take pictures and videos to share on social media.

Sabrina exclaimed, "Stephanie, this is amazing! You've really outdone yourself!" The other ladies nod in agreement, expressing their admiration for Stephanie's hard work and dedication to the business.

Megan said, "I am emphatically impressed with your herculean effort and seeing you grow and maturate into such an amazing business professional. I absolutely love how you are taking pride in what you're doing. This is truly amazing work you have truly a gift."

Stephanie blushed, feeling grateful for the support and encouragement from the ladies. "Thank you, guys. I couldn't have done it without you all. Since the moment I've met you all you all have been a tremendous inspiration to me not only to work for but just as women in business it's so inspiring. You guys have given me a support system that I've never had, and I feel like I'm part of a sisterhood. We're going to keep growing and taking this business to the next level!" she says confidently.

The ladies all cheer and raise their glasses to toast to the success of the business and to their friendship. They all feel grateful to have each other and to be able to share in each other's successes and struggles.

Megan speaks up, "Steph, once again I just want to say how proud I am of you. You've shown us all that anything is possible if you put your mind to it. And you've done it all on your own, without relying on anyone else. You're a true boss babe! Let's meet tomorrow because I'm going to promote you to Chief Marketing Officer. You've shown initiative, you've shown drive, you displayed you are capable, and you take tremendous pride in what you do. That is what we are all about is lifting each other up inspiring one another that's always what I wanted for each one of us."

The other ladies nod in agreement and continue to shower Stephanie with praise and encouragement. They all feel inspired and motivated to continue working hard and chasing their dreams.

The next day Stephanie was feeling very confident and excited at the potential of what her new role is going to be. The ladies have decided to have a meeting at Megan's place to discuss farther about Stephanie's new role.

As Stephanie arrived at Megan's place, she's greeted with smiles and hugs from all the ladies. They all sit down at the table, and Megan started the meeting by congratulating Stephanie on her new role as CMO. "We're all so proud of you and what you've accomplished in such a short amount of time," Megan said, smiling at Stephanie.

Megan hands Stephanie a white envelope and she opens it with shock and amazement it's a bonus check for fifty thousand dollars.

Megan asked, "Her how does it feel to earn your own money now and not getting it handed to you?"

Stephanie was overwhelmed with emotion as she took the bonus check from Megan. "Thank you so much, Megan. It feels incredible to earn my money and to know that all of my hard work was paying off," Stephanie said, smiling. "I'm grateful for this opportunity and for all of you for believing in me." She got up and hugged each one of the ladies.

Megan nods, smiling. "We believe in you, Stephanie. And we want you to know that we're here to support you in any way we can. This is just the beginning, and we're excited to see where you take the business next."

Stephanie nods, feeling grateful and inspired by the support of her sisters in business. She takes a deep breath, feeling ready to take on her new role as CMO and continue to grow the business to new heights.

Stephanie asked Megan a question "Can you teach me how to invest half of this? I want to be like you guys."

Megan said, "I would be honored let's set aside a time to do that."

Amber pulled Stephanie aside and said, "When you have your own money, you can open up your legs for a man you desire, that's what a true queen does elevate your worth never settle for less."

Stephanie looked at Amber, surprised by her bold statement. "I see your perspective" she said, feeling a bit uncomfortable. "I believe that a true queen values herself and her worth, and that means not settling for less than she deserves. It's not about opening your legs for a man, it's about finding someone who respects and honors you for who you are."

Amber nodded, understanding where Stephanie was coming from. "You're right, Stephanie. It's important to value yourself and not settle for less than you deserve. I just meant that when you have financial independence, you have more freedom to make choices that are right for you."

Stephanie smiled, feeling grateful for the support and guidance of her friends. She knew that with their help, she could achieve anything she set her mind to.

Stephanie felt a deep personal sense of accomplishment and for the first time in life she felt like she'd found purpose. Working with Megan, Amber, Bridget, Elena, Bethania, Jacqueline, and Sabrina joining their world has transcended Stephanie into someone she never thought she could be. Stephanie felt a sense of gratitude towards the ladies for believing in her and giving her the opportunity to prove herself. At times she dealt with low self-esteem and what she wanted to be but now she felt like she'd found her true calling. She's grateful for the challenges that she's faced, as they've allowed her to grow and learn, and she's excited to see where this new role will take her.

Megan told, "The ladies you know what's next?"

Amber said, "Now that Stephanie has put together our first business event you know what that means ladies it's time to go shopping. I'm already going to give Jorge and Javier a call to do our hair."

Megan chimed in, "Yes! And we need to make sure we have the perfect outfits for this event. I'm thinking of something elegant and sophisticated. Maybe we should even consider hiring a stylist to help us out."

Bridget nods in agreement, "Yes, we want to make sure we make a statement and leave a lasting impression on our guests."

Jacqueline adds, "And let's not forget about the decorations and the ambiance. We need to create an unforgettable experience for everyone who attends."

Stephanie listened carefully to their ideas, taking notes and thinking of ways to bring their vision to life. "I'm on it, ladies. I'll start making some calls and putting together a plan."

Bethania told Stephanie "Hold up a second, I have something I wanted to share with you."

Bethania told her "I found you a really nice place you can stay its on West Ave. You want to go look?"

Stephanie's eyes lit up with surprise and gratitude as she listened to Bethania. "Wow, that's so kind of you, Bethania. Thank you so much," Stephanie said, feeling touched by the gesture. "I would love to take a look at it.

As Bethania and Stephanie arrived to look at this gorgeous apartment that overlooks the water. She can't believe how nice it is

Stephanie looked around the apartment in awe, taking in the beautiful view of the water and the sleek and modern decor. "Wow, Bethania, this is amazing. I can't believe you found this place for me. It's perfect," she says, smiling at Bethania. She walked around the living room, admiring the furnishings and the spaciousness of the apartment.

Bethania nods, smiling. "I'm so glad you like it. I knew you needed a fresh start, and this place is perfect for that. It's close to your work and it's a great neighborhood. Plus, the building has all the amenities you could ever need," she said, gesturing to the gym and pool areas.

Stephanie looked around again, feeling grateful for Bethania's generosity and thoughtfulness. "Thank you so much, Bethania. This means the world to me. I can't wait to move in," she said, beaming.

The next day Elena and Colin arrived back in Miami as an engaged couple. The ladies was so excited to finally get to see the engagement ring and catch up with them. So, they planned a dinner date with Maxwell and Megan, Amber and James, Charles and Sabrina,

Bethania and William to have dinner with Elena and Colin. They wanted to know how Norway and meeting Colin family was and how surprised she was when he proposed.

As everyone gathered around the table, the excitement was palpable. Elena and Colin are beaming, and everyone is eager to hear about their trip and the engagement. Over dinner and drinks, Elena told the story of how Colin proposed to her at Vigeland Park in Norway. She shows off the stunning ring on her finger, and everyone oohs and aahs over it.

Colin chimed in, telling everyone about how nervous he was to propose and how he had planned the perfect day for it. He thanked everyone for their support and kind wishes, and the group raised a glass to the happy couple.

Charles and Sabrina share about their trip to Sag Harbor, NY to meet Sabrina's parents. They talk about how beautiful it was there and how welcoming her parents were. Sabrina's mother cooked a delicious dinner, and her father showed them around the town. Charles adds that he enjoyed learning about the history of the area and seeing the old whaling ships. Sabrina mentioned that her parents were impressed with Charles and thought he was a great match for her.

Maxwell and Megan talked about how it was being in Manhattan and seeing Megan old SOHO condo for the first time. Maxwell shared how Megan told the story of how she invited Amber, Bethania, Jacqueline, Sabrina Elena and Bridget for her New Years Party and that's how you guys became friends.

Megan chuckled and nodded in agreement, "Yes, it's funny how one small invitation turned into such a wonderful friendship. I'm grateful for each one of you," she said, smiling at the group.

Maxwell adds, "And speaking of parties, I heard Stephanie did an amazing job organizing the business marketing. I love the billboard downtown I wish I could have been there to see it."

Stephanie blushes and thanks Maxwell for the kind words. "It was a team effort, and I couldn't have done it without the support of everyone here," she says, looking around the table.

The ladies listen attentively as Bridget shares about her trip to Nashville and how much of a help Cole was during her time there. "He's been amazing, and my family absolutely adores him," Bridget says with a smile. "It was tough seeing my dad sick, but having Cole there made it a little easier." The other ladies nod in understanding and express their support for Bridget and her family.

The ladies got up from the table and went to the ladies' room and shattered in the ladies' room. Also, William Cole James Maxwell and Charles were all congratulating Colin on the engagement.

As the ladies' head to the restroom, the men continue to chat and congratulate Colin on the engagement. William asks Colin how he proposed, and Colin told the story about he originally planned of how he wanted to surprise Elena on a hike in Norway and proposed to her on a mountaintop overlooking the fjords but decided Vigeland Park was a better idea. James comments on how romantic that sounds, and Maxwell asked, "if they've set a date for the wedding yet?

Colin said, "they haven't decided on a specific date yet, but they're thinking of having it next year in Turks and Caicos."

Meanwhile, in the ladies' room, the women are all gushing over Elena's engagement ring and asking about her trip to Norway. Bethania asks Elena if she's thought about the wedding dress yet, and Elena admits that she hasn't even started looking. Bridget chimed in and offered to take her dress shopping and even suggests some bridal boutiques in the area. The ladies continue to chat excitedly about the upcoming wedding, and Stephanie can't help but feel grateful for the strong bond she's formed with this group of amazing women.

Stephanie mentions to the ladies "I'm so glad you're back Bridget and Megan because since I've launched a new marketing campaign with the new billboard downtown, we have been getting so many inquiries for a new business The ladies look at each other with excitement, happy to hear the news."

Megan exclaims "That's amazing, Stephanie!" "I knew our new marketing strategies would pay off," she adds, smiling at Stephanie.

Bridget nodded in agreement and said, "Yeah, the website looks great, and the billboard is such a cool way to advertise.

So as the ladies made their way back to the table, Colin and Maxwell made an announcement.

Maxwell told everyone at the table "since Colin is a Software Engineer, I'm going to be subcontracting some work out to him."

Colin told Elena that he was going to be now officially living in Miami full time working from home so he's going to need to look for a new place since he now landed his new contract to work with Maxwell.

Elena looks thrilled and gives Colin a big hug. "That's amazing news! I'm so happy for you, and it's great that we'll finally be living together in the same city. Let's start looking for a new place together!" she says excitedly.

The other ladies congratulate Colin on his new opportunity and welcome him to Miami full-time. They start brainstorming ideas for places he and Elena could check out, offering recommendations and sharing their own experiences with apartments in the area. It's clear that they're all excited to have Colin living in Miami.

So as everyone leaves for tonight everybody's feeling all excited about the first company event that Stephanie has planned. The ladies are all excited as everyone has their attire so they can't wait till where for the event and network and meet so many different new people. Stephanie was somewhat nervous as event planning is not something she's done before in a professional setting, she's always hosted parties, but this was different. As she reviews the guest list and make sure all the invitations have been sent out to the VIP's. She had been promoting quite heavily through social media. She's also taken the time to hire one of the best caterers in Miami to serve food and drinks.

The night was finally here Stephanie had arranged private cars to pick up Amber and James, Bethania and William, Charles and Sabrina, Megan and Maxwell, Elena and Colin, and Bridget and Cole. Everyone was absolutely impressed as they got out of their respective cars, they noticed there was a red carpet for them to walk on as they went in the entrance there was a photographer and videographer for the event. They were so impressed with how Stephanie organized and orchestrated the event and perhaps became extremely resourceful.

As the guests made their way into the event, they were greeted by friendly staff and an elegantly decorated venue. The music was lively, the drinks are flowing, and the food is delicious. Stephanie was busy making sure everything was running smoothly, but she can't help but feel proud of herself for putting together such a successful event.

As the night progresses, the guests start mingling and networking with each other. They exchange business cards, discuss their companies, and even make plans for potential collaborations. Stephanie was thrilled to see that her event was not only a success but also helping her fellow businesswomen connect and build their networks.

As Megan was walking around at the party greeting the guests and she was surprised to see that Abigail has arrived. In the back of her mind Maxwell didn't mention that she was coming,

Megan walked over to her and said, "Hi and says it's good to see you again Abigail, I did not know you were going to be here tonight."

Abigail said, "I was in Palm Beach meeting with a potential client that I've known for a long time, and I remember Maxwell had mentioned that you were launching your first company event. I wasn't feeling too tired I decided to come down here and mingle and say hello."

Then Abigail asked Megan, "Who is that In the tan dress with the blonde streaks in her hair?"

Megan said, "That's my Chief Marketing Officer Stephanie she's the one who planned and coordinated this whole event."

Abigail said, "Wow I'm impressed she's gorgeous and talented." Abigail asked Megan, "Would you mind introducing me to her?"

Megan was somewhat perplexed at how Abigail was looking at Stephanie. As they walk towards Stephanie notices them walking in her direction.

Megan smiled and introduced Abigail to Stephanie, "Stephanie, this is Abigail Lawson. She's a potential client and Maxwell's Business Partner. Abigail, this is Stephanie Toro, my Chief Marketing Officer." Stephanie smiles warmly and extends her hand, saying "It's a pleasure to meet you, Abigail. Thank you for coming to our event."

Abigail shakes Stephanie's hand and said, "It's my pleasure, Stephanie. Megan has told me a lot about you, and I'm impressed by what you've accomplished with this event. I'd love to talk more about your marketing strategies and how you plan to grow the company."

Stephanie nodded and said, "I'd be happy to discuss that with you, Abigail. Let's exchange contact information and set up a time to chat soon." Megan watched the conversation, feeling slightly relieved that Abigail's interest in Stephanie seems to be purely professional. She made a mental note to follow up with Maxwell later about his relationship with Abigail.

Abigail said to Stephanie "You're very beautiful I love your hair and that smile and that dress, I would love to meet with you for lunch or dinner sometime.

"Thank you, Abigail, for the compliment. I appreciate it. As for meeting up, I'd be happy to discuss marketing strategies and business opportunities with you, but I prefer to keep things professional. I don't think lunch or dinner would be necessary at this stage, but I'm happy to exchange phone numbers and set up a time to talk further." Stephanie took out her phone and exchanged contact information with Abigail.

Megan breathed a sigh of relief, feeling reassured that Stephanie was maintaining a professional boundary with Abigail. She made a mental note to talk to Stephanie later and ensure that she felt comfortable with the situation. Megan also decides to talk to Maxwell and clarify the nature of his relationship with Abigail.

Megan decided to approach Maxwell and pulled him aside "What do you know about Abigail besides her being your business partner? I have a feeling she was hitting on Stephanie.

Maxwell pulled Megan closer and said, "This stays between us but Abigail is only into women."

Megan nodded and thanked Maxwell for confiding in her. She felt relieved to have a better understanding of Abigail's preferences and realizes that confirmed her suspicions regarding what happened earlier. Now that Megan knows what Abigail true intentions are. Megan contemplating whether to tell Stephanie she spoke with Amber, Elena, Jacqueline, Bridget, Sabrina, and Bethania on the rooftop to get their opinion on how to approach this situation.

Megan decided to approach Stephanie and explained the situation to her, making sure to maintain Abigail's privacy.

Megan approached Stephanie and said, "Hey, can I talk to you for a moment? I just wanted to clarify something about Abigail that I think might help clear up any misunderstandings."

Stephanie looked at Megan curiously and said, "Sure, what's up?"

Megan took a deep breath and said, "I spoke to Maxwell, and he told me that Abigail was actually into women. I just wanted to let you know that her earlier compliments were likely intended as friendly and professional, but I can tell from her demeanor it was flirtatious."

Stephanie looked surprised for a moment and then nods, "Oh, okay. Thanks for letting me know, Megan. I appreciate it. I wasn't sure what to think earlier, so it's good to have some clarity."

Megan nodded and said, "Of course. I just wanted to make sure that everyone is comfortable and on the same page. Let me know if there's anything else I can do to help."

Stephanie smiled and said, "Thanks, Megan. I appreciate your concern. I'm good now, but I'll let you know if anything comes up."

Megan felt relieved that she was able to clear things up with Stephanie and that the situation was resolved. She's glad that she talked to her friends and gathered their opinions before approaching Stephanie, as it helped her to handle the situation in a thoughtful and respectful way.

As Stephanie headed to the bathroom, she noticed Abigail checking her out, then she ran into Jacqueline, Sabrina, and Amber in the ladies room.

Amber asked Stephanie "What's that look on your face?"

Stephanie said, "I just caught Abigail checking me out."

Amber laughed and said, "Looks like you've got an admirer, Steph!"

Sabrina chimed in and said, "Abigail's definitely got good taste. Jacqueline adds, you're looking fabulous tonight, girl! don't let it go to your head though. We're all here to network and make business connections."

Stephanie chuckles and nods in agreement, "Of course, Jacqueline. But there's no harm in a little harmless flirting, right?" The group giggles and continued to freshen up before heading back out to the event.

Megan and Bridget decided to gather all the guests around and give a speech as the night was coming to an end.

Megan speech says,

"Thank you all so much for coming to this event tonight. It means the world to us that you took the time to come out and network with us. We hope you had a great time and that you were able to make some valuable connections. We also want to take a moment to thank our amazing event planner Stephanie for putting together such a fantastic evening.

As some of you may know, our company was started by a group of friends who all had a passion for entrepreneurship and creativity. We are thrilled to see how far we have come and are excited for what the future holds.

We also want to take a moment to recognize the importance of diversity and inclusivity in the business world. It's so important to create spaces where everyone feels welcome and valued, regardless of their background or identity.

Thank you again for coming out tonight and we hope to see you at our future events."

So later that night after the event ended everyone was at home cuddling with their partners. Stephanie received a text from Abigail asking her, "Are you free tomorrow for drinks?" Stephanie doesn't know how to respond to this, especially based off of the information Megan shared with her earlier. Stephanie replied to her and said, "The night is still young how about we meet tonight?"

Abigail responded quickly and agreed to meet up with Stephanie later that night. Stephanie was a bit nervous but also curious about Abigail's intentions. They agreed to meet at a popular bar in the downtown area.

As Stephanie arrived at the bar, she sees Abigail already sitting at a table with two drinks in front of her. Stephanie took a deep breath and walked over to the table. Abigail greeted her with a warm smile and invited her to sit down.

As they started talking and catching up, Stephanie brought up the topic of Abigail's sexuality. Abigail looked a bit surprised but then admitted that she's attracted to women and has been struggling to come to terms with it. Stephanie reassured her that it's okay and that she doesn't have to label herself if she doesn't want to.

Abigail said, "I'm considered an outsider by my family because I left my ex-husband, and I didn't want to have children with him. And that's when I knew I had always had a thing for women but growing up where I'm from it's very taboo to have an open conversation about those things."

Stephanie listened intently and shared that she could relate to feeling like an outsider at times. She encouraged Abigail to embrace her true self and surround herself with people who accept and support her. Abigail thanked Stephanie for the advice, and they continued talking for a few more hours, enjoying each other's company.

Stephanie asked Abigail why did you really want my number? Abigail said, "As much as I was trying to keep it professional, but my intentions were more personal."

Stephanie told Abigail, "I just came out of a relationship" and Abigail said, "I'm recently divorced so I can absolutely sympathize with what you're going through."

As they were sitting in the booth together Abigail gave Stephanie a very seductive look then she slides over closer to Stephanie wearing quite a revealing dress that Abigail cannot stop looking at her.

Stephanie told Abigail, "You're not the first woman who's tried to hit on me"

Abigail said to her, "What intrigued you to want to meet me tonight? I couldn't tell at the party if you were picking up what I was giving off."

Stephanie said, "I was picking it up, but my boss was right there who made the introduction I wanted to keep it professional in front of her."

Abigail was also wearing a very revealing sexy dress and Stephanie started to notice what she was wearing.

Stephanie said, "I love your style and taste I like your earrings and those red bottoms that you're wearing." Stephanie notices that Abigail has started putting her hand on her leg and slowly caressing it.

Abigail said, "I haven't been with anyone since my ex-husband" Stephanie said, "I haven't been with anyone since my ex."

Stephanie wanted to tell Abigail to stop playing with her leg but then she started to actually really like it. Then these two gentlemen abruptly interrupt them walking over from the bar one of them said, "We have been noticing you beautiful women for a little bit."

Abigail immediately in interrupts them and said, "Thank you gentlemen, but we are not interested in men."

The men seem taken aback by Abigail's response, but they quickly apologize and walk away. Stephanie looked at Abigail and said, "Thank you for that, I wasn't sure how to handle it." Abigail smiled and said, "No problem, I'm used to dealing with unwanted attention." Stephanie nods, feeling a bit guilty for not realizing how difficult it must be for Abigail at times.

Abigail said to Stephanie, "Let's close our tab let's go somewhere else quieter so we were not interrupted."

Stephanie said, "What did you have in mind? Abigail responded, "How about we go back to your place?"

Stephanie said as she pauses for a moment takes a sip of her drink and said, "Let's go." So as they hop into Stephanie's car and go back to her place on the ride back Abigail asked, "Stephanie where are you from?"

Stephanie said, "I was born in the Bronx, but my parents moved to Boca Raton but when I was a kid."

Stephanie said, "What about you?"

Abigail responded and said, "I'm a Texas girl from McKinney."

As they arrived at Stephanie's place Stephanie said, "Forgive me I'm still settling in I just recently moved in."

Abigail said, "I love your place wow what a magnificent view"

Stephanie said, "Bethania is quite an amazing realtor she found this place for me. As Abigail opened the sliding door and walked out on the balcony I love the Miami skyline.

Stephanie said, "Can I make you a drink?"

Abigail said, "What do you have?"

Stephanie said, "I can make you a Margarita."

Abigail said, "That sounds like a plan to me."

Stephanie walks towards the kitchen Abigail continues to check out Stephanie.

Abigail said to her "Girl your legs and body it's absolutely gorgeous." Stephanie said to her, "Thank you I can say the same about you."

Stephanie was making her drink Abigail walked back in closes the sliding door.

Stephanie hands Abigail her drink looks at Abigail said, "What are we doing here?" Abigail told her hold that thought may I use your restroom?

Stephanie had sat down at her dining room table, has a sip of her drink still intrigued and cannot believe that she brought Abigail over to her place but she's just going with the flow and see where the night takes her. and then Abigail walks out of her bathroom with no clothes on still in her heels. Stephanie looks at her with amazement and gets up from the table and Abigail said, "I didn't want to be alone tonight either."

Abigail begins to passionately kiss Stephanie and slowly takes off her dress. As Abigail and Stephanie embrace each other, their bodies entwined in passion, Stephanie feels a rush of excitement and desire. She had never been with a woman before, but something about Abigail's boldness and confidence was irresistible.

As they continued to kiss, Abigail led Stephanie towards her bedroom. The room was decorated with candles and soft music playing in the background, setting the mood for their encounter.

Abigail slowly pushed Stephanie onto the bed and began to explore her body, tracing her fingers along every curve and contour.

Stephanie moaned in pleasure as Abigail's touch sent waves of excitement through her body. She had never felt so alive and free. Abigail moved down towards Stephanie's nether regions, expertly teasing and exploring her with her tongue.

As Stephanie reached the peak of her pleasure, she couldn't help but cry out Abigail's name. Abigail crawled back up towards her and they shared a deep, passionate kiss. Stephanie knew that this was only the beginning of their night together, and she couldn't wait to explore more with Abigail.

As they explore each other's bodies, Stephanie feels a sense of liberation and freedom, as if she had been holding back her desires for too long. She surrenders to the moment, lost in the pleasure and intensity of the experience.

As the night progresses, Stephanie and Abigail engage in a steamy encounter, exploring each other's bodies with passion and intensity. They take turns leading and following, each eager to please the other. As the sun begins to rise, they finally collapse onto the bed, exhausted but satisfied.

Stephanie looked over at Abigail and smiled, feeling a sense of contentment she hadn't experienced in a while. Abigail returned the smile and whispers, "That was amazing. I can't believe I'm admitting this, but I couldn't achieve an orgasm with my ex but you giving me three in one night."

Stephanie chuckled and said, "I'm glad I could help." They both share a laugh and cuddle together under the blankets.

Abigail looked at Stephanie and said, "You know, I didn't expect to connect with someone like this so soon after my divorce."

Stephanie replied, "I didn't expect it either, but I'm glad we did." They continue to talk into the early hours of the morning, getting to know each other on a deeper level. As they drift off to sleep in each other's arms, Stephanie realizes that this unexpected turn of events may be the best thing that has ever happened to her.

As they began to wake up and start the morning Stephanie told Abigail, "I would love to see you again, but we have to be discreet about this. I know we're both just coming out of relationship, so I know I'm not ready for anything serious but if we can keep it cordial like this it works for me."

Abigail nods and agrees, "I understand completely. I'm not looking for anything serious either, but I really enjoyed our time together last night. And I agree that we should keep it discreet, at least for now."

As Abigail leaves, Stephanie reflects on the events of the night, feeling a mix of excitement and uncertainty. She knows that her life will never be the same after this encounter, but she's ready to embrace whatever comes next.

Chapter 12

So it was Saturday morning Amber texted the girls talking about last night's event. Amber suggested that we should add Stephanie to our group chat. I believe she's earned the right to be a part of our family. Bridget, Jacqueline, Elena, Bethania, Megan, and Sabrina agreed to add Stephanie and Amber said, "let's all meet this morning at the gym. After all that food and drinks from last night we could certainly work it off."

The ladies were getting ready for the gym, Jacqueline said, "I can't hang out too long since Harry's parents are flying in town today. I need to make sure I get my place ready since I'm cooking dinner for everyone tonight."

As they parked their cars and arrived at the gym Stephanie was excited to work out with them for the first time as they greeted one another.

Stephanie said, "What are we training on?"

Elena said, "Since I'm getting my body ready for my wedding, I downloaded this workout called 300."

Stephanie raised her eyebrows in surprise and asked, "Is it that intense?"

Elena laughed and said, "Oh yeah, it's no joke. But trust me, it's worth it. You'll feel amazing after."

The rest of the girls nod in agreement and Sabrina chimed in, "Plus, it's a great way to burn off all those calories from last night."

Stephanie grinned and said, "Alright, let's do this!" And with that, the ladies headed into the gym to tackle the intense 300 workout. They did a combination of exercises such as squats, lunges, push-ups, burpees, and other high-intensity movements. The workout was challenging, but the ladies pushed through it, motivating each other along the way. As they finished the last set, they all high-fived each other and took a moment to catch their breath. Stephanie was impressed with their stamina and dedication to fitness.

Stephanie said, "I'm so impressed with you ladies you work hard professionally still make time to do fitness and keep these amazing figures that you have."

The ladies smiled and said, "Thank Stephanie for the compliment."

Bridget said, "It's all about balance. We prioritize our health and fitness because it helps us feel good in all aspects of our lives."

Jacqueline adds, "Plus, it's a great stress reliever."

After their workout, they hit the showers and got dressed. As they were leaving the gym, Sabrina suggested they grab a smoothie from the juice bar next door. They all agreed and headed over to the juice bar, chatting and laughing along the way.

Stephanie asked, "So what does everyone got planned for their weekend other than Jacqueline who will be occupied entertaining?

I know I must do some work and follow up on all the leads that we've collected last night and since we've launched our new marketing campaign."

Bridget chimed in and said, "I'm planning on going to a concert tonight with Cole. We're seeing one of my favorite bands perform."

Elena said, "I'm going wedding dress shopping and help Colin find a new place, which I'm excited about."

Bethania said, "William and I are going out to dinner and then seeing a movie."

Megan said, "I'm furniture shopping and working from home."

Sabrina said, "I'm actually planning on just relaxing at home and making some dinner for Charles. Maybe catching up on some Netflix shows."

While Stephanie was working at her Home Office checking all the leads, she noticed a name that looked very familiar to her in the database. Her name was Divya Katdare, her and Stephanie were so extremely close in high school but lost touch when she got accepted to Cornell. Stephanie decided to give the number on file a call and she answered Stephanie told her she's following up on a lead, but your name sounded familiar like someone I used to know back in high school.

Stephanie asked her, "Did you go to the same high school as I?" Divya said, "Yes I did."

Stephanie said Divya, "This is Stephanie Toro I know it's been too long."

Divya was surprised and excited to hear from Stephanie after all these years. They catch up on each other's lives and reminisce about their high school days. Stephanie told Divya about her business and how they're expanding their marketing efforts. Divya, who works as a Managing Direction for a large corporation, offered to give Stephanie some advice on how to improve their campaign.

They made plans to meet up for lunch the next day to discuss it further. Stephanie was thrilled to have reconnected with an old friend and is looking forward to catching up more.

Stephanie group texted the ladies and said, "Bridget I have a hot lead that's old friend of mine who's interested in buying a home. She's already filled out the mortgage application on our website. I know you need to review it before you approve and Bethania, she's looking for house in South Florida preferably Ft. Lauderdale."

Bridget replied, to the group text, "Great job, Steph! I'll make sure to review the application as soon as possible and get in touch with her to discuss her options."

Bethania responded, "Thanks for letting me know, Stephanie. I have a few great listings in Ft. Lauderdale that I think she'll love. I'll send them to her as soon as Bridget approves the application." The other ladies also chime in with words of encouragement and congratulations for Stephanie's successful lead.

Stephanie told the ladies, "Business in all three divisions were expanding with Bethania killing it on real estate, Bridget now the mortgage side of the business is growing and investment services thanks to Megan has always been solid."

Megan said, "I'm proposing ladies we might have to start looking at office space. What do you ladies think?"

Bridget responded, "I agree, it's time we start thinking about expanding our physical presence as well. We can't keep working out of our homes forever. An office space would make us look more professional and could attract more clients."

Megan added, "I also think having a centralized office space would make it easier for us to collaborate and work together on projects. Right now, we're all working independently, and it can be challenging to coordinate everything."

Elena chimed in, "I have a friend who works in commercial real estate. I can ask her for some recommendations on office spaces in the area."

Sabrina agreed, "That would be great, Elena. Let's start exploring our options and see what's available in our budget."

Stephanie said, "Ladies our business model is mostly doing finance and real estate, we need to be looking for office space in Brickell with all the other major key players. I already know a few places that are available that I think you guys would love the office space. The reason how I know is because Amir's friend used to rent out the commercial space, but he sold his company."

Bridget replied, "That sounds like a great idea, Stephanie. We need a dedicated space for our business operations. Brickell is the perfect location since it's a hub for finance and business in Miami. Can you send us the information about the available spaces you found?"

The rest of the ladies chimed in with their agreement and excitement about the potential move to a new office space. Stephanie quickly sent over the information to the group chat and they discussed the pros and cons of each space.

After some deliberation, they finally settle on a spacious office in a prime location in Brickell.

Bethania said, "I've contacted the property management firm we have an appointment for Monday to take a look at the space." The ladies are excited to see this office space that Stephanie knows about.

On the other side of town Jacqueline had been spending a significant amount of time preparing her place, getting the food ready for Harry's parents. As she hears a knock on the door, she just gathers herself for a minute, takes off her apron, checks herself in the mirror and opens the door.

To her surprise, it was Harry's parents standing outside her door with flowers and a gift basket. "Hi Jacqueline, we couldn't wait to see you and Harry," they said, giving her a warm hug. Jacqueline was delighted to see them and invited them inside.

As Harry's dad hugs Jacqueline step back and looks at her and says Harry you are quite a lucky man, she is gorgeous.

Harry's dad said, "You look like Halle Berry in that movie swordfish with John Travolta one of my favorite movies of hers."

Jacqueline blushed and thanked Harry's dad for the compliment. She tells him that she's a big fan of Halle Berry and that it's a huge compliment.

After catching up with Harry's parents, Jacqueline led them to the living room where they sat down and get to know Jacqueline more and vice versa. They all sat down and enjoyed a delicious meal while reminiscing about old times and sharing stories. As Jacqueline tells Harry's parents that Harry has been a true gentleman, he's absolute godsend he's always treated me like a queen. Jacqueline tells the family excuse me for a moment I just need to check on the food and make sure it's all ready. As she gets up she just so happens to look at Harry's father and she catches him checking her out.

Jacqueline tried to ignore the awkward moment and quickly went to the kitchen to check on the food. She takes a deep breath and composes herself before returning to the living room to continue the conversation with Harry's parents. Jacqueline announced that dinner is ready.

They all head to the dining room where Jacqueline has prepared a feast for everyone. The table is set with a beautiful centerpiece and candles flicker creating a warm and inviting atmosphere. As they enjoy the delicious food, they catch up on each other's lives and share stories Harry's parents were impressed with Jacqueline's cooking and her hospitality.

After dinner, Harry's parents complimented Jacqueline's place and said they absolutely love the view and the layout. Jacqueline started telling them about the Paramount building.

Jacqueline said, "The Paramount is a beautiful building with stunning ocean views. It's one of the most sought-after buildings in the area, with top-notch amenities like a spa, fitness center, and 24-hour concierge service. I've been trying to get Harry to move in with me, but he's hesitant to leave his current place. Maybe you guys could talk to him and convince him!"

Harry's mom laughed and said, "Oh, we've been trying to get him to move closer to us for years, but he's stubborn like his father. Maybe you can have more luck than we did!"

While Jacqueline and Harry's mom were cleaning up from dinner and doing the dishes. Jacqueline happened to overhear Harry's dad and Harry talking about Jacqueline.

Harry's dad says son, "that is a fine piece of brown sugar you got there I'm proud of you and she makes her own money that is a rare commodity right there."

Jacqueline, who overheard the conversation, felt a bit uncomfortable but tried to brush it off. She continued helping Harry's mom with the dishes and making small talk. After a while, Harry's parents thanked Jacqueline for the lovely dinner and said their goodbyes, promising to stay in touch.

As they left, Jacqueline felt relieved but also a bit uneasy about the comment she overheard. She decided to bring it up to Harry and express her discomfort. Harry was understanding and reassured her that his dad is just old-fashioned and sometimes says things without thinking. Jacqueline appreciated Harry's support and felt grateful for their open communication.

As the ladies arrived on Monday to check out the office space, they were absolutely blow away at how amazing it was and the views of Miami from each office.

Bridget said, "Wow, this is incredible. It's exactly what we need to take our business to the next level." Megan adds, "And the location is perfect for meeting with clients and attending financial events in the city." Elena chimed in, "And can you imagine how impressed our clients will be when they see our stunning office space?"

Stephanie smiled and said, "I'm glad you guys like it. I think this is the perfect space for us to grow and expand our business." Bethania nods in agreement and said, "I've already spoken to the property management firm and they're willing to work with us on a lease that fits our needs."

The ladies spend the rest of the afternoon touring the office space and discussing potential plans for the layout and design of the office. They leave feeling excited and motivated for the future of their business.

The office space is located on a high floor with stunning views of the Miami skyline and the ocean. The entrance leads to a reception area with a sleek, modern design and comfortable seating for guests. The walls are adorned with art pieces that give the space a creative touch.

There are several private offices with glass walls that allow natural light to flow in and provide views of the cityscape. The offices were spacious and equipped with comfortable furniture, large desks, and plenty of storage.

There was also a conference room with a large table and comfortable chairs, perfect for meetings with clients. The room was equipped with a projector and a large screen, making presentations easy and impressive.

The common area is a spacious lounge with comfortable seating, a kitchenette, and a dining area. It's perfect for lunch breaks or informal meetings with colleagues. The walls of the lounge are adorned with colorful artwork and motivational quotes that create a positive and inspiring atmosphere.

Overall, the office space was modern, elegant, and functional, designed to inspire creativity and productivity. The ladies are impressed and excited at the prospect of working in such a beautiful environment.

Megan tells the property management firm after she had reviewed what the terms and conditions are of the lease. "We'll take it" Stephanie just so happens to have a bottle of champagne and some plastic champagne flutes and her purse just in case.

She tells the ladies I'm so happy that I can contribute to being and asset to this group you guys have inspired me from day one. I absolutely love Amber, Megan, Jacqueline, Sabrina, Bethania, and Elena.

Stephanie said, "I thought about this space for Elena as well because I know she's an OBGYN now she can do virtual and also bring in her new patients in Miami."

Elena was thrilled at the idea and says that having a separate office space would allow her to better serve her patients and also give her more flexibility in her schedule. She thanks the ladies for their thoughtfulness and support.

Amber said, "well let's have a toast ladies, our journey started in Brickell when we first got here together and now we're back in Brickell all together once again. We are officially a Brickell Boss now ladies."

The ladies were grateful for the opportunity to work together and build something meaningful. They had each other's backs and supported one another through thick and thin. They knew that success was not just about making money, but also about creating something they could be proud of, something that made a difference in people's lives.

As they sat together in their beautiful new Brickell offices overlooking the city, they raised a toast to each other and their shared success. They knew that there would be more challenges ahead, but they were confident that with each other's support, they could overcome anything.

The group takes a moment to savor the accomplishment and celebrate with some drinks and snacks on the rooftop. They toast to their friendship and success, feeling grateful for each other and excited for the future of the business.

Megan said, "So ladies I want to hear about what's new with you guys. How did it go let's start with you Jacqueline tells us how things went with meeting Harry's parents?"

Jacqueline responds, "It went really well! I was nervous at first, but they were both so kind and welcoming. We had a great dinner and chatted about everything from family to work. Harry's mom and I even got a chance to do the dishes and bond over our love for cooking. Overall, it was a great weekend and I'm happy it went so smoothly. I caught Harry's dad checking me out a few times and told Harry I was fine piece of Brown Sugar"

Amber said, "Ladies I'm late on my cycle and I don't know how to tell James."

Bethania responded, "Amber, take a deep breath. It's important to be honest with James, but it's understandable that it can be difficult to bring up. I think it's best to just tell him in a calm and direct manner. Maybe you can sit down with him and have an open and honest conversation about it. Remember, we're here for you and will support you no matter what." The other ladies nod in agreement and offer their support as well.

Stephanie said, "She has reconnected with an old high school friend her name is Divya Katdare. I'm going to meet up with her today after this and see her for the first time since high school."

Bethania asked, "What was she like in high school, Stephanie?"

Stephanie responds, "Oh, she was always very smart and driven. She was in all the advanced classes and was always involved in different extracurricular activities. I haven't spoken to her in years, but I saw on LinkedIn that she's been working at an investment firm, so I'm excited to catch up with her and hear about what she's been up to."

Megan chimed in, "That sounds great, Stephanie. Let us know how it goes! "

Megan also asked Stephanie "how did it go the rest of the night at the event with Abigail?"

In the back of Stephanie's mind, she automatically knows she could never disclose the truth of what happened that night with such an amazing romantic encounter.

Stephanie hesitates for a moment, knowing that she can't reveal the true nature of what happened with Abigail at the event. She decided to keep it vague and said, "It went well, we had a good time chatting and getting to know each other better."

Megan raised an eyebrow, sensing that Stephanie was holding something back, but decided not to press the issue. "That's great, I'm glad you had a good time. "

Stephanie said, "Ladies this has been a wonderful day I'm so glad we were able to get this accomplished I'm looking forward to transitioning into our new office space. Wow I don't mind volunteering to plan and coordinate the move and get office furniture. But I must go now I told Divya I would meet her at Bayside in Coconut Grove."

As soon as Stephanie gets out of her car in Coconut Grove, she automatically sees Divya. Stephanie called her name as she was walking up to the restaurant, and she turned around and immediately they start running towards each other so excited to see one another. After hugging and greeting one another

Divya looked at Stephanie and said, "Wow you are more gorgeous now than you were the last time I saw you. Wow girl you are filled out in all the right places and kept that thin waist. I love that your hair is blonder now you look like a young Argentinian young Jennifer Lopez."

Stephanie said, "Thank you so much, Divya! You look amazing too. Girl, I love your hair and this outfit somebody has been hitting the gym look how cut your arms and your legs are. You're still a vegan right? I can't believe it's been so long since we've seen each other. How have you been?"

Divya responds, "Yes, I'm still a vegan! It's been a journey, but it's worth it. And thank you, I've been working out a lot lately and trying to stay healthy. I've been good, just busy with work and life. How about you, what have you been up to?" Stephanie replied, "Same here, just keeping busy with work and trying to balance everything. But I'm glad we were able to make time to catch up.

Stephanie asked Divya, "What happened to us after high school? I can't believe we lost touch, but I know when you got accepted to Cornell that was a huge accomplishment for you."

Divya said Stephanie, "I owe you an apology and I never actually admitted this to you until now but a part of me was very jealous of you in high school you had all the guy's attention you were prom queen. I wanted the attention you got. After I graduated I just kind of wanted to leave high school behind and start fresh and new. After I graduated from Cornell I moved to London and worked over there for a while at a foreign investment firm. I wanted to get some international experience. I was in a relationship that lasted almost two years, I thought we were going to get married, and things fell apart. I just recently got back from India visiting my family yeah mom and dad decided to retire and leave Florida and move back home."

Stephanie listened attentively and nodded in understanding. "Divya, please don't apologize. I completely understand how you felt. I'm sorry if I ever made you feel that way. High school can be tough, and we all have our own insecurities and struggles. But I'm glad we're reconnecting now and that you're doing well. London sounds amazing, and I'm sorry to hear about your relationship. But I hope you've been able to find happiness since then. It's so funny you say that about your family my family is still in the Boca Raton."

Stephanie told Divya "I can't wait for you to meet these ladies who have become friends even though they're my bosses they are just incredible businesswomen and human beings. If I hadn't met them I would still be in a very empty place, I was in a relationship with someone that I didn't truly desire but he just spoiled me I feel like I was in that relationship trying to fill a void of insecurity and then when I met these ladies they taught me so much about myself and elevated me in ways I never thought I could be elevated."

Divya smiled and said, "I'm so happy for you, Stephanie. It's amazing to have such strong and supportive women in your life. I can't wait to meet them and learn from them too."

Stephanie nodded and said, "You'll love them. They're all so different but have such unique perspectives and experiences. And I'm sure they'll be just as excited to meet you and hear about your adventures in London."

While Stephanie and Divya continued to catch up, Elena and Colin were riding around looking at different places where Colin would want to move. They stopped by just one place in North Miami. Colin liked that it was on the beach, but Elena felt like she wanted to make a suggestion and see what he thought about it.

Elena asked Colin, "What do you think about us living together? We're engaged now and we have a lot of wedding planning to do. Plus, there is plenty of room for you to build your office at my place. I know you have a lot of upcoming meetings with Maxwell and Abigail."

Colin took a moment to think and then said, "Honestly, Elena, I think that's a great idea. We are engaged now, and it makes sense for us to start building a life together. And you're right, we do have a lot of wedding planning to do, so living together would make that process much easier. And I appreciate the offer to build my office at your place, that would save me a lot of time and money. Let's do it."

Elena smiled and they share a hug before heading back to her place.

William surprised Bethania and said he got club seats to the Dolphins game tonight and wants to invite all of the ladies and their partners. He also said, "I have two extra tickets for Stephanie if she wants to bring a friend."

Bethania was thrilled and thanked William for the invitation. She immediately group texted the ladies and told them the exciting news. Everyone was excited about the game and agreed to go, except for Stephanie who is still catching up with her old friend Divya.

However, when Bethania tells Stephanie about the extra ticket, she gets excited and decides to invite Divya to the game. Stephanie knows that Divya is a huge football fan, and she thinks it would be a great way for her to get to know the rest of the group. Stephanie texted Bethania back, "Hey girl, thank you so much for the invitation! I'm catching up with Divya today and she would love to come to the game."

So as everyone arrived for the game and made their way into the club seats. Stephanie and Divya decided to ride together, they were the last to get to the club seats as they walked in.

Stephanie said hi to everyone and immediately Cole interrupted Stephanie and said, "Divya" and Charles, James, Harry, and William were all absolutely shocked to see her.

Stephanie said, "You guys know each other?" As all the ladies in the room look at each other suspensefully.

Cole said, "Yes William and Divya dated in London."

James tells Divya "Wow you look so different now"

Charles said, "It's truly a small world and even more in Miami." William had a dear caught in the headlights look on his face and Bethania slapped him on the leg to get his attention. William introduced Bethania, my lady to Divya. As Bethania smiled and checked out Divya and Divya does the same. Stephanie does not know how to process the moment. Bridget, Megan and Jacqueline stir in silence while.

Amber said, "William, I see you don't discriminate who's next Ms. Azerbaijan?"

James looked at Amber and said, "How do you know about her?" Amber chuckled said, "I'm messing with you, but really?"

Divya chuckled nervously and said, "Well, it's great to see all of you again. It's been a while."

Stephanie breaks the awkward silence and said, "Divya and I go way back, we were high school friends." Colin jumped in and said, "Pleasure to the meet you Divya, this is my fiancé, Elena."

Elena said, "Nice to meet you" Everyone agreed, and they settled into their seats.

Stephanie turned to Divya and introduced her to the ladies, "And this is my dear friend Divya, we go way back to high school. "Jacqueline, Bridget, Sabrina, Megan, Amber and Bethania greet Divya warmly, introducing themselves and exchanging pleasantries.

Stephanie adds, "These are the women who have been my greatest inspiration and transformation. They have helped me grow both personally and professionally, and I couldn't be more grateful to have them in my life." Divya smiles and thanks the ladies for their warm welcome.

During the game, they all had a great time cheering on the Dolphins and enjoying the food and drinks. Bethania and Divya hit it off and started chatting about their interests and careers. William felt relieved that everything was going well and tried to focus on the game. Bethania was now intrigued and wanted to get to know more about Williams' past.

After the game, they all head out to a nearby restaurant to grab some dinner. As they sit down to eat

Stephanie pulled Divya aside and said, "I had no idea that you and William used to date. Are you okay?"

Divya smiled and said, "Yes, it was a long time ago and we're both happy with our lives now." Stephanie nods and said, "Okay, just making sure." They both smiled and headed back to the group.

As soon as Bethania and William got into the car together to head home.

Bethania said, "I like Divya, she seems nice it's really nice to get to know your past a little bit. Well, how did you guys meet in London? How come things didn't work out she seems like a great girl?

William looks at Bethania and takes a deep breath. "Divya and I met through work. We were working for the same investment firm and were on the same team. We hit it off quickly and started dating. But after a while, we realized that we had different goals and aspirations for our lives. She wanted to travel and experience different cultures, while I focused more on work and transition to working for the Prime Minister. We ended things amicably and remained friends, but our lives took us in different directions."

Bethania nodded understandingly and said, "It's great that you guys were able to stay friends. It says a lot about your character and how you handle relationships. and I'm happy that you're in my life now."

William smiled at her and took her hand, "Me too, Bethania. You're the best thing that's ever happened to me."

Cole, James, Charles, William, and Harry group text each other about Divya and couldn't believe how different she looks now.

Cole said, "Guys I couldn't believe that was Divya, she looks like a fitness supermodel."

Charles said, "Miami will have that effect on you, look our women we are so lucky."

James chimed in, "She always had the looks, but now she has the body to match."

Harry said, "I can't believe she and William dated in London, small world indeed."

William, who had been quiet during the conversation, finally speaks up, "Yeah, it was a long time ago. We were both young and it just didn't work out. But she seems happy now, and that's what matters."

Cole said, "she aged like a fine wine, but I was worried how Bethania was going to take, did she question you?"

William replied, "She did but it's to be expected, we were all blindsided tonight. Bethania knows about my past relationships, and we trust each other completely."

Amber group text the ladies "what did y'all think about Divya? Bethania are you ok? Why did they have to dress like its New York Fashion week to a football game?"

Jacqueline said, "Amber jealous party of 1"

Bridget responded to Amber's text, "I thought Divya was nice, and she looked amazing. As for the dressing up, I think it's just their personal style."

Megan chimed in, "Yeah, I agree. They all looked great, and it's not like they were the only ones dressed up in the club seats."

Jacqueline adds, "And let's be real, Amber, you always look fabulous no matter what you wear."

Bethania texts, "I'm fine, thank you for asking. Divya seems nice, and it was interesting to learn about William's past."

So as Megan is heading home from the game, she gets an interesting phone call from concierge saying, "Do you know someone named Melanie? She says she's your sister. Megan was so surprised that her baby sister is in Miami, and she didn't tell her she was coming.

Megan's heart skips a beat as she hears the name of her younger sister. She hadn't seen Melanie in years and didn't even know she was in Miami.

She quickly responded to the concierge, "Yes, Melanie is my sister. Is she okay? Why is she at the hotel?" The concierge explained that Melanie had come to Miami for an event and had decided to surprise Megan by staying at the same hotel.

Megan was relieved that her sister is safe and well and felt a rush of excitement at the thought of seeing her after so long. She thanked the concierge for letting her know and made plans to meet up with Melanie later that evening. As she hung up the phone, Megan couldn't help but wonder what her little sister has been up to all these years and looks forward to catching up.

After she hangs up the phone, she told Maxwell "I've got to go back to my place my little sister who I haven't seen in forever is in the lobby."

Maxwell asked her, "Why has it been so long since you've seen your little sister?"

Megan said, "Long story short she got pregnant my father kicked her out my father's a very old school man he had very strict rules in the house. My sister laughed and vanished it's been almost twelve years since I've seen her."

Maxwell nodded sympathetically and said, "I'm sorry to hear that. It must have been hard for you to lose touch with her like that. Are you excited to see her again?"

Megan replied, "Yes, I am. I've missed her so much. I can't wait to catch up and see how she's been doing all these years."

Maxwell smiled and said, "That's great. Let's head back to your place so you can see her."

Megan nods and they head back to the One. As they walk into the lobby, Megan spots her sister Melanie standing there looking nervous and uncertain. Megan rushed over to her, and they embraced a long overdue hug.

Megan said, "Oh my God I cannot believe you're standing right here, how did you find me?"

Melanie said, "Social media plus you have a huge billboard of you and these ladies downtown Miami." Megan introduced Maxwell to Melanie and Melanie said, "So you're dating Boris Kodjoe I see."

Maxwell chuckled and said, "No, I'm not Boris Kodjoe, but I'll take that as a compliment."

Megan laughed and said, "Maxwell is my boyfriend."

Melanie looked surprised but happy for her sister. She said, "I'm glad you found someone who makes you happy, Meg."

Megan said, "Well let's go up to my place so we can catch up." Maxwell said, "I am going to head home for tonight I think you girls probably want to be alone." Melanie nodded in agreement and thanked Maxwell for his understanding. Megan and Melanie then made their way up to Megan's apartment.

Megan said, "I see you're staying here on the hotel side. Tell me what happened after you left? You just vanished; I had always wondered where you were."

Melanie said, "After father kicked me out, I couldn't even stay with my boyfriend because his parents didn't want anything to do with me. We broke up a few weeks later the only money I had at the time was what grandma left me before she died. So, I decided to get on a bus and head West, and I got off in Phoenix AZ. I didn't even know where I was going to stay or what to do but I knew I was on my own. I was able to get a job working in fast food and get a place close by luckily, I was 16 so I had a driver's license and that allowed me to be able to work. A few months later from all the stress of working I miscarried. I ended up gaining a lot of weight but my coworker who became an amazing friend at the time wanted me to stay with her she was worried about me."

Melanie continued, "I felt so alone and abandoned I had contemplated suicide. There were so many times I wanted to call home, but I was afraid if I tried to reach you, father would cut you off. I eventually worked up the courage to get my GED and I enrolled into University of Arizona. At this time, I was working two jobs trying to make it through school and didn't really have much time for a social life, just trying to survive. Around the holidays, Thanksgiving and Christmas seeing friends of mine go home to their families it was lonely for many years having Christmas and Thanksgiving alone. At this point stage my self-esteem, self-worth was just at an all-time low I started doing drugs. And then I met someone that I worked with that made me feel like I was worthy of love. And we started going to the gym together. He would meal prep and teach me about nutrition and I started losing a lot of weight and my body just changed my health improved. His mom took me in because she was a psychologist, so it was easy for me to open up and talk to her. One night we had just left a concert coming home and as we were walking back to the car these guys jumped us, they robbed him and sexually assaulted me. We were never the same after that."

Megan was sitting in her living room listening to her sister speak and she started crying and feeling guilty feeling like she could have done something.

Melanie continued, "After that, I just couldn't stay in Arizona anymore. I needed a fresh start, a new environment. So, I moved to Los Angeles and started over. It was tough, but I found a job and started going to therapy to work through everything that had happened to me. And now, here I am in Miami, trying to get back on my feet again." Megan wipes away her tears and takes her sister's hand, "I am so sorry, Melanie. I had no idea that you were going through all of this. I wish I had been there for you. But now, I am here, and I am not going to let you go through anything alone anymore. We are going to get through this together." Melanie smiled and hugged her sister, "Thank you, Megan. I missed you so much. And I am glad that you are here for me now."

Melanie asked Megan "I never thought you would ever be living in Florida. I thought you would always be in New York, you always wanted to live there ever since high school. I'm so proud of you for all your success. I'm just glad to see you're doing well. Have you talked with mom and dad?"

Megan replied, "Thanks, Mel. It's been a wild ride, but I'm grateful for where I am now. And no, I haven't talked to Mom and Dad in a while.

Megan said, "I never forgave dad for kicking you out I thought he was being too harsh. But when I left to go to Philly for school, I knew coming back home wasn't going to be that often. I'm thankful for our upbringing because it made me very tough and competitive, it's the reason why I have so much fire to be successful. The love that I wanted I felt like dad couldn't give it to us. So, I shared it to my wonderful girlfriends who are all living with me now in Miami."

Megan asked, "how do you like living in Los Angeles? Which part of LA are you living in? Melanie replied, "I live in the Westwood area near UCLA. It's a nice neighborhood, and I love the fact that I can walk to all sorts of great restaurants, cafes, and shops. I also love that it's close to the beach and to other cool neighborhoods like Santa Monica and Venice. Overall, I really enjoy living in LA. It's a vibrant and diverse city with so much to offer."

Megan said, "You look absolutely phenomenal I noticed that the gym has paid off."

Melanie replied, "Thank you sis it was a rough ride to get here, but after I became vegan life forever changed. Once I started making money, I will admit I wasn't looking good. I went and got some cosmetic procedures to help elevate my look I didn't feel confident in myself. I'll admit the drugs took a toll on me, but once I got my mental health right. I learned the most important thing is to look in the mirror and know how to love yourself. That started a long healing process for me, I started going to church in LA and my church family has been really very supportive."

Melanie said, "Sis I know it's late I'm going to go but I'm so happy to see that you're doing well, I wanted you to know that I'm OK."

Megan hugged Melanie and said, "I'm so glad you're here, and that you're doing well. Let's stay in touch and catch up more soon." Melanie hugged her back and said, "Yes, let's do that." They exchanged phone numbers and said their goodbyes. Megan watched her sister leave, feeling a mix of emotions. She was happy to have reconnected with her sister, but also sad about the difficult experiences

Melanie had been through. She made a mental note to keep in touch with her sister more often and offer any support she could.

Just before Melanie walked out the door, Megan asked her "what are you doing tomorrow?"

Melanie said, "I was going to check out Wynwood and probably just hit the beach." Megan said, "Can I join you?"

Melanie smiles and said, "Of course, it would be great to spend some time with you."

Megan and Melanie made plans to meet up the next day and explored Wynwood and the beach together. They hugged and said their goodbyes for the night, and Melanie heads back to her hotel. Megan sits on the couch, reflecting on the conversation she had with her sister. She realizes how much she missed her and is grateful to have reconnected with her.

On the other side of Biscayne Bay, James had noticed that Amber hadn't been feeling like herself lately.

He asked Amber, "What's going on sweetheart? You certainly haven't been yourself lately."

Amber said, "Why do you think that?"

James replied, "You haven't been wanting to be intimate lately."

Amber takes a deep breath and said, "I'm late with my cycle and I'm afraid to take a pregnancy test."

James put his hand on Amber's arm and said, "It's okay, Amber. We'll figure this out together." He told her that no matter what the result of the test revealed, they will face it together and make a plan for their future. Amber felt comforted by James' words and they both agreed to take the test together the next morning.

The following day, they head to the drugstore to pick up a pregnancy test. Amber was nervous and James was supportive, holding her hand while they waited for the results. The test came back positive, Amber burst into tears, feeling overwhelmed and scared.

James held her tightly, telling her that they would figure everything out and that they would make a great team. He assured her that they would be good parents and that they would love their child unconditionally.

Over the next few days, Amber and James discussed their options and made plans. They decided that they wanted to keep the baby and started preparing for the arrival of their child.

Despite the initial shock, Amber and James were excited and happy about becoming parents. They know that there will be challenges along the way, but they are ready to face them together as a team.

The next day, Amber couldn't sleep too much through the night thinking about becoming a mother, she was processing myriad of thoughts and emotions. Megan was lying in bed thinking about everything her sister shared with her. Bethania was thinking about all that transpired at the game. Jacqueline was thinking about organizing a trip to Chicago, so Harry could meet her family. Sabrina and Charles were discussing on the way home last night about his parents coming to Miami, she started wondering will his family accept her the way her family accepted him.

Cole called Bridget and said, "I have a surprise for you I didn't want to share it last night are you free if I come over?"

Bridget said, "Sure are you hungry? I can make some breakfast." He replied, "Breakfast sounds lovely I'll be there in about 30 minutes."

Bridget said, "Wonderful I'll let concierge know you're coming, and I'll leave the door open." After Bridget hung up the phone, she was wondering what's the prize could this be. It didn't seem like a bad surprise according to Cole's voice that she was pondering in her mind.

Bridget heard the front door open, and Cole surprised her with a cute little golden retriever named Marley. Cole said, "Marley this is your mommy."

Bridget said, "She's cute and adorable let me hold her." As Marley stared at Bridget with her golden fur and big, dark eyes, Marley was an adorable little pup who loves to play and cuddle.

Cole said, "She's full of energy and loves to run around, play with toys, and explore her surroundings."

Bridget said, "You know me so well oh my gosh I love dogs." Bridget gave Cole a hug and said, "Give me a kiss. Marley leans over and starts licking Bridget and Cole's face."

Cole chuckled and said, "Looks like Marley already approves of us as her new family." Bridget nods and smiled, "She's a sweetheart, I can already tell." Cole then tells Bridget that he adopted Marley from a local shelter and that she was one of the few remaining puppies there. Bridget's heart melts at the thought of giving Marley a forever home, and she thanked Cole for the wonderful surprise. They spend the rest of the morning playing with Marley and bonding as a new little family.

Megan group texted the girls and said, "Let's all get together for lunch I have so much to share since last night at the game." The ladies replied.

Bridget said, "Sounds good, what time and where should we meet?"

Jacqueline says, "Count me in! I'm free anytime today."

Sabrina replied, "I'm in, but I have a meeting until 1 pm. Can we meet after that?"

Bethania said, "I'm free for lunch, just let me know the time and place."

Amber chimed in, "I might be a little late, I have a doctor's appointment this morning, but I'll join you guys as soon as I can."

Elena mentioned "I'll be there I may be there I'm just helping Colin finish move some of his stuff in getting his office set up."

Stephanie said, "I should be able to the movers are moving in our new office furniture today."

Megan said, 'How about we meet at that new seafood place downtown at 2 pm?"

Bridget said, "Perfect, see you all there!"

Megan decided to text her sister and said, "Can you meet me for lunch downtown it's near your hotel at around 2:00 PM?"

Melanie said, "Sure, that works for me. Where should we meet?" Megan shared with her the details and said, "I'll see you in a little bit."

So, when the ladies arrived for lunch they hugged and greeted each other. As the hostess walks them to their table and after they set down Bridget looked at Megan and said, "What's the surprise?" There comes Melanie walking into the restaurant Megan saw her. Megan noticed she looked so much different than last night. Melanie was dressed in a very gorgeous revealing dress with some very nice stilettos. Megan said, "Ladies this is the surprise this is my sister Melanie we finally reunited after so many years of losing contact."

The ladies stood up and introduced themselves and hugged Melanie.

Amber said, "Wow Megan I see gorgeous women just run in your family." Jacqueline agreed, "I agree, Melanie you are so beautiful how did you find and reconnect with each other?"

Melanie said, "Thank you ladies it's an absolute pleasure to meet each of you. To answer your question Jacqueline, it was literally through social media and then you can't miss the huge billboard that you guys have of yourselves downtown. You guys are the wonderful ladies my sister was telling me about. Congratulations to each of you all on your success it is truly inspiring and very inspirational."

Sabrina asked "What do you do for work? I'm sure you're quite talented just like your sister."

Stephanie walked in running a little late and said, "I'm sorry guys but all the furniture has been moved into our new office space. I have already tested the Internet to see if it's working so we can start moving our stuff in when we're ready. I'm sorry to interrupt who is this beautiful lady?"

Melanie said, "I was literally just wondering the same thing" While Stephanie was checking out Melanie and Melanie reciprocated.

Megan chimed in and said, "Stephanie, this is my sister Melanie. We just reunited after many years."

Stephanie said, "Oh wow, it's so nice to meet you, Melanie. Welcome to our group."

The ladies all smiled and continued with their introductions and small talk. They ordered their food and drinks, catching up on each other's lives and sharing stories from their week.

While they were eating, Melanie said, "My apologies Sabrina let me answer your question I'm fashion designer I have my own store in LA. This dress I have on is one of mine that I designed. There's a music artist on tour here in Miami that wanted to wear my line for the concert and upcoming music video I'm just overseeing my team making sure everything goes smoothly."

Sabrina was impressed and said, "Wow, that's amazing! You must be talented."

Melanie nodded and thanked Sabrina for her kind words.

Stephanie chimed in, "I would love to see your store next time I'm in LA. Do you have a website or social media page where we can check out your designs?"

Melanie smiled and said, "Absolutely, I'll share my information with you all before we leave today."

The ladies continued to chat about fashion, design, and business, exchanging ideas and tips.

Elena said, "I need a wedding dress and dresses for the bridesmaid which are all these ladies here do you think you can design all of that for us Melanie?"

Melanie smiled and said, "Of course, I would be honored to design your wedding dress and dresses for your bridesmaids, Elena. I can guarantee that the dresses will be stunning and will make your special day even more memorable." The ladies chimed in and expressed their excitement at the prospect of having Melanie design their dresses.

Melanie shared a little about her life and more about her work. They all listened attentively, impressed by her accomplishments and her positive energy. It's clear that Melanie has made a great first impression on the ladies and they're excited to get to know her better.

Melanie said, "Excuse me ladies I need to use the ladies' room.

Stephanie said, "I'll join you." Melanie caught Stephanie checking her out. As they walked to the restroom together, they chatted.

Melanie turned to Stephanie and said, "I couldn't help but notice you checking me out earlier. Is everything okay?"

Stephanie blushed and said, "I'm sorry, I didn't mean to make it obvious. It's just that you're so beautiful and I couldn't help but admire your dress."

Melanie smiled and said, "Thank you, that's very sweet of you to say. You look phenomenal, by the way."

Sabrina said, "Megan I see success just radiates in your family." Megan replied, "Thank you Sabrina but her story of how she got to where she is baffling and emotional so much more inspiring than mine that's a true survivor. My father kicked out Melanie when she was 16 and to see where she is now it's incredible. Her and I are six years apart in age, with some parts of me feeling like I should have fought more to try to find her."

As Stephanie and Melanie returned Melanie said, "I absolutely love how each one of you all are dressed so classy regal beautiful." The ladies thanked Melanie for the compliments and smiled at each other.

Amber said, "Ladies I have an announcement, but I want you to know I'm having mixed emotions. It's confirmed I am pregnant." The ladies were excited and overjoyed but Amber is not so much.

Amber said, "James is more excited about the news than I am. I know he will be a phenomenal father he's an amazing boyfriend."

Megan laid a comforting hand on Amber's arm and said, "It's okay to have mixed emotions, Amber. Having a baby is a big life change, and it's natural to feel a bit overwhelmed. But you have a great support system here, and we'll all be here to help you through it."

Sabrina chimed in, "And just think of all the cute baby clothes and toys we can spoil your little one with!" The ladies share a laugh, and Amber can't help but smile. She felt grateful for her friends and their love and support.

As the ladies continued to enjoy their lunch suddenly

Sabrina said, "James is here."

Amber turned and noticed James was walking towards their table. Amber said, "James what's wrong what are you doing here?"

James said, "Ever since you told me the news that you're pregnant Amber I can't see myself being with anyone else but you."

James got down on one knee, Amber was completely surprised, and the ladies were in shock. James displayed a small box from his pocket and opened it, it revealed a beautiful diamond ring.

He looked up at Amber and said, "Amber, you're the love of my life and I want to spend the rest of my life with you. Will you marry me?"

Amber was speechless for a moment, tears welling up in her eyes. She looked at James and then at the ring before she nodded her head and said, "Yes, James, I will marry you!" The ladies were cheering and clapping as James slipped the ring onto Amber's finger and they share a kiss.

Stephanie said, "Oh my gosh, this is the best news ever!" and the ladies agree. They all congratulated the newly engaged couple as they were holding hands and smiled at each other. Amber said, "I can't believe this is happening. I'm so happy."

The rest of the lunch was filled with excitement and chatted as the ladies discussed wedding plans. It's a memorable day that they'll never forget.

Stephanie said to the ladies, "After a day like today I think I'm just going to hit the beach and relax."

Melanie said, "That sounds fabulous you mind if I join you?"

Stephanie said, "Sure my friend Divya is going to join us."

Bridget said, "I would love to join you, but I want to see Cole he got us a puppy name Marley she's so adorable. Bridget shares pictures of her with the ladies from her phone."

The ladies all said, "aww" over the pictures of Marley and Bridget's face lights up with joy.

Jacqueline said, "I'm up for some beach time too, count me in." Sabrina said, "I'll probably hit the spa and get a massage, you ladies enjoy the beach."

Amber said, "I'll join you Sabrina, a massage sounds amazing right now."

Elena said, "I think I'll join you ladies at the beach, I could use some sun."

Megan said, "You have to bring Marley to the office, and we could definitely use that little bundle of joy as we're working. Also, ladies tomorrow let's meet at the office so we can talk about which offices were going to be setting in bring your stuff as well."

As the ladies head out Stephanie told Elena, Megan, Jacqueline and Melanie "I'm just going to shower and change and get my beach stuff you guys just want to meet at Megan and Elena place since they live right on the beach? I'll let Divya know to meet at the One hotel."

Jacqueline, Elena, Divya Stephanie Melanie met at Megan's, Stephanie introduced Melanie to Divya then Megan escorted them down to the beach. As the ladies got settled, they found a perfect spot for some sun.

Melanie said, "That might have been the most eventful lunch I've ever attended. Amber announces she's pregnant and gets a proposal that is a lot to take in."

Stephanie said, "Divya you missed a very interesting lunch."

Divya said, "Oh my what happened?"

Stephanie said, "Remember Amber from the football games the tall blonde looks like Margot Robbie?"

Divya said, "Oh yeah she definitely has a sense of humor."

Stephanie said, "She told us she's pregnant and then probably no more than 30 minutes later after the announcement her boyfriend now fiancé proposes to her at the lunch."

Stephanie also said, "Colin and James have great taste in engagement rings Elena and Amber you guys are so lucky."

Megan said, "Elena I'm still laughing and chuckling at times thinking about how you and Colin first met when we were all at Kiki on the River. I can't believe you got up from our table walked over to that bar and hit on him."

Elena said, "it got me a ring didn't it."

Divya ask the ladies "Who is that tall redhead walking this way she looks like she knows us."

Megan said, "That's Abigail my boyfriend's business partner."

Melanie said, "Do all the women in Miami look like they're ready to pose for Playboy?" All the ladies turned to her and said, "Yes." As Abigail walked over and said, "I thought that was you Megan, Elena, Stephanie, Jacqueline, and who are these other two beautiful ladies?"

Megan said, "This is Divya and my little sister Melanie."

Abigail smiled warmly and greeted each of them, making small talk and exchanging pleasantries. Divya can't help but notice the way Abigail seems to radiate confidence and charisma and feels a twinge of jealousy.

As they chat, Melanie spokes up and said, "So, Abigail, do you always look like you're ready to pose for Playboy centerfold?"

The rest of the ladies' groan and roll their eyes, but Abigail just laughs it off. "I'll take that as a compliment," she said with a grin. "But no, I don't always dress like this. I just like to make a statement, you know?"

Melanie nods, impressed by Abigail's confidence. "I hear you. You make a statement."

Elena asked Abigail, "So what brings you back to Miami?"

Abigail said, "For two reasons, I wanted to meet your fiancé since he's going to be subcontracting with us and second, I'm looking for a second home down here. Maxwell said I need to contact Bethania."

Stephanie said, "That's awesome Bethania is great to work with when it comes to finding the right home."

Elena nods, "That sounds great. I'm glad you were able to come down and meet Colin. And yes, Bethania is definitely the person you want to talk to about finding a second home here in Miami. She knows the market inside and out, and she'll be able to help you find the perfect place."

Abigail smiled, "That's what I've heard. I'll be reaching out to her soon."

Stephanie chimed in, "And if you need any help with the design or renovation of your new place, let me know. I have a lot of experience in that area."

Abigail was impressed, "That's great to know. I'll definitely keep that in mind."

Megan said, "How about you join us Abigail says well thank you very much I would love to."

Abigail asked, "Melanie so are you talented just like your older sister?"

Melanie responded, "My sister is one-of-a-kind, but I hold my own."

Abigail said, "What do you do?"

Melanie said, "I'm a fashion designer I have my own boutique and Los Angeles and possibly thinking about expanding to the East Coast."

Divya and Abigail said, "Really what's your website and social media?" Stephanie laughed how ironic both of you all say that at the same time.

The ladies pulled out their phones and checked out Melanie's website and her social media and they were emphatically impressed at Melanie's fashion designs. The scroll through pictures of beautiful dresses, chic outfits, and trendy accessories.

Divya speaks up, "Wow, Melanie, I'm loading up the cart right now. Your creations are absolutely stunning."

Melanie smiled, "Thank you, Divya. I've always been passionate about fashion, and I'm so glad that I can share my designs with others."

Stephanie adds, "These outfits are so unique and stylish. I love the way you mix and match different fabrics and textures."

Elena nodded, "Yeah, and I love how your designs are so versatile. They can be dressed up or down, and they work for so many different occasions."

Abigail chimed in, "And the accessories are just as amazing as the clothes. I love the statement jewelry and the bold purses."

Melanie said, "Thank you so much ladies it was a long hard journey to get here. Whatever you guys order I'm all make sure to reimburse you for the shipping that's on me. I have a fashion show that I'm putting on but with the pandemic restrictions still in Los Angeles I think I'm going to move it to Miami."

The ladies all smiled and nodded in agreement, expressing their excitement at the prospect of attending Melanie's fashion show in Miami.

Divya said, "That sounds amazing, Melanie. I'd be happy to help you with any logistics or planning you might need. Just let me know what I can do to assist."

Melanie was grateful, "Thank you so much, Divya. That would be incredible. I'll take you up on that offer."

Abigail adds, "And if there's anything I can do to help with the event planning or promotion, please let me know as well. I have a lot of connections in the fashion industry down here in Miami."

Melanie nods, "That's great to know, Abigail. Thank you. I'll keep that in mind."

Megan said, "Make sure each of you get my sister's number I appreciate each of you supporting her and you know I'm about to load up that cart. I already see some fashion that will suit me here in Miami."

Jacqueline said, "I'm pulling out my credit card now."

Megan told the ladies, "I'm going to have to go back inside I need to do some work from my home office." The rest of the ladies decided to stay a little while longer and chat.

Abigail asked Melanie and Divya, "What are two gorgeous women like you doing here? Where are your boyfriends at? Are you guys single ready to mingle?"

Divya said, "Dating in South Florida is very challenging just look at all the competition you have to deal with all the women here are so gorgeous especially in Miami so it makes it hard to find a really good guy that's all about you."

Melanie said, "Yeah and the dating scene in Los Angeles certainly has its challenges as well but I'm in a relationship with my business. We all can't be lucky like Bridget, Elena, Megan, Bethania, Amber and Sabrina."

Melanie looked directly at Elena and said, "Megan told me the back story of how you guys found these amazing men y'all haven't even been in Miami a hot minute."

Elena said, "I will admit ladies it wasn't like we were all just looking but we certainly got lucky I feel very fortunate to have found Colin."

Divya asked, "Where is Colin from?"

Elena shared, "Colin Sorensen is from Oslo, Norway we just got back from meeting his family that's where he proposed to me. It was at this beautiful park that he used to go to a lot growing up. I feel he is truly godsend he so attentive and caring and loving and supportive and he just understands me. The thing I love about him the most he's consistent and I think that's one of the things that that we love about the men we're with is they are very consistent."

The ladies responded with nods and murmurs of agreement.

Abigail said, "Consistency is key in any relationship, for sure. And it sounds like you all have found some real gems in your partners."

Divya adds, "Yeah, I think it's important to have someone who really gets you and supports you, especially in a city like Miami where it can be so competitive and fast-paced."

Melanie chimed in, "Absolutely. And it's nice to see that you guys have found love in unexpected places. Maybe there's hope for the rest of us yet!"

Elena shared some advice with the ladies, "The most important thing is as long as you're working on yourself prioritizing yourself the right man is going to come along he's going to match you where you are. Colin is a very good-looking man he can get any woman he wants in Miami. I told him I'm not your average girl and he respected that and once he truly started to get to know me we realize that we were more right for each other. I took him out of his mental hemisphere of what he's normally used to. I'll admit I had always envisioned myself being married but I never envisioned my husband could possibly look like him."

Stephanie said, "When I saw him at the game I was like OK Elena I'm not going to even lie I had some jealousy vibes he is very gorgeous."

Divya said, "I agree with Stephanie he had a very humble spirit about him he wasn't cocky or arrogant. Normally guys who look like that they're ego is the size of the Statue of Liberty."

Abigail said, "Show us a picture of you guys."

Elena pulled out her phone and showed a picture of them.

Abigail said, "Yeah he is gorgeous he definitely looks like Thor." Elena laughed and said, "Yes, I can see the resemblance. But he's even more handsome in person, trust me. Well ladies it has been a pleasure chatting with you all I'm going to get home and relax and see what my man is up to since we just moved in together, we're still getting settled in."

Jacqueline said, "I'm going to head home too, have fun ladies."

Stephanie said, "You get to look at that every day we're living vicariously through you and Jacqueline."

The ladies laughed and nod in agreement as Elena and Jacqueline bid them farewell and headed out. As she walked to the One, Elena thought about how lucky she was to have found Colin and to be living in such a beautiful city with great friends.

Divya said, "I noticed how you two have been looking at each other so let's address the elephant in the room what's going on?"

Melanie also said, "I noticed that vibe too."

Stephanie and Abigail were shocked at Divya comments.

Divya also said, "Stephanie, I know you I know it's been a long time, but some things don't change."

Abigail said, "Divya are you good at keeping secrets?"

Divya said, "We're adults and we're amongst friends your secrets are safe with me it."

Abigail said, "Stephanie and I hooked up once."

Stephanie had her hands over her face in total disbelief at what had just transpired.

Divya said, "I knew something was up by the way you looked at Stephanie when you were walking this way."

Stephanie took a deep breath and said, "Yeah, it's true. We had a moment. We decided to keep it between us. It was a one-time thing."

Abigail nods in agreement and adds, "We didn't want it to affect our friendship, so we agreed to keep it a secret." Divya said, "I totally get it"

Melanie said, "It's all good but you guys are very gorgeous. Miami is such a very special place I mean the women here are just breathtakingly gorgeous since I've been here, I almost wanted to get a few girls numbers."

Melanie said, "Well since we are the single ones in the group you guys want to go out tonight?"

Divya, Stephanie, Abigail looked at each and said, "What did you have in mind? How about we check out Mila Lounge tonight?"

Melanie said, "Yeah, I was thinking of checking out Mila tonight. It's a great spot for drinks and dancing, and I've heard they have a good DJ tonight."

Divya said, "Sounds like fun, count me in!" Stephanie and Abigail nod in agreement, and Abigail adds, "I haven't been there yet, so I'm excited to check it out." Melanie said, "Awesome, it's settled then. We'll meet at Mila at 10 pm tonight.

Sabrina and Amber were enjoying their wonderful spa treatment together.

Sabrina asked Amber, "How were you taking it all in? I know you've been having mixed emotions about being pregnant and now being engaged. These are some major life decisions when you first got to Miami, you said you didn't want to be locked down or in a relationship and here you are pregnant and engaged. What changed?"

Amber said, "Sabrina I'm seriously just trying to take it all in it's so much the process right now. I haven't even told my parents yet, but James is different than any guy I've ever been with the way he looks at me, the way he wants to understand me, I've never felt so desired so differently. It's crazy because I wasn't looking for any of this and I don't know if it's the universe telling me I really need to accept all of this, and this is what I need. You and I are both very blessed to have the men that we have, and we got good men and it's so hard to find. James truly desires me, and he desires wanting to have this baby and a life with me what scares me the most is my level of desire doesn't match his."

Sabrina nods and listens attentively. "It's understandable to feel scared and uncertain, especially when you're not sure if your desires match your partner's. But remember, relationships are about compromise and communication. It's important to have an open and honest conversation with James about your feelings and concerns. That way, you both can work together to find a solution that works for both of you."

Sabrina takes a deep breath and adds, "And as for telling your parents, just know that they love you and will support you no matter what. It might be scary, but it's important to be honest with them and let them know what's going on."

Amber nods, as she listened to Sabrina's words to heart. "Thanks, Sabrina. You always know what to say. It really sucks that I can't have a drink right now because I need one the most but I'm popping prenatal vitamins like popcorn in the movie theater. I just need to give myself a little time to process all of this before I can really have a heart to heart with James."

Jacqueline and Harry decided to spend the evening together smuggling on her day bed on the balcony of her place. She told Harry it's time for us to go to Chicago so you can meet my family.

Harry smiled and said, "I'd love to meet your family, Jacqueline. I've heard so much about them from you and I'm excited to see where you grew up and meet the people who shaped you into the amazing person you are today." He leaned in and gave her a kiss on the forehead.

Bethania finished up with work early and she decided to hit the gym for a little bit now she's working on her new routine. When she arrived home, she decided to take a quick shower and she was going to surprise William. She texted William and asked him, "Will you be home in couple of hours?"

William said, "Sure I'll be finishing up my work out by then." She replied, "Perfect I'll see you soon."

Bethania decided she was going to wear this new lingerie that she hadn't had a chance to wear yet and was going to surprise William. She found a beautiful black lace push-up bra that had intricate details and a matching thong with a strappy design on the back. She also picked up a black satin robe with lace detailing to complete the look. The bra and panties were both comfortable and sexy, designed to accentuate her curves and make her feel confident. The robe added an extra touch of elegance and sophistication to the ensemble. Overall, it was the perfect combination of sexy and classy, and Bethania couldn't wait to surprise William with her new lingerie.

Bethania left her place and walked to her car only having the satin robe and her red bottoms. She arrived at Williams place, as she got out of the car and walked up she gets to the concierge desk she says I'm here for William Edwards the concierge opens the elevator let her up to William floor. As she exits the elevator, as random men and women pass her and can't help but to turn their heads and admire the view. She knocks on William door, and he opens the door with absolute shock and amazement as she slowly walks into his place.

William said, "Bethania Diaz I can't believe you came over here only wearing that robe" as she slowly unties the robe Bethania said, "I bet Divya never came over like this" as she slowly takes the robe off. William is stunned and speechless as he took in the sight of Bethania in her lingerie. He finally managed to say, "Wow, Bethania, you look stunning. I can't believe you went through all this trouble just to surprise me." Bethania walked towards him with a seductive smile and said, "Anything for you, William." William pulls her into a passionate embrace as they share a steamy kiss. Then he takes her by the hand and escorts her to his bedroom.

Bethania can feel her heart racing with anticipation as they make their way to the bed. William turns to face her and takes her hands in his, "Bethania, I want to make this a night you will never forget," he says with a loving gaze. Bethania nods, lost for words as William begins to caress her body, starting with her neck and shoulders and moving down to her breasts, tracing the contours of her lingerie with his fingers. They spend the night exploring each other's bodies, lost in a world of passion and desire.

Elena arrived home from the beach she was surprised to notice that Colin had made dinner, there are rose pedals on the floor, candles are lit and soft music is playing in the background. Elena was taken aback by the romantic atmosphere that Colin has created.

She asked, "What's all this, Colin? You've really gone all out."

Colin responded with a grin, "Just wanted to do something special for you tonight. I hope you like it." Elena felt her heart skip a beat and tears begin to form in her eyes. She's touched by Colin's thoughtfulness and effort to make her feel special. They sit down to eat the delicious dinner that Colin has prepared, and as they eat, they talk and laugh and enjoy each other's company. After dinner, Colin surprised Elena with a gift a beautiful necklace that he had picked out especially for her. Elena was overwhelmed by the gesture and threw her arms around Colin in a tight embrace.

Elena said to Colin "Come with me as the walk to their master bathroom" she runs the waterfall shower.

She told Colin, "Come join me" Colin smiled and followed Elena into the bathroom. As they both stepped into the shower, the warm water cascaded down their bodies, relaxing their muscles. Elena turned around and looked at Colin, her eyes filled with desire. She ran her hands through his wet hair and leaned in to kiss him, their lips meeting in a fiery embrace. The steam from the shower filled the bathroom as their passion intensified. As they continued to kiss, Colin slowly moved his hands down Elena's back, feeling the curves of her body. Elena moaned softly as his touch sent shivers down her spine. They both know that this is just the beginning of a long, hot, and steamy night together.

Maxwell and Megan decided they were going to ride and take a look at the new office space and see Megan's new office. Megan was curious about how Stephanie had organized the furniture and she just couldn't wait to see it the next day.

On the ride over Maxwell said to Megan, "How are things going with Melanie?"

She mentioned, "Things are going quite well thank you so much for asking I'm still very touched and bothered by her story of where she is now from where she started." Megan slowly started to have a tear come down her face Maxwell starts to reach over with his hand on her leg and rubs it and said, "Hey I understand."

When they arrived at the building and entered the elevator Maxwell said, "This is a great location." They were both carrying a few boxes that Megan had for her office, as they walked into the office for the first time she is completely blown away by how well Stephanie and the movers and everyone organized everything. Megan walked into her corner office set the box down her and Maxwell were just mesmerized by what they saw.

Megan looked around her new office with a mix of excitement and awe. The space is well-lit with natural light pouring in from the large windows, and the view of the city skyline is breathtaking. The office furniture was sleek and modern, with a large desk and comfortable-looking chairs. On one wall, there is a bookshelf stocked with books and decorative items, while on another wall has a large whiteboard for brainstorming and planning.

Maxwell looked at Megan and said, "This is quite the setup, Megan. I think you're going to love working here."

Megan nods, a smile spreading across her face. "I already do, Maxwell. I can't thank you enough for helping me tonight."

Maxwell walked over to Megan and said, "You can thank me now" he lifted Megan and set her on her desk slowly starts kissing her on her cheek and down her neck as he slowly undresses her. Megan feels a shiver run down her spine as Maxwell's lips move down her neck. She wraps her arms around his shoulders, pulling him closer to her. As he slowly undressed her, he whispered sweet nothings into her ear, sending chills down her body. Their bodies entwine as they give in to their passion, the office becoming a playground for their desires. The large windows provide a backdrop of the city lights, as they explored each other's bodies in the dimly lit room. Megan moaned softly as Maxwell's touch sends waves of pleasure through her. Their bodies moved together in a perfect rhythm as they give in to their primal urges. Hours pass, and they laid naked on the office floor, both exhausted but satisfied. Megan looked up at Maxwell, a content smile on her face. "I never expected my first night in the new office to be like this," she said with a laugh.

Maxwell looked down at her, a grin on his face. "Well, we can't let this beautiful space go to waste," he said, pulling her in for another kiss.

Megan giggles and wraps her arms around him. As they lay there,

Megan's heart races with excitement. She can feel the heat building between them as they become more and more intimate.

Maxwell's hands roam over Megan's body, exploring every curve and contour. She moans softly as he finds all her sweet spots, sending waves of pleasure through her body. Megan ran her fingers on Maxwell's head, pulling him closer to her as their passion intensifies.

Finally, as they stand there naked and breathless,

Maxwell whispers in Megan's ear, "I've wanted you for so long, Megan. You're everything I've ever wanted in a woman."

Megan smiles, feeling overwhelmed with emotion. Megan said, "Let's go back to my place you can tell me more about that."

Cole, Bridget and Marley are making it a movie night as they are enjoying Marley as their new little addition. Bridget suggested to Cole "Marley can stay with me full time I know you're going to be busy with work at the hospital."

Cole said, "OK if it becomes too much, we can split the time and I can get a dog sitter at times." Bridget leaned to kiss Cole. Marley stands up on her hind legs on the couch demanding some attention as well.

Cole said, "I'm going to go take a shower real quick freshen up"

Bridget said, "OK" as Marley sat on her lap.

Bridget and Marley relaxed on Cole's couch the moment she hears the shower run and she slowly gets up from the couch she told Marley, "Stay right here I'll leave the movie running I'll be right back." Bridget walked towards the bathroom where Cole was taking his shower, she slowly starts removing her earrings and articles of clothing, enters in the bathroom and gets in the shower and told him I don't think I properly thanked you for Marley.

Cole was surprised to see Bridget entering the shower with him, but he couldn't help but be turned on by her bold move. As the warm water cascaded over their bodies, Bridget began to kiss him passionately. Cole responded with equal enthusiasm, running his hands over her smooth skin.

Bridget breaks away from the kiss and looked into Cole's eyes. "I really appreciate everything you've done for Marley and me, Cole. You're such a kind and caring person."

Cole smiled at her and said, "I just want to take care of you both. You mean a lot to me."

They continued to kiss and explored each other's bodies under the running water. The steamy shower becomes a haven for their desire as they lose themselves in the moment.

As Melanie, Divya, Abigail, and Stephanie get ready for girls' night. Melanie started a group text for all the ladies,

Melanie asked the ladies, "You ready for a wild night tonight in Miami?"

 Divya replied, "Yes, can't wait for the first round of drinks!"

Abigail chimed in, "Definitely, I need a break from work and some fun."

Stephanie responds, "I'm so excited, we should try that new rooftop bar, and everyone's been talking about then to Mila."

Abigail said, "First round of drinks is on me."

As the ladies gather at the rooftop bar, Divya catches everyone's attention with her black mini dress that perfectly hugs her slim figure, featuring a plunging neckline and a thigh-high slit. Stephanie's dress is a showstopper too, a red halter-neck gown with a low-cut back, revealing just enough skin to turn heads. Abigail stuns in her shimmering gold wrap dress that highlights her figure, and Melanie's bold choice of a bright purple cocktail dress with a deep V-neckline and a daring slit up the side makes her stand out from the crowd. All four ladies look confident, sexy, and ready to have a wild night in Miami.

Abigail asked, "Why is it we didn't invite any of the other ladies out tonight?"

Melanie said, "They're all in wonderful, committed relationships we are single and ready to mingle and have some fun. Relationship girls can't do what single girls do."

Divya giggles and adds, "Yeah, we're just living our best lives and enjoying our freedom."

Stephanie nods in agreement, "Exactly, no need to worry about anyone else's schedule or plans. We can just go where the night takes us."

Abigail raised her glass, "Cheers to the single ladies!" The other ladies clink their glasses together and take a sip of their drinks.

As they chatted and enjoyed the atmosphere of the rooftop bar, a group of men approach their table. One of them, a tall and handsome man, introduced himself to the ladies and asked if they would like to join them for a drink.

The ladies exchange glances and smiled, and Melanie said, "Sure, we'd love to!" As they follow the men to their table, they feel a sense of excitement and anticipation for the night ahead.

Chapter 13

It's the ladies first day in their new Brickell headquarters. Each of them was ecstatic to get settled into their designated offices. Bethania brought in some artwork that she thought would look good with the décor.

As they walked into their respective offices, they were greeted with a blank canvas. Each of them began to think about how they could decorate and personalize their space. Bethania, who had a keen eye for design, immediately went to work. She had brought along some artwork that she thought would look great with the office's decor.

Bethania carefully placed the artwork on the walls, taking care to choose the perfect spot for each piece. She stepped back and admired her work, pleased with the way it added a pop of color and personality to the room.

Megan walked by, stopped and took notice. "Wow, Bethania, that looks amazing! I love how it ties in with the rest of the space."

Bridget, who was also nearby, agreed. "Yeah, it really makes the room feel more inviting and comfortable."

Elena, Sabrina, Amber, and Jacqueline soon joined in, admiring Bethania's artwork, and discussing their own plans for decorating their offices. They all wanted to make their space reflect their unique personalities and styles.

Stephanie soon walked in the office and admired what was transpiring feeling slightly a bit hungover from last night with Melanie Divya and Abigail. As she tried to maintain her professional appearance without any of the other ladies noticing that she was out last night. Megan instantly congratulated her and said, "You did a job well done handling the logistics helping us find this office space and coordinating with the movers."

Stephanie couldn't help but smiled at Megan's compliment, even though she was feeling a bit rough from her night out. She tried her best to hide her hangover and maintain her professional demeanor.

"Thank you, Megan," Stephanie replied. "I'm glad everything went smoothly with the move. And I'm excited to see what we can accomplish in this new space."

Bridget, who had overheard their conversation, chimed in. "Yeah, this office is amazing. And it's all thanks to you, Stephanie. We couldn't have done it without you."

Stephanie felt a wave of relief wash over her. She had been worried that her colleagues would notice her less-than-stellar state, but their compliments had boosted her confidence. She was proud of the work she had done to make their move to the new office a success.

As the ladies continued to settle in and decorate their offices, Stephanie made a mental note to be a bit more careful with her drinking in the future. But for now, she was happy to bask in the glow of her colleagues' appreciation and get back to work in their new and improved space.

Stephanie stopped by Elena's office and told her, "The equipment and everything you need to set up your OBGYN space should be on its way today and tomorrow. Let's just go over the checklist one more time to be sure you have everything you need."

Elena smiled at Stephanie, grateful for her help in setting up her new OBGYN practice. "Thank you so much, Stephanie. I really appreciate all of your hard work in making this happen."

Stephanie nodded. "Of course, Elena. I want to make sure you have everything you need to get your practice up and running smoothly."

They went over the checklist together, double-checking that all of the necessary equipment and supplies had been ordered and were on their way. Elena was impressed by how thorough and organized Stephanie was and felt confident that everything would be in place by the time she was ready to start seeing patients.

Elena said, "Thank you again, Stephanie," as they finished up. "I couldn't have done this without you."

Stephanie smiled. "It's my pleasure, Elena. I'm excited to see your practice take off and become a success."

Megan walked around the office and said, "Ladies while the IT guys are setting up our computers video conference equipment and everything that we need let's all meet in the conference room."

Megan said, "As first order of business let's just take a deep breath and take all this in and let's remember where we started and where we are now and look at each other around the room. We are a quintessential example of when we stick together work together support each other we can accomplish anything."

The ladies nodded in agreement, looked around the room at each other with proud and grateful expressions on their faces. They had come so far together, from their early days of struggling to make ends meet to now having beautiful new office space and successful businesses.

Sabrina spoke up. "Megan, you're right. It's amazing to see how much we've grown and accomplished together. I'm so grateful for each and every one of you and the support we give each other."

Elena chimed in. "I couldn't agree more. It's been such a journey, and I'm so proud of all of us for getting to where we are today."

Amber added, "We're like family now, and I wouldn't have it any other way. I know I can count on all of you for anything."

Bridget smiled. "And we have so much more to look forward to. I can't wait to see what we'll accomplish next."

Bethania nodded in agreement. "The sky's the limit for us. We've proven that we can overcome any obstacle when we work together."

Jacqueline spoke up. "I'm just so grateful for this opportunity and for all of you. Let's keep pushing forward and achieving our dreams together."

Then Megan turned and looked at Stephanie and said, "From the moment I met you to what I see now I am just in shock and awe at your growth and maturation you have so many hidden talents. I'm so glad that we could be an inspiration to you."

Megan continued, "Ladies well let's now get down to business, first I've been noticing in my emails I've been getting a lot of phone calls we have a lot of follow-ups still from the first event. I know each of you are still balancing doing your other jobs as well as working the business. What do you think we need? We need someone to help assist us to make sure we keep a fine balance so we're not too overwhelmed when it comes to growing this business."

Stephanie said, "I think we should hire an Executive Assistant manage our schedules you know answer the phones you know clients that come in who want to meet with us."

Bridget chimed in, "Yes, I agree. Having someone to manage our schedules and handle administrative tasks would free up a lot of time for us to focus on the growth of the business."

Sabrina nods in agreement, "I think that's a great idea. We could also look into using project management tools to keep track of our tasks and deadlines. It would help us stay organized and on top of things."

Amber suggested, "What about bringing in interns or freelancers to assist us with specific projects or tasks? It could be a great way to get some extra help without having to hire full-time employees."

Bethania concluded, "I think we have some great ideas here. Let's take some time to research and discuss these options further, and then we can decide on what will work best for us and our business."

Stephanie said, "I might know someone who could be a great receptionist and handle all the administrative tasks."

Megan said, "Sounds good Stephanie bring them in and let's set up an interview. Sabrina, I like your idea we're going to need some project management tools especially for the construction projects we got to do on that apartment building we just bought. Jacqueline when can you bring in that contractor that you know?"

During the meeting Cole texted Bridget saying, "I've been requested at the hospital, Can I drop off Marley at the office?"

Bridget said, "Absolutely bring that little bundle of joy here." Melanie texted Megan saying, "I'm in Brickell and finished meeting with a client and wanted to stop by and see the new office space." Charles surprised Sabrina and dropped off some roses in a beautiful vase for her office. Jacqueline had two potential new athletes that were stopping by to sign their contracts so she could be their agent. Amber just landed a new cosmetic surgeon that wanted her to be Pharmaceutical Representative. Bridget real estate development business in Orange Country was having trouble with a project and she was trying to juggle handing new potential clients with mortgage lending business.

As the ladies looked at their calendars and realized how busy they were going to be they all looked at Stephanie and said, "How soon can you get that Executive Admin Assistant in for an interview?

Stephanie said, "I'm going to contact Divya right now because she mentioned she knew somebody that was looking for that kind of work."

Stephanie quickly pulled out her phone and sent a message to Divya and asked for the name of the recommendation she knew for the Executive Admin Assistant. Divya responded almost immediately with the contact information of her friend who was looking for a job in that field. Stephanie thanked her and quickly reached out to schedule an interview.

Meanwhile, Megan suggested that they each prioritize their tasks and make a to-do list for the day to ensure they stay on track. She also suggested that they delegate tasks, if possible, to lighten the load. Sabrina agreed and offered to help Jacqueline with the contract signing for her new athletes.

As they each go back to their respective offices to tackle their workload, they realized how important it is to have a strong support system and team in order to achieve their goals. They all felt grateful for each other and the progress they've made as a team so far.

Stephanie told the ladies "I have good news they are available for an interview with us later this afternoon can everybody meet in the conference room at 4pm?"

The ladies agreed to meet at the conference room at 4pm for the interview with the potential Executive Admin Assistant.

Megan told Sabrina, "We need to research and outsource a good human resource consultant for our business. Sabrina since you're our General Counsel I'm sure you know just the person."

Sabrina nodded and said, "Yes, I have a few contacts that I can reach out to. I'll make some calls and see who's available and who would be the best fit for our company culture." She quickly took out her phone and started making some calls.

Meanwhile, Elena chimed in and said, "I think it's important for us to have a clear code of conduct and employee handbook in place before we start hiring more employees. That way, everyone knows what is expected of them and there are no misunderstandings."

The ladies nod in agreement and Megan adds, "Absolutely, we need to make sure that we're providing a safe and comfortable work environment for all of our employees."

First day in the new office space handling phone calls or checking emails trying to get stuff done. Sabrina noticed the ladies hadn't eaten much at all day so she ordered some food for everyone. She knows her and Bethania are vegan and made sure it accommodated them as well.

As the food arrived, the ladies gathered in the break room to have a quick lunch break. They chat about their busy schedules and how important it is to take a moment to refuel and recharge. Bethania complimented the food and thanked Stephanie for being considerate of her dietary needs. Elena shared some tips on how to stay energized during long workdays and suggested some healthy snacks that she usually keeps in her office. Amber agrees and adds that taking breaks throughout the day is crucial for productivity and mental health.

Megan smiled and said, "I'm glad we're all on the same page. We need to take care of ourselves to be able to take care of our business."

Stephanie just got a message saying our Executive Admin is here to interview. I'll go to the lobby and escort Victoria up.

Stephanie heads down to the lobby and greets Victoria, the Executive Admin candidate. She introduced herself and escorted her to the conference room where the other ladies were waiting.

Megan stood up and greeted Victoria, thanking her for coming in to interview for the position. They go through her resume and asked her some questions about her experience and qualifications. The ladies were impressed with her professionalism and organization skills.

Megan said to Victoria, "As impressive as you are I'm not understanding why it is you're available."

Victoria said, "I've worked in some environments that weren't so accommodating for me. I'll be very direct with you because I really am impressed with how this interview has gone and you ladies seem like the type of women I would love to work for. Most of the environments that I've worked in in the past did not feel comfortable because I'm transgender."

Megan smiled and said, "We don't discriminate here, Victoria. We believe in equal opportunities and diversity. If you can perform the job, that's all that matters."

The other ladies nod in agreement, and Sabrina adds, "We want to create a safe and inclusive workplace for everyone, and we're happy to have you join our team if you're interested." Victoria visibly relaxed and thanked them for their understanding and acceptance. The ladies continued with the interview, impressed with Victoria's qualifications and experience, and offered her the position at the end of the meeting.

Amber says to Victoria, "I know what it feels like when people can't see you and accept you for who you are but only willing to accept you for who they want you to be I've been in those shoes. and let us know if there is anything that we can do to make this environment more accommodating for you."

Elena asked Victoria, "What questions do you have for us that we can answer?" Victoria asked about the company culture and values, and how the team collaborates and communicates with each other. She also asked about any potential challenges or projects she would be working on in the role, as well as opportunities for growth and development within the company. The ladies answered her questions and provided more information about the company culture, emphasizing teamwork, open communication, and a focus on continuous improvement and learning. They also discuss potential projects and responsibilities for the role, as well as opportunities for career advancement and professional development.

Megan said, "Welcome Victoria we've heard great recommendations from Divya, she said you guys used to work together you did great work with her."

Victoria smiles and nods, "Yes, Divya and I worked together at my last job, and I'm grateful for her recommendation.

Stephanie showed Victoria her new desk, "I'll make sure we can get your phone and e-mail Sabrina will handle all her paperwork and getting you properly onboarded."

Megan says Victoria "I would be honored if you could join me in the ladies tonight at Komodo we're going to have dinner we would love to get to know more about your life story."

Victoria felt grateful for the invitation and accepts, saying she's looking forward to getting to know everyone better. The ladies congratulated her on joining the team and headed out to their respective offices for the day. As Victoria settled into her new desk, she felt a sense of relief and excitement for this new opportunity with a company that values diversity and inclusion.

Bridget goes down to the lobby to meet Cole and get Marley. After kissing Cole goodbye, she saw Melanie walking into the building. Bridget greeted Melanie and they had chat for a few minutes before heading up to the office together. Bridget walked in and introduced everyone to Marley. Everyone falls in love with her cute puppy eyes.

Melanie couldn't resist Marley's cuteness and immediately asked Bridget if she can hold her. Bridget hands Marley over to Melanie, and the little puppy snuggles up to her. The ladies looked and admired Marley and asked Bridget about her breed and how old she was. Bridget happily answered their questions and told them that Marley is a golden retriever and just turned 3 months old. They all take turns holding and playing with Marley, enjoying the little break from work.

Bridget introduced Melanie to Victoria, and they had a chat for a bit before Megan invited them both to join her and the rest of the ladies for dinner at Komodo later that evening.

Melanie happily accepted the invitation, and they all discussed what time to meet up. Stephanie offered to make the reservation and suggested they meet at the restaurant at 7 pm. Bridget told Melanie she was excited to catch up with her and hear about her latest projects, and Melanie said she's looking forward to it as well. As they wrap up their conversation, Bridget heads back to her office to catch up on some work while Melanie heads to the lounge area to relax for a bit before dinner.

Victoria received a phone call at her desk telling Jacqueline that her clients are finally here in the lobby after running late. Victoria thanked the caller and relayed the message to Jacqueline, saying, "Jacqueline, your clients have arrived. They were running a bit late but they're here now." Jacqueline thanked Victoria and quickly headed to the lobby to meet her clients.

Melanie and Megan are meeting in her office,

Melanie said, "I don't know how much work you plan on getting with that amazing view."

Megan said, "Did you forget I used to live in New York I'm used to having views. I'm true to this I'm not new to this."

Melanie laughed and said, "Okay, you got me there. But still, this view is something else." Megan nodded in agreement and said, "It helps to have a beautiful workspace to be productive in. Plus, it's great for impressing clients."

Melanie shared with Megan, "I've picked up enough clients in Miami to open up a second boutique store, so it looks like I'll be flying back and forth from Miami to LA a lot."

Megan nodded and said, "That's great news, Melanie! I'm sure your business will thrive in Miami too. And it'll be nice to have you here more often, even if it's just for a short while."

Melanie smiled and said, "Yes, I'm excited about the new opportunities. And it'll be nice to spend more time with you and the rest of the ladies."

Victoria knocked on Megan's door and Megan waved for her to come in.

Victoria said, "There's an important contractor that I have on hold he knows Jacqueline but she's in a meeting right now with two clients."

Megan said, "Yes I definitely need to speak with him I'm sorry sis I need to take this important phone call."

Melanie asked, "Is there some place where I can work and answer emails until it's time to go to dinner?"

Victoria said, "Come on I'll show you where the lounge is you can work in there."

Victoria and Melanie are walking to the lounge, Melanie complements Victoria dress and shoes. Victoria smiled and thanked Melanie for the compliment. She told her that she loves fashion and always tried to dress her best for any occasion. Melanie nodded in agreement and said to her that she can definitely tell that Victoria has great taste in fashion.

As they arrived in the lounge Melanie said, "This is the most luxurious lounge, I've ever seen in an office space."

The lounge is a spacious area with modern decor and comfortable furniture. The walls are painted in a soft neutral color and decorated with abstract art pieces that add a touch of elegance to the space. Floor to ceiling windows allow plenty of natural light to flood the area and offer a breathtaking view of the city skyline. The furniture includes plush sofas and armchairs, coffee tables, and side tables. The seating is arranged in small clusters to encourage casual conversations and collaboration. The lounge is also equipped with a large flat-screen TV, a coffee machine, a fridge stocked with refreshments, and a small kitchenette with a sink and microwave. The overall design of the lounge was sleek, stylish, and inviting, creating a comfortable and welcoming environment for all who use it.

Melanie handed Victoria her business card and said, "I'm a fashion designer this is all my information check out my website I would love to hear your input."

Victoria said, "Thank you Melanie I can't wait to see what you have to offer."

Victoria was walking back to her desk and saw Divya in the waiting room talking with Stephanie. Divya turned around and hugged Victoria and congratulated her on the job "I'm so glad that you were able to land this opportunity to work with these amazing ladies. I'm sure this will be a very safe workspace for you."

Victoria smiled and thanked Divya for her kind words. "I'm really excited to be here and work with all of them," she mentioned. "It already felt like a great environment, and I can't wait to see what we can accomplish together."

Stephanie chimed in, "We're so happy to have you on board, Victoria. You have some big shoes to fill, but we have faith in you. Victoria thanked them again and heads back to her desk, feeling grateful to be part of such a supportive team.

Amber walked down to Elena's office and asked her if she had a minute to talk. Elena said, "Sure" Elena looks at her face can tell there was some concern.

Amber said, "I know you're still setting up your office and exam room for all your patients, but would you be my doctor? I just want to know the status and the health of the baby. "

Elena said, "I would be honored to give you an examination and let's see how the baby is doing. I'll finally have everything set up by tomorrow afternoon."

Amber smiled and thanked Elena, "That would be great, Elena. Let's schedule it for tomorrow then."

Elena nodded and they discussed the details of the appointment, including the time and what Amber needs to bring. After their conversation, Amber felt relieved and grateful to have Elena as her doctor.

As the ladies finished their first full day in the office Megan said, "Ladies you ready to get some dinner?" Amber, Bethania, Stephanie, Jacqueline, Bridget, Melanie, and Victoria were all excited to have dinner.

Bridget said, "I'll meet you there I just have to take Marley home and feed her."

Megan said, "No problem, Bridget, we'll wait for you." The group headed to a nearby restaurant called Komodo. As they sit down, Megan suggested they start by sharing some appetizers. Bethania told the waiter that she and Sabrina are vegan, and Megan assured her that they have plenty of vegan options on the menu. The group orders a variety of dishes, including vegan options for Bethania and Sabrina.

Amber asked Victoria, "Where are you from? What brought you to Miami? How long have you and Divya known each other?

Victoria replied, "I'm originally from Seattle, but I've lived in several different cities over the years. I moved to Miami a few years ago for a job opportunity and fell in love with the city. Divya and I met at our previous job and worked together for about two years. We became good friends and have stayed in touch ever since."

She took a sip of her drink and continued, "I'm really excited to be working with all of you. I've been following the success of your company and I'm honored to be a part of it now. You guys have such an interesting story I've never been part of an organization that is pioneered by all women dominating a multitude of different fields and for each of you to come together and collaborated to build a company together is quite impressive. What inspired you to start a company together?"

Megan smiles and said, "We all have different backgrounds and experiences, but we shared a common goal of creating a company that empowers and uplifts women in all industries. We wanted to create a space where women can thrive and support each other, rather than compete or tear each other down. It wasn't easy, but we all believed in the vision and worked hard to make it a reality."

Bethania adds, "We knew that by coming together, we could bring a unique perspective to the business world. We wanted to challenge the traditional male-dominated workplace and create a more inclusive and diverse environment."

Amber said, "Ladies time to raise your glasses even though I can't drink with you, but I need y'all to have a toast another day and a successful milestone that we are now and professional office space growing once again."

The ladies all raised their glasses and cheered for the success and growth of their company. They discussed their plans and their excitement for what's to come. As the night goes on, they enjoy each other's company and laughter fills the air. It's clear that they have not only built a successful business together but also formed strong friendships. The dinner ends with hugs and goodbyes, and the ladies head home, excited for what the future holds.

Chapter 14

The next day James and Amber were ready to meet with Elena to see the ultrasound of the baby. As they arrived at Elena's office, they walked to the exam room. Elena walked in and explained the procedure and began the ultrasound. James and Amber watch in awe as they saw their baby on the monitor for the first time. Elena points out the different features and organs and checks to make sure everything is developing properly. She reassured them that the baby looks healthy and is growing at a normal rate. James and Amber were overjoyed and thanked Elena for her expertise and care. As they leave the room, they can't stop talking about how amazing it was to see their baby on the ultrasound.

Amber said to James, "We need to fly to San Diego to see my family I want to break the news to them in person and not over the phone."

James nodded and said, "Of course, I completely understand. When do you want to go?"

Amber replied, "I was thinking this weekend if that works for you. We can make a little trip out of it and stay for a few days."

James agreed and said, "That sounds like a great idea. I'll make the arrangements for the trip." They both smiled at each other, excited to share the news with Amber's family in person.

Melanie stopped by the office to say goodbye to everyone, and she'll be back in a few weeks to start logistics of opening new store in Miami, she told Amber and Elena I've already started working with my team in LA to customize your wedding dresses. Megan hugged her and walked with her to the car.

Megan said, "I'm so glad that we reconnected after all these years but if you need anything you make sure to call me."

Melanie responded, "Of course, sis. You know I'll always have your back too." She hugged Megan one more time before getting into her car and driving away.

Megan headed back into the office, feeling a bit nostalgic about her time with Melanie.

She turned to Amber and Elena and said, "Can you believe how far we've come? I mean, just a few months ago we were all working from home, and now we have this beautiful office space and so much momentum. I'm so grateful for all of you and excited for what's to come."

Victoria walked to Amber office and said, "You need me to book your tickets to San Diego for you and James?"

Amber smiled and said, "That would be amazing, Victoria. Thank you so much!" When James left Amber's office, he stopped by Bethania office and said, "I need to look for house for Amber and I."

Bethania responded, "Oh, that's exciting! Are you looking for something specific? Any particular neighborhood or type of house?"

James replied, "Well, we want to be close to the office, but also in a quiet neighborhood. We were looking for a place with at least three bedrooms and a backyard for the baby."

Bethania said, "I know a few areas that would be great for you guys and I'm sure Bridget can get you a great mortgage for your home too."

James nodded and said, "That would be great. We're looking for a home that we can really make our own, and it sounds like Bridget can help us with financing. Thanks, Bethania." He smiles and heads out of her office, feeling optimistic about the house-hunting process.

Victoria walked into Stephanie office and said, "I would like to help plan the baby and wedding Shower for Amber and Elena."

Stephanie smiled and responded, "That's a great idea, Victoria! I was thinking about organizing a shower for them as well. We could work together on the details and make it a special event for both of them."

Maxwell and Abigail stopped by the office they introduced themselves to Victoria. Maxwell said, "I was just seeing if Megan was available, we just happened to be in the area."

Abigail said, "She wanted to see Bethania and make an appointment to look at some homes."

Victoria said, "I know Bethania is meeting with a client right now and Maxwell I'll let Megan know you're here I'm sure she'll be glad to see you."

Maxwell nodded and thanked Victoria, while Abigail made a note of the appointment with Bethania. As they wait for Megan,

Maxwell looks around the office and says to Abigail, "This is quite the setup, isn't it? I can see why Megan is excited to work here."

Abigail agreed, admiring the sleek design and modern furnishings.

As Megan walked into the office, Victoria let her know that Maxwell and Abigail were here to see her. Megan greeted them with a smile and welcomed them to the office. After catching up for a few minutes, Maxwell brought up the topic of dinner plans, suggesting they all go out to try a new sushi restaurant he's heard good things about.

Abigail agreed saying "She's been wanting to try it as well."

Megan said she's up for it and they made plans to meet up later that evening.

Stephanie walked over to Victoria while she's sitting at her desk and tells her "since Maxwell Abigail and Megan are going out later, I want to see if the ladies could stay a little late in the office. We all need to meet in the conference room and begin to plan out Megan's birthday since it's coming up."

It's the end of the day Stephanie wanted to meet with Amber, Bethania, Jacqueline, Elena, Victoria, and Sabrina while Megan is out. Also, she conferenced called in Melanie, Colin, James, William, and Charles. She even invited over Divya to come to the office,

Stephanie said, "Thank you everyone for making time today, I really want to plan something quite spectacular for Megan's birthday and I want it to be a surprise. She has done so much and has been the leader and the rock for making all this happen. She's one of my greatest inspirations for helping me in my journey. I want us to have a great brainstorming session of thinking of some phenomenal ideas that we can do to host a birthday party for her here in Miami. What are ideas that each of you have we can do?"

Amber suggested, "What if we throw her a pool party at a luxurious villa in Miami Beach? We can have a catered BBQ, cocktails, and music."

Bethania adds, "That's a great idea! We can also rent a yacht for a sunset cruise around the bay and have a DJ onboard."

Jacqueline said, "I love that idea, but what if we add a little adventure? We can rent jet skis and go parasailing."

Elena chimed in, "That sounds amazing, but we should also make it a pampering experience. We can book a spa day for all of us and have massages, facials, and other treatments."

Victoria contributed, "We can also plan a surprise performance by a local artist or DJ. That would make it extra special."

Sabrina adds, "And we can decorate the venue with beautiful flowers and balloons to give it a festive look."

Divya said, "I love all of these ideas! What if we also create a custom birthday cocktail for Megan and have a mixologist teach us how to make it?"

Colin said, "That's a great idea! We can also make a video montage of all the fun moments we've had together with Megan and play it during the party."

James suggested, "We can also have a photo booth with fun props for guests to take pictures in." William adds, "And we can have a dessert table with all of Megan's favorite sweets and treats."

Charles said, "We can also have a gift table where everyone can leave a personal message and gift for Megan to show our appreciation."

Stephanie said, "Wow, these are all great ideas! I think we have the making of an amazing party for Megan. Let's start planning and get to work!"

Stephanie also sent a text message to Abigail saying she would like to have a conference call with her and Maxwell, the two discuss we're going to do a surprise birthday party for Megan.

Abigail responded to Stephanie's text message, "Sounds great! Maxwell and I are in. When would you like to schedule the conference call?"

Stephanie replied, "How about tomorrow at 3 pm EST? That should give everyone enough time to come up with some ideas." Abigail agreed and said she would mark her calendar for the call.

Stephanie also called Bridget since she couldn't make the meeting since she was with a VIP client and let her know what's going on and wanted to get Bridget's ideas for Megan birthday.

Stephanie greeted Bridget over the phone and updated her about their plan for Megan's surprise birthday party. She also mentioned that she wanted to get Bridget's ideas for the party since she was not able to make it to the meeting earlier.

Bridget thanked Stephanie for including her and said she has a few ideas for the party. She suggested having a beach party with a bonfire and some live music. She also recommends having a photo booth with fun props for guests to take pictures with. Stephanie agreed and thanked Bridget for her input.

They also discussed food and drinks for the party. Bridget mentioned having a buffet-style setup with different types of cuisines to cater to everyone's preferences. She also recommended having a signature cocktail for the night. Stephanie loved the idea and asked Bridget if she can work with the caterer to finalize the menu and drink options.

Victoria Stephanie Maxwell, and Divya decided to meet and gather all the ideas that have been collected for Megan surprise birthday.

Stephanie said, "I want to be able to see how we can compile all these cool ideas everyone shared into one venue.

Stephanie said, "We're going to reserve the Seafair Mega Yacht downtown Miami as the venue."

Maxwell said, "Whatever the cost is just send me the invoice. We'll get a DJ and some live music, catered buffet style, let's hire a photographer."

Stephanie said, "Victoria, I need you to start preparing the guest list let's make sure we invite all of our VIPs and get a hold of Megan's parents.

Victoria nodded and said, "Got it, I'll start working on the guest list and sending out invitations. I'll also reach out to Megan's parents and make sure they're able to attend."

Divya chimed in, "I can help with the decorations and make sure everything looks amazing on the yacht."

Stephanie nodded and said, "Great, and Maxwell, can you take care of the drinks and the bar setup? And make sure we have plenty of options for everyone."

Maxwell smiled and said, "Absolutely, consider it done." They all agreed to divide up the tasks and start working on their assigned responsibilities to make sure Megan's surprise birthday party is a huge success.

Afterwards, Stephanie and Divya make their way to Wynwood, the ladies take in the colorful street art and lively atmosphere. They stopped for a drink at a trendy bar and danced to the music, enjoying the vibrant Miami nightlife.

As Stephanie and Divya made their way through the streets of Wynwood, they were surrounded by colorful murals and street art.

The area was buzzing with energy and excitement, and the ladies could feel the vibrant Miami nightlife all around them.

They decided to stop at a trendy bar, where the music is pumping, and the drinks are flowing. Stephanie ordered a round of shots for the two of them, and they clink glasses before downing them in one go.

As they took a break from dancing, they ordered a few more drinks and chatted about their lives and the upcoming party for Megan. They both agreed that it's going to be an amazing celebration, and they can't wait to see Megan's face when she realizes what they've planned for her.

As the night went on, the girls continued to chat and catch up with each other. They talked about their different backgrounds, their careers, and their experiences with dating and relationships. Divya, was still trying to find her footing in the dating world, was particularly interested in hearing about the other Stephanie experiences.

The bar was packed with people, and Stephanie and Divya could feel the excitement in the air. They joined the crowd on the dance floor, moving to the beat of the music and enjoyed the lively atmosphere.

Amber and Jacqueline, we at home packing their bags for Chicago and San Diego. Both never brought a significant other over to meet their families. Amber was rehearsing in her mind how to break the news that she's pregnant and engaged. Jacqueline this was her first time being in an interracial relationship and first time bringing a man home to meet her family. They both planned on leaving after Megan's surprise birthday party.

The night of the event is finally here for Megan's surprise birthday party, Stephanie and Victoria arrived early at the Seafair Mega Yacht to ensure everything is in order. They decided to tell the guest on the invitations to be there an hour early and Megan was going to arrive an hour later. Maxwell was going to be picking her up and pretending like they were just going to go out for a date night, but he requested her to dress fancy.

As all the guests arrived, they were mesmerized at the decorations the food the DJ the band as they walk around the entire yacht.

Taking in the breathtaking views of the Miami skyline from the water. The yacht was beautifully decorated with balloons, streamers, and flowers in Megan's favorite colors. The catered buffet was set up with delicious food and drinks, and the DJ is playing Megan's favorite songs.

As the night goes on, more and more guests arrive, including Megan's family and close friends. Everyone is having a great time dancing, chatting, and enjoying the festivities. Stephanie and Victoria are keeping an eye out for Maxwell and Megan's arrival, and as the hour approaches, they start to get nervous.

Finally, they spot Maxwell's car pulling up to the dock, and they hurried to get everyone in place for the big surprise. As Megan stepped onto the yacht, she was stunned to see all of her friends and loved ones gathered together to celebrate her birthday.

She was moved to tears as she hugged every one of them, feeling overwhelmed with gratitude and joy. She instantly hugged Maxwell and gave him a kiss and then walked over to Stephanie, Jacqueline, Bethania Sabrina, Elena, Bridget, Victoria, Divya, and Amber for hugs. As she steps back smiling with tears, her sister Melanie hugs and surprises her from behind. Megan was overwhelmed with emotions and couldn't believe someone planned all of this.

Then everyone gathers around as all the ladies are shocked as they look at Maxwell on one knee holding a gorgeous diamond ring.

Maxwell said, "There is no other woman for me I knew it from the moment I met you."

Megan was shocked and speechless as she looked down at the ring in awe. She nods her head yes and Maxwell slides the ring onto her finger. Everyone cheers and claps as the newly engaged couple embraces each other. Stephanie walks over to them with a champagne bottle and pours glasses for everyone to toast the happy couple.

After the excitement settled down, the party continued with dancing and more celebration. The DJ played Megan's favorite songs and the band performed a special song for the newly engaged couple. The food is delicious, and the drinks keep flowing as everyone enjoyed the beautiful Miami skyline from the yacht.

Megan walked around greeting and thanked the guests for coming out. She was just trying to take in the moment and then suddenly as she walked up to the top of the yacht, she saw her parents and she was absolutely shocked that they were here. As Melanie slowly walked up behind her, she was even surprised to see her parents. It's been a long time since they have spoken.

Megan and Melanie walk over not as happy and thrilled to see them. Megan's father said, "I'm going to address the elephant in the room I owe both of you all a tremendous apology I know I was hard on you all I made some decisions and choices that I deeply regret. I thought about my actions and how I was treating you all was setting you up to be tough in the real world when I should have been more loving caring understanding and supportive."

As a tear begins to shed down her father's face of guilt and sorrow. Megan and Melanie and their mom started crying too, their father looked at Melanie, said, "I especially owe you an apology I should have been more protective of you. What I did was wrong your mother almost left me she didn't forgive me until I agreed to come on this trip when I got the invitation from your assistant Victoria and Stephanie."

Megan and Melanie were both overwhelmed with emotions as their father spoke. It's clear that his words were sincere and coming from a place of regret and remorse. They both hugged their father, forgave him for the pain he caused them in the past. Megan's mother also joined in the hug and the four of them embraced each other for a long moment.

Megan's father then handed her a wrapped box and said, "I also wanted to give you this. It's something that belonged to your grandmother, my mother. She always said it was a special piece and I think you should have it." Megan opened the box and found a beautiful gold necklace with a diamond pendant. She was touched by the gesture and put the necklace on immediately.

Megan's father handed Melanie an envelope and says to her, "I can never get back the time that we lost but I hope this makes up for it and we can start a brighter future together." Melanie was very emotional, speechless, didn't know what to say.

She looked at her father and said, "You don't know what I've been through to get to this very moment for so long I hated you and then I hated myself." As Megan put her arms around Melanie, Maxwell slowly walked up and saw it was a very emotional moment happening.

Maxwell looked at Megan and Melanie and asked, "Is everything alright?"

Megan said, "Yes Maxwell this is my father and mother Jericho and Beatrice Babineaux."

Maxwell greeted them warmly and introduced himself. He said he's glad to see Megan and her family have reconciled and that family is important. Megan's father thanked Maxwell and said he's grateful for his role in bringing them all together. They all continued to talk and caught up, sharing stories and memories. The party continued and everyone enjoyed the rest of the night, dancing, eating, and celebrating Megan's birthday and the newfound reconciliation between her and her family.

Elena, Amber, Bridget, Jacqueline, Sabrina, and Bethania were setting down and talking yeah eating while their men were standing at the bow chatting.

Amber said to Bridget Jacqueline Sabrina and Bethania, "So which one of you is next because if you all can all get engaged, we can just share these wedding expenses and get it done the same day, you can join Elena, Megan and I." They all looked at chuckling Amber and said, "Girl it will happen when the time is right." I'm sure they're feeling the pressure.

As the party was coming to an end Megan decided to gather everyone around and give a speech.

Megan said, "First I want to thank everyone for coming out to celebrate this monumental occasion. I did not expect a surprise birthday party and to be proposed to on the same night I don't think I'm going to be sleeping the rest of the weekend. Let's give a round of applause to my Chief Marketing Officer Stephanie Toro, her friend Divya Katdara, my new Executive Assistant Victoria Lake, lastly my fiancé Maxwell St. John a round of applause for planning and coordinating this event today."

The crowd applauded, whistled and cheered Megan continued her speech, "But tonight it's not just about me. It's about all of us coming together, setting aside our differences, and celebrating the love and connections that we share as a family and as friends. I know that we've all had our ups and downs, but I hope that tonight serves as a reminder of the strength of our bond and the importance of forgiveness and second chances. Let's continue to support and uplift each other as we navigate through this journey called life." The crowd cheers and Megan raises her glass, "Here's to love, family, and new beginnings. Cheers!"

Megan continued, "I also want to take a moment to thank my sister Melanie for being here tonight. It means the world to me. And to my parents, Jericho and Beatrice Babineaux, thank you for coming and apologizing for everything. It's been a long journey, but I'm so grateful that we can start to move forward and make up for lost time."

Megan looked around at all of her friends and family and felt overwhelmed with gratitude. She said, "This night has shown me the power of love and forgiveness, the importance of family and friendships, and the beauty of life's surprises. I feel so blessed to have each one of you in my life. Thank you for making this a night I will never forget."

The group cheered and raised their glasses to Megan, wishing her a happy birthday and a lifetime of love and happiness with Maxwell.

As Megan was riding in the car back home, she told Maxwell, "Take me to your place I want to spend the night with you."
Maxwell smiles and said, "Of course, my love. Whatever you want." As they drove to his place, he reached over and took her hand, admiring the ring on her finger. "You deserve every bit of this," he said, "and so much more."

Megan looked at him with tears in her eyes and said, "I never thought I would find someone who loves me like you do. Thank you for everything, Maxwell."

As she stared at her ring, she cannot believe how big it is,

Maxwell smiled at Megan and said, "It's a 7-carat princess cut diamond. I wanted to get you something that matched your radiance and beauty."

Megan looked at him and said, "It's stunning, Maxwell. I can't believe it."

Maxwell took her hand and said, "And I can't believe how lucky I am to have you in my life. You make me so happy, Megan."

Megan leaned over and gave him a kiss, saying, "I feel the same way, Maxwell. I'm so grateful for you and everything you do for me."

Melanie shared with her parents about how she felt neglected and unsupported when she needed them the most, and how she struggled to cope with the trauma of losing her baby. She explained how she moved to a new city, started a new job, and slowly worked on healing herself. She talks about the therapy she went through and how it helped her cope with the grief and the guilt. Her mother starts crying and apologizes for not being there for her daughter when she needed her the most. Her father nodded in agreement and said he wished he could go back in time and be a better father to both Melanie and Megan.

Melanie stopped in front of their hotel and turned to her parents. She says she forgave them and wants to start a new chapter with them. As she hugged her parents' goodbye, she felt a sense of closure and a renewed sense of love and connection with them. She walked back to her own hotel, feeling grateful for the unexpected reunion and the chance to start a new relationship with her parents.

Melanie arrived back at her hotel she decided to go to the hotel bar and have a drink. She opened the white envelope that her father had given her in the envelope, it's a letter and a check.

The letter said, "I was so ecstatic to hear about Megan having a surprise birthday and they told me that you were we're going to be invited I was scared how you might react if you saw me again. I wanted to do something to make up for not being the best father I could be. I realized kicking you out was not the right thing to do. I hope this makes up for lost time and you can use it towards whatever you need."

Melanie stared at her check for two million dollars from her father. She was absolute shock and disbelief. Melanie said to herself, "I know exactly what I'm going to do with this as she folds the check and puts it in her purse continued to sit at the bar and just reminisce."

The bartender brings over a drink and Melanie said to him, "I didn't order another round this round is from someone else. Then she saw a very attractive handsome gentleman walking in her direction.

He walked up to her and said, "I saw you were drinking alone would you like some company?

Melanie said, "Sure" the gentleman said, "My name is Enrique and yours?" Melanie said, "Melanie" as they shook hands, he sit down next to her.

Enrique said, "I saw you looking at me earlier."

Melanie replied, "I was" then Enrique responded, "You're looking at me now."

As he smiled and she chuckled Enrique said, "What's the special occasion? I love your dress."

She responded "It was my sister's birthday party and what about you? I love your suit."

Enrique said, "I was at a private party at the W, you live in Miami?" Melanie said, "I live in LA, but going to open a location of my business in Miami. As much as I love talking to you and you're very good-looking I'm not in the mood for small talk. I'm only in town for a good time not a long time if you catch my drift."

Enrique said, "Let's go to my room then" Melanie said, "No, let's go to mine."

Enrique smiled and said, "Lead the way." As they exit the bar, Melanie's mind races with anticipation and a tinge of nervousness. She led Enrique to her hotel room and opened the door. Inside, the room is dimly lit and cozy. Enrique looked around, impressed with the decor. Melanie walks over to the mini-bar and pours them each a glass of champagne. As they clink glasses, Enrique leaned in and kissed her neck as she slowly took her dress off, causing her to shiver with excitement. She turned to face him, and they kissed deeply. As she took off his shirt she gasped at the sight of his chiseled chest and abs. Enrique, sensing her desire, picked her up and carried her to the bed, where they continued to kiss with increasing passion. Melanie couldn't believe how quickly things had escalated, but she couldn't resist the pull she felt towards Enrique.

Enrique began to explore Melanie's body with his hands, trailing kisses down her neck, over her breasts, and down towards her hips. As he slipped off her panties, he positioned himself between her legs and began to pleasure her in ways she had never experienced before. Melanie's moans filled the room as she writhed with pleasure, her hands tangled in Enrique's hair.

Enrique took her by the waist and lifted her onto the bed, their lips never leaving each other.

Melanie felt the weight of Enrique on top of her, and his lips trailed down her neck and onto her collarbone. She moaned with pleasure as his hand traveled up her thigh.

Enrique flipped her over and entered her. Melanie gasped as he filled her up, and she started to ride him hard. The sound of their bodies slapping together echoed in the room as they both moaned in ecstasy.

As they both reached their peak, they collapsed onto the bed, breathing heavily. Hours passed, and they lie entwined in each other's arms, sated and content.

As the sun begins to rise, Melanie realized that she must leave for her flight back to LA. She gently wakes Enrique and tells him that she has to go. They exchanged phone numbers and promised to keep in touch.

Melanie left the hotel, she texted Megan and asked her if they could meet before she headed to the airport. Megan said, "sure sis come on over I'm at Maxwells I'll send you the address." As the cab approaches Maxwell's home in Morningside, Melanie walks up to the door and Megan answers Melanie gave Megan the envelope her father gave her last night and said, "I need you to invest this for me when I double my return cash me out."

Megan took the envelope from Melanie and nodded. "Sure thing, sis. I'll take care of it. Is everything okay?"

Melanie takes a deep breath and nods. "Yeah, everything's fine. Just trying to move forward and make things right."

Megan smiled and hugged her. "I'm proud of you, Mel. You've come a long way." They chat for a bit before Melanie must leave for the airport. As she hugs Megan goodbye,

Melanie told her, "Take care of yourself, sis. I'll see you soon." Megan watched as the cab drives away and heads back inside to continue her day with Maxwell.

Amber and James are in route to the airport along with Jacqueline and Harry both ladies are feeling extremely nervous about their men meeting their parents for the first time. They both couldn't even sleep last night as James and Harry were concerned for them.

Harry told Jacqueline, "Everything is going to be fine let's enjoy ourselves in Chicago."

James was also comforting Amber, Amber said, "Ever since I got pregnant, I have been hungry all the time, my breasts are swelling nipples are still sensitive.

James responds "It's normal, honey. Your body is going through a lot of changes right now. We'll make sure to grab some snacks for the flight, and maybe we could even get a massage at the airport to help you relax."

Jacqueline chimed in, "That's a great idea. I could use a massage too; I've been feeling so tense lately."

Harry nods in agreement and said, "Let's make sure to book a spa session once we get to Chicago, we could all use a little pampering."

Harry tells James "Thank you all so much for allowing us to ride with you guys to the airport."

James and Amber hugged Harry and Jacqueline at the airport and wished them safe travels.

Harry said, "Make sure you guys take plenty of pics."

James said, "Same for you guys."

Jacqueline smiled and replied, "We will take lots of pictures! And we'll send them to you guys too."

James adds, "And don't forget to try some deep-dish pizza while you're in Chicago."

Jacqueline laughed and said, "Oh, we definitely won't forget about that!" As they say their goodbyes and head off to their respective gates,

Amber turned to James and said, "I can't believe we're doing this. Meeting each other's parents for the first time."

James nodded and said, "I know, it's a big step. But we'll get through it together." They shared a kiss and headed off to their gate, ready to start their new adventure.

Cole spent the night at Bridget's, and they wake up with Marley somehow jumped in the bed in the middle of the night and decided to snuggle in the middle of the bed between both of them. As they looked at each stunned how that happened when she was in her bed when they went to sleep.

Bridget said, "I am going to go in the office today and do some work since you're working at the hospital, I appreciate you coming to Megan birthday last night."

Cole nods and said, "No problem, I had a great time celebrating with everyone." As Bridget gets ready to head to the office, Cole got up and got dressed as well. Before he left, he gave Marley a pat on the head and said goodbye to Bridget.

As Cole arrived at the hospital, he's greeted by his colleagues. They chat for a bit before Cole headed to his shift. It's a busy day at the hospital, with several emergencies and surgeries that need to be attended to. Cole worked hard, putting his medical training and skills to good use.

William and Bethania spent the night at her place, William sneaks out of bed and decided to make her breakfast in bed. Bethania woke up to the smell of breakfast and saw William in the kitchen.

She was pleasantly surprised and said, "William, you didn't have to do this. Thank you so much!" They sit down to eat and chat about their plans for the day. Bethania mentioned that she has a few appointments with clients and a meeting. William said he had some meetings at the office as well. Before they parted ways,

William asked, "Do you have plans tonight? I was thinking of taking you out to dinner." Bethania smiled and said, "I would love that. "I know you have to get ready and head to the office since real estate business is so busy for you, but I wanted to surprise you.

Charles received a surprise phone call from his parents saying they are staying in downtown Miami. His parents said they're looking forward to meeting him and Sabrina. Sabrina is in the shower and Charles can't believe he has to break the news that they have arrived in Miami. This is Charles first time introducing someone to his family.

Charles took a deep breath and decided to tell Sabrina about his parents' surprise visit. He knocked on the bathroom door and said, "Hey, babe, can I talk to you for a minute?" Sabrina responds from the shower, "Sure hon, what's up?"

Charles cleared his throat and said, "So, my parents just called, and they're already in Miami. They surprised me with a visit." Sabrina quickly turns off the shower and said, "Oh my gosh, when are they coming over?"

Charles checks his phone and responds, "They said they're staying downtown and want to meet us for lunch today."

Sabrina looked nervous but tried to stay positive and said, "Okay, love I'm looking forward to meeting them.

Charles nodded and said, "Thanks, babe. I really appreciate your support." They both quickly get ready and head out to meet Charles' parents for lunch.

Charles and Sabrina walking around trying to figure out what they would wear for lunch. Sabrina was hoping that his parents would love to appreciate and accept her just the way her family did.

Stephanie, Victoria Bridget and Bethania all decide to work in the office when they all thought they were going to have the office to themselves on a Saturday. When each of them arrived, they were shocked to see that someone else is in the office working too.

Bridget asked Victoria "What are you doing here? This is your first week."

Victoria said, "We have so many leads that I need to follow up on and get them scheduled in each of your calendars."

Bridget said, "I know I'm going to follow up with some clients today."

Victoria also says hi to Marley and surprised Marley with some doggy treats that she brought in.

Stephanie was shocked as she walked in to see Victoria and Bridget, Stephanie tells them "I've been so occupied planning have Megan's surprise birthday I need to get back to focused on work."

Then surprisingly Elena walked in and said she has a few clients that are coming in today to see her. as she greets everyone.

Victoria said, "I also put a few other new appointments in your calendar."

Bethania said, "Wow we have a full house today I know I have a few clients wanting to come in."

Victoria said, "Would you ladies like some coffee?"

Stephanie said, "An espresso for me."

Bridget said, "A latte for me please."

Bethania requests a cappuccino, and Elena said, "I'll just have a black coffee."

As Victoria heads to the kitchen to prepare the coffee, Marley follows her wagging her tail in excitement.

Once the coffee was ready, they all settled down to start their work for the day. Stephanie goes back to working on her client's marketing strategy, Bridget starts calling up some potential clients, Bethania prepares for her upcoming meetings, and Elena reviewed some new patient profiles. Victoria checked in with each of them throughout the day, making sure they're on track with their tasks and offering assistance when needed.

The ladies decided to take a small break and meet in the lounge.

Stephanie asked "Well what did you guys think about Megan's surprise party last night? I didn't know it was going to get emotional when her and Melanie saw their parents."

Bridget said, "It was a beautiful moment. You did an amazing job, Stephanie. Megan was very happy."

Bethania agreed, "Yes, it was a great party. I especially loved the decorations and the music. Everything was perfect."

Victoria adds, "I'm glad I got to meet Megan's mom last night. She's such a sweetheart."

Stephanie smiled, "Thanks, guys. I'm glad it turned out well. It was a lot of work, but seeing Megan's reaction made it all worth it."

As they finished their coffee, Bethania checked her phone and realized that she had a missed call from one of her clients.

She apologized to the others and said, "I must go call this client back. See you all later." The others nod and say goodbye as they head back to their office.

Meanwhile Charles and Sabrina have finally arrived to meet his parents, both feeling antsy and nervous. Charles spotted his parents already have been seated in the restaurant they get up as soon as they see him and Sabrina walking toward them with smiles on their faces as they introduced themselves to Sabrina, his mom gives her a wonderful warm hug and told her how beautiful she is.

Then his father that gives her a hug and said, "So this is the woman that has made my son a better man I can't wait to get to know more about you Charles has told us that you're an Attorney and Entrepreneur. I'm impressed with what Charles has told us so tell us more about yourself personally."

Sabrina was blushed and flattered by the compliments from his parents she tells them she lived in Korea until she was four years old and grew up in New York, she's always had a passion for law and loves being a Corporate Lawyer. She shared with them that she's a vegan and loves fitness. She also said, "Charles has been an absolute gentleman I never met a man like him before you've done an exceptional amazing job raising him."

Charles smiled and felt proud hearing Sabrina's kind words about him. His parents were also impressed by her and asked more about her work as a Corporate Lawyer. Sabrina told them about the company her ladies had started and how it's one of the fastest growing companies in Miami and her plans. Charles' parents nodded, impressed by her ambition and dedication.

They also asked about Sabrina's family, and she disclosed to them about her parents and siblings. They exchange stories and get to know each other better over lunch, and by the end of the meal, they all feel more at ease and comfortable around each other.

Charles decided to get on one knee in front of his parents, everyone in the restaurant observed what was happening.

Charles takes Sabrina's hand and looks into her eyes. "Sabrina, I love you more than anything in this world. You've brought so much happiness and love into my life, and I can't imagine spending a single day without you by my side."

Sabrina's heart was racing with anticipation as Charles continued. "I want to spend the rest of my life with you, building a future filled with love, joy, and adventure. Will you do me the honor of becoming my wife?"

Sabrina's eyes fill with tears of joy as she nods and said, "Yes, Charles, I will marry you!"

Charles slides the engagement ring onto Sabrina's finger as his parent's cheer and congratulate the happy couple. Sabrina feels overjoyed and grateful to have found love with Charles and to be welcomed into his family.

His parents congratulated them and hugged them both, thrilled to witness the proposal.

Charles' mom said, "We're so happy for you two. We can see how much you love each other." His father adds, "And we're proud of you, son. You've found a wonderful woman to share your life with." Sabrina and Charles feel a sense of joy and relief wash over them, knowing that they have the support and love of each other and their families. They finish their meal, chatting and laughing about their future and all the adventures they'll have together.

Charles held Sabrina's hand and looks at her with a loving gaze, "I can't wait to spend the rest of my life with you, Sabrina." She smiled back at him, feeling grateful and excited for what the future holds for them.

As they walked out of the restaurant, Charles' mom pulled Sabrina aside and whispers, "You're a wonderful woman and we're so glad Charles found you. We're looking forward to seeing more of you." Sabrina thanked her and smiled, feeling grateful and relieved that the meeting went well.

Charles and Sabrina walked hand in hand, feeling closer than ever. He told her how impressed and happy his parents were to meet her, and Sabrina said to him how grateful she is for his support and love.

Sabrina shared with the ladies in group text that Charles proposed in front of his parents I'm officially engaged. I can't believe first Megan get engaged last night and now me.

The group chat explodes with excitement and congratulations for Sabrina.

Megan said, "Oh my god, another engagement! Congrats, girl!"

Elena adds, "That's amazing news, Sabrina! So happy for you and Charles."

Amber chimed in, "Yay! More weddings to plan and more dresses to buy!"

Bridget and Bethania also send their congratulations and share their excitement for the upcoming wedding.

Stephanie said, "Wow, two engagements in two days! What are the odds? Congrats, Sabrina! Can't wait to celebrate with you." Jacqueline, who had been quiet for a while, finally speaks up, "I'm so happy for you, Sabrina. You deserve all the love and happiness in the world." The group continued to share their congratulations and excitement for Sabrina's engagement.

Maxwell and Megan planned a special surprise for her birthday weekend. They've rented a private boat and are going to take a romantic ride along the coast. The sun was shining, and the water was calm as they set off, enjoying the peaceful scenery and each other's company.

Maxwell packed a picnic basket full of Meghan's favorite foods and drinks, and they enjoyed a delicious lunch as they sail along. Megan was overwhelmed by the effort that Maxwell has put into making her birthday special, and she told him how much she loves him.

As the boat sails into a quiet cove, Maxwell drops anchor.

Megan chuckled and said, "I like where this is going." He quickly removed his beach shorts and jumped into the water. Megan followed suit, taking off her bikini top and jumping into the water as well. They both swim around for a bit, enjoying the warm sun and clear water. After a while, they get back on the boat and sit on the deck, enjoying the beautiful view of the ocean. Maxwell wrapped his arms around Megan and kissed her neck, telling her how much he loves her. Megan leaned back into his embrace, feeling so happy and loved.

Megan said, "Tell me what you love about me I love hearing it when you tell me, and I'll tell you what I love about you. Maxwell you're a good-looking guy a tall handsome successful you can have any woman you wanted why you choose me and fall in love with me?"

Maxwell smiled and looked deeply into Megan's eyes, "I love your beautiful smile, your kind heart, your intelligence, and your adventurous spirit. You always know how to make me laugh and bring light to my day. I love the way you care for others and are always willing to lend a helping hand. Most of all, I love the way you love me, flaws, and all. I didn't choose you because of what you look like or what you can do for me, I chose you because I love who you are, Megan."

Megan's eyes fill with tears of joy as she listens to Maxwell's words, "I love how caring and supportive you are, Maxwell. You always know how to make me feel loved and appreciated. I love the way you make me feel safe and protected, and I feel like I can be myself around you without judgment. You're also an amazing listener and always know how to comfort me. I love how we can be silly together and never take ourselves too seriously. I feel so lucky to have found someone like you."

When Harry and Jacqueline finally made it to Chicago, Jacqueline decided to check them in and a nice hotel she knew right on the Magnificent Mile.

Jacqueline looked at Harry as they were walking to their room and getting settled in, she said to him, "How are you feeling? What do you think about Chicago you excited to be meeting my family?"

Harry replied, "I'm feeling a bit tired after the long flight, but I'm excited to be here with you. Chicago seems like a beautiful city, and I'm looking forward to exploring it. I'm also a bit nervous about meeting your family, but I'm sure it'll be great getting to know them."

Jacqueline smiled and took his hand, "Don't worry, my family is going to love you. They've been asking about you ever since I told them I met someone special. And I can't wait to show you around the city and try some deep-dish pizza. We'll have a great time."

Harry nodded and returned the smile, "I'm sure we will. I'm just glad to be here with you."

Jacqueline said, "I told my family to meet us at this nice restaurant for dinner, in the meantime let's take a shower relax, I'm going to hit the gym before we go out."

Harry and Jacqueline decided to take a little nap since they were a little jet lagged before getting ready to meet our family. As they wake up from their nap

Jacqueline said, "Let's go to the gym I got us a few pre workout protein shakes."

Harry said, "Let's do it."

They entered the gym in the hotel they were impressed with how nice it was.

Jacqueline told Harry, "I'm going to train my legs and do some core."

Harry replied, "I'll be your workout partner."

Jacqueline nods with a smiled and they begin their workout.

As they finish up, Jacqueline said, "That was a great workout, I feel so energized!" Harry agrees and they head back to their room to get ready to meet her family.

While they were walking back to their room Harry couldn't help but notice and couldn't stop checking out Jacqueline and how sexy her body was in her workout attire. Harry said, "Baby I love watching you walk in front of me it's such a magnificent view."

Jacqueline said, "After dinner when we get back to the room, I'm going to give you a view you won't forget,"

Harry giggled and said, "Oh really? You better be ready to deliver on that promise, Ms. James." Harry winked at her and they continued walking back to their room, both feeling excited about what the rest of the night had in store for them.

While they were getting dressed, Jacqueline said to Harry, "A little bit about her family and what to expect. My family is big and loud, but they're also very welcoming and friendly. I know they'll love you," she explained with a reassuring smile.

Harry nods and takes a deep breath, feeling a little nervous but excited to meet Jacqueline family. "I'm looking forward to it," he said.

As they exited out of the hotel, Jacqueline held Harry's hand and they made their way to the restaurant. Harry felt a sense of anticipation building up inside him as they approached the table and Jacqueline saw her mom, dad, aunt, uncle and older brother. Jacqueline said, "Family this is my wonderful boyfriend Harold Wellington from Devon England, you can call him Harry."

Harry greeted Jacqueline's family with a warm smile and a handshake, feeling a bit nervous but trying to hide it. Jacqueline's mother complimented Harry on his accent and asks him a few questions about his background and interests. Harry answered politely and engaged in small talk with Jacqueline family, trying his best to make a good impression.

Jacqueline's father then turned the conversation to Harry and Jacqueline relationship, asking how they met and how long they've been together. Harry shared the story of how they met at Brickell City Center in Miami and how he fell for Jacqueline beauty and intelligence. He also expressed how much he enjoyed spending time with her and getting to know her better.

Jacqueline's brother said, "You look like Henry Cavill."

Harry smiled and said, "Thank you, I've been told that before friends tease me and call Harry Cavill." He then asks Jacqueline's brother, "What do you do for a living?" and the conversation continues as they all settle into their seats and order their meals. Harry enjoyed getting to know Jacqueline family and hearing about their experiences living in Chicago.

Jacqueline family is equally interested in Harry's life in England, and they asked him many questions about his upbringing, his career, and his interests. They find out that Harry was a successful businessman who has traveled to many parts of the world. He shared some of his travel experiences with them and they are all fascinated by his stories.

Jacqueline's mother told Harry how impressed she was with his manners and how he treated her daughter with respect. Harry thanked her for her kind words and tells her that he feels lucky to have met Jacqueline. They all continued to chat and enjoy their meal, sharing stories and laughs.

As the night winds down, Jacqueline's father told Harry that he's welcome to come back and visit anytime. Harry thanked them and said he's looking forward to getting to know the family more. Jacqueline gave Harry a knowing smile and a squeeze of his hand, silently communicating how happy she was that he was getting along so well with her family.

Amber and James finally made it to San Diego, and she tells James "I can't believe I'm so hungry these pregnancy cravings are unreal, you won't believe how my breast feel and I'm horny all the time, please forgive me I just need vent my hormones are all over the place." As the ride in the car on the way to hotel, she texted her family that they arrived safely, and they want us to come over for dinner.

James smiled and said, "Of course, we'll make sure to have dinner with your family tonight. And don't worry about venting your hormones, I'm here for you." He reached over and gently rubbed her belly, saying, "Our little one is growing so fast, it won't be long before we get to meet them."

Amber leaned into James and sighed, feeling comforted by his touch. "I can't wait to introduce you to my family," she says. "They're going to be so excited to meet you and the baby." She took a deep breath and adds, "And I'm sorry about my mood swings, it's just been a lot to handle lately."

James nodded understandingly and said, "Don't worry about it, Amber. I'm here to support you and take care of you, no matter what." They arrived at the hotel and check-in; James ordered some room service for Amber since she's been so hungry since getting off the flight.

Amber said, "I need to take a shower" as she started removing her clothes and looking in the mirror, she noticed how her body is changing seeing the baby bump and her breast are getting bigger. James stared at her and just loved how beautiful his fiancé looked, he felt like the luckiest man.

Amber said to him, "Do I still look good to you? I feel so heavy, but she started to embrace the new version of herself, a surreal moment coming to grips that the old Amber is gone and new Amber has arrived.

James replied, "You look more beautiful to me now than ever before. Seeing you carrying our child and going through all these changes just makes me fall in love with you even more."

He walked up to her and placed his hands on her growing belly, feeling the baby move. "And look at this, we have a little one on the way. You're amazing, Amber."

Amber replied, "I love you James, but I don't know why you still have clothes on I am so horny right now."

James smiled and said, "Well, in that case, let me take care of that." He quickly removed his clothes and joined Amber in the shower, embracing her as the water poured down on them. They share a passionate moment together before leaving for dinner with Amber's family.

They departed the hotel on the way to Ambers parents' house Amber was rehearsing in the back of her mind what to tell her family first that she's getting married and they're about to be grandparents. They were walking up to the door nervously and her mom answered. Her mom gave Amber big a hug and kiss and said, "Who's the handsome gentlemen?"

Amber said, "This is James Holland my fiancé" then Amber lifted her hand and showed her mom the ring and totally shocked and grabbed Amber by the hand and told James to come in. Amber mom yelled for Amber's Dad and siblings to come to the living room. They all greeted and hugged each other, and her mom said Amber is getting married.

Everyone in the room is excited and congratulates Amber and James on their engagement.

Amber's dad asked James about his family and his background, while Amber's siblings asked about the proposal and wedding plans. Amber and James shared some details about their relationship and their plans, including the fact that they're expecting a baby.

There's a moment of stunned silence, followed by cheers and hugs from everyone in the room. Amber's mom starts asking questions about the baby, and Amber and James happily answer them.

Amber dad said, "Lets come to the backyard and have dinner."

He's been cooking on the grill.

Amber's dad said, "You didn't tell me James looks like a young Brad Pitt." Amber's family started asking James all kinds of questions about his family and where he grew up.

James happily answered their questions and shared stories about his childhood and family. Amber's family seemed to be enjoying getting to know James and they all sit down for dinner in the backyard. Amber's dad grills up some delicious burgers and hot dogs, and they all chat and laugh together while enjoying the food.

During dinner, Amber's mom turned to James and said, "So, when are you planning on marrying my daughter?"

James looked at Amber and smiled, "I was hoping to ask for your blessing tonight, Mrs. Alexander. Amber and I have been talking about getting married soon, and I want to make it official and start our family together."

Amber's mom looked thrilled and gave James a big hug. "Of course, you have my blessing, James. I couldn't be happier for you both. When were you planning on doing it?"

Amber said, "Right now with everything going on with the baby we're still working on logistics of where we're going to live at there's a lot going on right now, so I haven't had a chance to start wedding planning."

Amber sister said, "I'd be more than happy to come to Miami and help you guys as much as I can."

Amber's dad said, "We are definitely coming to Miami."

Amber said, "Dad, you said you never like Florida."

He replied, "I'll like it more now that my grandchild will be there."

Amber and James felt overwhelmed with love and support from her family. They discussed their plans and how they can work together to prepare for the baby and the wedding. Amber's sister excitedly takes out her phone and starts showing them pictures of wedding dresses, venues, and decorations. Amber's dad started asking James about his plans and offered him advice on how to provide for his family.

Amber was so relieved and grateful for her family's love and support, and she knew that they will be there for her and James every step of the way. She felt blessed to have found a man like James who loves her unconditionally and is willing to support her through all the ups and downs of life. Together, they will face the challenges that lie ahead and build a beautiful life together with their child. The rest of the evening was spent enjoying a delicious dinner and catching up with Amber's family.

Back in Miami, Elena and Colin are excited that they have officially set a date for their wedding. They've also decided on a venue which will be at the Vizcaya mansion in Coconut Grove. Elena and Colin spend their evenings researching vendors, discussing wedding details, and creating a guest list. Elena spent hours scrolling through Pinterest boards, looking for the perfect wedding dress ideas to send to Melanie, while Colin focused on the logistics of the wedding day. They decided on a beautiful outdoor ceremony by the water, followed by a reception in the mansion's grand ballroom.

Elena answered her phone, it was her family saying that they were going to be flying into Miami. Elena was so happy to hear that news because due to the pandemic restrictions it was difficult for her to fly home to see her family. She was so ecstatic and elated that her family was finally going to meet Colin face to face, video conferencing just doesn't do it justice she felt.

Elena shared the news with Colin and they both started making plans to show her family around Miami and made sure they had a great time. Elena suggested taking them to the beach, visiting some of the popular tourist spots in the city, and of course, trying out some of the delicious Cuban food Miami is known for.

Colin was excited to meet Elena's family and get to know them better. He suggested taking them out on a boat tour of the city and showing them some of the beautiful waterfront homes and famous landmarks from the water. Elena loved the idea and can't wait to show her family how beautiful Miami is from the ocean.

Colin also shared some exciting news with Elena, that he's looking forward to meeting the VIP clients that Maxwell has set up for him.

He felt that this is a very good lucrative opportunity to expand his business. He's looking forward to flying to Washington DC and finally getting some government subcontracting experience under his belt. Elena was happy to hear that Colin's business was expanding and growing, and she knows how much he's been looking forward to getting into government subcontracting. She tells him how proud she is of him and how much she admires his hard work and dedication to his business. They spent the rest of the evening discussing Colin's plans for his trip to Washington DC and their upcoming wedding.

Charles decided he wants to go over to Sabrina's because he has a surprise for her. He called her and asked her if she's available,

Sabrina says, "Sure I'm just doing some work at my Home Office." As Charles arrived, he said, "Sweetheart I have a special surprise that I want to do for us." Sabrina heart starts racing with anticipation, Charles tells her "I have booked us a trip to Paris." What you said to my family was very special and I want to do something special for us. We're going to be staying close to the Eiffel Tower with a nice view every night that we're staying there.

Sabrina was overjoyed and couldn't believe that Charles has booked a trip to Paris for them. She gave him a big hug and kissed him, saying "Thank you so much, Charles. This is the best surprise ever. I can't wait to explore Paris with you and see the Eiffel Tower every night."

Charles said, "I'm glad you like it, my love. I want to make more memories with you, and I think Paris is the perfect place for us to do that." Sabrina can't stop smiling and feels so lucky to have Charles in her life. They spend the rest of the day planning their trip and dreaming about all the things they will do in Paris.

Stephanie decided to call Divya and see what she was up to. Divya answered feeling sad that her business is not well, and she lost a major client and potential investor. Stephanie listened to Divya's concern and offers her support. She reminds Divya that setbacks are common in business, and that it's important to stay positive and keep working towards her goals. Stephanie said, "How about I invest a small minority stake in your business plus with my marketing skills I can help draw clients to your business. Girl, you know I have a large following on social media."

Divya was taken aback by Stephanie's generous offer and thanked her from the bottom of her heart. She felt grateful to have a friend like

Stephanie who not only listened to her problems but also offered practical solutions. Divya agreed to Stephanie's offer and they both discussed the details of the investment and marketing strategy. They make plans to meet up in person to finalize everything and celebrate their new partnership. Divya feels a renewed sense of hope and motivation, knowing that she has Stephanie by her side to help her overcome any obstacles in her business.

William decided to pay Bethania a surprise visit when he noticed that she seemed off and could tell she had something on her mind.

He asked her "oh I can tell something is on your mind if you're not ready to talk about it I understand."

Bethania said, "Ever since Megan surprise birthday party I saw how her and her family finally made-up for a lost time. It got me thinking about needing to go home and try to see if I can set out and talk with my father, we haven't been on speaking terms and a long time."

Bethania asked William "Would you be willing to go to New Jersey with me to meet my family?"

William smiled and held Bethania's hand, "Of course, I would love to go with you and support you in any way I can. It's important to try and make amends with family, and I'll be there for you every step of the way."

Bethania looked relieved and grateful, and they started making plans for their trip to New Jersey. They discussed possible dates, transportation, and accommodations, and William promised to help Bethania with anything she needs during the trip. They both feel excited and hopeful about the upcoming visit, and they can't wait to see what the future holds.

As Jacqueline, Harry, Amber, and James returned to Miami, the ladies felt a tremendous weight lifted of their shoulders breaking the news to their family. Amber especially felt relieved with her family's support and excitement that they're going to be grandparents.

Amber said to James, "We need to meet with Bethania and Bridget we need to buy a home and I would prefer we get a single family with a yard."

James said, "Don't worry I've already let Bethania know I need to buy a home."

Amber said, "In the meantime our places are not big enough to accommodate us plus a child."

James said, "Let's tell Bethania the type of home you want, and you can connect with Bridget on getting us a good deal on mortgage." Amber said, "We'll just rent out current places for additional income."

Bethania decided to give Stephanie a call, she asked Stephanie "I need to go out of town for a few days do you mind covering my real estate clients while I'm away and if you need any help or anything just call me on the phone."

Stephanie happily agreed to help Bethania out with her real estate clients while she's away. She assured Bethania that she would take good care of her clients and that she can call her anytime if she needs any assistance or advice.

Megan says to Maxwell, "I have some business I need to handle but before I leave. I want to know why it is you don't talk about your family much. I know you said your mom and dad separated when you were little. I would like to come to DC with you and meet them."

Maxwell said, "The reason why I don't talk about them much I was angry with both of my parents and why they were not together for so long and they never actually shared with me why they divorced. My father wasn't a very loving type of father, he didn't show a lot of affection, he was old school in that regard kind of like how your dad was. But it made me want to be a better man and the future father from my family because I learned what I didn't want to do from him. My dad and stepmother live in Potomac MD now and my mom she's retired in Charleston SC."

Megan nodded and listened attentively as Maxwell explained his family background.

She said, "I understand why you might have felt angry and frustrated with your parents, but it's great that you've been able to learn from their mistakes and use that as motivation to become a better person and future father. I would love to meet your family and get to know them better. Just let me know when you're ready I'll make accommodations to go with you."

Maxwell said, "I want you to meet my mother first, I need to get my mind ready before I introduce you to my father."

Megan said, "Very well" she gave Maxwell a kiss as she left and headed to the office. As Megan was driving to the office, she felt thankful that Maxwell decided to open a little bit about his family. She can truly understand what it's like dealing with family drama or unresolved issues. Then her thought process shifted as she thought about all the money that Melanie wanted her to invest for her. Megan decided once she arrived to her office, she was going to give Melanie a call and discuss more about this.

When Megan arrived in the office Victoria, Bridget, Stephanie and Divya were all in the office. Megan greeted everyone and saw how everybody was doing.

Victoria said, "I put a few appointments on her calendar and there are a few messages for you." She thanked Victoria and says she's going to be in her office working and needs to call her sister. Megan settled into her office, and she picked up the phone and calls Melanie.

Melanie answered and Megan said, "Sis how are you?"

She replies, "I'm good I'm just looking at some emails with work and notice that Amber and Elena have sent me some ideas on their wedding dress."

Melanie said, "That's right plus Sabrina wants me to do her dress too. So, what do I owe the pleasure of this call?"

Megan said, "I can't believe you want me to invest 100% of this money that dad has left you."

Melanie said, "Yes, I want to make double the return and then I want to return the initial $2 million back to him. What father is trying to do he thinks writing a check is going to recompense him from his guilt. I told dad this you made it very blatantly clear what the rules are I broke the rules and got pregnant, and I suffer the consequences I'm not mad at you I just am mad at myself for making a dumb decision. But that one dumb decision wouldn't have made me who I am today as strong and resilient and smart and successful and that's where the greatest reward in my peace is with it. I don't want father to feel like he needs to feel guilty about anything he is who he is he's never wavered from that. once that investment doubles just pull out the initial investment and just send it back to the father."

Megan listened to Melanie and nodded along. She said, "I understand where you're coming from, sis. It's not about the money, it's about the principle. I agree that Dad shouldn't feel guilty or like he needs to make it up to us in that way. I think it's also important to remember that everyone copes with things differently. Dad may not know how else to show his love and support for us. While we don't need his money to be successful, it's still nice to have that safety net."

Megan continued, "That being said, I think your plan is a good one. Doubling the investment and then returning the initial amount is a smart way to handle it. I'm going to start in looking at some aggressive ways to invest this and get it back to you. Megan looked down at the floor as she was hanging up the phone with her sister. She noticed her underwear was in the floor. Then she starts having flashbacks of that hot steamy passionate night her and Maxwell were in our office and couldn't find her underwear they decided to leave the lights off.

Bridget knocked and walked into her office at the same time Megan is picking up her underwear and having it in her hand.

Bridget said to Megan "Why are your underwear in your hand?" As Megan's face looks completely disheveled. As the door is still open Divya and Victoria over here their conversation with their faces looking into Megan's office.

Megan quickly tries to compose herself, feeling embarrassed and caught off guard.

She stammers and says, "Oh, um, I was just...I needed to adjust them, they were bothering me."

Bridget looked at her skeptically but decided not to push the issue. Megan quickly tried to change the subject and asked Bridget about the progress on the current real estate deals they are working on. Divya and Victoria, who were eavesdropping, quickly pretend to be engrossed in their own work as Bridget updated Megan on the deals. After the meeting, Megan took a deep breath and realized that she needs to be more careful in the future.

Moments later Elena walked in all happy and jubilant she said her and Colin had finished lining up the wedding plans. She asked all the ladies to be bridesmaids, she's also decided on the theme and color for the wedding.

Megan said to Elena "I can't believe we got rings on our fingers."

Elena said, "I know right I'm just thankful that our men love values and appreciates us the right way."

Elena also said, "It's the first time me being in a relationship where I never had to felt insecure or question anything Colin has always made me feel secure, he's easy to talk to he's a great listener he truly understands me he's very empathetic."

Stephanie said, "Well don't forget good looking."

Elena said Stephanie, "You're right that's truly a bonus but I just wanted a man that can truly compliment me match energy and have some substance and plus I love his family values."

Megan nods in agreement and says that she felt the same way about Maxwell. She said that she's never been with someone who respected her opinions and valued her the way he does.

Divya chimed in and said that she's happy for both of them and that she hopes to find someone like that someday. Victoria adds that she's happy for Elena and Colin and that she can't wait to see how beautiful the wedding will be. Elena thanked everyone for their kind words and said that she can't wait to start planning the wedding with all of them. She says that she's already picked out the color scheme and theme, and she's excited to share it with everyone.

As Elena and Megan walked into the waiting area, then a very interested distinguished handsome gentlemen entered the office said he has an appointment with Bethania. Victoria, Divya and Stephanie look at each other as they slowly start checking him out. Victoria asked him his name and, "Who was your appointment with?"

He said, "My name is Enrique Estevez, I'm here to meet with Bridget Berry and Bethania Diaz I'm looking to buy a home."

Victoria said, "Yes I spoke with you on the phone it's nice to meet you, have a seat I'll let Bridget know you hear."

Victoria walked to Bridget office and said, "Your supermodel Enrique is here, I know Stephanie is covering for Bethania I'll let her know."

Bridget chuckled and said, "I'll be there to take him to the conference room."

Victoria walked to Stephanie office and said, "Bethania has a fine appointment waiting for you since you're covering for her."

Divya said, "We can talk later go enjoy some eye candy."

Stephanie laughed and said, "I don't know if I can handle that kind of distraction, but I'll go see what Enrique wants." She gets up from her desk and heads to the conference room where Enrique is waiting.

As she entered the room to join Bridget, she could feel her cheeks turning pink as she takes in his striking appearance.

She clears her throat and introduces herself, "Hi, I'm Stephanie Toro, I'm covering for Bethania today, how can I assist you?"

Enrique smiled and said, "It's a pleasure to meet you, Stephanie. I'm looking to buy a home in this area, and I was hoping to get some information on available properties." Enrique was trying to remain professional but couldn't help but check out Stephanie, looking at her long hair, beautiful lips and legs as he watch her walk on the other side of the conference room.

As Enrique and Bridget go over the details of the home buying process, Enrique found himself struggling to focus on the conversation. He kept stealing glances at Stephanie, who was busy at her desk working on her computer. As he ogled Stephanie couldn't help but admire her beauty and wondered if he would have the chance to get to know her better.

As Bridget finished up with Enrique, Enrique asked Stephanie about her role at the company, and they engaged in a brief conversation about her work. Stephanie was impressed by Enrique's professionalism and the way he carries himself.

Enrique asked Stephanie "Excuse me for being so forward but you're just so extremely gorgeous would you be interested in having lunch or dinner with me?"

Stephanie said, "Normally I don't mix business with pleasure but since you are Bethania's client and I'm covering for her I'll be willing to have dinner with you."

Enrique smiled and said, "Thank you, Stephanie. I appreciate your willingness to have dinner with me. How about tomorrow evening at 7 pm? I know a great Italian restaurant nearby." Stephanie agreed and they exchanged numbers to confirm the details.

As the meeting concluded, Enrique headed to Bridget's office to discuss the new mortgage process, while Stephanie couldn't help but feel excited about her upcoming dinner date.

As Stephanie watches Enrique leave the conference room, she noticed Victoria Elena and Megan looking at her.

Megan said, "Keeping business and personal separate, are we?" Stephanie said, "He's good looking and I know how much money he makes he's qualified I'll go on a date."

Victoria said, "uh-huh that's a new policy in the company handbook."

Elena chuckled and said, "Well, there's nothing wrong with a little bit of romance outside of work as long as it doesn't affect our jobs."

Megan nodded in agreement and said, "Besides, Stephanie deserves to have a little bit of fun and romance in her life. We all do."

Victoria shrugs and said, "I suppose you're right. Just be careful, Stephanie. We don't want to see you get hurt."

Stephanie smiled and thanked them for their concern. She felt happy and excited about her upcoming date with Enrique but also knew that she needed to be careful and keep her personal and professional life separate.

Bethania and William just finished packing their bags getting ready to head to the airport to meet her family. Bethania had been feeling some anxiety about trying to settle things with her father in the past, but she's also excited to see her family and introduce William.

Bethania warned William, "If you notice some tension between me and my father, he has not been happy with me since I dropped out of college. Every day I wake up feeling like I need to prove to him that I can make it and I did but he's old school and they only think if you go to college, it's guarantees you a pathway to success. my little brother and sister are going to love you and I'm sure you will like my mom."

William responded by saying, "I understand how important this is for you, and I'll be there to support you no matter what. And as for your father, I'm sure he'll come around eventually. You've accomplished so much and built a successful business, which is something to be proud of. I'm excited to meet your family and I'm sure I'll get along great with your brother and sister. Let's focus on enjoying our time with them and making new memories."

Bethania smiled and said, "Thank you, William. Your support means everything to me." They grab their bags and head out the door to the airport.

Elena and Colin are excited that Elena family were arriving in Miami. They were getting their place ready since they'll be staying in the guest bedroom. Elena says to Colin "do you think we have enough room? I don't want it to be too crowded."

Colin reassured Elena, saying "Don't worry, love. We have plenty of space. Plus, your family is only here for a short time. It'll be nice to have them stay with us."

Elena smiled, feeling grateful for Colin's positive attitude. She knows he always knew how to make the best of any situation. "You're right, it'll be great to spend time with them and show them around Miami."

Colin nods in agreement. "We can take them to some of our favorite restaurants and maybe even go to the beach," he suggests.

Elena's face lights up at the idea. "That sounds perfect," she said. "I can't wait to see their faces when they see the ocean for the first time."

Colin took Elena's hand and smiled at her. "It's going to be a great visit," he says. "We'll make sure they have the time of their lives while they're here."

While Stephanie was getting ready for her date with Enrique, she felt that something was telling her this doesn't feel right to go on this date since he's a client of the company. Then she starts having impure thoughts about Enrique which made her feel more compelled to want to go on this date with him. Then Stephanie said to herself, "It's just one date and that'll be it."

She arrived at the restaurant; she handed her keys to valet all the men outside of the restaurant were checking here out. Stephanie noticed Enrique as she stood by the hostess. She couldn't believe how good-looking he was in his suit, and she noticed his hair and smile. Enrique was looking at her in this dark purple dress as he was checking her out from head to toe. Stephanie felt a rush of excitement and nerves as she saw Enrique looking at her. She tried to compose herself and walked towards him with a smile on her face. As they sat down at their table, Enrique complimented Stephanie on how beautiful she looked in her dress. Stephanie thanked him and said she loves purple. They begin to talk, and Stephanie finds herself enjoying Enrique's company. They have a lot in common and she finds him easy to talk to. As they finished their meal, Enrique asked if Stephanie would like to go for a walk with him. Stephanie agrees and they take a stroll around the city, talking and laughing.

Enrique asked Stephanie, "If she would like to go out with him again?"

Stephanie said to Enrique "I would absolutely love to go out with you on another date, but it doesn't feel right knowing that you're a client of the company."

Enrique said, "I understand, and I respect that but what made you decide to come out tonight?"

She said, "I tried to talk myself out of it but I did want to see your handsome face again."

Enrique smiled and said, "Well, I'm glad you decided to come out tonight. And don't worry, I won't pressure you into anything that makes you uncomfortable."

Stephanie smiled back and said, "Thank you for being understanding. I had a great time tonight."

Enrique said, "Me too. How about we plan something for next week, but as friends, just to hang out and get to know each other better?"

Stephanie said, "I'm not ready for the night to end so let's go over to this lounge I know close by and let's get some more drinks." Enrique said, "Lead the way," As they arrived at the lounge and sat down.

Stephanie said, "Don't judge me, I'm going to have to take my shoes off my feet are a little sore from walking."

Enrique said, "I'm sorry to make your feet suffer I used to do massage therapy I don't mind giving you a foot massage."

Stephanie paused for a moment and looked at Enrique and smiled and said, "I can't believe I'm about to say yes but I really could use that foot massage."

Enrique said, "It'll be my pleasure this is a very nice quiet and I love the ambiance."

Stephanie said, "Yes it's quiet a hidden gem sometimes I come here when I just want to drink and be alone."

Now she asked Enrique "What is a good-looking guy like you doing single?"

As the waiter comes over to take their drink order

Stephanie said, "I'll have a grey goose martini dirty."

Enrique said, "I'll have a Moscow mule."

Enrique said, "To answer your question I got out of a relationship a year ago with someone I thought I was going to marry. She told me she had a change of heart about getting married and having children."

Stephanie was absolutely enjoying this foot massage she said, "This feels so intimate even though we are just friends."

Enrique looks at her and said, "That depends on your definition of friends."

Stephanie blushed and said, "You really make this difficult for me" Enrique says, "Trust me it's mutual."

As they continue to talk you could sense the sexual tension and energy building between them, Stephanie and Enrique. Trying to do everything possible to keep impure thoughts from circumventing in their minds. Stephanie couldn't help but continue to check out Enrique, she loved how attractive his hands looked, his statue his hair he smelled so good as he continued to massage her feet and work his way up her leg. She wanted to get him to stop but every fiber of her being said just kept going. Enrique couldn't stop checking her out, especially her legs as he was enjoying massaging her feet and touching her soft radiant luminous skin.

Stephanie noticed she's started to get turned by the soft touch of Enrique she's knows it's been so long since a man touched her in a way that stimulated her.

She tells Enrique "I normally don't allow a man I just met to touch me in this way."

Enrique said, "I'm very honored to be so privileged, would you like for me to stop?" As he looked Stephanie in her eyes, and she stared back into him.

She said, "No keep going, I thought it was a foot massage, but my legs are enjoying your hands."

Enrique smiled at her and continued massaging her legs, making sure to be gentle and attentive to her reactions. Stephanie couldn't help but feel a rush of pleasure and anticipation as she let herself enjoy the sensation of his touch. She knew that she should stop him and maintain some level of professionalism, but her body had responded to him in ways that she can't ignore.

Enrique noticed Stephanie's body language and senses that she was feeling aroused.

He leaned in closer and whispers in her ear, "I can tell that you're enjoying this. If you want me to stop, just say the word." Stephanie's heart races as she feels his breath on her neck, and she knows that she should stop him, but she can't bring herself to do it.

Instead, she takes a deep breath and said, "No, don't stop." Enrique smiled and continued massaging her legs, moving higher and higher up her thighs. Stephanie's breathing becomes faster and shallower as she felt his touch getting closer to her most intimate areas. She knows that this is wrong, but she can't resist the overwhelming desire she feels for him.

Finally, Enrique leaned in and kissed her softly on the lips. Stephanie responds eagerly, deepening the kiss and wrapping her arms around his neck. They both know that this is a bad idea, but they can't help themselves. The sexual tension that has been building between them since they first met has reached a breaking point, and they both give in to their desire for each other.

Stephanie said, "I'm going to close the check and let's get out of here." They both went back to Stephanie's car and headed to her place. While Stephanie was driving Enrique decided to continue to touch her leg while she was driving.

Stephanie said, "You're making it hard for me to concentrate but I just love the way your hands touch me."

Enrique said, "I can't resist touching you, Stephanie. You're so beautiful and captivating." Stephanie blushes and said, "I can't believe I'm doing this. I'm not usually this impulsive."

Enrique said, "Sometimes it's good to be impulsive. Life is short, and we should make the most of it."

Stephanie nods in agreement and they both smile at each other.

As they arrived at Stephanie's place, she invited Enrique in. They sit on the couch, still feeling the intense chemistry between them.

Stephanie said, "I don't usually do this, but I feel like I can trust you."

Enrique responded, "I feel the same way about you, Stephanie." They share a passionate kiss and begin to explore each other's bodies.

As Stephanie takes off Enrique's shirt unbuttoning every button, she loved how incredibly in shape his body was. She ran her hands along his six pack Enrique slowly unzips Stephanie's dress. They're both so visually enamored and turned on, then Enrique started kissing Stephanie on her neck and then he slowly goes down to her chest as she removes her bra. Enrique can't get over just how incredibly soft her skin and how beautiful she looks. He decided to pick up Stephanie and carried her to her bedroom. As he slowly lays her on the bed and begins to remove her panties. He begins to go down on her.

At that moment, Stephanie gasps in pleasure and she can feel the heat and intensity building up inside of her. She arched her back as Enrique continued to pleasure her. After a few minutes, Stephanie pulled him up to kiss him deeply, their tongues intertwining as they shared a passionate moment. Enrique then slowly entered Stephanie, and they both moaned in pleasure as they start to move in sync with each other. The room is filled with the sound of their bodies colliding and their heavy breathing. Stephanie could feel the tension building inside of her and she knows that she's getting closer to her climax. Enrique could feel her getting closer too, and he started to move faster and harder. Soon, Stephanie reached her peak and cries out in ecstasy. Enrique continued to move inside of her until he reached his own climax and collapsed next to her, both breathing heavily. They lay there for a few moments, catching their breath and enjoying the afterglow.

Stephanie looked over at Enrique and said, "That was amazing, thank you." Enrique smiled back at her and said, "No, thank you. You're incredible."

Bethania and William are getting settled in to go meet and see Bethania's family in Hoboken NJ. So many thoughts are running through Bethania's mind knowing she hasn't been on speaking terms with her father. Bethania called her mother to let her know they're going to be coming over and her mom was ecstatic to see her and her siblings since it's been so long. She asked about her father, but her mother said, "You know how your father is."

Bethania said, "We'll be shortly, so I'll see you soon."

As they made their way to Hoboken, William noticed that Bethania seemed a bit anxious, and he asked her if everything is okay. She tells him about the situation with her father and how she hasn't spoken to him in a long time. William listened attentively and offered his support, telling her that he'd be there for her no matter what.

When they finally arrived at Bethania's family home, her mother and siblings welcomed them warmly. "Everyone this is William Edwards this is my mom, brother, and sister."

William greeted them all with a warm smile and introduced himself, shaking their hands. Bethania's family seemed to like William immediately, and they started asking him questions about himself and his life. Bethania noticed that her father is not around, and she asked her mother about him. Her mother shared with her that he's at work and won't be back until late. Bethania looked disappointed but tried to enjoy her time with her family.

As they spent time with her family, Bethania started to feel more relaxed and comfortable. She and William joined in on the family's activities and shared stories about their own lives. They had a nice lunch together and spent the afternoon catching up. Later in the evening, when her father returned home, Bethania was hesitant to see him, but her mother encouraged her to talk to him.

Bethania takes a deep breath and goes to see her father. They exchanged awkward greetings, and Bethania tried to explain why she hadn't been in touch. Her father listened quietly, and then told her that he's sorry for the way he acted and that he wanted to make things right. Bethania was surprised but relieved, and they hugged.

Bethania told her father "I want you to come to Miami I want you to see everything that I've accomplished. I didn't turn out the way you expected I turned out better."

William watched from a distance, feeling happy for Bethania that she's able to make amends with her father. He noticed how much she loved her family and how important they were to her. As they leave her family's home that evening, Bethania thanks William for being there for her and supporting her through everything. They shared a sweet moment together, feeling even more connected than before.

Elena and Colin were greeting Elena's parents as they were visiting Miami for the first time. As they walked into their home Elena's parents absolutely marveled at how gorgeous her place was they loved the view being able to see the whole Miami skyline. Colin takes their luggage and Elena decides to give them the grand tour of her place in the One hotel building.

Elena showed her parents around the spacious living room, the cozy bedrooms, and the modern kitchen. Her parents were impressed with the luxurious and elegant design of the condo, and they express how proud they were of Elena for accomplishing so much. They also complimented Colin for being such a gentleman and helping Elena with everything.

As they settled in, Elena's mother asked about Colin's background and what he does for a living. Colin told them about his business as a Software Engineer doing Subcontract work for the Department of Defense and how he's been working in the industry as a Software Engineer for several years. Her father seemed interested and started asking Colin about his business, which leads to an in-depth discussion about the government and technology. Elena watched as Colin was impressed by her father with his knowledge and expertise.

After the tour, Elena and Colin showed her parents the pool so they could relax and get some sun before going out to dinner at a local seafood restaurant. While at the pool, Colin takes off his shirt and Elena's mother can't believe how in shape he is.

Elena's mother said, "Colin you got a body like a superhero." Colin laughed and thanked Elena's mother for the compliment, saying that he tries to stay in shape by exercising regularly and eating healthy.

Over dinner, they catch up on family news and share stories about their lives. Elena's parents express their gratitude for Colin taking such good care of their daughter and making her so happy. Colin smiled and thanked them for their kind words, saying that he feels lucky to have Elena in his life.

As the evening ends Elena parents were getting ready for bed, Elena's parents tell her how much they enjoyed dinner and how proud they were of her and happy that Colin will be their future son-in-law.

Monday morning, all the ladies were getting ready to head into the office. Everyone had a phenomenal weekend. Bethania felt like a new woman after seeing her family, Jacqueline still feeling ecstatic after her family absolutely loved Harry. Elena felt good that her family was still in town, and they loved getting to know Colin. Megan felt good that she's finally reached a turning point with Maxwell and she's going to be meeting his family soon. Bridget felt very good about Marley and Cole, back home she felt very good about how things had turned out. Amber was over the moon feeling so good about becoming a mother and her family was excited and her and James were finally going to be looking for a home with Bethania help. Sabrina can't wait to go on her trip to Paris with Charles. Victoria was feeling very good for the first time she's working in an environment that makes her feel appreciated and accepted and she's financially making the most money. Divya has a meeting with Stephanie and Megan she has a proposal she felt very confident she wanted to present to them. Stephanie was still feeling good and reminiscing over her wild romantic extravaganza with Enrique.

As the ladies walked into the office, they hugged and greeted each other, then they started rubbing Amber belly. Megan decided let's all meet in the conference room and just briefly catch up and see how everybody is doing. The ladies shared their amazing stories as they laughed and cried just feeling so thankful that everyone was doing well.

As they break from the conference room, Divya arrives for her appointment with Megan and Stephanie. Megan and Stephanie greeted Divya, Megan said, "Well come in my office let's talk. As they sat down the first thing Divya did was hand Stephanie a check in an envelope and said, "Thank you for supporting and believing in me but I decided I want to go in a different direction."

Divya looked at Megan and said, "I would like to come work for your company my background is in finance have experience and global wealth management I have some clients in London and in New York that are willing to work with me."

Divya said, "Megan I know how extremely successful you are in finance I would like to learn a lot working under you and bringing value to this company."

Megan looked impressed by Divya's offer and took a moment to consider it. She nodded and said, "I was wondering when you were going to ask, I already knew you were qualified I'm open to the idea of you joining our team, Divya. We'll also need to discuss the terms of your employment."

Stephanie chimed in, "I think it's great that you're considering working with us, Divya. We can use someone with your expertise and connections.

Divya smiled and thanked Stephanie, "Thank you for your kind words and understanding, Stephanie. I truly appreciate it. I look forward to discussing the opportunity further with you and Megan."

As Divya and Stephanie leave Megan's office, Stephanie saw Enrique. She was surprised to see him even though they had been texting each other. As she walked over to greet him, she maintains a professional demeanor even though in the back of her mind she's thinking about how well Enrique rearranged her cervix over the weekend.

Enrique greeted Stephanie with a warm smile, and they exchanged pleasantries. Stephanie tried to keep the conversation professional, but she couldn't help feeling the sexual tension between them. She took a deep breath and reminded herself that they are at work and needed to maintain a professional relationship.

Enrique said, "I'm here to sign off on my mortgage papers with Bridget and I'm supposed to see two different places with Bethania this afternoon."

While Stephanie and Enrique were talking in the waiting area, Melanie surprise visits everyone as she walks in. Victoria greeted Melanie shocked to see her once again, Enrique turned around and saw Melanie,

Melanie looks at him and said, "Enrique wow it's a small world."

Enrique was shocked and startled to see Melanie, then Melanie greeted Stephanie looking at Enrique and Melanie.

Stephanie asked, "So how do you all know each other?" Enrique with a shocked look on his face Melanie remains silent for a moment.

Melanie changed the conversation quickly and said, "It looks like you two know each other" and there is an awkward amount of silence especially knowing that Enrique has slept with both of these women.

Melanie said, "Wow Miami is truly a small town you can't be surprised if you're riding on the same saddle with somebody else."

Stephanie and Enrique both look at Melanie with surprise and a bit of discomfort at her comment.

Stephanie quickly changed the subject, asked Melanie, "How she's been and what brings her to the office?"

Melanie replied that "She's in town for a few days for a business conference and thought she would stop by to say hello" They made small talk for a few minutes before Melanie excused herself, saying she needs to get going to see Megan. After she leaves, Stephanie and Enrique both feel a bit awkward and uncomfortable about the situation.

Stephanie looked at Enrique and said, "Well, that was unexpected." Enrique nods in agreement, still feeling a bit taken aback by seeing Melanie again.

Meanwhile Divya, Jacqueline, Victoria and Bridget overheard that conversation, and then

Bridget said, "Enrique I'm ready whenever you are."

Enrique told, "Stephanie it was good seeing you again."

Stephanie said, "likewise congratulations on your new mortgage." As Stephanie was walking back to her office, she sorts of realized that she and Melanie both slept with Enrique.

Divya and Victoria walked into Stephanie's office and said, "Are you ok? What was that all about with Enrique and Melanie?"

Stephanie chose to not disclose the truth regarding that, so she said, "It looks like Enrique and Melanie seems to have dated at some point." Divya and Victoria look at each other skeptically but decide not to push the issue. They change the topic and start discussing work-related matters. As they submerged into their tasks, Stephanie couldn't help but feel a bit uneasy about the whole situation.

When Melanie left Megan's office, she stopped by Stephanie office and told her, "I went on a date with Enrique, but I told him I wasn't looking for anything so he's all yours. He's definitely good looking you too make a great couple." Stephanie instantly felt better after talking with Melanie and couldn't wait to call Enrique after work.

Bethania walked into Stephanie's office and asked her, "Could you show this property to Amber and James I'm double booked today, it's in Coral Gables?"

Stephanie nodded and said, "Sure, I can show the property to Amber and James. Let me just check my schedule to make sure I have time. When are they available?"

Bethania responded, "They're free this afternoon at 3 pm. Will that work for you?" Stephanie checked her calendar and saw that she had a meeting at 2 pm, but it should be finished by 3 pm.

She nodded and said, "That should work. I'll meet them at the property at 3 pm."

Victoria showed Divya her new office, Divya was excited to be working with Megan and ready to learn a lot. Victoria gave Divya a tour around the office, pointing out where she could find the supplies she needs. She also gave Divya a rundown of the company's policies and procedures and told her about the projects she'll be working on.

Divya was thrilled to be working with Megan and was eager to learn as much as she can. She thanked Victoria for showing her around and said she couldn't wait to get started. Victoria told her to take her time settling in and to let her know if she needed anything.

As Divya started to unpack her belongings and set up her workspace, she couldn't help but feel a little nervous. She knew she had a lot to learn and wanted to make a good impression on Megan and the rest of the team. But she was also excited for the challenge and feels grateful for the opportunity to work at such a prestigious company.

While Divya was getting set up in her new office the new human resource consultant dropped off and updated the offer letter signed by Megan. She looked at it and couldn't believe how much her new updated starting salary was. Megan wrote a personal note that said, "Stephanie and your clients gave you a phenomenal recommendation."

Divya was overjoyed and felt grateful for the opportunity to work at such a great company. She thanked the human resource consultant and took a moment to reflect on how far she had come. She felt excited to start her new role and make an impact in the company. She decides to call Stephanie and thank her for the recommendation and support. Stephanie was happy to hear that Divya received the offer and congratulates her on her new position. They discussed some of the upcoming projects and Stephanie offers to help Divya with any questions or concerns she may have. Divya felt grateful for the support and encouragement from Stephanie and can't wait to get started.

While Victoria was working at her desk, she received a very surprising phone call from the local channel 10 news Miami wanting to interview Megan and the team on being one of the fastest growing companies in Miami. They tell Victoria, "When would be a good time that we can come into your office and do an interview?" Victoria puts them on hold and goes to see Megan,

Victoria knocks on Megan's office door Megan looks at her and said, "Why are you so excited?"

"I have channel 10 news on hold they want to schedule an interview with you Bethania, Jacqueline, Amber, Stephanie, Bridget and Sabrina regarding being one of the fastest growing companies in Miami and talk about your community outreach work."

Megan was thrilled at the opportunity and thanked Victoria for letting her know. She quickly gathered the team in her office and shared the news with them. Everyone was excited but also a little nervous about being on camera. Megan reassured them that they will do great and that they can use this as an opportunity to showcase the amazing work they've been doing. She also assigns specific topics to each team member so they can prepare their talking points. They set a date and time for the interview and Megan encouraged everyone to dress professionally and be well-prepared.

Megan told Victoria, "We need to hire a public relations consultant to properly prepare us."

Victoria also received another call same day from the Mayor of Miami saying he would like to meet with Megan. Victoria was taken aback by the call from the Mayor of Miami, but quickly composed herself and asked when the mayor would like to meet with Megan. The mayor said to her that he would like to schedule a meeting for the following week, as he has heard about the success of Megan's company and would like to discuss potential opportunities for collaboration. Victoria thanked the mayor for reaching out and promised to schedule a meeting at a time that works for both parties.

After hanging up with the mayor, Victoria rushed to Megan's office to tell her the exciting news. Megan was thrilled and immediately asks Victoria to schedule the meeting with the mayor's office as soon as possible. She also asked Victoria to make sure Bridget, Elena, Amber, Sabrina, Bethania, Jacqueline, and Stephanie accompanied her to the meeting. Victoria nods, excitedly, and heads back to her desk to get started on the preparations.

Megan also called back to Victoria once again, I want to schedule our company's first corporate off-site trip. I want to take me, Sabrina, Bridget, Amber, Stephanie, Jacqueline, Elena, Divya, and you on a trip Vail Colorado. We'll make an end of the year Ski Trip, just book it on the company credit card. Tell the ladies to clear their schedules.

Victoria was thrilled with the news and immediately started making arrangements for the ski trip. She sent out an email to everyone on the list, informing them of the upcoming off-site and asking them to block their schedules for the trip. She also included a tentative itinerary and asked for any suggestions or preferences.

In the email, Victoria writes, "Hello everyone, I hope this email finds you well. I'm excited to announce that Megan has planned our first corporate off-site trip, and we'll be heading to Vail, Colorado for an end-of-the-ski-season trip! The trip will be fully covered by the company, so all you need to do is pack your bags and get ready for a fun-filled adventure.

I've included a tentative itinerary for the trip, but please let me know if you have any preferences or suggestions for activities. Also, please block your schedules for the dates of the trip, so we can all enjoy this experience together. Let's make it a trip to remember!"

Victoria sent the email and waits for the responses, excited to plan the trip with the rest of the team.

All the ladies were excited to share the news with significant others. Sabrina calls Charles, Amber calls her fiancé James, Jacqueline called Harry, Bethania calls William, Elena called her fiancé Colin, Megan decided to take a break and give her fiancé Maxwell a call and inform him of the good news that she's going to be premiering on a television interview for the local news and the mayor of Miami would like to meet with her.

Megan said, "Hey babe, how's your day going?"

Maxwell said, "It's going well, how about yours?"

Megan explains "It's been crazy busy, but also really exciting. I just got a call from Channel 10 news in Miami, and they want to do an interview with me and some of the team about our company being one of the fastest growing in the city."

Maxwell replied "Wow, that's amazing! Congratulations, love!"

Megan says, "Thanks, it's a big opportunity for us. And that's not all, the mayor of Miami also wants to meet with me."

Maxwell said, "What?! That's incredible! You're really making a name for yourself and the company."

Megan said, "Yeah, it's surreal. I wanted to share the news with you first, you always support me in everything."

Maxwell replied "Of course, I'm so proud of you. Let's celebrate when you get home tonight."

Megan says, "Sounds good to me. Love you."

Maxwell said, "Love you too."

Meanwhile, the other ladies are also excitedly chatting with their significant others, sharing the news of the upcoming TV interview, meeting with the mayor, and the corporate off-site trip.

As Megan leaves her office she walks around and tells everyone let's meet in the lounge Victoria grab one of those bottles of champagne and bring some glasses we have much to celebrate. As everyone gathers in the lounge.

Megan said, "Ladies no matter what they print in the news about us we couldn't have made it without each of us working together. I love our synergy, the culture, the environment and most of all I love you not only as colleagues but as sisters and our sisterhood that we built for one another. I always want us to continue to build this culture and make it better not only for us but all the new people that join us. What we have right now is so precious is the reason why we are gaining so much recognition."

Victoria said, "As she starts crying, I just thank you all for being so considerate and fostering such a healthy culture to work in. This has been the only opportunity I've ever had where I was excited to come into the office on the weekend and now, you're considering taking me on a corporate off-site trip I'm extremely flattered."

Megan looked at Victoria and said, "I knew you fit the culture the moment we interviewed you and I'm honored that you're working with us and now you're part of the family."

Jacqueline adds, "I just want to say how proud I am to be a part of this team. We have accomplished so much together and it's because we all bring unique strengths and perspectives to the table. I think it's important to continue to encourage diversity and inclusion within our company and make sure everyone feels valued and supported."

Bridget chimed in, "I agree, and I also want to thank Megan for being such a great leader. Your vision and passion for this company have inspired all of us to work harder and aim higher. I feel so lucky to be a part of this journey with you."

Elena nods in agreement, "I just want to say that the community outreach work we've been doing has been so fulfilling. It's amazing to be able to give back and make a positive impact in people's lives. I hope we can continue to prioritize this aspect of our work."

As the champagne was poured and glasses clink together, the group shares a toast to their success and to the bright future ahead.

Chapter 15

As wedding season had officially commenced, it's Colin and Elena wedding day. The ladies looked so gorgeous in their bridesmaid dresses; Elena couldn't believe how beautiful the wedding dress that Melanie designed for her was with the shoes.

Melanie and her team designed a wedding dress fit for a princess by its regal and grand appearance, featuring luxurious fabrics and intricate details. The dress is designed to make Elena feel like royalty on her special day.

It's a full, voluminous skirt with layers of tulle, organza, and silk giving it a dramatic and ethereal quality. The bodice is embellished with intricate beading to feature a sweetheart neckline for a romantic touch.

The back of the princess-style wedding dress is adorned with a corset, adding to the regal feel of the design. It also features a long train, adding to the grandeur and elegance of the overall look.

The veil that accompanies the dress was long and flowing, with intricate lace adding to the overall romantic and ethereal feel of the outfit.

After all the ladies had put on their makeup, Elena comes walking out of the room to see all of her bridesmaids. The ladies just simply dropped their jaw because they could not believe how stunning and beautiful Elena looked in her wedding dress. They were all smiles some started to tear up.

Amber said, "Elena you literally look like a Princess marrying royalty today."

Megan was simply astonished at how talented Melanic was and told Melanie "Whatever the cost is to make my dress beautiful like this I don't care."

Amber said, "I second what Megan just said."

Elena said, "The most important thing that I love about today is not only am I marrying such an incredible man, but I wouldn't be here if it wasn't for you incredible women in this room from where we started to where we are right now. I couldn't have asked for a greater support system and sisterhood." Elena's mom starts crying in the moment, as they all hugged each other.

Elena said, "Our bond is rare that's always protected and have each other's backs."

The moment was filled with love, joy, and gratitude. Elena's wedding dress had not only stunned her bridesmaids but had also brought them closer together as they shared her happiness. The dress was undoubtedly a masterpiece, perfectly designed to complement Elena's natural beauty and personal style.

As they hugged and shared tears, it was clear that the bond between the women in the room was unbreakable. Elena's wedding day had not only been a celebration of love between her and Colin but also a testament to the power of friendship and sisterhood.

Melanie, the talented designer who had created Elena's stunning wedding dress, had proven herself to be a true artist. Her work had left a lasting impression on the bridesmaids, who were already planning their own weddings and wanted Melanie to design their dresses as well.

In that moment, everything seemed perfect, and the love and support between the women in the room shone brighter than ever. It was a day that they would all cherish and remember for years to come.

About the Author

Mac Harvey is an IT Consultant Software Developer, Writer, World Traveler, Investor and Entrepreneur. Born and raised in the United States from Virginia, he has always been passionate about exploring new cultures and expanding his horizons.

Mac's interest in technology began at a young age when he started tinkering with computers and programming languages. As he grew older, he decided to pursue a career in software development and attended college to study Network and Communications Management. Prior to graduation, he landed his first internship with IBM, where he quickly rose through the ranks and became a lead developer and Project Manager within a few years.

Despite his success in the tech industry, Mac felt a strong urge to explore the world and experience different cultures. He took a sabbatical from work and spent several months traveling around the globe, immersing himself in new environments and meeting people from all walks of life. His travels inspired him to write a book about his experiences.

During his travels, Mac decided to start his own software development and IT Consulting company, leveraging his expertise and network to build a successful business from scratch.

Throughout his career, Mac has remained committed to the principles of hard work, innovation, and personal growth. He is known for his unwavering dedication to his craft, his insatiable curiosity about the world, and his boundless creativity and energy. His impact on the tech industry and the world at large is a testament to his vision and tenacity, and his legacy as a trailblazer and innovator will continue to inspire generations to come.